continued . . .

O9-AIC-199

WANDERLUST

"Fast-paced and thrilling, *Wanderlust* is pure adrenaline. Sirantha Jax is an unforgettable character, and I can't wait to find out what happens to her next. The world Ann Aguirre has created is a roller-coaster ride to remember."

—Christine Feehan, #1 *New York Times* bestselling author of *Dark Peril*

"The details of communication, travel, politics, and power in a greedy, lively universe have been devised to the last degree but are presented effortlessly. Aguirre has the mastery and vision which come from critical expertise: She is unmistakably a true science fiction fan, writing in the genre she loves." —*The Independent* (London)

"A thoroughly enjoyable blend of science fiction, romance, and action, with a little something for everyone, and a great deal of fun. It's down and dirty, unafraid to show some attitude." —*SF Site*

"Once in a while you come across certain characters that just remain with you long after you've finished a book. For me, I found those characters in the cast of *Grimspace* and *Wanderlust*." —*Dear Author*

"Emotions run high in *Wanderlust*, and the many twists and turns will leave readers hungry for more."

—*Darque Reviews*

"Vivid world-building accented with gut-wrenching action ensures that following Sirantha Jax through her first-person adventures will leave you breathless." —*Romantic Times*

GRIMSPACE

"A terrific first novel full of page-turning action, delightful characters, and a wry twist of humor. Romance may be in the air. Bullets, ugly beasties, and really nasty bad guys definitely are."

—Mike Shepherd, national bestselling author of the Kris Longknife series

"An irresistible blend of action and attitude. Sirantha Jax doesn't just leap off the page—she storms out, kicking, cursing, and mouthing off. No wonder her pilot falls in love with her; readers will, too."

—Sharon Shinn, national bestselling author of *Quatrain*

"A tightly written, edge-of-your-seat read."

—Linnea Sinclair, RITA Award–winning author of *Rebels and Lovers*

"An unflinching tale of survival, redemption, and serious ass-kicking. Jax's brutal eloquence will twist your heart when you least expect it."

—Jeri Smith-Ready, award-winning author of *Bring on the Night*

"An exciting, evocative, and suspenseful science fiction romance, reminding me of *Firefly* and *Serenity*. Characters and a world you'll think about long after the book is done. Fascinating!"

—Robin D. Owens, RITA Award–winning author of *Heart Journey*

Also by Ann Aguirre

Sirantha Jax Series

GRIMSPACE
WANDERLUST
DOUBLEBLIND
KILLBOX

Corine Solomon Series

BLUE DIABLO
HELL FIRE

KILLBOX

ANN AGUIRRE

ACE BOOKS, NEW YORK

THE BERKLEY PUBLISHING GROUP
Published by the Penguin Group
Penguin Group (USA) Inc.
375 Hudson Street, New York, New York 10014, USA
Penguin Group (Canada), 90 Eglinton Avenue East, Suite 700, Toronto, Ontario M4P 2Y3, Canada
(a division of Pearson Penguin Canada Inc.)
Penguin Books Ltd., 80 Strand, London WC2R 0RL, England
Penguin Group Ireland, 25 St. Stephen's Green, Dublin 2, Ireland (a division of Penguin Books Ltd.)
Penguin Group (Australia), 250 Camberwell Road, Camberwell, Victoria 3124, Australia
(a division of Pearson Australia Group Pty. Ltd.)
Penguin Books India Pvt. Ltd., 11 Community Centre, Panchsheel Park, New Delhi—110 017, India
Penguin Group (NZ), 67 Apollo Drive, Rosedale, North Shore 0632, New Zealand
(a division of Pearson New Zealand Ltd.)
Penguin Books (South Africa) (Pty.) Ltd., 24 Sturdee Avenue, Rosebank, Johannesburg 2196,
South Africa

Penguin Books Ltd., Registered Offices: 80 Strand, London WC2R 0RL, England

This is a work of fiction. Names, characters, places, and incidents either are the product of the author's imagination or are used fictitiously, and any resemblance to actual persons, living or dead, business establishments, events, or locales is entirely coincidental. The publisher does not have any control over and does not assume any responsibility for author or third-party websites or their content.

KILLBOX

An Ace Book / published by arrangement with the author

PRINTING HISTORY
Ace mass-market edition / September 2010

Copyright © 2010 by Ann Aguirre.
Cover art by Scott M. Fischer.
Cover design by Lesley Worrell.
Interior text design by Laura K. Corless.

ISBN: 978-0-441-01941-0

ACE
Ace Books are published by The Berkley Publishing Group,
a division of Penguin Group (USA) Inc.,
375 Hudson Street, New York, New York 10014.
ACE and the "A" design are trademarks of Penguin Group (USA) Inc.

PRINTED IN THE UNITED STATES OF AMERICA

10   9   8   7   6   5   4   3   2   1

For Andres, always.
Because we got lost in Interlomas in the dark and you hate that zone.
We only had my dubious sense of direction to find the way home.
("I think I recognize that wall, veer right!")
But you cranked Shakira and made it a party.
Plus, you bought me a new 360 the day after mine died.
Now, that's love.

ACKNOWLEDGMENTS

Thanks to Laura Bradford—for everything. I talk about her at the beginning of every book, and this one is no exception. In my mind, there will always be something magical about signing with her. She pulled my manuscript out of the slush pile; I didn't come with a recommendation. I didn't have gold stars beside my name. So what we've accomplished together feels miraculous. She will always be a fairy godmother in my eyes. With *Killbox* in particular, she provided valuable insight in resolving a plot issue, which involved a lively discussion about nanites; there is no end to her talents.

Here's a big thank-you to Anne Sowards, who edits with a keen eye and asks questions that I don't. For all you readers who wonder about these things—she's the reason the answers exist. I've learned so much working with her, and my books are better for it. In fact, I still find it hard to believe I'm lucky enough to tap her expertise.

It's beyond time to acknowledge the Schwagers, who copyedit the Jax books. Their positive comments mean the world to me; when people have read (and worked on) as many novels as they have, it renders approbation that much more momentous. I also appreciate their diligence in ensuring each book is as good as it can be.

I'm fortunate in that I have a cadre that offers support whenever I need an ear. So big gratitude to Bree Bridges, Lauren Dane, Donna Herren, Megan Hart, and Carrie Lofty. At one time or another, you've all talked me down, listened, and/or helped me brainstorm. Whenever I'm in panic mode, you ground me and make me laugh. You all rock for that; I hope I've been as good a friend in return.

Thanks to my family for being patient and supportive. I often spend my time in a world other than the one we live in, but they don't seem to mind. Without such great kids and a great husband, things would be tough, and I couldn't accomplish as much as I do.

Finally, I thank my readers for making Jax a success. Even now, I'm a little starstruck at how far she's come. She isn't your typical heroine, and I thank those who loved her from the beginning. Your e-mails thrill me—please keep writing. That's ann.aguirre@gmail.com.

CHAPTER I

Grimspace blazes through me like a star gone nova.

I'm the happiest junkie who ever burned chem because this is where I belong. Kaleidoscopic fire burns against the hull, seeming as though it should consume us, but we are the only solid thing in this realm of ghosts and echoes. Sometimes I think this place holds all the potential for everything that ever was, everything that ever shall be. It's a possibility vortex, and thus it lacks any shape of its own.

I glory in the endorphins pounding through me. Cations sparkle in my blood, marking me as unique, even among thrill-seekers. You see, my life started here.

Unfortunately, the rush is fleeting, and I need to carry us safely through. I focus on the beacons; they pulse as if in answer to my command. Here, I feel powerful, damn near invincible, however much a lie that proves to be. Jumpers almost never die old and gray.

March swells inside me, filling my head with warmth. My pilot, who is also my lover, feels natural there. Anybody else would wonder at that, but if you're a jumper, you get used to sharing mind-space. In fact, I'm lonely without him there.

He manipulates the ship so we can jump. The phase drum hums, all juiced up, and we swing out of grimspace. Homesickness floods me at once, but I battle it back. No point in dwelling on what can never be—staying in grimspace would kill me. But at least I'm jumping again. Not too long ago, I thought I'd have to choose between my addiction and my life. The decision isn't as obvious as you might think.

I unplug, still savoring the boost, and check the star charts. *Oh, nice, a clean jump.*

"Good work." March grins at me and steals a kiss.

I'm so happy that he wants to.

He's not as pretty as the men I've been with before. I used to have an eye for the lovely, androgynous ones, but I guess deep down, I don't mind a bit of the brute. March has strong, angular features and a nose that's obviously been broken. But his eyes, his eyes shine like sun through amber. I could spend hours looking at him.

Business before pleasure, however—I have an important message to send. With a jaunty wave, I leave the cockpit and head for my quarters. I share the space with March. Despite cohabitation, it's still an austere environment: plain berth, terminal, lighting fortified with solar simulators to compensate for lack of nutrient D3 if you spend too much time on board.

Constance greets me, flickering into a holo projected from my terminal. She's everywhere and nowhere, blazing her way through the ship from terminal to terminal. I don't know if we'll ever convince her to come back to a physical shell now that she's tasted the power and freedom a starship can offer. She's either fused with the vessel's limited AI or overridden it. Regardless, I suspect there's something illegal in what we've done, and I couldn't care less.

"All systems indicate a smooth arrival, Sirantha Jax."

I smile. "You got that right."

Since we jumped from Ithiss-Tor to the beacon closest to New Terra, the crew could be forgiven for thinking we intend to land there. That's what our orders demand. Instead, we're heading away from the planet. We're not operating on the Conglomerate's credits, and this is a vessel out of Lachion, so I can do something I've been longing for since the minute I acceded to that rock-and-a-hard-place decision. Jael—the merc who betrayed us all on Ithiss-Tor—was right about one thing. People seem to think it's fine to force me to choices that range from bad to worse.

No longer.

I add, "Activate comm. I need to bounce a message to Chancellor Tarn."

"Acknowledged."

The system glimmers to life before me, and I sit down to record. This won't take long. Constance zips through the protocols, leaving the proper software in place. In the shadowy light, I can see myself in the terminal, and it's an eerie feeling, alone but not.

I could make this a lot more detailed. Instead, I go with blunt, which is my favorite style of communication. If I never have to dissemble again, that will be wonderful. My time on Ithiss-Tor damn near killed me, figuratively and literally.

I imagine Tarn playing this message and smile. Then I deliver two words: "I quit." Satisfied, I stop the program and tell Constance, "Send it right away, please."

"My pleasure, Sirantha Jax. Do you require anything else?"

"Not at the moment. Feel free to go back to exploring the ship."

Like she needs my permission. She's been blazing through the circuits since Dina—our ship's mechanic and my best friend—set her free from the memory spike. Under her direction, the long-haul fuel system has increased efficiency by 14 percent. Though I had no hope of the merchants on Ithiss-Tor doing so, Constance might even improve the phase drive from the inside out.

Standing, I consider the consequences of what I've just done.

Tarn may reply with bluster and words of obligation; he might say I have a duty during mankind's darkest hour. Maybe he'll even accuse me of turning tail when the chips are down. Once, those accusations might have even been true.

Now my skin is too thick with scars for such barbs to draw blood. I know my own mettle. I've glimpsed my breaking point. And Tarn will never, ever have my measure.

I choose not to serve the Conglomerate as an ambassador, but that doesn't mean I've given up on humanity. Surrender isn't a word in my personal lexicon; there are other ways and means. If nothing else, Ithiss-Tor taught me there's always a choice.

Now we're heading for the last place anyone would ever look for us, Emry Station. It will be a long haul in straight space, but this isn't a frequently traveled trade route, and there's nothing here to attract pirates and raiders. We should pass unnoticed.

After the Morgut attack, Surge—one of March's old merc buddies—and Kora, his Rodeisian mate, turned the place into a virtual fortress, complete with junker tech that will prevent the docking of Morgut vessels. Just thinking about them, the ravening monsters, brings to mind a memory too vivid for me to staunch.

After Vel shines the light both ways, I don't have an opinion, but I do know my skin is crawling all to hell. It feels like I'm passing through wisps of webs, not enough to entrap me, but it does stick to my face. I refuse to let myself start slapping at my skin, a complete breakdown of impulse versus intellect. I won't be the one to go nuts and flee shrieking in the dark.

The hum of machinery grows louder as we make the turn Jael suggested. Maybe we can find a terminal here, so Vel can patch in and see how many we're looking at. I'd rather know the odds, straight-out. I saw the bounty hunter handle a full clutch of Morgut on board the Silverfish, so maybe our chances are good. Maybe.

I continue the silent pep talk as we continue, step by step. The coppery stink increases, the closer we come. By the time we hit maintenance, I have to cover my nose and mouth with my shirt.

Mary, no.

I don't want to look, but it's a compulsion as Vel lifts his light. I register impressions as flashes that burn themselves into my retinas. I'll see this room again, frame by frame, in my nightmares, as if rendered on some old-fashioned film.

They've been here. Chunks of flesh litter the floor. I imagine the hunger, the frenzy that drove them to this. I imagine the spilled blood as an intoxicant, reacting on their alien body chemistry.

I fight my way out of the flashback to find March studying me. He recognizes the signs in someone else, but he doesn't say anything. We're broken in complementary ways, thus rendering our damage comprehensible to each other. Instead, he merely sets a palm on my back, centered heat to let me get my head on straight. I take a deep breath.

We had been forced to take shelter at Emry Station, when Kora gave birth on our Conglomerate ship. Grimspace damages unformed minds, so you can't jump with a child less than two turns old on board. Emry offered the only sanctuary within our hauling range, but once we docked, we found the place infested with Morgut. I'd never forget the trouble that followed. Nor would Surge and Kora, so they'd taken defensive measures. Therefore, we couldn't find a safer place if we searched the whole galaxy, but we're not going there just to hide or to see old friends, although that's part of it.

I step out into the corridor and nearly run into Vel. He goes without human skin these days, more often than not. I hope that means he feels sure of his welcome.

"I wanted to tell you that I've nearly completed the simulator you requested."

My brows arch. "Already?"

"It was not difficult," he tells me with a flex of his mandible. "All Farwan's data is now a matter of public record."

"And you can build anything I might want from a schematic." I try to restrain a smile. From anyone else, that claim would seem like bragging.

"I am unfamiliar with artificial intelligence," he says then.

Right. So he can't build an android from the plans. Good to know.

"Thanks. Will you find Argus for me? I want to talk to him."

I've got an idea. Maybe it's crazy, but then again, some of the best ideas are. Can you imagine the reaction they gave the guy who first found phase-drive technology? This is certainly less radical.

Vel inclines his head, then heads off down the hall.

Later, I'm ensconced in the starboard lounge when Argus finds me. He's young, one of Keri's distant cousins, and he has the J-gene. Doc confirmed it for me today. The kid first came to my attention when I was investigating a murder attempt back on Ithiss-Tor. Argus broke the rules and slid planetside to get a glimpse of the unknown. Too bad for him, he couldn't figure out how to leave the spaceport.

He strides up to my table and offers an awkward bow. His earnest courtesy makes me want to smile, but I don't. I know how easily these kids bruise. I want his willing cooperation, so I'll need to deal with him carefully.

There are others in the break area, mostly clansmen, and a few of them raise their brows when they see the captain's lady invite a young man to join her. Tough. Mary knows, they'd talk even more if I did this in my quarters.

"Have a seat," I invite.

Argus takes me at my word and drops down into the chair opposite me. Wariness wars with excitement in his young face. I think he knows already that I have a reason for summoning him. This isn't a social visit.

"Good to see you again . . ." He trails off, unsure what rank to use for me and unwilling to presume the intimacy of my name.

"Jax is fine. I have this idea," I continue. "Maybe jumpers can be trained outside an academy. If a starship were outfitted with a simulator, a lead jumper could take on an apprentice and spend the downtime in straight space teaching him the ropes. It might also be possible to tweak the nav computer so that both jumpers could jack in at once."

His excitement spikes to painful levels; his smile becomes blinding. "Do I think it's possible, or do I want to sign on?"

"Let's start with the first question."

Argus nods. "I think it could work. We teach kids to drive in vehicles like that dirtside. Why not up here?"

I go on. "I think you're right. It wouldn't take too much to tweak this ship into a training vessel. That way, the lead jumper is there to make sure things go smoothly. Like any apprentice-ship, it would have a training period and a commencement."

"I want in," Argus says. "I'll do it."

"It may be a while before I have all the technology in place," I warn. "We have good people on board, but I won't risk a jump unless the gear has been perfected, and I'm sure you're ready."

"Whatever you think best," he answers.

Well, that's a good start.

"The good news is, I have a simulator standing by. It'll give you a feel for grimspace and replicate the pulse of the beacons. At the Academy, we trained on those for years before ever touching a ship."

He grimaces a little. "Well, I hope it doesn't take *years*, but I know a jumper has to be well trained. I would never put the ship at risk."

There's good steel in this one. We talk a little longer, but he's eager to be off to tell his friends that he's been accepted as an apprentice jumper, the first in this new program. Whether he knows it or not, Argus Dahlgren will make history; he'll be the first of his kind—a jumper trained outside of Farwan's academies. It'll be up to me to make sure he does the role proud.

"So you did it," March says from behind me. "You think he'll be ready in time?"

We've talked about this at length. It's his idea, his dream, and I'm going to make it happen. Not the way they originally intended, but sometimes paradigms must be adapted and improved.

"I hope so," I say quietly. "We need this if we have any hope of winning the war against the Morgut."

His big hands on my shoulders feel hard and warm. I lean back against him, resigned to a long haul. But at least I can use the time working with Argus.

Mostly, I'm tired of taking orders. It's time for me to decide my own destiny. And that's just what I'm going to do.

CHAPTER 2

We've been cruising for about four days, heading away from New Terra, when disaster strikes.

I awaken to the sound of Klaxons. Next to me, March bounds to his feet and starts scrambling into his clothes. His face seems all hard planes in the half-light, softened by the shock of dark hair and his hawk's eyes. Though this is new to me, I recognize the warning, even without Constance on the comm.

"This is not a drill or a technical malfunction. Your vessel is under attack." She sounds so polite and unruffled that I cannot help but smile.

My hands feel clumsy as I tug up my black jumpsuit. Mary, it feels good to be back in familiar gear. "What do you want me to do? We can't jump from here."

"Check in with Dina at weapons," he says over his shoulder, already on his way out.

No time for other niceties.

The ship rocks. In a vessel this size, that can't be good. Even without seeing it, I know we're taking heavy damage. It doesn't make sense, though. We're not a merchantman or a freighter. We're not hauling contraband, and we're well off the beaten path.

I take off for the gunnery bay at a dead run. Dina's already there when I burst in. She's got lasers, but she can't work those as well as the particle cannons. We also have old-fashioned projectiles from an ancient rail gun, but those are best directed at personnel attempting to board, not ships.

"I'll take cannons," she snaps. "Get your ass in the chair. Besides March and me, you're the only one with any interstellar live combat experience."

High praise, indeed.

"Is that why you're not trying to keep this thing in one piece up in engineering?"

"The only reason," she mutters. "I hope those clansmen know what they're doing."

"How're we holding up?"

"Better than expected. Our hull's been reinforced."

I bring the sighting apparatus down over my head, and suddenly I'm out in space, part of the fight in a way that scares the shit out of me, even though it's not my first time. I tap the panel, and the system whines, telling me it needs time to power up. This is a hell of a cutter we're fighting, slim but fast, and outfitted with enough ordnance to destroy a small planet. Whoever these assholes are, they're serious. To my eyes it looks like a Silverfish adapted for spaceflight, but I don't know if that's possible.

Their shots nearly blind me, but they soar wide, striking the Gunnar-Dahlgren vessel far starboard. I don't know what they were aiming at, but they missed weapons. Maybe our engines?

I can see but not hear Dina's first volley; she hits the other vessel in a clean blow that takes out the aft shields. This is more advanced than the technology on the *Folly*, the first ship March ever owned. For a second I can't breathe because of all the black space around me. There's no air here.

With sheer will, I choke it back and tell myself this is only a sim. *Focus on the other ship.* The system cycles, then shows ready. I just have to point and shoot.

"Do we want to disable or disintegrate them?"

Before her next shot, Dina taps the comm. "Use deadly force?"

March's voice fills the room, giving me courage as if he's beside me. "Confirmed. We are at war."

That's all I needed to know. I spin the sight and target the panel where they're trying to restore shields. A tap magnifies my target, then I fire until the lasers whine, telling me they're out of juice for the time being.

It's oddly pretty.

And there's no boom.

But a panel flies wide. They have a hull breach. We probably do, too, but we've given them something to think about.

Muffled through my headgear, I hear Constance on the comm. "I have identified the vessel. According to the registration on the hull, this is the *Blue Danube* out of Gehenna. Data on the ship is scarce, but I found reference to an unpaid tariff on trade goods."

"Speak plainly," I mutter.

"In its hold, the crew had concealed four human females, two Rodeisians, and three male humanoids of unknown origin, possibly from some class-P world."

Slavers. Well, shit.

It makes sense they'd be getting bolder along with everyone else, and Gehenna does a brisk business in the flesh trade. I just didn't realize they do it literally. I thought it was more of a rental than a purchase. But what the hell are they doing here in the middle of nowhere?

"Did they have slaves on Tarnus?" I ask.

"Yes." Dina is too distracted to care I'm prying. "Aren't those lasers ready to go yet?" She lets fly another burst from the particle cannon, focusing on the weak spot. More bits of metal break off in slow, graceful chunks.

Our ship spins, and I wonder how much damage we've taken. I can tell it's March or Hit in the pilot seat because we're taking evasive action that has us rolling and twirling. If nothing else, our fliers outclass theirs.

"Almost. Any critical systems where we're aiming?"

I can hear the evil grin in her voice. "Only little things like power and life support."

"No wonder we're shooting that way."

Slavers. Random evil. They're not part of any grand conspiracy. They just want to buy and sell us like livestock.

Like hell.

I'm ready for round two. Red beams burst forth, slicing the dark between the pearly gleam of our hulls. Luck or Dina's calculations—either way, I hit a stress point, and the back half of the ship cracks wide, the stern going dark, adrift in space. At that point, the *Blue Danube* starts trying to pull away from the fight. Their engines are crippled, which is a good thing; otherwise, they'd leave us sniffing their trail.

There could be slaves on that ship.

I wonder if March has thought of that. It reminds me unpleasantly of Hon's Station, where he tried to save people who were beyond hope of rescue. In doing so, he proved himself a hero, but he also endangered all of us. Back then, it never would've even occurred to me to look. But now, here I sit, worried that we might be blowing innocent people to cosmic dust.

My breath skitters. I shouldn't say anything. I absolutely should not.

Even as I think it, there's a warm tingle at the back of my neck. He's there. The gun bay must be just below the cockpit, or he wouldn't be able to do this. His gift has a limited range.

What's wrong, Jax? You're worrying me.

No turning back now. *There could be innocents on that ship.*

His surprise crackles through me like footsteps on fresh snow. I know what I've done. Seconds later, I hear his voice on the comm. "Dina, belay the order for deadly force. We have to board."

"Are you out of your mind?" she snarls.

"No," he answers. "Take out engines and weapons array if you can. I'll get the tow cables on them to hold 'em still."

"You heard the man," she says, yanking the headgear off me. "He wants precision, and for that I need lasers. I guess you're done here."

"I'll go prepare the boarding party."

"You'll need me," Dina calls. "Don't leave without me."

I'm already thinking about who else we should take. Hit, March, and Vel for their hand-to-hand skill, Doc in case anyone is wounded. Dina and I round out the group. Of them all, I'm the most expendable. That's an interesting sensation.

Once, I'd have protested the stupidity of this. We should've just blown them to atoms and gone on to Emry Station. For good or ill, I don't think that way anymore.

It doesn't take me long to assemble my gear: shockstick, torch-tube, a few packets of paste. You never know when that will come in handy. If we manage to save anyone over there, they might be starving. Slavers aren't known for their kindness.

Once prepared, I head over to the hatch to wait. With the tow cables in place, we'll launch the boarding apparatus and connect to their hatch doors. Vel has the expertise to get us in, even from the outside. I pull on the full-compression suit but leave the helmet off. It gets sweaty in there fast, and I don't want to wear it longer than I have to.

I'm slightly queasy over the idea of entering the boarding array. It's no more than a few thin centimeters of an alloy allegedly perfected for use in space. Seeing how Far-wan "perfected" other technology, it leaves some room for concern.

One by one, I notify everybody who'll be going with us. I don't need to check with March on that. I know he'll agree with my call. Too many, and we'll hinder each other in the close confines of the smaller ship. Too few, and we won't have the skills we need to make this work. It's a delicate balance.

Maybe that's the mistake we made on Hon's Kingdom. We tried to do it on our own. I just hope history's not repeating itself because it was *my* idea this time.

CHAPTER 3

Everyone's suited up.

People I've come to know better than my own family
look alien to me, clad in the dull gray suits that will protect
us in case the seal is faulty. As I mentioned, I'm not eager to
risk my life on the reliability of the docking tube, so this is
a commonsense precaution.

March does a quick head count; then, satisfied, he leads
the way to the hatch and inputs the codes to pop it open.
The pressure door gives with a hiss, and Vel slides past.
Though we can't gain access without him, sending him first
makes me uneasy because he's the only nonhuman among
us. It smacks of prejudice: humans thinking we're the most
important race in the galaxy and everyone else should line
up to serve.

"There's no reason this has to go bad," March is saying
to the rest of us. "Just limit the shooting as much as possible
because it'll be tight quarters."

"No shit." Dina grins, visible even through her helmet.
"I'd rather not catch one in the back."

"We're looking for human cargo," he goes on. "I don't
want to spend a long time over there, so let's make it fast.
This may be a target-rich environment, and you're authorized to do whatever you need to. Clear?"

I etch a salute. "Sir, yes, sir."

A smile flickers in his eyes, but he doesn't let it touch

his mouth. Instead, his gaze sweeps the rest of our boarding party. Everyone seems sharp and ready.

My comm beeps, then Vel says, "I have disengaged the locks and manually opened their hatch."

March gestures toward the door. "Let's go."

We cross one at a time. Vel's already there, and Hit follows to give him solid backup. When my turn comes, I try not to think about the way the tube bows beneath me. It's safe. It could hold ten times my weight.

Still, I'm relieved when I step past the lip of the door with Vel's help. He's already taken readings, verifying that the ship's air is safe for us to breathe and that force fields have sealed off the breaches, so I pull off my helmet and shove the hair out of my face. I didn't have time to work up a sweat. But it's not pure vanity or comfort motivating me here. Helmets limit your peripheral vision, and I'll be damned if I let some slaver sneak up on my six.

The rest of the team arrives quickly and efficiently, leaving us clustered in a narrow hallway. Little as I like it, it makes sense for us to split up and search. If we don't, this will take longer, and every moment we waste standing around, we increase the possibility the slavers will reach somebody inclined to aid them. Plus, there's the chance that catastrophe will strike this damaged ship. March gives a slight nod to show we're on the same page.

"From here, we split," he says aloud. "I want a brawler in each team. Jax, you're with me. Vel, go with Doc. Hit, stay with Dina. We meet back here in twenty . . . Set the timer on your comm if you need to. Call if you find anything, or you need backup."

Their ship was in good shape before we shot it up, I note. Of course, the same could be said of ours. I focus on staying behind March as he leads the way down the corridor. Overhead, the lights flash irregular and sparky. We need to be prepared for failure of life support. That was, in fact, our goal before I complicated matters.

"It's cold in here," March says softly.

"Not too much for humans yet. But the systems are hay-wire. It will get worse." I duck beneath coils of wire and step over fallen ceiling panels. We really rocked this section.

"Agreed."

We come to a door. March taps the button beside it, and it swishes open. Looks like somebody's quarters, but all the belongings lie scattered on the floor. We're not looters, so I don't poke through any of it. Moving on.

In that same vein, we canvass our part of the ship. In the last cabin, a wild-eyed man greets us with laser fire. I dive wide, landing to the left of the door, and March goes in shooting. I hear a cry, then he comes out alone.

"Slaver," he murmurs. "He didn't want to talk."

"No kidding." I offer a shaky smile.

My time as an ambassador has left me soft, more accus-tomed to handling trouble with my mouth than wading in like I once did. The way things stand, I need to rewire that impulse in a hurry. Passing by, I smell charred flesh, but it doesn't rouse the visceral horror it used to. I'm in control, no crazy knocking at the windows of my brain. I don't know if it speaks well of me or poorly that, despite what I've been through, the stink doesn't bother me anymore.

"Well," he answers aloud. "I already told you, Jax. You're strong."

Whatever I might've said has to wait because from another part of the ship comes the sound of combat.

March is already on the move, so I fall in behind him. We find Hit and Dina pinned down in a hallway; black marks score the floor nearby. More shots come in as we creep in from the intersection on the other side. Before us, two sla-vers crouch down, eyes on our crewmates. I shake my head silently. They're not paying attention to the rear at all.

Not smart.

I'm hardly even breathing at this point, not wanting to alert them. They stink so bad I can smell them from here: eau d'garlic and dirty man-sweat. Before March can say a word, I crawl far enough to get a shot and take one in the back. He cries out, his back sizzling into a mass of open sores. Horrible as that is, it's nowhere near as bad as a disruptor-inflicted wound. His mate turns, but March and Hit fire as if they've choreographed it, dropping him in a smooth motion.

"You two okay?" I step forward and tug Dina to her feet. Not that she *needs* my help. Mary, she'd kick my ass if she thought I meant she couldn't get up on her own.

"Fine," the mechanic answers. "We were about to push through."

I'm glad they didn't have to. Warmth curls through me. For once, we were in time.

"Any luck?" March asks.

Hit shakes her head. "Nothing but scumbags so far."

Then Doc's voice comes over the comm. "I think you'd better see this."

He gives us directions and, after a number of turns, we wind up heading toward the stern. That worries me a little, especially given the way the ship wobbles. Who knows what might give way? Or when?

I watch my step as we come up to a storage room. Vel stands in the corridor outside, and I can hear weeping just inside. Guess he scared the folks worse than the slavers. That sends a pang through me because I know it hurts him.

"You all right?" I pause beside him.

"I have a face that frightens small children."

Is that a joke?

"They're just not used to you. Don't worry about it." I touch him lightly on the arm as I pass by and find Doc kneeling amid seven or eight small people.

Kids. None of them older than ten turns. I'm not the best at estimating ages, though. Three boys, four girls. They peer around Doc, trying to get a glimpse of the monster in the hall.

Poor Vel.

"Mother Mary," Hit breathes.

The tall woman curls her hands into helpless fists, faced with upturned, teary eyes. I'm a little relieved that she, too, wears a trapped look, as if she could fight off a whole crew of slavers but has no idea what to do with weeping children.

I know the feeling.

Doc manages to coax their sobs into sniffles, and they cluster around his stocky form like he has pockets full of sweets. Beside me, March wears a look of quiet horror. I don't need to be Psi to know what he's thinking.

How long have they been enslaved? I ask him. *Do they remember their families?*

If so, we can get them home, March replies silently. *If not, I don't know what the hell we're going to do with them.*

What if it's worse than that? What if their parents were the ones who sold them?

He has no answer for that.

"Hush, now," Dina says, kneeling. "We're here to help."

A little girl peeps from between her fingers up at the mechanic. "You are?"

"Yep," March says. "Promise. But you have to be brave for a little while longer. Can you do that?"

"Yeah," she answers. "But . . . will you let the monster get me?"

The others quiet, watching the proceedings with big, damp eyes. They want to know the answer to this question, too.

"Sometimes," I say quietly, "there are monsters who look like people . . . and they do bad things." *Like sell kids for fun and profit.* "And other times, there are people who seem scary, but they're nice on the inside."

"You can't tell who's nice by looking at them," she tells me, too wise for her years.

"Pretty much."

"You ready to go now?" Dina asks.

They're remarkably brave. They have nothing to pack, and there's no time to exchange names. I grab a child at random and settle him on my hip. In the other hand I carry a pistol, just in case we didn't get all the slavers.

Mary, I hope we don't have to fight our way out.

"We have to get them off this ship," Doc says. "It's doomed."

As if in answer, the vessel shudders beneath our feet.

CHAPTER 4

We're halfway there when the lights go out.

That means life support's gone down. We only have the oxygen present in the ship, and it won't be recycling, so when we use it up, we'll be breathing carbon dioxide instead. Hopefully, we won't be here that much longer.

Without breaking stride, Vel snaps a torch-tube and navigates our course back to the hatch. He's unencumbered, so it makes sense for him to lead the way, but again, I don't like it. March and Doc are both weighted down with two kids each, so they won't be much help in a fight. The burden of defense falls on Vel and, to a lesser degree, Hit and me, though we can only offer one-handed backup.

If it comes to it, we'll have to drop the children and hope they have the sense to stay down. I'll certainly order mine to stay put, but my experience in the crèche on Gehenna taught me that children don't always do as they're told.

"Almost there," Vel says.

Foreboding shimmies down my spine.

Then, from the darkness beyond, a low voice says, "Don't move."

I don't, not so much as a millimeter. But I can speak. "Why the hell did you attack a bigger ship? And what are you doing out here anyway?"

I'm trying to buy time for Vel to assess the situation. With him holding the light, they can see us, but we don't have a target. There's no telling how many of them there are, either. There's no denying the fact that this doesn't look good for us. But maybe we can flip it somehow.

"Your shields are good. We didn't detect your weapons until it was too late." I hear the shrug in his voice. "As to what we're doing here, you can frag off."

"Probably waiting on a rendezvous with a buyer," Hit says softly.

Mary, I wish she didn't know that.

"What do you want?" March asks, as if *they're* the intruders.

"I'm the captain of this ship. Obviously, I want my cargo back and the *Danube* repaired, but that's not going to happen. So I'll take your ship instead."

Dina actually laughs. "You really think that'll work? Have you seen the size of our ship? It's teeming with trained soldiers."

That might be a stretch for most of the clan, but they're certainly more familiar with battle than the average crewman. Unless there are a lot more bodies here than I sense breathing in the dark, they won't be able to hold the ship. The boy on my left hip lets out a whimper, and I try to reassure him silently with a pat on the back.

"Then it's just as well I'd planned to take hostages. They won't move against us if there's a chance to save their beloved officers."

He might be right about that, but he's out of his mind if he thinks we'll go along with it. I'm not letting this asshole get on our ship. He's been bullying civilians too long if he believes it's as simple as surprising us and then we cave to his demands.

"I have infrared," Vel says in Ithtorian. "There are four of them, two meters away."

Just a few clicks and chitters, nothing that would make sense to any other human. I smile as the enemy captain gets nervous.

"What was that?"

Warmth prickles down my neck as March surges into me. He knows about my translation implant, proving handy even off Ithiss-Tor. *Vel has a plan?*

He has intel. I relay it silently, wishing I had the vocalizer, which would allow me to speak Ithtorian as well. But I can't respond, only understand what Vel says. *Be ready.*

"What's the matter?" Hit taunts. "Scared of the dark? You're worse than these kids. That must be embarrassing."

I'm not sure that's wise, but she succeeds in distracting him.

"Enough of this," he snaps. "I want you to line up and start crossing, or I splatter your brains on the wall, one by one."

"We all want a peaceful resolution to this," Doc says in a conciliatory tone. "Why don't you tell us who you want to cross first?"

While they try to decide who poses the most threat, Vel addresses me in Ithtorian. "On my mark, get everyone down." He shifts a little. I can hear the movement, but it's hard for me to see with him holding the light. And then: "Now."

"Down," I shout.

Mary bless them, the others all hit the floor at the same time. I cover the boy with my body, trying to shield him from the worst of the fight. The kids are crying again, quiet, hiccuping sobs that hurt me because they sound so weary and desperate. Vel's torch-tube hits the floor, sending a sickly green glow spinning all over us, and I roll onto it. He'll do better in the dark.

I can hear Vel fighting, but I'm not afraid. A few stray shots singe the floor nearby, but they don't have targets anymore. From the wet, sucking noises, he's using his blades on them. It's beyond eerie, lying in the blackness, listening to them die.

It can't be longer than a minute, but it feels like an eternity before Vel says in universal, "We can go now. The way is clear."

When I move off the torch-tube, I can see the corpses piled a few meters away. Vel stacked them facedown so the children wouldn't have to see the entrails. That strikes me as uncommonly sensitive. Around me, the others clamber to their feet, each picking up a kid.

One of the girls who had been clinging to Doc takes a step forward. She stares up at Vel for a few seconds, then she holds out her arms. *That's right. He's a good guy.*

He doesn't move for a moment, then he emulates the rest of us, lifting her with one arm and settling her against his armored side. He's not snuggly but she doesn't seem to mind. I guess defeating the bad guys went a long way toward raising his stock.

"Can we be sure the seal is intact?" I ask.

These kids don't have pressure suits. If the movement of the doomed ship has wrenched at the seal between our hatches, the tube may not be safe. I'll be damned if we went through all this just to have them die in vacuum. From the others' expressions, they've already thought of this.

"Readings indicate it is," Doc answers.

But there's no way to be sure it won't pull apart during the crossing, March tells me silently.

There are six of us, seven of them. Too many for them to squeeze in with us, one-on-one. But two kids can fit in one suit, if we had a spare. That leaves one kid to squeeze in per person. I start peeling out of mine.

Having gleaned my idea, the rest of the crew help their children wiggle down into the pressure suits with them. They make interesting bulges, but the fabric is tensile and fastens over them. That's what makes these pressure suits adaptable for many humanoid races. They're forgiving of odd lumps and extra appendages.

March puts a hand on my shoulder, stilling me. "What're you doing?"

My eyes meet his. "You know what I'm doing. Somebody will need to carry the two kids in this suit. They won't be able to see well enough to walk."

"I'll do it," Hit says quietly. "For lightest body weight, I'm the strongest."

That's undoubtedly true.

We intended to run back across for extra suits if we found survivors, but the whine of the engines renders that impossible. This vessel doesn't have long; soon it'll be dead in space. The magnetic tow cables will keep it within reasonable proximity, but wreckage makes that dangerous as well. We don't want the dying ship to collide with ours, so we need to finish this as quickly as possible and cut it loose.

I help the kids into my suit and fasten them up. The little boy puts on the helmet because he's taller; the little girl snuggles against his back. Resemblance makes me think they might be brother and sister. I give a nod, and Hit picks them up. With a kid on her chest, she can't be elegant, so she drapes them over her shoulder.

"I'll go first," she says. "And I can run back with the suit once everyone else is across."

The ship rocks again, making the tube bounce. I shake my head. "We don't have time. Just go."

One by one they leave. March says nothing. I don't know if he's too angry to protest, or if he just can't think of any- thing to say. Doc is next to last. Before he takes his turn, he hands me something from the first-aid kit.

"Oxygen patch. Seal it over your nose and mouth before you make the run, just in case. It won't protect you from vacuum, but it will offset some of the cyanotic effects."

It may keep me conscious long enough to get where I'm going. I can't think of anything more horrible than choking to death in the array, just a few seconds from safety. Maybe I'm worried over nothing. Maybe the seal will remain intact. But I'm not testing it on the kids.

From a science standpoint, they should be able to recover from a few seconds' exposure out there. But what if they don't? They might have some medical condition we don't know about; they're probably weak from maltreatment.

What if they die? I'm not willing to take the risk unless it's my own skin on the line. That's mine to gamble.

Finally, my turn comes. I'm the last one here. As Doc suggested, I slap the patch over the lower half of my face, push past the hatch and into the tube.

Then I run.

CHAPTER 5

I'm halfway across when I hear the snap behind me.

Mary help me, the other ship has gone into a dead roll, tearing away from the tube. That end flails in open space and pressure closes in on me from all sides. I don't have the strength or the traction to make it up the rest of the way. Despite the patch, the oxygen isn't flowing through my blood anymore. I have ten seconds before the lights go out.

Something latches onto my waist, but I can't see anymore.

The next thing I know, I'm aboard the ship, with everyone clustered around me. My breath comes in hard, choking gasps, and stars fill my vision. Doc is working on me while Dina barks orders about jettisoning the tube and unlocking the tow cables.

"Vitals returning to normal," Doc says at length. "I think we got her out in time."

"What happened?"

"March went back for you," Vel says.

Dina adds, "And I went for him."

"And I went out for her," Hit finishes.

There's something sweet, if suicidal, in this. We're bound by chains of love, but they don't weigh us down. Instead, they allow us to be bigger and better than we are.

"We joined hands," Doc says. "Vel and I stood anchor here, and we pulled you up."

Mary curse it, I feel tears rising in my eyes. I didn't mean to endanger anyone else. I didn't realize they'd risk everything for me. I mean, I suspected March would, but not the rest of them. It makes me rethink my ideas of friendship. Is it truly being willing to die for someone else? Is that the high-water mark?

I struggle into a sitting position and find I can't see March because he's at my head. He draws me back against him, and I feel him trembling—not so anyone else would notice, but in his arms, I feel it. He puts his face against my hair and still says nothing. I'm a little alarmed by that.

Someone has summoned Rose—Doc's lover from Lachion—to take charge of the children, and they follow her out of the bay without question. The others disperse one by one with a little pat or a word of encouragement. Eventually, it's just me, March, and Doc, putting away his implements.

"You'll be fine, Jax. Just take it easy for a few days. And stay out of the simulator."

I start guiltily because that was the first thing I meant to do. "Fine."

Then Doc takes his leave as well, probably to help Rose with the kids. I wonder if they've ever considered having a big family. I'm guessing not. As I understand it, they spent long periods separated, first by his education, then by the mission he undertook with March to try to develop an alternate training program for jumpers, so they could break Farwan's monopoly on interstellar travel. I'd hate to be in Rose's shoes, left patiently at home, waiting for my man to return. Yet from what I can tell, she appears to adore him, and I guess that means doing whatever it takes to be with him. Mary knows, she left her home and went out into the stars, just to stay close. I imagine her saying to him, *You're not leaving me behind again.*

The silence spreads into subtle discomfort. At last he says, "Is that what it's like, living with *me*?"

Wow, I didn't see that coming. I answer cautiously, "Did you think I was trying to teach you some kind of lesson?"

Behind me, he shakes his head. I can't see his face, which is frustrating, but he won't loosen his arms around me enough to let me turn. "No. I think you've just changed for the better, but . . . it's going to kill me if you make a habit of it."

I get it now. Nobility and self-sacrifice sound wonderful in theory, but now he's seen how it feels. A dead hero is still dead at the end of the day, and you're still alone.

Gently, I run a hand along his thigh. "Sucks, doesn't it?"

"I've never been so scared in my life."

"You guys saved me. It worked out. And we got every one of those kids back here safe and sound." Which might not have happened if we'd done it any other way.

"That's the worst of it," he mutters. "You did the right thing, and I hate it."

"Because I might do it again?" How funny, he's chiding me indirectly for developing a moral compass.

"Oh, you'll definitely do it again." March sounds utterly wretched.

"Thing is," I say softly, "so will you. There are no guarantees."

"I can't even yell at you about it because you're the smallest and lightest. It made *sense* for you to go last."

"I know. That's why I volunteered." I pause, thinking about what happened. "If it had been anyone else, the tube might've given way sooner. No hope of rescue."

A long breath puffs into my hair. "And that's why I didn't protest."

"Done is done," I murmur. "Just . . . love me, and let tomorrow look after itself."

"I can do that," he whispers.

He permits me to turn then, and I wrap my arms around his neck. March kisses me with a delicacy and heat that work their way into my nervous system. His hair spills against my cheeks, too soft for such a hard man. If he knew how rakish it makes him look, I'm sure he would shave it off.

"Thanks for saving me."

His mouth brushes my jaw. "Didn't I promise?"

"You did." I can't help but smile over the rarity of a man who keeps his word. And he's mine. "Can we go now? It's a little chilly in here."

March murmurs an assent and swings me into his arms. Soon I'm not cold at all.

*In the days that follow, I find people treat me differ-*ently. It's a subtle distinction, but I'm not sure what to make of it. Eventually it dawns on me—most of them call me Sirantha now, as Vel does. I'm a person to them at last, not Jax the nav-star. Only March still calls me Jax, but spoken in his deep voice, it becomes an endearment.

It's been so long since I jumped that thinking of it evokes a toe-curling ache. I want it more than sex and food combined, almost more than I want to breathe. To combat the feeling, I throw myself into training with Argus.

Even though I know it isn't real, the simulator offers a panacea for what ails me. Argus shows up early every time. I head for the training room at 0900, and find him already there. He occupies his chair with eager impatience. While I was resting from the rescue mission, the shunt in his wrist has had time to heal properly.

"You ready to do this?"

"I'd rather jump for real, but I guess I have to start somewhere."

With some effort, I control my smile. "Got that right. Jack in, and we'll begin."

"Right."

The world fades into an imitative swirl of color. It's as much like real grimspace as anything can be, but if you've been there for real, the sim leaves you a little hungry. Nonetheless, it's a convincing enough replica for our purposes.

I give him a few seconds to acclimate to the inundation of the senses. *Find the nearest beacon for me.*

Argus responds well to having me in his head. No overt shock. He has a strong, impetuous mind, teeming with ideas that skitter like schools of fish. With some effort, he stills his thoughts—good, it takes some jumpers ages to learn that trick—and then focuses. Argus has a harder time with distance here; all normal measures are relative. What is "close" in grimspace?

How do I know? Wouldn't that be dictated by our destination?

Yes, I answer. *That's your first lesson . . . There is no distance in grimspace. We have no equipment to measure it. Everything is predicated upon the goal in straight space.*

Shouldn't you have given me a route, then?

In time. For now, just take me to a beacon. Any of them. Your choice.

The simulator acts in lieu of a pilot, following Argus's directives. Soon he's delivered us smoothly to a beacon in the Outskirts. I've made this jump fairly often, as it's the one nearest to Gehenna. Colors swim all around us, seemingly in response to the beacon's pulse. In true grimspace, I don't notice that as much, overwhelmed by the sweetness and the seduction of the far horizon.

Minutes trickle into hours as he practices. Every now and then I correct his course, show him where he went wrong. The sim-pilot logs it all, and we'll deconstruct it later. Eventually, I call a halt to the day's work. He'll be shocked to find his body weak and shaky when he unplugs. Even in the virtual world, grimspace takes its toll.

Argus surprises me with his compliance. Once we're both out of the sim, I shut it down. He actually salutes me. "I'm honored to be studying with you, ma'am."

I don't know if I'm flattered or alarmed. Just what did he see while we were both jacked in? As if he senses my confusion, a smile plays around his mouth.

I narrow my eyes. "Dismissed. Go get something to eat and report back here same time tomorrow."

His silver-gray eyes twinkle at me. "Yes, ma'am. Whatever you say, ma'am."

Great, my first student is a smart-ass . . . just like me. On some level, I know this serves me right.

I resign myself to a long, rocky apprenticeship.

.CLASSIFIED-TRANSMISSION.
.ACCEPTANCE.
.FROM-EDUN_LEVITER.
.TO-SUNI_TARN.
.ENCRYPT-DESTRUCT-ENABLED.

Chancellor Tarn,

After careful consideration, I've decided to accept your offer of employment. I will arrive on New Terra shortly. At that time, we will need to negotiate terms, as I am sure you understand the sole right to my expertise does not come cheap.

There are a few codicils to my agreement. One: My true function can never be revealed in this administration. You may call my position whatever you desire, so long as it doesn't reflect my real purpose. I will provide a certain amount of busywork to prevent any of your colleagues from putting the pieces together. Let them think my job results from governmental bloat. Two: You will immediately destroy all classified communications from me. Three: You will create a convincing alias. Certain factions would recognize my real name, and accomplishing anything on New Terra thereafter would become problematic. Four: You will comply with my suggestions, rare though they may be. I don't appreciate anyone wasting my time, not even you. Five: You will not inquire into the business of my past employers. If anything has bearing on our situation, I will volunteer the information. Otherwise, confidentiality must be maintained. If you can accept these conditions, then you may consider we have a deal.

As a gesture of good faith, I am attaching my findings regarding raider activity in Delta Tau. You'll find ship numbers and losses, along with a dossier of names and their likely whereabouts and known associates. This intelligence took me years to gather, which I have done for purposes I will not reveal to you. If you find it helpful, understand it is only the tip of that which I can offer you.

Do not mistake me: You will not win this war without my help. I trust you will take that into consideration when we negotiate my salary.

That said, I look forward to working with you.

Edun Leviter

.ATTACHMENT-RAIDER_INTEL-FOLLOWS.
.END-TRANSMISSION.

.COPY-ATTACHMENT.
.FILES-DOWNLOADED.
.ACTIVATE-WORM: Y/N?

.Y.
.TRANSMISSION-DESTROYED.

CHAPTER 6

Our arrival at Emry the second time is much different from the first.

The station looks different now; more lights have been welded to the exterior. Though I know it's false cheer at best, the place no longer looks so forbidding. Kora has probably transformed the inside as well. If they have to stay there with their daughter for the next several turns, there's nothing wrong with making it homier. Sirina won't be old enough to survive a jump with her brain intact for a while yet, and we don't have toddler protective gear on board.

Surge answers our first call within seconds. "You made good time. I'll open the docking-bay doors for you."

In a larger vessel like this one, the long haul doesn't bother me as much. There's more to do on board, and of course, I keep busy with Argus. He's going to be good someday; I can already tell that much. The kid has great instincts, and I'll add in the additional factor of navigating the right beacons when we get a little further along.

At this point I'm just keeping March company. There's no reason for me to be in the cockpit, which is three times bigger than I'm used to. This ship will be great for testing the apprenticeship. There's room in here for an extra chair, which could be used for a trainee pilot or jumper. We'd just need an extra jack.

"Standing by," March tells him.

I imagine the clunk of metal as the massive door rolls back, then he guides the ship smoothly through the gap. Even the bay area has been renovated to some degree. Last time we were here, this station looked on the verge of going derelict; but they've deployed bots to sand away the worst of the rust from years of spillage and coated the metal with fresh sealant. The ship sets down, taking up almost the entire compartment.

"Good work," Surge says. "You didn't even scratch the paint."

March smiles, and it does something to my heart to see the light in his eyes. Oh, he's not healed completely. The war he fought on Lachion—up close and personal—nearly cost him his soul. He came back to me broken almost beyond repair and ready to take up his old life as a merciless killer. Lucky for him, I don't give up easy. His complete recovery will take time, of course, and he'll have fresh emotional scars, but he's on the path. He can laugh now, at least, and stand to be touched again. For my credits, that's worth everything.

He taps a panel and switches from outbound comm to shipwide announcement. "We've arrived at Emry Station. Any crewman who wishes to disembark for R and R may do so. There's not much to do here, but you're welcome to it."

I hear laughter in the corridor beyond, greeting his words. For the first time, I realize I'm serving on a ship where everyone present volunteered. Nobody was drafted, assigned, or picked from a pool, and there's a camaraderie present like nothing I've ever known before.

"Ready to go?" I ask him.

March nods. "Let's locate our crew."

He doesn't need to tell me he means Dina, Hit, Doc, and Vel. Argus might tag along, and so might Rose, but they don't comprise the core of us. They haven't come through fire with us and emerged whole on the other side.

Things have been cool between Doc and me after the way I threatened him on Ithiss-Tor. The fact that he didn't have to do what I asked doesn't change the fact that I asked it. I know what I did—and for March I'd do a whole lot worse. I'm not sure if I should apologize for that.

We step into the hallway, and March shakes hands and pats shoulders in passing. They're mostly clansmen who wanted to see a little of the universe before settling down on Lachion. Right now they seem so young, full of conviction in their own immortality. And they scare the shit out of me.

They don't realize what he suffered for their sake, or how he clawed his way out of hell twice over to keep a promise. To them, he's simply their captain. That's all they need to know, and they'd follow him into the pit if he asked it.

He catches my expression, and I feel the telltale warmth that says he's reading me. I don't even mind anymore. Once you get used to it, there's a certain comfort in not having to explain yourself.

"Don't," he says quietly. "I'm no hero."

I smile. He really has no idea.

"You are to them."

What is it they say? History is writ by the victors, and in the legends of Lachion, March will be known as their crown prince, a chieftain who never ruled and who will come again in times of need, or perhaps simply the savior that came from the skies. It's a romantic fable. Even now I can see its genesis in the admiring eyes of young men who strive to walk like him.

His arms go around me, and though we have things to do, I stand quiet while he sinks his hands into my hair. I've learned what some people never do—not to take for granted what I have, while I still have it. I came within a whisper's breath of losing him, so if he wants to hide his face against my head to cover his embarrassment, I'll let him.

I feel his heart thumping steadily against mine. The sounds aren't quite in rhythm. His comes slow and steady while mine has a funny little skip every fifth beat. I could probably ask Doc what that means, but I don't need to go looking for trouble when I already have a heaping helping on my plate.

March raises his head, and his eyes search mine for a long moment. His lips brush mine in a prelude to sweeter things, but we both know we have to belay the urge to retreat to our cabin for a week. *Our cabin.*

Simply thinking it sends a little ripple of pleasure through me. *He's mine again.* Maybe even more mine than he was before because I certainly did my best to emblazon myself into him so deeply he'll never be free. Was that wrong, I wonder?

"I don't mind," he says softly.

I grin. "You wouldn't. You've been trying to tie me down since the minute you set eyes on me."

"Not quite," he answers. "Close. I think from when you first thought about dropping a giant rock on me." He traces the pattern on my throat and shakes his head. "If anybody else had done this to you, I'd be asking you to get it lasered off."

On Ithiss-Tor, Vel put a tattoo around my throat as camouflage for marks March left during one of his nightmares. If I'd shown up to a council meeting so damaged, they would've taken it as a sign of weakness, and it would have hurt my status. From what other Ithtorians said, I think the pattern and its placement might have some deeper meaning, but I never asked Vel what it signifies. I figured he'd tell me if he wanted me to know.

"Just as well you're not asking. I wouldn't do it. Call the others?"

With a nod, he does.

Our crew meets us at the door. My gaze touches on them one by one: Hit in her dark beauty, with Dina pale as the moon; Doc, stocky and broad enough to bear any burden, with red-haired Rose by his side. Vel stands slightly apart, listening to them talk, but I can tell he's attentive.

As we exchange greetings and make ready to head on station, Argus comes down the hall toward us. His stride slows as if he's afraid of presuming too much. I don't think for a minute he intended to join us. I think he just wants to explore the station. He's a navigator to the bone. Since I understand him so well, I smile, seeing myself in him.

"You ready?" I ask him.

March raises a brow. It's not sexual jealousy. He's secure enough for that. Instead he's curious at why I've included the kid. Argus hasn't seen enough of the universe to be useful yet, and he's not a trained jumper, so strategic deployment is out.

I shrug. *He's my apprentice. That makes him one of us.* I can't offer more explanation than that, but it seems right that he attend the meeting with us. My gut feeling's apparently enough.

"Let's move out," March says.

In an hour with Surge, we'll get more straight talk about galactic affairs than we would in a year of working for Tarn. Placed at Emry, Surge and Kora have been monitoring the bounce satellites that cover the region. At this point, they know what's been going on close to New Terra better than the Conglomerate.

Of course, that's not saying much.

I'm braced for the worst. We were here; we saw the evidence of Morgut passage. But braced isn't the same thing as prepared. You can *never* be prepared for that.

With the exception of those looking after the kids, the rest of the crew will enjoy some time off, doing whatever they damn well please. As for us, we'll be planning for war.

CHAPTER 7

The station has been rehabbed from top to bottom.

As we pass through the corridors, the last trace of my unease uncoils. Though it's not a rational fear, and I know Emry has been well guarded by Surge's family and the skeleton crew provided by the Conglomerate, I can't help but remember echoes of horror. Surge didn't see the worst of it, so it's probably not as bad for him. The former merc ran with March once; he's a sturdy man with a rough face and a shock of curly hair.

He greets us in the mess hall, a large open space filled with tables and chairs. Even the gunmetal walls have been enlivened with swaths of color, Kora's doing no doubt. She's taken liberties that Farwan would never have permitted. The result is cheerful and chaotic, much like the Rodeisian female herself. She bares her teeth at us in a smile, but her incisors are blunt. For all their size, her people are herbivores, slow and peaceful, which makes the grievous offense Ambassador Fitzwilliam gave their empress so many years ago that much more inexcusable. You just don't visit a larger-than-human race and open with a fat joke, then compound it with comparisons to Old Terran livestock. As I understand it, they objected more to his denigrating their apparent intelligence.

Kora bears her daughter, Sirina, in one arm. The baby has grown since we saw her last. Now she can propel herself around; she's a fat little cherub with tufts of fur on her head. We exchange hugs as if this were a family reunion—and as Dina and I stand as godmothers to her child, perhaps it is. When I lean over to accept a one-armed embrace from Kora, Sirina snags her fingers in my hair and pulls, hard.

"Siri!" her mother chides, disentangling.

Ah. The unexpectedness of it blindsides me. I'm not prepared for the pain, and it tears through my chest like a metal hook. The last baby I had charge of didn't end up so well. Quite simply, Sirina is a vivid reminder of my failure with Baby-Z, the lizardling who died on Hon's Kingdom. March puts his hand on my shoulder, knowing without being told, and I take some comfort in that. I school my features to something bland and quiet. Conversation washes over me, blurring into one vague noise, until:

"We should take the lift up," Surge says. "There are things you need to hear."

Messages, most likely. And hearing them spoken will offer more impact and insight than if he tries to sum things up for us.

March nods, answering for all of us. Once, that irked me to no end. Now I simply appreciate that he is willing. "Lead on."

We follow Surge en masse to the second deck, where he leads us to the communications center. Display screens line the walls, leaving one big console in the middle as the control. It's a tight fit, standing room only, but nobody offers to step out. We're all in this; we all have a stake.

"Play back relay 111647, second shift," Surge tells the computer.

"Accessing."

An electronic crackle slides from the terminal, then a grainy image pops up. Through the static and interference I can't make out much more than a man's face. It looks as though he's injured, but the image is of such poor quality I can't be sure.

"This is the *Perseus Queen*, a cargo vessel out of New

Terra, en route to Venice Minor. Our shields cannot hold. We are under attack and request immediate assistance. We have no weapons on board. I repeat—"

The message ends there.

"By the time New Terra got this, they were toast," Dina says into the silence.

Nobody looks at me, but I know what they're thinking. Farwan's fall left a huge gap out here. The Conglomerate doesn't have the ships or resources to patrol and respond to cries for help as efficiently as Farwan did. The loss of this ship—and countless others—can be tracked back to me. I made the choice to take them down because they went too far in murdering a whole shipful of ambassadors, diplomats, and council representatives. My lover also died in that Farwan-engineered crash, and I couldn't let the injustice stand, but like all major decisions, this one has had far-reaching effects.

"Do we know who did this?" Doc asks.

"Any one of the usual suspects," Surge answers. "Pirates, raiders, Syndicate, Farwan loyalists."

"But not the Morgut," Vel says. "They do not blow vessels up. They board them."

A slow shudder works its way through me. I'm not sure I can stand to see the rest of this grim collection, but Surge has more for us. In the time we've been gone, he's accrued an impressive collection of bounced misery and woe.

Another plea fills the screen. The picture is slightly better this time, so I can see the young woman with the strong jaw and short, fair hair. She isn't pretty. Most people would call her masculine. Her eyes are dark, her mouth compressed into a thin white line. She gazes at us, probably through the veil of death, determined to deliver her message.

"The captain is gone," she says quietly. "I am the only officer left. This is Second Lieutenant Evelyn Dasad of the Science Corps, sending this as a record. At 2200 hours, a Morgut vessel came through." The steadiness of her voice drives the horror home, more than if she wept or sobbed.

There is acceptance in the face of Evelyn Dasad, too deep for grief. "They use the beacons with more precision than we can muster. This is not a known jump zone. A brief battle ensued, and our vessel was rendered dead in space. The magnetic tow cables hit our hull at 2245. It is 2304, and they are coming for me. Mary have mercy on us all."

The message shows Evelyn reaching for her weapon, then she turns off the feed. I can hardly breathe for the ache in my throat. I fight the need to weep, which seems absurd, given that I don't know this woman. So many personal losses, and I rarely cried, but this one is too much.

"Do you think she killed herself?" Rose asks in a small voice.

Doc's lover has rarely been off Lachion. She has never seen the Morgut. Her terrors had been limited to what one planet offered. I don't know if he's done her a kindness in giving her the universe, but I do know she wouldn't have let him fly away without her again. I understand *that* completely.

Kora juggles Sirina against her shoulder. Her broad face is impassive. Doubtless she has heard these messages many times, and she's already felt everything she can feel. There comes a point when numbness is all you have left.

"No," Vel answers. "I believe she went down fighting. It has been my experience that some human females do not give up, even when the situation seems beyond desperate and devoid of all hope."

March flicks a look at me, smiling. "Well said."

I turn to Vel. "See what you can find out about Evelyn and her ship. Official records, unofficial, whatever you can dig up."

"As soon as we are finished here," he answers.

I muster my strength, then address Surge. "Is there more?"

There is. So many cries for help went unanswered. Sometimes they tell us it's a Syndicate hijacking before the screaming starts. In other bounces, we hear nothing but cries of anguish and despair. Final tally: twenty ships in this sector alone.

By the time we're done, I feel battered. Nobody else looks any better than I feel. Rose cries silently against Doc's shoulder when Surge powers the terminal down. The room feels close and warm, full of salty sweat and tears, and silence burns like a brand.

Nobody has the answers. I don't even know where to begin. The space between tier worlds is impossibly vast. We need well-armored ships with powerful weapons and trained crews to man them. We need battle-seasoned pilots and combat jumpers who know how to handle themselves.

There haven't been any combat jumpers since the Axis Wars.

I don't think I've ever been so sorry that I didn't just go down easy like Farwan wanted. Whatever their flaws—and they were legion—they did keep the star lanes safe. Now it's a giant free-for-all, and the body count just keeps piling up.

"Things are seriously fragged up," Hit says at last.

That prods a smile out of me.

"They sure are," Surge says. "And it's breaking my heart to listen to this shit without being able to do anything about it."

March would be pacing if there were room. Since there isn't, he stirs beside me restively. "We need a militia to replace Farwan's patrols, one with access to the emergency sats, so we could relay distress calls, allowing the closest vessel to respond."

I nod. "That's how Farwan did it. And they destroyed all enemy vessels, even if they couldn't save the beleaguered ship. They were big on object lessons."

"They'd chase you to the ends of the earth," Dina mutters.

I get the feeling she has some personal experience with that.

"An undertaking like that would require extensive capital," Vel points out.

Surge glances at him. "You got a spare fortune lying around?"

The former bounty hunter inclines his head. "As it happens, I do. But even so, it would not be sufficient for this cause."

"No kidding." Argus speaks for the first time. "Ships cost a sweet bundle, and that's just one good one. For a whole armada . . ." He trails off like he can't imagine the outlay.

To be honest, I can't, either.

Before Vel can answer, Surge taps the comm array and glances over at me. "Jax, you just got a message from Chancellor Tarn. They forwarded it from the ship."

I shrug. "I don't care. I don't work for him anymore."

Hit says, "Not as an ambassador. But . . . you might want to keep your options open."

I really don't like the way they're looking at me. This is how it begins. "Oh?"

"Maybe we should take a look." March glances at Surge. "Can you play it for us?"

"Got it queued up already."

"What the hell," I say. "Let's see what he wants."

CHAPTER 8

"Ms. Jax, I accept your resignation." Suni Tarn has sur-prised me once again. His image on the terminal looks composed, not insulted. Perhaps he is one of the rare politicians who has more sense than ego. "Given your personality, I would not have employed you as an ambassador had there been any other viable alternative at the time. Nonetheless, you performed well, and the Conglomerate is grateful."

He pauses, as if trying to find the words.

"Oh, yeah?" I mutter. "Then why do I feel you're buttering me up for something?"

"Because he is?" Dina offers.

I motion her to silence as Tarn goes on. "Though I hesitate to ask, we could use your help again."

I sigh. "Here it comes. What now?"

"I am given to understand that your partner is a former mercenary with a wide web of contacts," Tarn says directly. "The Conglomerate needs to build a fleet of starships capable of offering protection to tier worlds, or everything we have accomplished to date will be for nothing. Mr. March, the remainder of this message is for you."

I sit back, relieved and pleased. For once, I'm not on the hook, forced into a Hobson's choice. Like Dina and Hit, I can just listen.

"We would confer upon you the title of commander and put you in charge of building said armada. As our resources are not unlimited and time is of the essence, we will not cavil if you must use creative methods. Please discuss the matter and use my private code for urgent communications. I wish to be able to report back to the representatives that I am actively pursuing a solution."

From what I can see, this is pure win for us. No more operating in the gray areas. By their expressions, Dina and Hit agree. The mechanic is glowing, and her lover looks almost as excited.

"They're offering you carte blanche," Dina says. "You'll be able to do almost anything you want. Confiscate ships in port for running contraband and turn them over to our people. You'll be able to build the Conglomerate fleet from the ground up."

Put that way, it sounds thrilling as hell.

"Why March?" I wonder aloud. "Doesn't Tarn know any other soldiers?"

"Doubt it," Hit answers. "There hasn't been a standing army for centuries. Everything filtered through Farwan. The only soldiers left are those who fight in private wars, and most of them die on Nicu Tertius or they're still there."

It's true. Besides Surge's salvage crew, I haven't met a lot of mercs who retired or moved on to other things. March has been running his own ship like clockwork for several turns, and despite many entanglements with Farwan, they never managed to haul him in. His credentials for executing this endeavor sound promising to me. For Tarn, he has to seem like the last chance to make the center hold.

I glance at him. March has been oddly quiet, his dark face thoughtful. He's staring at the screen, gone blank now. I touch him on the shoulder.

"What do you think?"

"I'd be dumb to turn it down," he says briskly. "It worries me a little to accept work with the establishment, but maybe that's suspicion left over from Farwan's regime. I want what will save lives, and if I can use the Conglomerate, if I can create some of the policies myself, I may be best placed with them."

"But you're not sure."

His breath puffs out. "No. I'll have a hell of a lot more people to worry about than just those on my ship. I don't know if I want that much weight, but I don't think I can walk away from it, either."

Vel has been listening silently, but at that, he inclines his head. "It is good that you recognize the opportunity does not come without its share of thorns."

March shakes his head wryly. "No free lunch, isn't that what they say?"

"Speaking of which"—I push to my feet—"I could eat."

March chooses to stay and talk with Surge, while everyone else takes a break. We disperse from fruitless brainstorming, and I sit by myself in the mess hall, nursing a cup of hot choclate. The room is big and empty, except for me. Overhead, the lights give a faint hum.

I like Kora's murals. They're abstract, but they brighten up the endless gray. You can look at only so much neutral without feeling your mood start to drop in answer. Farwan officials would've had a fit.

I can see the faint reflection of my face in the silvered tabletop. My features look monstrous, elongated, with great hollows where my eyes should be. The surface also shows me the glimmer of movement over my left shoulder.

I greet Vel without turning. "You discovered something?"

He rounds the table and sits down beside me, then places his handheld on the table. "Evelyn Dasad worked for the Science Corps. Since Farwan's fall, they operate unaffected by the collapse. They had their own budget and financial officers, so they have continued their research. Recently, they filed with the Conglomerate to be recognized as a nonprofit, nonpolitical organization."

"How long did she work for them?"

"Eleven years, four months, and twenty-three days." It seems he anticipated my question.

But then, he knew I wanted to learn more about her. Her face, as she leans over to turn off the terminal, haunts me.

Such resolution there, such finality. I don't know if I could offer such composure in the face of death.

"What did she study?"

"She specialized in biomechanics," he tells me.

"Like . . . cybernetics? Or ways to improve the fusion of man and machine?"

"Both. She was instrumental in the perfection of nanite technology." He pauses, reading on in the file, then continues: "Her IQ was 162. She painted in her spare time. And she liked choclate almost as much as you do."

Such bare-bones facts to sum up a woman's life. I put my fascination with Evelyn Dasad aside for the moment. There are other lines of inquiry to pursue.

"How many ships has the Science Corps lost in the last month?"

He didn't anticipate that one, so he has to tap on the handheld a few times. "Three."

My fingertips drum lightly on the table. It's not an alarming number, so why am I alarmed? What would the Morgut be doing with human scientists, besides eating them?

"How many to slavers or pirates?"

Vel shakes his head. "The Morgut took all three vessels."

"There's some connection we're not seeing."

"That is almost always the case."

I offer a wry half smile in acknowledging the point. "Let's go at this from another angle, then. What was Dasad's ship working on? What were they doing in this sector?"

It's possible that I have a hold of the wrong end of the stick. Maybe the Morgut were hungry, and the Science Corps ship was there. But I don't think so. From what I've seen and heard, they prefer to prey on outposts, not ships. Hole up somewhere and wait for more prey to come to them. If times are tough, and they're starving, they do board, of course, but it's not their preferred method.

A few moments pass while Vel searches for information. At last he comes up with a curious expression, mandible flexing. "It is classified."

I prop my chin on my hand. "Who would have the power to do that? Science Corps is autonomous now, accountable to no one."

At least until their credits run out. Let me tell you— there's a scary thought. Scientists running amok in the galaxy, unfettered by rules, regulations, or bureaucracy.

Vel looks uneasy—and uncertain with it. "I do not know."

If Dasad specialized in biomechanics . . .

"Could it have anything to do with wetware?"

The Morgut have to jack in, just as we do, to navigate grimspace. That requires particular biomechanical technology. Unlike us, they don't need both a navigator and a pilot. Their physiology is such that they can split their vision to do two things at once.

"Anything is possible." I can tell from the movement of his claws, he finds my thought processes random and disorderly. This isn't going anywhere, at least not now. I don't have enough information to ask the right questions.

"What about Psi-Corp?" I ask. "What's their status?"

More tapping. I wait and sip my choclaste with poorly concealed impatience.

Eventually he says, "The Conglomerate assumed control of the facility the day after we revealed the Farwan conspiracy. As of now, training proceeds on schedule, though the Conglomerate has hired independent auditors to review processes put in place by Farwan."

That's good, at least. I'm happy to hear we don't have a legion of half-trained Psi running around out there. The unleashed scientists are disturbing enough.

"None of this helps us afford a militia and reinstate regular patrols, does it?"

"No." He considers the problem at length while I finish my drink. "It would seem to make sense to choose one raiding faction and deputize them."

I think I see where he's going with this. "Forge an alliance and formalize their presence? We could ask them to go after other raiders and keep what they take."

"When you deal with criminals," Vel points out, "there is considerable risk of betrayal."

"That's a problem. So how would we make them conform to the agreement?"

Right now it's all just speculation anyway. First we would need to determine the least bloodthirsty faction, then we'd have to make contact. Worrying about their breaking the deal seems futile since we're so far from that point.

Vel lifts his shoulders. "One problem at a time, Sirantha."

He's right. This is too big for us alone. Thankfully, we have official sanction to solve the problem however we see fit—and Conglomerate backing to make it happen.

"Maybe we should focus on something we can deal with for right now."

"Like finding out where those kids belong?" March drops down on the other side of me, looking remarkably cheerful. "I've been talking to Surge about them. Long story short, he's bounced scans of them to a database that monitors missing children. Most of them were able to tell us where they came from, so that'll help."

I smile. "Thanks. Glad to hear it." Quickly I fill him in about how the Morgut seem to be targeting science vessels.

His face darkens. "I can't think of any circumstances in which that could be good."

"That's pretty much what we said. So what's the plan?"

"We need credits, which the Conglomerate is willing to provide—to a certain point. The budget Tarn forwarded doesn't leave me room to do a lot of shopping. With what he's willing to spend, I'll be lucky to make payroll. That doesn't cover ships," March adds quietly. "There's no easy way to make this happen. So far, there *is* no plan. I know what we need, but I'm not sure how to get us there." He pauses, gauging my expression, I think. "But . . . my first instinct is to start raiding the pirates. Hit them where it hurts."

I don't love the idea, but I don't discount it out of hand. "If we're going to do that, we need a home base other than Emry. It doesn't make sense to work from here. We need something closer to the high-traffic beacons."

"Agreed," March says. Then he turns to Vel. "Any ideas?"

"On how best to embark upon a career in piracy?"

March grins at him. "Technically, I think we'd be privateers. We have the equivalent of a letter of marque. Otherwise . . . in a word: Yes."

The three of us talk strategy for a while, and then it's time to return to the comm room and give the Chancellor his answer. Without further discussion, March leans forward and taps the terminal. His message to Tarn is as terse as mine. "I'm in."

CHAPTER 9

Once we bounce the message, a celebratory feeling swells among us. The comm room is crowded again, but the mood lightens. I raise my brows at March. "This calls for a party, don't you think, Commander?"

With the promise of action ahead, I don't let the grim memories of Emry Station get to me again. Maybe we can replace them. Kora's gone a fair ways toward that with redecorating. Even the walls in here are no longer plain gray metal. A quote comes to me; I can't remember the source: *Eat, drink, and be merry, for tomorrow we may die.* Yeah, that. Exactly. After Ithiss-Tor, we need to burn off steam.

March grins at me. "Already wasting Conglomerate resources? Don't make me dock your pay."

I widen my eyes at him. "I get paid? Since when?" But that reminds me. "Hey, Tarn promised to recover my assets if I did that job for him. So where are my credits?"

Vel's already at work on his handheld. I don't know my account numbers by heart, but that only slows him down by a few seconds. By the twitch of his mandibles, he actually seems surprised when he glances up. "They've been restored to your account, Sirantha."

He kept his word? Well, I'll be damned. That bodes well.

"I'm not broke anymore?"

In answer, Vel shows me the machine, which gives me

the balance. Everything I had, plus what I can only assume is a performance bonus. It's not a fortune, but I'm no longer destitute. That's a fabulous feeling.

"You said something about a party?" Hit prompts.

"Can you two handle it?" I ask.

"It was your idea," Dina grumbles. "And you want us to do all the work?"

I smirk. "Yes."

"Come on." Hit tugs on her hand. "It'll be fun. We could all use the chance to cut loose before we jump into this with both feet."

She's right about that. And a party will show the crew we appreciate them. Call it an exercise in morale building. Besides, the old Jax is anxious to drink and dance. I haven't let her have any fun in months.

Dina nudges March with her shoulder. "This cleared with you, Commander?" She gives the last word a subtly mocking stress, but it's affectionate.

He nods, and the other two women head out to prepare for the night's festivities. Vel excuses himself shortly thereafter. I think he senses when March and I need to talk; Vel and I share a connection, too, though it's different, nothing I could articulate. Once we're alone, March turns to me, his face raw with worry. There's certain magic in that; he won't show this look to anyone else. To the rest of the crew, he's captain, commander, savior, or whatever title they've hung on him.

He won't let himself be vulnerable with anyone else.

"It's just so big," he says quietly. "I thought the Academy was too much for me to handle . . . and look how that turned out."

I'm torn between the urge to smack him and the urge to curl up on his lap and tell him everything will be okay. Since I'm not really the nurturing sort, I offer a thump on the shoulder as a compromise.

"Don't be an idiot."

He blinks. Clearly he was expecting something else.

"I'm training Argus," I remind him. "It's not a genetically engineered race, or a new training academy, but it's a beginning. It might even be *better* than an academy. Training jumpers on ships makes sense. If it catches on, we could offer an on-the-job training program as part of the incentive package for people who volunteer." Seeing his expression lighten a touch, I go on. "And okay, so we haven't fixed the burnout problem, but you know that with Doc it's just a matter of time. Maybe instead of breeding a hybrid species, he could do something with the jumpers we already have."

"Tweak their DNA, you mean."

I nod. "Maybe. Maybe he can use *me* for that. I don't mind donating samples as long as he doesn't dissect my whole brain." I offer a fleeting smile. "Though some might argue the fact, I still need that."

"You always put things in perspective for me. Just when I start feeling like we haven't accomplished anything—"

"How can you *ever* feel like that?" I'm honestly astonished. "Since I've known you, we've toppled the order of the universe, set Gunnar-Dahlgren as the undisputed leadership of Lachion, and forged an alliance with Ithiss-Tor. Even if Emry Station blows up *right now*, we'd still go down in history."

Not that I give a shit about that, but March does. Men always want to be remembered whereas women realize that requires being dead.

I continue. "And now we're going to start trying to set things back on their axis."

"I wish you hadn't said 'axis.' " But he's smiling faintly.

I refuse to be derailed. "One good war deserves another, right? We'll slap some human raiders back in line, recruit the rest, and see what we can do about the rest of the galaxy as we get there."

"That's my first step," he says, nodding. "I'll take care of that right now."

As I watch, bemused, he sends out a message on a smugglers' channel, telling them he can offer profit and amnesty to any interested captain. They're to report to Emry Station for more information.

"And now we wait for our ships to come in?" There's so much to do, so much to organize. The endeavor seems impossible when you examine it from a distance. So we'll just take it step by step.

"No." He snags me around the waist and kisses me. "Now we celebrate."

CHAPTER 10

Hit and Dina really know how to throw a party.

By the time I arrive, they've bedecked the lounge with extra lights left over from station rehab. Music comes piping in through the comm system, and everyone looks to be having a great time. March is already there, waiting, but I've been working with Argus, and we lost track of time.

I tilt my head in wry acknowledgment, as he'd predicted that would happen. Argus pauses in the midst of scoping out his crewmates; he has his eye on a petite blonde who works with Dina. "You think I'm in trouble?"

"Nah. It's not your fault. Enjoy the party . . . but not too much. We'll be back to it first thing in the morning."

Wisely, Argus excuses himself as March claims me and leads me onto the dance floor. His eyes are laughing. "Surprise."

"You didn't dance with me on Hon's Kingdom."

"I wasn't ready to call you mine then." He spins me as the music picks up.

I arch a brow. "You are now?"

Once, I would have protested the verbiage. Now I know there are ways to belong to someone that don't take anything away. A relationship shouldn't impose limits—and if it does, then it's wrong. A lover should help you exceed your potential, not clip your wings. Pity I didn't know that when

I married Simon. I spare a fleeting thought to wonder what became of him.

"You know the answer to that." In March, the dark is only ever a breath away, and for a moment, something sharp and feral stares out of his eyes. His gaze touches my throat.

Yes, I know how he feels about that, but I'm not changing my stance. Maybe I don't know exactly what the mark means, but between Vel and me, it's a measure of trust. He saved my ass on Ithiss-Tor, and I'll wear his colors as proudly as I do my scars.

Other people join us on the floor. Dina twirls light and graceful in Hit's arms; the taller woman moves with sinuous grace. Together, they offer such intensity that it feels slightly illicit to watch. With their eyes locked, I can see the love and longing circulate on a closed circuit, fed by proximity.

"You think that's permanent?" I ask softly.

March nods. "I've never known her to stay with anybody so long."

On some level, that makes me happy. Though our second visit to Lachion was disastrous, those two would never have met without that trip. So maybe it was worth it—everything we went through—just to see Dina this happy now.

I catch the station doctor regarding Dina with regret and yearning. It seems she remembers their fling with more than fondness; but our mechanic made a habit of having a girl in every port, before she met Hit. Those days are done now.

Doc's dancing with Rose. Surge and Kora are nowhere to be found, so I guess they're helping with the kids we rescued. I hope we're able to get them home soon. They've adopted Tiera—the girl we saved the first time we visited Emry—as their own, and she seems to be doing well enough, despite the trauma of the Morgut attack.

Eventually Argus persuades the blonde to give him a shot, and that makes me smile, too, because she made him work for it. They seem impossibly young. At their age, I was still at the Academy, resenting Farwan's leash. At their age, I had Sebastian.

"Who?" He has the grace to look slightly embarrassed at tapping my thoughts, but he doesn't rescind the question. "It's not the first time you've thought of him."

"My first love."

March misses a step. I suppose he thought he'd known everything about me, but a woman doesn't reach my age without leaving a few men behind her. In my case, more than a few, but most of them didn't matter. Sebastian did.

"Did he die?" he asks warily.

I know what he's thinking: another ghost for him to fear, another man whose perfection he can't touch.

"No." I gaze over his shoulder for a moment, lost. Then I meet his gaze squarely. "At least not so that I know anything about it."

"Then what did happen?"

"Are you going to tell me the names of all *your* lovers?"

In fact, I don't care. It's best not to think about anyone who came before me, or I might drive myself crazy like March.

"I couldn't," he says quietly. "I didn't know their names, only how much it cost for an hour of their time."

That he'd paid more often than not made me hurt for him. Had nobody but his sister ever loved him, before me? I find myself hoping there might've been a woman who cared; maybe she just wasn't brave enough to tell him so.

"Oh. Well, Sebastian was a musician back on New Terra. I ran off from the Academy every chance I got and found him playing the saxophone in Wickville. Remember, I came from money, and I'd never met anyone like him." Years distant, I remember our last fight: his pretty face and wounded eyes. "Eventually, it came down to a choice between him and grimspace, as we always knew it would."

"Poor bastard."

"Yeah."

We finish the dance in silence, then two more. To my surprise, I'm not tempted to drink to excess. I did that when I needed to forget, and for a change, I have things I want to remember. Despite the looming threat, there's no shadow on the night. We all seem to realize this may be our last chance to be carefree before the war begins in earnest, so we seize it with both hands.

Hours later, the food is gone, the crew has departed, and the san-bots begin cleaning up the mess. Before we leave, I cut the music off, and it leaves a profound silence. I tug March by the hand, tipsy, but in no way impaired.

"Where are we going?" he asks.

I smile and say nothing.

It pleases me when he doesn't ask again. Instead, his fingers tighten on mine, and he follows my lead. He's genuinely surprised when I take him to the comm room instead of our quarters. Amusement stretches my smile—Mary, it's good not to worry about offending anyone by showing my teeth.

"Constance pinged me earlier," I say. "But I didn't want to interrupt the party."

She slips from ship to station and back again, riding the beams like a ghost in the wires. Has anyone ever used a PA like this before? For good or ill, she monitors all the information coming and going; she looks for patterns and presents her findings, as I asked her to on Ithiss-Tor.

His dark face becomes wary. "Tell me it's good news."

"She only said we'd already gotten a response to your broadcast." I lean in and activate the message she's left queued up.

An image flickers to life on-screen, good quality compared to the distress calls we've been watching. The man is a little older than March, skull-cut black hair and a darkly handsome face. At first I don't recognize him, then he smiles. The two gold teeth are a dead giveaway.

"Hon," March breathes. "I thought he was too smart to get blown up on station. He wouldn't have trusted the Conglomerate to get close enough to kill him before he ran."

The pirate looks older with his locks shorn off, but no less appealing. "Surprise," he greets us. "I'm tired of lying low. Farwan destroyed most of my resources, so I'm willing to consider a truce, *if* you make a good offer. Let me know."

I glance at March. "Do you trust him?"

"Not any farther than I can throw him." He grins. "But he'll make a strong ally. His name still has power in the Outskirts, and where Hon goes, others will follow."

"He won't like working for you, Commander." I add his rank in a teasing tone.

"But he'll like legal raids . . . and seizing property in an official capacity. What we're talking about is Conglomerate-sanctioned piracy, turning smugglers to our purposes."

"So you'll tell him to come?"

In answer, he tells the computer: "Bounce a reply immediately: Record on."

"Acknowledged." To my surprise it's Constance.

"My offers stands," March says. "It applies to *any* captain and crew. Report to Emry for more details." He pauses, then adds, "I'm glad to see you, man."

Really? I wouldn't have thought so.

He's so much a part of me now that there's no warm prickle because he's almost always touching my mind lightly, so March answers aloud without even realizing what he's done. "He's one of the few people who remembers Svet. I could talk about her with him."

Anyone who wasn't a jumper would find that constant presence awful and invasive, but I'm used to it. Part of me wishes I could do that for him, too, outside the nav computer, so he could know that comfort, too.

"Didn't Dina know her well?" She's been with him the longest, as I recall.

Doc came later, after he finished his medical training off Lachion. Of us all, Keri has known him longest, but never met his sister. And despite her leadership of the clan, he doesn't think of her as someone he could lean on. She always turns to *him* for help.

March shakes his head. "They met once or twice on Gehenna, I think, before Svet went to work for Farwan. But you know how Dina is when we put into port."

I grin. "I know how she used to be. But I take your

point—Hon's the only one left. No wonder you want to see him."

There's weight in those words. People only live as long as someone remembers them, and for a while, March thought he was the only living soul with memory of his sister. Maybe there are ex–Farwan employees out there somewhere who knew her, but how would he find them? And what would he say if he did? You can't reminisce with a stranger.

"This is a good omen." March pushes to his feet and reaches for me. "Any other urgent messages I need to see before we retire?"

I smile up at him. "Nope, that's the only one. But there will be more." Leaning my head against his chest, I close my eyes for a moment, just enjoying his warmth. "Tarn couldn't have done better than you for this job. I hope you know that."

"You're biased. Anything else on the agenda, Jax?"

My smile widens into a grin. "Maybe."

"Shall we talk about it in private?"

But in our quarters, there isn't much talking tonight.

.CLASSIFIED-TRANSMISSION.
.NEGOTIATION.
.FROM-SUNI_TARN.
.TO-EDUN_LEVITER.
.ENCRYPT-DESTRUCT-ENABLED.

Mr. Leviter:

I agree to your terms. In anyone else, I would call your confidence arrogance, but I've seen what you can do. If the royalists on Tarnus had the wit to employ you, I have no doubt they would still be in power. Your résumé is . . . impressive, to say the least. I hope you can turn the tide for us, because as Mary knows, we can use the help.

As you requested, I've set up an alias for you on world. You'll be slipping into the identity of Corin Underwood, a minor Conglomerate official. He died off world, but I've managed to suppress that news, and when you arrive, you will take over his life. Naturally, you'll need some cosmetic work to make it feasible, so I'm attaching an image. You'll want to take it to your own surgeon; I trust you know someone who does good work. From the tone of your letter, I collect you've done this sort of thing before. I know— I'm not to ask about it, and so I won't.

We'll conduct the negotiations for your salary after you arrive. You'll find I can be a very generous benefactor, but it would be wrong of you to assume you can get your way in all things simply because I have done what I must to get you on the Conglomerate payroll. The simple fact is: We cannot afford to have you working against us.

Corin Underwood has recently been appointed Minister of Diplomatic Relations in absentia. The position awaits your arrival. Is that nebulous enough? I thought it best to give no indications of your function, even in the title. That one should permit you to travel off world as needed.

I'll expect your first status report once you've had a chance to get settled in your new life. Truthfully—and as you can probably tell by the image—Underwood was a bit of a nebbish. I spent no time with the little weasel when he was alive, so you and I will not confer in person either. I know you function best independently, and I'll let you do so. Information will help us win this war, if anything can, and our fate is in your hands.

Mary grant you grace as you make your way, sir.

Tarn

.ATTACHMENT-CORIN_UNDERWOOD-FOLLOWS.
.END-TRANSMISSION.

.COPY-ATTACHMENT.
.FILES-DOWNLOADED.
.ACTIVATE-WORM: Y/N?

.Y.
.TRANSMISSION-DESTROYED.

CHAPTER II

The days fall into a routine on station.

Mostly, I work with Argus in the simulator. I train him longer hours than the Academy endorsed, and we do a lot more practical application than theoretical study. Maybe I'm the minority, but I learn things a lot faster by doing them than by reading about how. Argus seems all right with my methods.

By the end of the first week, he has a better grasp of the process than I could've ever expected. But it's taking a toll on both of us. He looks tired, even in the mornings now. Maybe I should give the kid a few days off.

Today when we break, he looks almost done in, as if he hasn't been sleeping well. And instead of excusing himself, he hangs around the cockpit. Well, I can take a hint.

"Something you need?"

"I was wondering . . . do you ever dream about it?"

"Sometimes," I admit. He doesn't need to tell me he means grimspace. Only one thing can affect a navigator this way—and it's not a love affair. "Not as much as I used to."

March has something to do with that, frankly. He takes up space in my head, leaving less room for other things. In this case it's good; I can't fixate on my addiction the way I used to. He doesn't let me. But most jumpers lack that buffer.

"I have these dreams," Argus says. "First I can't sleep for

seeing the colors, then once I drop off, they're all I see, and I'm convinced there's something past the light. Something I need to see, so I can understand everything."

I must confess I'm worried. If Argus is already feeling the jones—and he hasn't even seen the real deal yet—what does that say about his longevity? Nothing good. He may be a strong candidate for early burnout—or maybe I'm just pushing him too hard.

Regardless, it can't hurt to have Doc take a look. Maybe now that he's isolated what makes me different from other navigators, he can give Argus a tweak to make him more like me. It would be highly experimental, but there are no other test subjects suitable for something like this. It would be up to the kid.

"Let's run by med bay before we head back to the station," I say then.

Argus just nods, which tells me he's seeing a problem, too. We find Doc working on Mary knows what, but he pauses readily for us. "What seems to be the trouble, Jax?"

Funny how he assumes *I* have the problem. I explain succinctly, and Argus adds a few things that he didn't see fit to mention earlier, like how he woke from the last dream near the simulator, with no memory of how he got there. That's really not good.

After a few tests, Doc mutters, "Abnormal activity in the amygdala . . . damage to the cortex. I'm afraid your initial diagnosis was correct. He's already begun the process."

A kinder way to say burnout.

"How is that possible? We haven't even done a real jump. Too much time in the simulator?" Oh, Mary, I ruined him. I was too rough, too impatient. Maybe Farwan had a reason for easing us into it as they did.

Argus looks sick now, his youthful eagerness replaced with fear and horror.

"Some subjects who possess the J-gene have less natural resistance to extreme environments," Doc says. It's a hypothesis, gleaned from years of study. He rambles on about brain structures and innate resistance, but I'm not really hearing him.

"Can you try gene therapy?" I ask. "I know you've isolated what makes me different. But can you give it to him?"

He gets a mad-scientist gleam in his eye. "Only with his permission. And you'd need to keep him out of the simulator until the process was complete."

"What are we talking about here?" Argus asks.

And I realize he doesn't know all that much about me. "My mother was a kinky freak, and I was conceived during a jump, leading to a mutation that lets me heal grimspace damage to my brain."

Doc interrupts then, explaining the benefits and risks of the ability. In short, this genetic mutation lets my body pillage other systems to renew my brain. It keeps me from burnout, but if it ransacks my heart or lungs, it could kill me. Thus far, I've been lucky and it defaulted to my skeletal system, resulting in a loss of bone mass. For a while, I was annoyingly fragile, but with treatment, that's been repaired, too.

"When I had time, I've been working on a regulator that will control the way her mutation functions," Doc adds. "Thus far it's not ready, but if you're willing to let me try gene therapy on you, I'll finish my work as soon as possible."

Ouch. He's still really pissed at me. Thanks, Doc, I get the subtext: I'm not worth the trouble, but if Argus joins my elite cadre of one, then he'll need a fail-safe.

"How risky is it?" the kid asks. "Worse than this?"

Unfortunately, I can't answer that. We both look at Doc.

Who shrugs. "I cannot answer that. Gene therapy can offer brilliant or unreliable results. However, I have no reason to believe it will worsen your circumstances."

Because—now that he's had a taste of grimspace—he's going to go crazy and die anyway, if we don't do something. Other than verifying the J-gene, I didn't run any genetic tests on Argus before popping him in the simulator. I didn't have Doc look at his brain scans to see if he was a good candidate. He had the ability, and that was enough for me. I let my distrust of Farwan tarnish my perception of all their methods. And that was a stupid, unforgivable mistake.

"Then let's do it," Argus says.

I offer my arm to Doc and he takes a sample. "It will take some time for me to work up a suitable vehicle for delivery." He offers a lot more technical information, but I don't care how it's done. I just hope it helps. "And keep him out of the simulator," he adds in unnecessary chastisement, as Argus leaves.

That does it. We need to have this out.

"I'm sorry," I say humbly. "I didn't go about this the right way. I should have had you run a profile on him before I began his training."

And once, I *would* have, but things haven't been right between us since Ithiss-Tor.

"That was stupid," he agrees. "You saw his nature and considered nothing else."

As it's true, I have no defense against that. "Will you help him?"

Doc sets down his tools with exaggerated care on the counter before him. "Do you think I'd let personal feelings impact my professional performance?"

Point taken. Such a petty revenge is certainly beneath him. He wouldn't let an innocent suffer, no matter how he feels about me. That would go against everything he believes in. His credo is "do no harm."

That's where we struck each other wrong, in fact.

"I'm sorry for what happened between us." That's not a proper apology, and by his expression, he knows it.

"You don't understand," he says quietly. It's then that I realize it isn't anger in his eyes. It's pain.

"Tell me."

"I always thought there was no wedge that could break me. I thought my conviction absolute. I always thought I would die rather than cause harm. And yet, Jax . . ." He sighs tiredly. "You found the weakness whereupon everything else crumbles. Under the right circumstances, I *am* willing to bear arms. A hypo in the right hands becomes a weapon, and I was ready to do it. Not pleased, but resigned."

"I thought it was our best chance to take Jael without him hurting anyone else."

He inclines his silver head, older in this moment than I've ever known him to be. "I know. But if I show willing at *any* point, if I falter in my convictions, then my prior refusal becomes nothing more than hypocrisy and cowardice."

Oh. I see the wound now.

"I'm so sorry."

"What am I now?" he asks, relentless.

"Have you talked to Rose about it?" Maybe she can comfort him.

He makes a sharp, angry gesture in the air, his hand like the blade of a knife. "She has never understood, though she champions me. She loves me, but there's nothing she can say. Fighting is a way of life on Lachion."

"I think it says something good about you," I say then. "That you *do* think it's wrong, but you're willing to scar your soul anyway for those you love. It says you put people ahead of principles."

Though it's never been the way between us, I hug him then. His arms come around me, and he feels sturdy as an old tree against me. We stand that way for perhaps three beats before he shoves me back.

"That helped."

"Are we okay?"

He nods. "Just don't cut me out of the loop again. The last time, March wound up in an Ithtorian prison—and now you've gone off half-cocked with this poor young Dahlgren." Doc gives me a half smile. "He's lucky I'm here to clean up after you."

"You said it," I agree with feeling.

CHAPTER 12

The smugglers arrive two days later.

To nobody's surprise, Hon gets here first. We await him and his crew outside the docking bay. This occasion feels like an odd juxtaposition of the last time we met, but I hope we don't have the same fallout here on Emry. Though it's no real reassurance, I can't think of any one faction that would have the ordnance to blow up an emergency station, now that Farwan has split into various splinter cells.

The Syndicate, March tells me silently.

Thanks. I needed that.

He flashes me a roguish grin as he steps forward to greet Hon with a handclasp. With his hair shorn, the pirate seems more warlike. Since that's what we're planning, I figure it's fitting.

"You bastard," Hon says to March. "You must have nine lives."

"You, too. You remember Jax, Dina, and Doc?" At Hon's nod, March introduces the others: Rose, Hit, and Argus.

"You're not still traveling with Fugitive scientists?" Doc asks warily.

Hon shakes his head. "Learned my lesson. Farr was too crazy, even for me."

I want to ask if he knows anything about those breeding experiments, but I suspect he'd just lie, and we're trying to work for a common cause now. Whether I like it or not, I have to follow March's lead.

The smuggler starts naming his crew, and I log a number of new faces. His jumper, Jory, is a tall, fair-skinned woman with dark hair and twinkling gray eyes. Ship's mechanic, Dobson, is a taciturn man, whose face has been weathered by the sun; he wears his iron gray hair in a braid down his back, and his dark eyes look like currants. But it's the fourth member of their group who holds my attention. He stands quiet at the back, still and watchful, but I think I know him. I *do* know him.

His hair is shorter now, shorn like Hon's, and his face shows hard living. Whatever he's been through, he's lost that untouched expression as well as his unearthly prettiness. But the deep blue eyes are the same.

"Loras," I breathe.

I remember how it hurt, letting him sacrifice himself for March and me. All this time, I never dared hope he might've made it. Between the raiders and Farwan blowing the space station, I didn't think he had a chance. Mary, I've never been so happy to be wrong.

The others start, conversations falling still. I push past Jory and Dobson toward him, intending to grab him in a tight, relieved hug—and then I realize he may not be happy to see us. After all, we left him to die. I draw up short.

Uncertain, I offer him my hand. I can't believe he's *here.*

Loras regards me for a moment. I can't read his expression. A glance at March tells me he's equally in the dark. Hit never even knew him, so she looks puzzled, while Dina doesn't seem sure what to say, either. He shakes my hand briefly, as if we're strangers, as if we never huddled in a corrugated metal shed together, afraid for our lives.

"I'm so glad to see you. We thought—" Well, I'm sure he knows. "Why didn't you get in touch with us? We'd have come for you, no matter where you were."

"Because he's *mine* now," Hon tells me. "I saved him, first from the beating he took from the raiders, then when Farwan attacked."

There's a sinking in my stomach because that's true. Because of physiological adaptation to a drug humans introduced on his homeworld, Loras belongs to whoever protects him best. So he won't be rejoining us; I failed him. But it's not about me. I'd rather see him safe with Hon than dead like a sacrificial goat.

"It's true," he says then. "Hon is my *shinai* now. It never occurred to me that any of you would want to hear from me."

As if he were a burden we couldn't wait to shift. Mary, we were such sorry bastards. We never made him feel welcome among us, never gave him the sense of belonging the rest of us enjoy. Beside me, March flinches. He used to joke about getting rid of him, and I can feel the guilt flowing off him in waves.

"I'm sorry," March mutters. "I didn't realize how you felt. I should have. Loras—"

"Forget it." Loras shrugs like it doesn't matter, but I can see it does.

I have to figure out some way to make this up to him. Hon and March get busy explaining to the others how we know each other. That story carries us from the corridor outside the docking bay back to the lounge. We lose a few along the way, as our crew decides to give Hon's a tour of the station.

Eventually, it's just me, March, Hon, and Loras. We settle in with drinks to talk terms. While I listen, March outlines the deal he's put together with Tarn's sanction.

"I can offer you full amnesty for all your past crimes, right now, on the condition you sign an agreement to act as a subcommander in the Conglomerate Armada."

Hon raises a brow. "The what?"

"We're building an army," I say. "And we need ships . . . but not *just* ships. If we have any hope against the pirates and smugglers—"

"You need them manned with clever crew," Hon finishes. "What's in this for us?"

March asks, "Besides a full pardon?" But even I know that's not enough. He grins and continues. "You'd be out there raiding anyway . . . without backup. You lost most of your ships running from Farwan at DuPont Station, so it's harder than it used to be. Plus, now you have Syndicate ships to contend with, along with other pirates."

"Tell me something I don't know." Hon takes a slug of his drink, eyes narrowed.

"We hire you to patrol," March says. "You answer distress calls, bounce messages to a closer ship if necessary, and act as the Conglomerate's eyes. You'll have the authority to treat your sector as a killbox, eliminate threats by any means you deem necessary. In addition, you can claim any hostile ship, including cargo and contraband, as hazard pay. In exchange, you leave the merchantmen and cargo vessels alone. You're already at war with other raiders, so you might as well do some good out there."

"You putting together an army full of mercs and smugglers." The pirate grins. "Only you would think of deputizing outlaws to uphold the law."

March shrugs, but by his expression he's thought of the irony himself. "We were never fighting the Conglomerate. It was always Farwan. If we don't step up, if we don't try to shape the authority that governs us, then we have no right to complain about it later."

"True," Hon says thoughtfully. "But I was never one to complain . . . *or* follow the rules. What makes you think I won't take your credits and do what I want out there?"

A tight smile curves March's mouth, but it doesn't quite hit his eyes. "There's a limit to my trust. We'll equip your ship with technology that logs your encounters with other vessels. As long as you act as we've agreed, we won't have a problem."

"Technology isn't infallible," Hon points out. "And what if there's a dispute regarding the way I handle a situation?"

It's sad he has to wonder about that, but it's a valid question. He could very well save some merchantman from imminent doom and have the asshole owner complain that he took too long about it.

"If any other ship lodges a complaint against an Armada vessel, we will send the matter before a review board comprised of randomly selected officers," March answers.

The pirate considers that, then inclines his head. "Well thought. It eliminates bribery, and it should be an impartial hearing. All right, I've heard enough."

"And?" I ask.

"I'm in. Draw up the contracts."

March nods, tapping his comm. "Constance, I need that agreement you worked up earlier. Forward it to me?"

"With pleasure," she replies.

"Who was that?" Hon perks up at the feminine voice I gave my PA back when she was just a little silver sphere.

I stifle a grin. *Not this again.*

Should we tell him? March asks me silently.

Maybe not just yet. I owe Hon for plying me with pheromones that made me think I wanted to sleep with him.

The lightning exchange takes only seconds, so I answer aloud, "Her name is Constance. Maybe you'll meet her later."

"Oh, I'll find her. Count on it, pretty." The pirate does everything but rub his hands together at the prospect of meeting the female that owns such a great voice.

Loras has been listening silently, as he used to, but he interrupts now. "Have you considered a uniform? Historical precedent suggests that any police force is taken more seriously by the populace if they offer conformity in their dress."

"I'm not covering myself in bars and symbols," Hon mutters. "This isn't worth going around dressed like a fascist ass."

"Something simple should work," I say. "Plain, but vaguely military. The important thing is that everyone wears it."

Nodding, Loras says diffidently, "I have some ideas."

March is busy beaming the contract to Hon's handheld, but he spares me a nod. "Do you mind working with him on this?"

Mind? I was hoping for a chance to talk to Loras alone. I smile.

"I think that's our cue. Shall we hole up somewhere and compare notes?"

CHAPTER 13

Wordless, Loras follows me to a small conference room, which has escaped Kora's touch, so it's as gray and soulless as Farwan left it. There aren't many such rooms on station, which means we're going to be hard up for space once the Armada starts growing, but for security, we couldn't do better. And ideally, we'll start rotating ships out, so we won't have the whole fleet docked here at the same time.

That would sort of defeat the purpose.

"Here," he says, getting right to business. He shows me a few images on his handheld. "Something like this could be adapted with a new logo designed to integrate the Conglomerate's symbol and something new for the Armada."

With an inner sigh, I realize he doesn't want to get personal. Fine, I can be patient if I must. Resigned, I examine some of the designs before tapping a forefinger lightly on the screen. "This is good, don't you think?"

It's a sleek uniform in midnight blue with fitted trousers, shiny black boots, and a plain shirt, covered with a matching jacket cut in relaxed but tailored lines. I'd wear it—and look good in it, too.

"That's the one I would pick," he admits. "Shall we work on a logo?"

"The Conglomerate symbol is a stylized sun crowned with a laurel leaf. Rather than change that, I'm thinking we should just add something to it."

We toss ideas back and forth for several hours, each subsequently worse than the other. I eventually patch Constance into the meeting via my handheld and she projects atop the table in a tiny version of the body that went defunct back on Ithiss-Tor. She listens to all of our terrible ideas, including flora and fauna, then offers a verdict:

"You are not thinking in terms of symbolism," she chides us. Or maybe I'm the only one who feels chided. Loras seems to be entranced. "Solar representations offer varied meaning in semiotics, heraldry, astrology, and many religions. In ages past, the Conglomerate chose it because it represents life, promise, and strength."

"What about the other part of the design?" Loras asks.

Well, I would have, too, given the chance.

"The laurel wreath represents victory or conquest," Constance tells us. "And the Conglomerate selected it for that association, though their conquests have long since been relegated to history."

"It's time to change that," I say with determination. "So looking at symbolism that fits, what can you offer?"

"Searching," she says.

"What's that?" Loras whispers, as if he's afraid of offending her.

"My PA," I say, sheepish.

"From Lachion?" His azure eyes widen. "Mair's old unit?"

How to explain? Well, it's better to just tell it all. So I do, summarizing our adventures since we parted ways, and that includes Constance's evolution.

"Is that *legal*?" he asks, when I'm done.

I shake my head ruefully. "Probably not. You gonna report me?"

He looks away. "You're Hon's allies. It would gain me nothing and incur his displeasure were I to do so."

Okay, that's it.

"You ass," I growl at him. "What does it take to get through to you, man? I thought you were *dead*. And don't give me any shit about *shinai* this, or in-your-debt that. You were my friend. I hope to Mary you still are."

If he says it is impossible for friendship to thrive when one person is wholly subservient to another, I don't know how I'll keep from smacking him. I never treated him like a slave. But then, I don't know how Hon's treated him.

Loras hesitates, staring at his hands, then finally: "I don't know what I am. It was different on Hon's ship."

I tense. "Different, how?"

Please don't let anyone have hurt him. Though I might've had an angry thought out of exasperation, I'd never harm him. If you have any decency, you can't lift a hand to the utterly defenseless.

"Hon said it best," he tells me tonelessly. "I belong to him. I do as he asks, whenever he asks it."

Oh. Not physical abuse, then. But a reinforcement of his belief that he lacks intrinsic value—that he's lesser because he can't bludgeon someone with a spanner in a fit of rage. Mary, I have to fix this.

"Loras . . ." I take his hand between the two of mine, marveling at the artistry of his fingers. For pure beauty, I've never seen any male anywhere to match him, not even the pleasure toys on Venice Minor. "If I could go back, if I could do it over, I wouldn't leave you there. I'd get ordnance from the ship and blow that door. We'd fight every last raider for you. And maybe you don't believe me . . . maybe you think I'm full of shit now, but I'm going to prove it. You're *not* just a bond servant to me."

He offers a very gentle return pressure before he slips his hand free, his face distant and cool. "The only way you can prove that is to set me free."

Shit, surely he doesn't mean he wants me to kill him. Fear jolts through my system. I can't do that—there's just no fraggin' way. I'm so unsettled that it draws March's attention, whatever he's doing now.

Jax? You all right?

I think so, I tell him. *Shhh.*

He quiets, but doesn't withdraw all the way, instead keeping half an eye on me.

"How?" I ask unsteadily.

He shrugs. "That's for you to worry about. But it's the only boon that will mean anything to me."

So saving his life is out. All that will do is transfer ownership back to me. He doesn't want that; he's sick to his soul of that. I've never met any others of his race, so I don't know if they all feel this way, or if Loras has extra steel in him that doesn't let him accept the yoke. Regardless, I have to try.

The obvious answer comes to me.

"Doc could try to work up a treatment," I say then. "It'd be risky, and no guarantee of success, but he's the original mad scientist. He's all for doing what's never been done before." And thank Mary for it—otherwise Argus and I would be doomed. "If it's proven to work on you—"

"The Conglomerate could offer it to my people."

"Along with abject apologies and reparations," I say quietly. "It's the least we owe. I can't make promises, mind, because I don't have any formal authority in this. But I swear to you I'll try."

Warmth surges through me. *Well-done, Jax.*

For the first time, Loras smiles. "That's all I could ask. You almost persuade me that I matter, Sirantha."

The pain behind his beauty makes me want to punch something. "You do."

Constance cuts in with, "I have resolved your query."

"I'm all ears," I tell her.

A beam of light skims over me. "You have only two, Sirantha Jax. Shall I present my findings?"

I'm hard-pressed not to laugh. Sometimes I swear she does stuff like that to be funny. "Please do."

"I recommend a lightning bolt. This has long been used to suggest authority, such as the gods themselves might wield. It also signifies power and knowledge. In a less abstract sense, I consider the symbol representative of Armada ship lasers standing ready to protect all Conglomerate citizens."

"That's perfect," Loras says. "We could tweak it, and add a line here to suggest the lasers themselves, and—"

"Two lines." I point to the left of the image. "And maybe it should pierce the sun?"

Constance brings up a three-dimensional logo beside her, incorporating our feedback until we have something that we agree is suitable for our purposes. I nod at the symbol. Right now, only the three of us know what it means, but one day, people will associate this abstract design with safety and security. That gives me an odd feeling.

I share a look with Loras, who seems to share my sense of wonder.

"That's it," I say at last. "Perfect."

"Saving," Constance tells me. "Shall I research the company best suited to fulfill a substantial order for the uniform emblazoned with this logo?"

I consider that. "Go ahead. But don't buy anything without checking with me first. We need approval before it'll become official. Just get me some numbers."

"Acknowledged. Is there anything else, Sirantha Jax?"

"Not right now. Thanks." Silly though it might be, I can't break the habit of treating Constance like a person, albeit one who lives in bytes instead of blood.

Then it's just Loras and me again.

"This will pass muster," he says with confidence. "We just set the tone for a new military presence in the galaxy. How does that feel?"

"Pretty damn good," I admit.

Not a thrill like jumping, but there's satisfaction in it nonetheless. For once, I've had a say in something important; I didn't shrug my shoulders and pass the grunt work off on someone else. I'm proud of myself for that.

I'm also stiff, sore, and hungry.

"Let's get something to eat," I add. "And then I'll talk to Doc."

CHAPTER 14

"Is there anything else, Jax? Perhaps a cure for Jenner's Retrovirus between now and breakfast? Would you like me to make the dead to *rise* again?"

Since we disperse the molecules of our dead, I know that's sarcasm. "Are you saying you can't do it?"

I don't want to tell Loras he won't even try when Saul has attempted so many other impossible things over the course of our acquaintance. If I had any skill with an imploring look, I'd employ it right now, but my face doesn't slant that way. So I regard him steadily.

While I wait, I take in the facilities. The ship they brought from Lachion is well provisioned, and he's set up an excellent mobile lab with machines and tools that I can't identify. If anyone can do this, he can.

"No," he says at last. "And since we've shifted away from the idea of engineering a new species, I will have the time to consider the problem."

"That's no longer on the table?" I ask, interested.

Doc shakes his head. "After extensive research I think it would be best to come at the problem via your mutation. If that proves efficacious, I might attempt to strengthen it with DNA strains from . . ." He pauses, his face softening. "Well, Baby-Z."

Once, I would've made a joke about his planning to turn jumpers into some freakish frogman hybrid. Not now.

We made Marakeq our first stop when we were gathering samples, so Doc could devise a better breed of jumper. DNA samples taken by Fugitive scientists had indicated that the genetic composition of the natives would offer a valuable longevity boost to those who possessed the J-gene. We'd only meant to take some samples ourselves; instead we wound up with a newborn hatched out of season, and our only choice had been to take him with us or let him die.

In the end, he'd died anyway—and I carry that failure close to my heart, where Baby-Z once rested. More than anything, I want to make that right.

"This can't be high on the agenda right now, but . . . eventually, I'd like you to clone him."

He quirks a brow at me. "If you wish to reproduce, Jax, there are easier methods."

"Funny." I hesitate, not knowing if he'll understand. "I want to take him home, if we ever get the chance. Once the war is over . . ." I trail off, thinking it sounds stupid.

But in order to move on from that loss, I have to make some attempt at restitution. I know it won't be the same, but I can't imagine turning up on Marakeq empty-handed. And I cannot imagine what other solace I can offer his bereaved mother. Maybe it won't be enough; maybe it's wrong, but I don't know what else to do.

"I understand. And yes, I can do that . . . someday." He doesn't mention that it's likely to be far in the future, when all we need to worry about is reparations, not plan for the destruction of our enemies.

But I understand that very well.

"Thanks. I don't know what we'd do without you."

"Sometimes I wonder." I turn to go, but he stops me with a tap on my shoulder. "Jax . . . how is Loras, really?"

"He's tired of being property." There isn't a lot I can do to dress that up.

"Then I'll give his problem equal time," he promises.

I nod in acknowledgment and step out of med bay. The ship lights have dimmed, simulating a more natural cycle, so I know it's late. At this point, I'm not sure if I should be in my quarters on the ship or if we've taken a berth on station. I'm too tired to hunt March down myself, but I don't want to go to bed without him, either. I've spent too many nights wishing for him by my side to let even one slip by now.

So I tap my wrist. "Constance, where's March?"

"Searching," she tells me. There's a brief delay of a few seconds, then: "I have located him in the officers' lounge on station. Shall I contact him for you?"

"No, I can do that." Well, I could if I *wanted* to. I think I'll surprise him. Looks like I have one last thing to do before I get some shut-eye.

"As you prefer, Sirantha Jax. I will return to my research now."

There's no end to her usefulness. Smiling, I make my way off the ship, through docking and into the corridors. Once, these halls were dark, guttering lights overhead, loose wires hanging. I remember the sickly sweet smell and the bodies. A little shiver rolls through me. Even with all the changes, it's still hard for me to be here by myself. More images fight to the forefront of my brain.

My knees feel like they're melting. Vel jerks me upright and gives me a shake that rattles my teeth in my head. When that doesn't help a whole lot, he slaps me full across the face. That stings enough that I try to fight back.

And that's when the things drop down from the ceiling.

My head spins too much to count them. When Vel knocks me flat, I have the sense to stay down, though the blow feels like it may have cracked a few ribs. Ironically, the pain clears my head to some degree.

I try to breathe through my shirt, and that helps a little, too. On my belly, I crawl along the floor, taking refuge behind a crate of machine parts. The fighting seems blurred and distant, too far away for where I'm hiding.

My vision can't be relied upon. I hear March swearing steadily as he fires. He's taken cover somewhere nearby. I hear the wet, splattering sound of the disruptor rearranging meat. The Morgut don't scream when they die; they keen.

Without March, it's harder to battle the memory back. I can still see the blood-spattered room and the monstrous Morgut with their bulging bodies and multiple hinged limbs. *I'm safe,* I tell myself. *Safe. Now, keep moving. Officers' lounge.* I know where that is. Everyone else seems to be asleep by now or at least retired to quarters, so I don't pass anyone as I make my way through the station. It's eerily silent, and I find myself making a game of trying to keep my footfalls quiet. That's why I can hear the voices long before I reach my destination.

I realize March isn't alone. Most likely I should stride up and announce myself—that, or back away before they know I'm here. But when I hear Hon's bass rumble in response, I decide I'm going to do neither. Instead, I slip a little closer and lean against the wall, waiting for March to answer.

"Sometimes, it's like I think she'll be back."

"It's hard," Hon says. "Back on DuPont, I didn't know. I would've said something. She was a good kid, your sister. I don't know what I'd do if anything happened to Shan."

That strikes a chord. I remember the glass dancer from Hon's Kingdom, a woman Hon didn't introduce me to. Though she doesn't favor the pirate, they share the same aura of absolute confidence. It makes sense he wouldn't want his enemies to know about her; she's a weakness. I wonder where she is now.

March makes a wry sound. "I know. But it wasn't like I was going to come in on a line like, 'Be nice to me for a change; I'm bereaved.'"

Hon laughs. "For a change? Who mistreats who again?"

"Frankly, I figure we're about even."

"I guess so. You said . . ." Hon's tone gains a delicacy I wouldn't have credited. "You want to talk about her?"

"It's more accurate to say I want to hear you talk about her. Tell me everything you know." Longing fills his voice— and I understand now how he feels about Kai. Oh, it's not the same *kind* of love; I understand that, but for the first time, I grasp fully that there's a hole in him I can never completely fill.

"Well, I never took her to my bed, so there's a limit to how accurate I can be." I can hear the smile in the pirate's voice.

A thwack as March hits him.

"All right, I'll tell you a story, man. She was a pretty thing. Looked nothing like you, bless her. I remember thinking you had to be joking me when you first introduced us, that there was no way you could be related to a fair little kitty like that."

"Don't call my sister that," March warns him.

"You want the story, you get my words."

I figure they're exchanging looks right about now, testing who's the most serious, but in the end, March agrees, "Fine."

"As I was saying . . . I'll confess now, once I tried to score her, but she knew your friends, and she was having none of it."

"You tried for my *sister*?" March sputters, torn between outrage and amusement that Svet shut him down.

Now I wish I'd met her. Small, fair? Does that mean blond? At any point, I could've called up a picture from Farwan's records. I don't know why I didn't, except that perhaps until this moment, Svetlana didn't seem quite real to me. Setting my handheld on mute, I tap a few commands and access the records via the station satellite uplink.

Within seconds, I have an image: heart-shaped face, mouth curved into a gentle smile, and eyes of a shade that wavers between blue and green. Warm, shallow seas have water like that. I can see nothing of March in her, but I know he loved her.

"After that," Hon continues, "I made point of looking out for her whenever I was on Gehenna. I stopped by that place she worked, two or three times a trip. We got to be friends, but don't go telling that around."

"Of course not."

"Most of all I remember she liked shiny things. Didn't matter if it cost ten credits or ten thousand; she loved the sparkle. Sometimes I'd bring her back a little something, just to see that smile. No strings," he hastened to add, doubtless forestalling March's wrath.

March lets out a heavy sigh. "Yeah. I've got a bagful of stuff I never gave her. I kept thinking I'd surprise her, then I'd take another tour working for some Nicuan asshole. It was always going to be, 'Just one more, and I'll be set. I can get a ship and get Svet out of there.'"

My legs are aching, so I shift quietly. I hadn't realized his guilt went quite so deep, but I should have. He blames himself for everything, even when it doesn't make sense. Thankfully, Hon is on his game.

"You can't beat yourself up over that. You didn't make her turn to Farwan when she got in trouble."

Wait, what? What trouble?

That's exactly what March wants to know. "What're you talking about?"

The pirate inhales sharply, and I can hear his chair rock back, a nervous shift. "I saw Svet for the last time on Gehenna, maybe five turns back. She didn't know about our contretemps on Nicu Tertius, so she still had a smile for me."

"And?" March demands.

"She was with child, man. I thought you knew."

CHAPTER 15

There's a crash from within the room, and I figure that's my cue. Pushing away from the wall, I head for the lounge at a dead run, and when I come in, I find March on the verge of pounding Hon's face in. Probably out of respect for March's shock, the pirate isn't fighting back, but he's not going to take a beating docilely, nor *should* he.

"Let him go." My tone brooks no refusal, but I'm still a little surprised when he listens to me. "Now, you two want to tell me what this is all about?"

March spares me a scathing glance. "Cut the crap, Jax. Do you really think I don't know anytime you're nearby?"

I hadn't, actually. I didn't realize his Psi worked in that way. Sheepish, I duck my head and shrug. "I didn't want to interrupt."

"Better to spy," he growls.

But I know he's just *angry*, not necessarily with me.

"Let's sit down and talk about this." I put my words into practice.

Hon straightens and gives March a narrow-eyed look. "You go after me again, for any reason, and I'm outta here, bwoy."

"I'm sorry," March says grudgingly. "I was just . . ."

"Shocked?" I supply, when it becomes obvious his clenched jaw it makes it hard for him to speak.

"What else can you tell me?" he asks at length.

Hon spreads his palms in a universal gesture. "Nothing. I never saw her again. Later, I heard she went to work for Farwan."

"Why didn't I know?" March whispers, looking inward.

"So you don't know what happened to the child." She might've lost it or had the pregnancy terminated.

"No." The pirate seems sorry, but he's telling the truth. There's no satisfaction in Hon at leveling March like this, which raises him in my estimation. "I think you two have some things to talk about. I'm gone." So saying, he makes good on the words and slides out of the lounge.

March buries his face in his hands, and though it's late, I take the precaution of securing the door. I don't want anyone else listening in like I did. *Do as I say, not as I do.*

Coming up behind him, I sink my hands into his hair, shaping my fingers to his skull. The warmth feels good, and he rubs his head against me like a big cat.

"Why didn't she tell me?" he asks.

"I don't know. Where were you, five turns ago?"

His jaw tightens. "Lachion. Mair had me on the road to recovery by then, but I hadn't earned off-world privileges yet. She didn't trust me not to return to Nicu Tertius."

Mair was Keri's grandmother, and the onetime leader of the Gunnar clan. She had saved March's sanity—and possibly his life—when her Rodeisian second, Tanze, stole Hon's ship with March aboard. Instead of just ending him, she'd worked to heal him and turn him from a ruthless killer to a decent human being. Being Psi had driven all the empathy out of him from years of unshielded exposure to people's worst natures. When you're fed nothing but ugliness, that's all you have to give back.

"That's why, then," I say aloud. "She couldn't get in touch with you."

"Whose fault is that?" he rages. "While she was growing up, I spent more time away than I did with her. And when she needed me most, I wasn't there, either."

Mary, this is going to bury him. I lean down and press

my cheek against the top of his head. In answer, he tips his face back, arms curling around me from an awkward angle.

"I think you're asking the wrong questions," I say softly.

"Oh?"

"You can't help Svet. There's nothing you can do for her now, and it doesn't matter why she acted as she did. You can't impact that."

"So what should I be asking instead?" Anyone else might be surprised to see him look to me for guidance; I'm the only one he'd let see him like this.

"What happened to her baby."

"Mother Mary," he swears, bolting to his feet. "Is it possible?"

By his expression, he's ready to take the ship and leave right now. I stay him with a hand on his arm. He looks at me, muscles coiled.

"There's nothing we can do tonight," I tell him, hating that it's so. "Put Constance on the problem, and maybe she'll have an answer in the morning. In the meantime, maybe you can look at this as a good thing?"

He considers, then shakes his head. "I can't see it."

"If you can find him . . . or her, this child will be like having a little of Svetlana back again. You won't be completely bereft of family anymore."

His arms enfold me then. "I'm not, Jax."

Well, I'm not sure if we could call ourselves family. After all, we're not married, and I don't want to be. That didn't work out so well the first time, and I have enough of Kai left in me that promises kept through desire mean more to me than those imposed by law.

We stand like that for another moment before I pull back. "Do we have a berth here, or should we head for the ship?"

"The ship," he says.

That's right; the kids are sleeping on the station.

As we walk, I fill him in on everything I've accomplished. Though he's still obviously distracted, he agrees the uniform is a step in the right direction. Knowing he won't get any sleep until I do, once we reach our quarters, I ping Constance one last time. How did we ever get along without her?

"Can you do me a favor?" Pointless—it's not like she can say no.

"Of course, Sirantha Jax. What do you need?"

"Can you do some digging on Svetlana March? She signed with Farwan . . ." I glance at March, who supplies the date.

That's when it occurs to me. March must be his *last* name. I've been with him this long, and I don't even know his name? The absurdity amuses me.

"Find out if there are any records of her giving birth. You may have to search a lot of different databases, so we understand if it takes time."

"Does this take precedence over the compilation of suitable manufacturers?"

I don't even need to look at March to answer. "Yes. The sooner you can tell us, the better off we'll be."

We get ready for bed. He doesn't have to tell me there isn't going to be any rolling around tonight. Hon killed the mood, as they say, but it's fine. I'm tired anyway. March is quiet, his face heavy with old regret.

Into the silence, Constance says, "I have the answer to your query."

I pause, shirt half over my head. Struggling through the black fabric, I glance at March, who's frozen in place. He looks half-sick at what he may hear.

"What did you find?" I ask.

"Svetlana Holder March spent four days in a private Farwan medical facility on New Terra on . . ." Constance names a date consistent with Hon's recollection. "Records indicate she bore a boy child, who tested Psi positive at four days old. *Highly* unusual for the gift to manifest so soon. The infant was remanded into Farwan's custody for crèche-rearing and eventual induction into Psi-Corp."

"I have a nephew," he breathes. "Where is he now?"

"I am sorry," she says, at length. "The data trail ends there. There are no records that I can access regarding his placement."

I watch him pace our quarters, not enough space to offer an outlet for his frustration. His deltoid muscles bunch with each movement. Finally, he slams a fist into the wall. The material dents, then flows back into shape. Starships have been designed to weather the occasional outburst.

"He could be anywhere," he bites out. "Constance, alert the crew. We're—"

"Belay that order."

March draws up short, his amber eyes sparking gold in his fury. His hands curl at his sides, and he's imposing as hell, but I stand my ground.

"You better have a damn good reason for that, Jax. That's my flesh and blood we're talking about."

"I know," I say softly. "But be rational. Where would we go? What can we discover by running around that Vel and Constance can't dig out in time?" I shake my head, sad that I have to be the one to point this out. It requires a deep breath and determination for me to go on: "We can't do this now; we're committed elsewhere. Your nephew or not, he's *one* child. Right now, we're looking after the fate of the human race. What's going to happen to that kid if we fail?"

For a moment, I fear he's too maddened to hear it, then the tension slides out of him in terrible, defeated resignation. I hope to Mary I never see that look on his face again, like an animal that's been wounded to the point that it expects nothing more.

"Good of the many versus the few," he murmurs. "I'm familiar with the concept. He's probably fine, whatever Psi-Corp training facility he wound up in."

"With the war on, he's better off on New Terra for now." I pitch my voice low, trying not to show how much it hurts that I can't wave a hand and fix this for him. "When we fight through, we'll find him, I swear, and make sure he's all right."

"And take Baby-Z home," he says bitterly. At my shock, he adds, "Oh, I know all about dreams deferred. But how *much* do we have to sacrifice before we're done?"

The question leaves me uneasy because I truly fear the answer.

.CLASSIFIED-TRANSMISSION.
.FIRST STATUS REPORT.
.FROM-EDUN_ LEVITER.
.TO-SUNI_ TARN.
.ENCRYPT-DESTRUCT-ENABLED.

Recruitment and War Effort

The campaign is going well. As Minister of Diplomatic Relations, I have access to all documents. At this time, we have nearly ten thousand bodies willing to go to war. The shipyards have started production, and the vessels will be built by the time the volunteers have completed their basic training. Allotment of seized Farwan resources should be sufficient to cover the first year of salary for all of these men, but alternate sources of income will need to be found. A recommendation on tariffs is attached. Said policy should not be implemented until the war is won. Should the war take longer than one year, other measures will need to be employed.

Syndicate Activity

Sigma Psi has the highest concentration of activity. A cadre of at least twenty ships hunts this sector; they appear to be interested in the same type of cargo though they are not above jacking whatever wanders into their web. In main, they target supply ships. By now the colonies are feeling the pinch, and a rescue mission here would go a long way toward repairing the Conglomerate public image.

Such a coordinated effort is unusual in independent raiders; therefore, it stands to reason that this group is affiliated with or contracted to the Syndicate. To date, these twenty ships account for 67% of all lost lives and loss of property in this region. Ship names and identification numbers are attached. Routes and plans will follow once I confirm the intelligence. You should feed this information to your commander, so he can schedule patrols accordingly.

Raiders

Since Hon-Durren went underground after the destruction of DuPont Station, they lack a unifying figure. Consequently, they've devolved into a disorganized group of thugs and ruffians. Their threat levels are insignificant compared to other factions in play. At best, they account for 15% loss of life over several galaxies. Because of limited resources, I suggest they are a minimal threat and should be recruited whenever possible.

The Morgut

All signs indicate they are mustering at a level we've never seen before. This is *not* a minor conflict. By my next report, I will be able to confirm whether I currently hold a piece of Morgut technology. They rarely permit their vessels to be taken. If it looks as though they will lose a conflict, sources report that the Morgut destroy their own ships to prevent their technology from falling into our hands.

I have pinpointed the location of their homeworld with reasonable surety, and all signs indicate this migration is not random chance but a calculated maneuver, a movement in some larger pattern. Experts state that this surge in Morgut activity indicates a great exodus. They do not plan on returning home again.

Against human beings, the Morgut have a 97% kill rate. This statistic includes both ship-to-ship combat and hand-to-hand encounters. More alarming, heretofore it has not seemed to matter whether they were facing a trained soldier or a civilian. A file detailing their physiological vulnerabilities is attached.

According to ancient Ithtorian writings, dating from before the Axis Wars, the Morgut are known to have four castes: workers, drones, hunters, and queens. More information is needed in order to properly assess the threat levels of each. I posit that the hunters are the ones currently terrorizing our colonies while the others move in once the local populace has been cleared and devoured. As to how this pattern works long term, I can only speculate.

One of my experts has synthesized a toxin he posits will reproduce the effects induced by contact with Ithtorian blood. Cost analysis of mass-producing said toxin follows, including components required. You will wish your troops equipped with it.

To date, information on the Morgut has been scarce. They are not a social race, except among their own kind. They are not hive-mind like the Jhihezu. To the best of my research, they exist to eat, breed, and claim territory. Their instincts seem primitive, but what we understand of their technology demonstrates they have capabilities superior to ours. Agents have retrieved miscellaneous apparatus from a dealer in such rarities, and analysis will tell us more.

This concludes my initial report. Please review the information and advise where you would like to focus our resources.

.ATTACHMENT-RAIDER_SHIPS-FOLLOWS.
.ATTACHMENT-PHYSIOLOGICAL_VULNERABILITIES-FOLLOWS.
.END-TRANSMISSION.

.COPY-ATTACHMENTS.
.FILES-DOWNLOADED.
.ACTIVATE-WORM: Y/N?

.Y.
.TRANSMISSION-DESTROYED.

CHAPTER 16

March doesn't come to me this evening.

I tell myself he's working, and it has nothing to do with my refusal to let him veer off from our mission to go looking for his nephew. In this, I'm playing the bad guy, and I don't like it. My heart is heavy, and sleep brings unquiet dreams. I can't remember what they were, but I know I was running from something.

The space is cool and empty when I wake.

After breakfast, I check in with the kids we saved. It doesn't seem fair for Rose to be stuck on nanny detail, though when I step into the dormitory, she doesn't seem to mind. Seven small faces turn my way, as I've interrupted a story.

I wave to show she should continue, so she does. I sit down at the back of the dorm. It's some legend I've never heard before, so I listen with as much interest as the children.

"Then Pyotr jabbed the pin into the giant's foot. The beast cried out in pain and hopped around, but what the giant didn't realize was—" She looks at the kids as if inviting them to guess.

"He was standing in front of a big hole!"

"There was a warrior behind him with a sword."

"He was at the edge of a volcano!"

They vie for her attention and her smiles for a good five minutes. By the time Rose finishes the tale of Pyotr and the Giant, they're cheering wildly. From their reactions, I gather there have been more tales about this particular hero prior to today.

When the kids notice me at the back of the room, they go from exuberant to timid, then a girl recognizes me. "You were with the people who took us off the bad ship."

I nod. "How are you guys doing?"

Her pointed chin dips. "I want to go home."

"I know. As soon as we can locate your parents, we'll take you."

A little boy gazes up at me, eyes wide. "So you're not going to sell us?"

"Sell you . . . No, of course not." Mary curse it, he must've heard the slavers talking. "Did you hear something on the bad ship?"

He nods. "They were talking about the people who ordered us."

The kids cluster around me, as if I can protect them. And I will. Nobody's going to hurt them while I'm around.

"What do you mean?"

The oldest child with heartbreakingly knowing eyes—she's ten, at most—answers, "They had buyers who wanted certain things: blond hair, green eyes, or . . . whatever. The slavers took us because we matched the descriptions."

I don't need to be told why. Now I'm twice as glad we killed those bastards. They stole these kids because they matched the requests made in some pervert catalogue. I don't doubt there are serious credits in it. A rich client with no moral compass would be willing to pay outrageous amounts for a perfect little toy.

Rose says softly, "You're safe, Hanna. Don't think about that now."

Good advice, but simply telling the monsters to back off doesn't always work.

The smallest kid sniffs. "They made us talk on the vid."

A virtual marketplace—horror roils in my stomach. "Is that all?"

"They kept us locked up, too," he answers.

Relief trickles in. It could've been much worse, but I don't tell them that. If they have any illusions left after this, I'll do my best to preserve them.

"Has someone taken down all your personal information?" Rose should have by now, but I double-check.

Hanna nods. "But some of the little kids didn't know much before they were taken, and we were on that ship for weeks."

So likely, the slavers were waiting for all buyers to approve their wares and agree to a certain rendezvous point to finalize the transactions. They might've been hanging around that sector for a while. By the time we arrived, our ship probably looked like it was Mary-sent for entertainment purposes.

"We've uploaded your pictures to the databases. If your parents have reported you missing, there will be a match, sooner or later." I smile in what I hope is a reassuring manner. "Don't worry, we'll get you home."

"Will Rose take care of us the whole time?" Hanna asks.

They know her. They trust her. So I can understand the question, but I have to be honest. "When we ship out, she'll come with us. But you'll stay on station, where it's safe."

A couple of lower lips start to tremble and Rose cuts me a sharp look. Hm, maybe I'm not the best person to deal with this. I thought it best to be straight with these kids, who probably have a bullshit detector after all they've been through. I don't want them to think we're just jerking them around, same as the slavers.

"I'll make sure you like whoever takes my place," she reassures them.

"You mean we get to pick?" Hanna seems to be the spokesperson for the group.

I can field that one. "Sure. We'll give you first choice of all hands remaining on station just before we ship out."

"I guess that'd be okay," Hanna says grudgingly. "But how long do you think that will be?"

I shrug. "Whenever we wrap up our business."

There's no way I can be more specific. I don't know how long the training and recruitment phase will take. That's up to March and the Conglomerate.

Rose pushes to her feet, running a hand through already tousled red-and-silver hair. "It's time for lessons now. Constance will be waiting for you in conference room one."

I must admit, I admire the smooth way she's organized them. They file out for their makeshift schooling. She must have some experience with children.

Apparently interpreting my look, she says, "Before the McCulloughs attacked, I was a teacher on Lachion."

Not Doc's medical assistant then. That was a wartime role, not her choice.

"You're good with them."

"You're not. They've been through enough—they didn't need to think about my leaving them right now. No matter how mature they seem, they're not adults, and you can't treat them as such. Don't spring news on them without running it past me first, please." That "please" is only meant to soften the order, not take the teeth from it.

"I'm sorry. I didn't realize—"

"Obviously not," she snaps.

I hold up both hands in a placating gesture. "Hey, we're on the same side here."

"That may be, but I don't come to the cockpit and tell you how to jump, do I?"

I restrain my annoyance. She hasn't liked me since we first met on Lachion, so I suspect she's overreacting to my visit. Anybody else would likely receive a more civil response. However, I can't argue that I upset the kids, at least a little bit, even if I didn't mean to, and I can't argue that results matter more than intentions.

"Sorry. I thought you might need a hand with them; but I can see you have things under control here, and I won't interfere again."

At that she relents a bit. "I'm a little overprotective of them, I guess."

"It's understandable. Let me know if you need anything?"

"Of course." Rose hesitates and then explains, "I've found it's imperative for them to have a sense of continuity. It eases the trauma if their routine is consistent and reliable."

"Are you saying you'd rather stay here on station with them?"

I don't blame her if she does. She wasn't raised on starships. She doesn't have the love of space travel pulsing in her veins.

Rose considers for several long moments. Many women have a strong maternal instinct, and it seems Rose is no exception. Mary, Doc will not be happy with me if I'm the reason his woman deserts him. But hopefully he'll understand.

She finally shakes her head. "No, I want to stay with Doc on the *Triumph*. If I don't, it makes leaving Lachion rather pointless."

Since you left because of him.

I nod. "Do you ever wish you hadn't?"

Her face is tired, new shadows beneath her eyes. Since we've been gone, she's aged, unaccustomed to the stresses we call normal. "Sometimes. There were a lot of gaps in our turns together, time he spent off world, and I wasn't part of it. I thought if I went with him, it would help me understand him."

"Did it work?"

She shakes her head. "Not really. I don't find him any easier to access out here."

There's not a lot I can say to that, as we're not friends or confidantes. So I merely nod and excuse myself.

As the weeks pass, and word gets out about Hon enlist-ing, more ships arrive. The first to join us is a sleek pirate vessel called the *Dark Tide*. Its crew seems none too thrilled, but they'd follow their captain anywhere. Finnegan wears a scar across his left eye socket, and no patch to cover it. His smile is infectious, and he has a booming voice.

"I never thought I'd see the day," he announces, after we sign the contracts. "Me, fighting for the establishment."

Hon grins. "Know what you mean. But some deals are too sweet to pass up."

Soon, more follow. A few vessels leave without signing on, and we let them go. But most take the offer of pardon and limitless Conglomerate-sanctioned booty. We may get a few who still hit freighters, but we'll deal with the transgressions as they happen. For now, at least we have bodies to fight and the start of a militia.

Between the two of us—with Constance's help—March and I organize the classes. There's so much to cover in a short time: ship-to-ship fighting, tactics, personal combat, weapons training, and more. And each ship needs a trained medic. Most pirate vessels don't bother with a full complement of crew; they just take whoever's handy and hardy and figure they can replace personnel easier than they can heal them. We can't treat our soldiers as that expendable. People die in war, but that doesn't mean we won't try to save them.

One month after Hon's arrival, the station hums with activity. Cadets head down the halls to various conference rooms, now converted to classrooms. It's funny to see hardened smugglers and pirates taking classes on how to obey orders. That's a simplification, but essentially what we're doing here. Tarn is sending men, too, as his New Terran recruitment campaign takes off, and he's spending seized Farwan assets on ships and equipment.

Such things take time.

CHAPTER 17

"I have information for you, Sirantha."

I'm in the exercise room, running in place. That seems like an unhappy reflection of our current situation, but I need the activity. March has too much on his plate to assist with the problems I've shouldered. Somehow I wound up in charge of enforcing discipline, and given my nature, I find it hilarious. Who am I to chastise some poor bastard for his failures? Yet we each have to bear our share of the weight or this unsteady structure collapses.

"What's up, Vel?" I don't stop running.

He comes alongside the machine, unfazed. "You wanted me to find out what happened to Evelyn Dasad, whether her body was ever recovered by salvage teams."

Oh. My steps slow. It seems disrespectful to listen to the tale of a woman's death while sweat runs down my back. I let myself cool down, then I step off the belt and head for the bench along the wall. This is a small workout room; it offers little in the way of amenities, but Farwan never expected to house so many people here at one time.

"Ready," I say.

"It is something neither of us expected," he tells me.

"She made it." Not a surety so much as a hope.

"She slipped past the Morgut and launched herself in a pod, wherein she set the life support to minimal so as to appear flotsam from the pitched battle that occurred prior to boarding. She drifted until they abandoned her ship and jumped. At that point, she reengaged life support and turned on her emergency beacon. A freighter rescued her when she had but four minutes of oxygen left."

All too clearly, I can imagine her terror, trapped in a tiny pod and barely able to breathe lest she use up too much air, wondering how long it will take for her enemies to clear off. Those hours, while waiting but not daring to hope for rescue, must have been interminable. Like me, she's a sole survivor.

"Where is she now?"

With a few taps, Vel checks the records. "Recovering from her ordeal on what used to be Perlas Station. It was the easiest jump for the freighter in that sector."

Then the fight took place in the Furlong galaxy, where you can also find Matins IV. That's where my love, Kai, and all my illusions about Farwan died. So Evelyn and I both survived a catastrophe in the same galaxy—the only ones who did—and we were both transported to Perlas for recovery. I only hope she didn't wind up in a cell, like me.

That's just too much of a coincidence, and I don't tend to see mystic cosmic connections, unlike my mentor on Gehenna, Adele. Now I can hear her whispering in my ear that this means something, that this is Mary's hand on both of our lifelines, entwining their threads. Maybe I'm not ready to make that leap, but a few more questions won't hurt.

"Who runs it now?"

"Nominally, the Conglomerate, but it is full of ex–Farwan employees," he says.

I don't know why that makes my flesh crawl, but it does, in a big way. Thankfully, it doesn't take my rational brain as long as it once did to make a connection between my primitive dread and the reason behind it.

"If the Syndicate sees the Morgut as a way to provoke a war, wouldn't Farwan loyalists feel much the same?"

Vel inclines his head. "At this time, all factions feel that unrest may strengthen their claim that their organization is best suited to govern during such difficult times."

"So Farwan could eventually step up and say, 'Yes, so we killed a few representatives . . . but look at the mess you're in without us.' And people would welcome them back with open arms."

"It is a regrettable situation, but plausible."

I shake my head fiercely. "No, that can't happen. They can't have Evelyn Dasad, after all she's been through."

Farwan might have some idea of what she was working on—and now they've got her under the pretext of sanctuary. Mary, are they subjecting her to dream therapy? No, they wouldn't do that if she has valuable information or expertise locked in her brain. They don't want to damage her.

"You seem to have a personal stake in this," Vel observes.

I acknowledge that with a quirk of my lips, pointless to deny it. "If she knows anything of value, we can't afford to let anyone else have it." Since the former bounty hunter regards me with a tilt of his head, his claws tapping a skeptical cadence, I add, "If nothing else, her work with nanites will prove a big help to Doc. He's researching two different problems that could be solved via their application."

"You do not need to convince me, Sirantha."

That's when I realize it; he knows my plan before I do. We're going after her. Maybe she knows something that can help us, but if not, well, I simply feel a kinship to her because of what we've both suffered. If she's not a prisoner, then security shouldn't be an issue. We'll slip in and get her out before anyone knows why we're there. I doubt they've moved on her yet. They'll want to build a sense of trust first.

Since she was a former Farwan employee, they think she'll jump at the chance to come back. They don't realize Science Corps is independent now. She doesn't have to take orders on how she goes about her research anymore, and that kind of autonomy is fiercely addictive. Mary knows, I wouldn't want anyone telling me where to jump.

"Which ship do you wish to commandeer?"

I consider that. March can't be spared from his work here. He's the only one who sees the big picture, who knows what we need to do. He's been studying old vids until his eyes look bruised from lack of sleep, assembling the Armada structure piece by piece. In addition, he needs to be here to come to terms with the smugglers, and more ships arrive every day. A certain amount of chaos is conducive to doing business; utter anarchy like we have now really eats into the profit margins.

"It'll have to be Hon's . . . and his crew," I say with some regret. "They've been training longest. The others have work to do here. But this will be a good dry run, best if we see how far we can trust him in a less-than-dire situation. A smaller ship will draw less comment on Perlas, too. The *Triumph* is far too memorable."

"Prudent," he commends. "But I do not envy you the task of explaining this mission to the commander."

I wince at his intentional emphasis on rank. "Can I rely on you to talk to Hon if I do the same with March?"

His faceted eyes meet mine in a cant of his head that once looked peculiar. "Sirantha, you may rely on me for anything."

Warmth surges through me as I push to my feet. "I'll let you take care of that. I want to leave as soon as Hon can ready the ship. Wish me luck."

"You will not need it," he says gravely.

Before going to see March, I stop at the comm array. Something about Evelyn's message has been bothering me. Surge isn't anywhere to be seen, but I remember how to queue up the vid. I watch it twice more before I put my finger on it. Because quality was poor, and there was interference, I didn't notice the first time. But in the background . . . I spot what could be a Morgut. Watching her. I see only its reflection in her wardrober, blurred and damaged. But unquestionably, *something* is there.

"Constance, can you clean this up?" I touch the screen where I want her to work on the image.

"Will make the attempt, Sirantha Jax. No guarantee of success."

A few minutes later, I have the proof I need. It's a monster in her quarters. Why was it just watching her record? That makes no sense; I've *never* known them not to attack. To them, we are meat, nothing more. But Evelyn had stayed its hand, so to speak. Does that mean she's the reason they have been targeting Science Corps vessels, specifically looking for her? What the hell does she know?

But she was cleverer than they gave her credit for—somehow she slipped away from them, then hid in a seemingly dead pod. We have *got* to get this woman before anyone else does. I call March to the comm room and reveal my findings, then explain why I think we need to make a rescue run.

He puts up a brief fight. "This is no different than my wanting to go look for my nephew."

At that I shake my head. "He's a child, and we don't know where he is. That's a waste of time and effort better served elsewhere right now. It's wholly personal. Evelyn Dasad is a resource we can't afford to have fall into other hands. Do you want Farwan perfecting that technology to use against us? The Morgut would be even worse. Imagine fighting them, improved by rapid nanite healing."

"Checkmate. You talk like a commander, Jax. Want my job?"

"Not for the all the choclaste in this sector," I reply with genuine horror. "I don't juggle *nearly* as well as you. Plus, I can't make the scary face."

He pulls his hard face into austere lines, his eyes like chips of amber. "This one?"

"Yep." I don't have to fake a shiver. "That's it. Keeps everyone in line."

"Everyone except you," he mutters. "You realize we're twenty-one days from a beacon, which is why we set up here in the first place. It's going to take you a long time to get there and—"

"Why?" I cut in.

March raises a brow. "Why what?"

"*Why* does it have to take so long to jump?"

By his expression, he thinks I've lost my mind. "Because it doesn't work that way. The phase drive only works in certain zones, you know that, and—"

"The first thing we learn is that there is no distance in grimspace, as relates to coordinates in straight space," I counter.

So why can't the phase drive power up anywhere and tap a beacon?

"Evelyn Dasad said in her message: 'The Morgut use the beacons with more precision than we can muster. This is not a known jump zone.' Constance, what information can you find on Morgut phase-drive technology?"

"Searching, Sirantha Jax." Several moments pass, then she says, "I can find nothing regarding recovered Morgut vessels. I can, however, offer information on their physiology. After the attack on Emry, the Conglomerate cleanup crew dissected several corpses in an attempt to devise more effective weapons to combat them."

That strikes a chord. "Emry was an emergency station before." I push to my feet, pacing as I think. March watches me, seeing I'm onto something, but he isn't sure where I'm going with this. Neither am I. "That means they probably did a lot of monitoring of signals for distress calls. Constance, were there feeds from outside the station?"

A brief pause, and then: "Affirmative, Sirantha Jax."

"Is there anything prior to the attack?"

She scans. Then a grainy image comes up on the comm screen. Before our eyes, the Morgut ship just appears at the edge of sensor range. No human vessel could do that—and no *wonder* they weren't detected hauling straight space before they hit Emry.

I meet March's worried gaze. He's come to stand beside me, face taut with the implications. "This means they can jump from anywhere, which is why they have no trouble hitting out-of-the-way outposts."

He looks horrified. "Places we think are safe because they aren't near a known jump zone. That means they can strike *anywhere*."

"We have to learn how, too. Now. Yesterday would be better." I'm brooking no argument, already on the move. I hear him protesting behind me, talking about safety, but no place in the galaxy is safe, not anymore.

"Dina!" I shout, tearing through the station at a dead run. "Dina!"

"What?" the mechanic demands in irritation, coming out of the lounge.

"We have work to do."

CHAPTER 18

I'm a little sick at the thought of this. It's been two weeks, and Dina has been crunching theoretical numbers with two other mechanics: Hobson from the *Dauntless* and the woman from the *Dark Tide*. I showed them the Morgut jump to Emry, then demanded they improve our phase drive, something humans have never been able to do. Constance has been helping.

I think we got limited technology from the ancients. There must be better models out there somewhere if the Morgut have it.

And now it's time to put all our effort to the test. I don't want Hon inside of me. As always my stomach churns at the idea of taking a new pilot. At least this time I haven't lost the old.

But the fighting's all done. March is furious with me, furious that I'm risking myself like this, and furious that I'm making the jump with Hon. But he's more commander than lover right now, and he knows I'm doing the right thing, the *only* thing. The delay chafes me, and makes me worry that someone else may have snapped up Evelyn Dasad in the meantime. We all feel that sending a message to inquire would alarm her if she's still hiding on what used to be Perlas Station. Better to go and plead our case in person.

"I don't know if this is a good idea," Dina says, as I settle into the nav chair. Mary, it's been a long time, and I fight a moan at the awareness I'll soon be back in grimspace. "We made the mods, but it's wholly untested. You could fry your brain."

"And mine," Hon mutters.

"If you're afraid, there are other pilots on station," I tell him, thinking of Hit.

"Like I'm gonna trust 'em with my ship."

And the fact is, we don't trust any of the other smugglers enough to run this mission with them. Even with Hon, it's not a sure thing, but we're banking he has some loyalty, and that he won't decide to sell Evelyn Dasad—and her secrets—to the highest bidder. As to that, I'll know as soon as he jacks in.

March leans down to kiss me, his mouth fierce on mine. *Come back,* he commands silently. *Come back to me.*

I'll do my best. I love you.

His answer comes in the form of a feeling so profound I have no name for it. Love dwarfs it because it's longing, need, desire, heat, and a complex sense of belonging coiled around one frail, strong person. Me. It brings tears to my eyes, then . . . he withdraws. I'm going to be alone in my head for the foreseeable future, and I miss him already.

"That's it," Hon says. "If you not a pilot or a jumper, get outta my cockpit."

Of our people, only Dina and Vel are coming with us. We may need the Ithtorian's deft touch with technology on station, and Dina is the only who can monitor what she did with the phase drive. *Please, let this work.*

Hon sits ready for clearance—when he hears that March has left the vessel, he starts the cross-check. He goes about it differently than March or Kai, but I can see he knows what he's doing. His cockpit is well-appointed and clean; the nav computer looks to be the latest model. Sweet; I've never jumped with one of these.

While we wait, I examine the coordinates in straight space. For what I want to do, no known jump site will do.

Five minutes later, Surge tells us, "You're clear, dock five. Mary guide you on."

There's reassurance in the way Hon maneuvers us out of the bay, smooth as s-silk. Once we've put some distance between the station and us, he turns to me. "Usually I'd say settle in for a long haul now, but you think you can do this another way?"

"I intend to try," I tell him, and sink the shunt.

In a vast wash of swirling light, the world dissolves; and then it's all darkness. But grimspace coils through my veins, tiny cations that render the negative void my seductive, irresistible opposite. It can no more refuse me than I, it.

Though he mutters a little, Hon jacks in beside me. To my relief, he's fully partitioned, granting me nothing. It's an impersonal touch, no more than what we must share to get the job done. After enough loss, most pilots develop that ability. Too many scars, and they don't want to give a fragile navigator anything they can't bear to lose.

His shunt offers only a neural link between him, the ship, and me, not the full virtual submersion my connection requires. Now, thanks to Dina, we've brought the phase drive into the nav computer that both Hon and I jack into. Combined with Constance, the separate units comprise a sort of ship consciousness that I dub the ship-net. At Hon's command, I sense it powering up. Instead of darkness, silver threads web the array in my mind's eye, and I find myself admiring the pattern: arachnid, like the Morgut spin for their prey.

Mary. I shudder at the alien touch of the phase drive. I've never felt it in quite this way before. Is it possible that the ancients who seeded this technology across the galaxy also bred the Morgut? But for what purpose? Regardless, here I glimpse the familiarity of design.

You doing all right?

Fine. I send him a vague reassurance because I can't afford distraction right now. I feel my way through the pattern, learning the twists and unnatural coils inside the ship-net. Constance walks me through it, showing me all the pertinent connections. At last I see we're missing a necessary, cation-rich link between the nav computer and the phase drive. The Morgut must have a complete, self-sustaining web. I can see now that despite the numbers and theories our mechanics posited, they couldn't complete the design on their own.

That's why we can't jump unless we're inside a known jump zone. And without that connection, the phase drive can't open a corridor to grimspace unless we reach a section of straight space where the cations gather naturally. I lack the mechanical knowledge to know how it needs to be built—how to get these necessary cations inside the wires—but I think I can jump-start it on my end.

There's not much actual energy, I tell myself. *And there's a certain amount in my blood from my conception in grimspace. So I can channel it. There's no danger.* Focusing, I push the wildfire in my veins toward the phase drive, willing it to quicken as if for a jump. I'm the vessel; I'm the missing link in the pattern—organic phase-drive component. *We're here,* I tell it. *I am the jump. Get ready.*

At distance I feel my body start to shake. There's wetness on my face, but I can't tell if it's sweat or blood. Beside me, Hon is cursing, but he's doing so out loud, staying out of my head as much as he can. I know there's self-interest in that because he doesn't want to die if I barbecue my brain.

When I think I can't hold the connection any longer, as I think I'll fry as Dina predicted, the phase drive roars to life. The power of the beacons blazes through me, as if I've channeled the corridor. I feel every particle of me glowing, burning from the inside out. It's bigger than pain—bright, hot, and profound.

Mother Mary. It's Hon inside me now, overflowing with awe. *We're through.*

Grimspace floods through me, cascading in all its glorious colors. My blood quickens in answer. In some fashion we are one. We always will be.

And thank Mary, I'm home.

This is going to hurt. Progress always does.

I'm not aiming for the nearest beacon anymore. I'm shooting for Perlas Station itself, using the beacons to *move* us, not navigate. The difference is miniscule to a layman, but I have a feeling it's going to be rough the first time. Best analogy I can offer: We're entering the stream of energy they emit and dissolving to reappear in another part of the galaxy. That's not exactly right, of course, but I don't know more than that. I'm riding on intuition here and hoping I don't kill us all.

For an instant Kai's face swims up from my consciousness, and he's smiling. I get the sense he's proud of me. Oddly, I feel closer to him here, as if grimspace could be the never-never that lies before the great and final gate. But it's not time for me to pass through, not unless I fail.

I can do this. I will. I have to. My work isn't done yet.

Though I'm intoxicated as always by the pulsation of energy, the wildfire blazing against our hull, I train my senses on one thing only: my goal. I'll do this or die trying. Mary, I'm glad we have a small crew.

My will alone must carry us through. I don't think about the far horizon, or what lurks beyond. I don't think about doors into infinite mystery. Instead, I find the beacon nearest Perlas.

Easy, I've made this jump before. But not there.

Here.

It's a twist, a wrinkle, and a fierce pain stabbing through my brain, but we pass through like a camel through the eye of a needle and sling wide. For me it's more than a little like giving birth. Agony blazes along my nerve endings in a merciless loop.

Hon's hands move furiously on the ship's controls. I can hear him struggling to interpret my signals. He's not trained for this, either, the poor bastard. Nobody is.

What the frag are you doing? he demands. *I can't do that. The ship doesn't—*

I am *the jump. And you will take me there.* There's titanium inside me. I will not be denied. This is *my* world, and here, I am queen. I feel the signal coursing through me once more, and to my astonishment, Hon obeys.

In defiance of what we used to believe was possible, the phase drive roars. The world goes dark again.

We're out of grimspace now, wherever I jumped us. My hands shake too badly to get the shunt out, so I reach out blind and manage to tap his shoulder. His fingers brush my wrist as he helps me, and my vision shudders back into focus. Everything looks filmy, and then I realize it's because I'm viewing the cockpit through a veil of tears.

"Where are we?" I rasp.

In answer he points out the view screen, unable to find his voice. Rising before us, just a few thousand klicks away, I see the lights of Perlas Station.

CHAPTER 19

Hon can't seem to meet my eyes.

There used to be playful camaraderie in his manner, but now his expression is edged with superstitious fear. As we're completing the docking protocol necessary for them to let us disembark on station, he keeps sliding me looks that I catch in my peripheral vision.

"What?" I demand.

Before he can respond, the port authority pings us. "*Dauntless*, what's your purpose at Perlas?"

"Just a little R and R," Hon answers smoothly. "We come off a salvage run, and the boys want to drink and spend a few credits."

The dock officer laughs. "I'm sure the vendors will be just fine with that." He follows with a list of questions of about hazardous materials and communicable diseases, which Hon answers by rote. "It'll take a few moments to complete the scan, but you should be good to go shortly."

"You were about to tell me why you keep staring at me like that." Courtesy of our pilot/jumper link, I think I already know. But I want him to say it.

"Was I?"

"Were you staring . . . or about to tell me? Yes, to both." Otherwise, we could go on like this all day.

"In the Outskirts, we tell this story," he says uneasily. "About one who holds in her body the key to the hidden

ways, life into death and back again. But when she comes, it
is not a blessing, for it means the end of all things."

"And you think that has something to do with me?" I can
see that he does.

"I don't know."

"*Dauntless*, you're clear. Enjoy your stay." The dock
officer saves us an argument. It won't do our mission any
good if I tell Hon he's full of crap.

"Let's get the lay of the land first. If we need Dina or
Loras, we'll beep the ship for them." Without further discussion, I push out of the nav chair and am pleased to find the
shakes have stopped enough for me to walk. I thread my way
past the pilot seat and step into the hallway.

To my surprise, Hon follows quietly. At my look, he
shrugs. "We still have a job to do, don't we?"

I grin, grateful for his pragmatism. I'm sure once he thinks
about it logically, he'll realize there's nothing metaphysical
or ominous in what I did. It's unique among humans, I'll
grant you, but the Morgut have been twisting like that for
Mary knows how long, and they haven't brought anything
to an end.

Not *yet*, at least—and they won't if I have anything to
say about it.

Though I don't know this ship as well as some, I find the
hatch without trouble. Maybe it would've made more sense
for Hon to lead, but I wasn't sure he was still on board until a
few seconds ago. I didn't know how badly I unnerved him.

Good thing he's not Psi. I'd have really pissed him off,
there.

The station looks different. It's lost some of the Farwan
homogeny, replaced with more grime and more character.
Each docking ship has brought its own flavor, and nobody has
made the san-bots erase it. Nonregulation lights bedeck the
corridors leading into the promenade, and on the dull gray
wall, some budding artist has painted vivid designs in azure
and citrine. Characters beside the picture draw my eye.

"It's Tarnusian," Hon answers. Mary, the last thing I need

is another pilot doing that, but at least he's just predicting my thought-path instead of sharing it.

"Can you read it?"

He shakes his head. I make a mental note to bring Dina by here, and we walk on. The promenade has turned into a long strip of bars, chem stands, and sex shops—some with live shows inside, others with toys and accoutrements offered boldly on display. Though I call myself an experienced woman, even I'm not sure what that two-pronged tasseled device is used for.

"Farwan would have a fit," I murmur, more to myself than to Hon.

My CO used to froth at the mouth on a regular basis at the way my moral turpitude reflected on the Corp. I wonder how he'd feel about Perlas's being chic with raider couture. Me, I kind of like the place. It exudes an energy that Farwan outposts always lacked.

"I dig it." Hon gazes around, breathing deep.

I realize it must remind him a little of the station-home he lost. Like everyone, the war has cost him dearly. No wonder he's looking for a little payback.

We continue on, exploring.

In the time since I escaped from a cell here, *everything* has changed. What used to be the officers' serenity garden has been turned into a marketplace. There's precious little tranquillity now, but all kinds of action.

"This is where we split, pretty. I can find out more without you sticking to me."

Personally, I think he just likes the look of the woman selling soy cheeses, but I don't protest. Since there's no danger I can see, it makes sense for us to cover twice the ground separately.

"Be discreet," I warn.

Hon raises dark brows. Okay, that was stupid. He stands over two meters, with lovely dark skin, a shaved head, and two gold-alloy teeth in front. People are going to remember him, no matter what he says or does.

I sigh. "Never mind. Let me know if you find anything."

First off, I call Dina. "You feel like some shore leave?"

"Sure," she says. "Where should I meet you?"

I give her succinct directions to the garden market, adding, "And do me a favor—can you read the Tarnusian characters on the wall on the way in from the docks?"

"You think it's important?" Surprise colors her voice.

"The patterns rang a bell for me, but I can't say where I saw them before. I thought maybe the accompanying message might clear it up."

It could be as simple as partisan propaganda. Regardless, on a station full of raiders, smugglers, freebooters, and Farwan loyalists, it doesn't hurt to sniff out the political climate. If a revolution is boiling up in the pot, I'd rather get in and out before we're caught in the middle of it.

"Got it. I'll input it word for word on my handheld. Anything else, boss?" Her tone carries a mocking lilt, but she's called me that before—and meant it. We both know it.

On impulse, I say, "Yes. Bring Loras."

People mill past, circulating through the marketplace. They're talking and shopping, making plans for later. I find myself watching them with envy because they don't have to worry about what goes on in the wider galaxy. Nobody's looking to them for help or guidance. Unless Perlas Station is attacked, they just don't care. Usually, I don't regret any of my choices, but for a moment, I can't help but wonder what that would be like.

But I have to be honest; I'd be bored stupid. I need the constant rush that comes from leaping from one catastrophe to another. I grin and content myself with experiencing a quiet life vicariously, via two girls talking about some guy they like.

By the time Dina and Loras catch up to me, I've bought a jaunty new hat, which thrills me because it's the first time I've used my own credits for anything in ages. The old Jax wants to proceed to the nearest bar and buy drinks until I'm the most popular person in the place, everybody's best friend. Ruthlessly, I crush her dreams.

"I have your translation," Dina says by way of greeting. " 'You heard my call once. Here I die until you call me again.' It's signed 'The oppressed shall rise.' That's this symbol." She indicates three wavy lines with a dot beneath them.

"What does it mean?" Loras asks.

We both glance at Dina, who shrugs. "If it's related to recent upheaval on Tarnus, I wouldn't know. I don't even look for updates on the vids."

Well, I can understand that. Dina was a princess in her former life, until revolutionaries deposed her family and exiled her from her homeworld forever. I wouldn't keep up with what was going on back home, either. Though I don't say it aloud, I hope there are no dissident factions waiting for us to hit the mix like spark to dry kindling.

"Maybe it's not relevant. Where should we start looking for Evelyn Dasad?"

"She won't be in the directory unless she received permanent status," Loras muses.

Dina runs a hand through her fair hair, thoughtful. "I don't think she'd still be in the infirmary unless her injuries were really severe."

I shake my head. "Vel made no mention of it." It goes without saying, he would. He's nothing if not thorough and precise. I didn't like leaving him on the ship, but we would attract less attention by doing so.

"A bar is the logical place to start," Dina says knowledgeably. "Let's ask a vendor which one has the best gossip and go from there."

CHAPTER 20

The consensus in the market is that we need to visit Rafferty's on the second level of the promenade. As soon as we hit the second level, the crowd and the flashing red signs point us the way to the "Pearl of Perlas." I'm partial to the animated clam accompanying that particular advertisement.

Music thrums from inside the bar. This is the kind of place I would've loved once—too bad I have work to do. I school myself to ignore the dancers and fall in behind Dina, who's best suited to shoving her way toward the bar. Her solid strength forges a path for Loras and me. When we shoulder up beside her, she's already ordering drinks.

Loras looks a little overwhelmed by the place, but he's drawing attention from all comers: male, female, and other. The man is simply too pretty for it to be otherwise, even now. I grin as one of them tries to chat him up.

Handing over her credit spike, Dina pays for our booze, and I snag mine, a pale amber something. If I know her, it'll put me on my ass if I'm not careful. I take a sip. Yep, it's potent, but I don't sputter as it blazes down my throat. After the homebrew I drank in Wickville, this is smooth in comparison.

When the servo whirs down the counter toward me, I tap the "personal service requested" button. Bots can efficiently mind a bar, but they're not good with questions, unless they're preprogrammed. Like, *Where's the hydroponics garden?* or *Where can I get a new shockstick?*

Dina leans over and whispers, "Should we rescue him?"

The woman who cornered Loras has a shock of bright red hair running in a striped tail down the center of her head. She's humanoid, but I don't think she's wholly human. Maybe she comes from a colony that interbred with the native population because she has heavy epicanthic folds and webbed fingers. Humans are wonderfully adaptive.

I shrug. "Not unless he looks to us for help, or she tries to drag him off."

We nurse our drinks for five minutes, waiting for someone to answer my page. In that time, two men and a woman try their luck with Dina. She puts them off politely but firmly. *Good on you, Your Highness. You really do love Hit.* For a few span, I consider teasing her about twu wuv, after all the shit she gave me about March.

Dina interprets my expression correctly, and her eyes narrow. "Don't start."

Before I can decide whether it's worth the risk, a man jostles me. I think he wants to order, so I ease back from the counter. When it happens a third time, I spin to face him.

"Do you *need* something?" I ask, trying to be polite.

We can't afford to get kicked out of here before we ask a few questions, but I can't stand being manhandled by strangers. My muscles are coiled, ready to knock a few of this guy's teeth out as an object lesson against hassling random women.

"Hey, it *is* you," the idiot exclaims.

"Huh?"

"You're Sirantha Jax."

A groupie. I would've thought people had a shorter memory. I'm not on the vids anymore. Shouldn't there be somebody who's replaced me by now?

To my dismay, he waves his arms excitedly until he has the attention of the whole room. "Guess what, folks? We have a celebrity here tonight!"

Oh, shit. I'd nearly forgotten about this.

My face heats as so many eyes are trained on me. Once, I gloried in this. I'd have jumped up on the bar and done a dance, given them what they wanted, until they were cheering me with wild enthusiasm. I give a halfhearted wave and step a little closer to Dina. Dammit, I wanted to be *discreet*—I mentioned it to Hon, for Mary's sake—and it turns out I'm the mission's weak point.

"Show us your tits, love!"

"I saw 'em on the vids," a drunk says. "They ain't so great. Not big enough."

Another agrees, "She's kinda old now, too. I bet they're starting to sag, unless she's getting Rejuvenex regular."

"Which one are you banging? The pretty bloke or the butch?" somebody shouts.

A wiseass near the back answers, "Both, if I know Jax!"

But they don't know me. None of them do.

I don't know how to defuse the situation because I can't give them what they want, and the mood seems to be getting uglier. They begin rumbling about how I was the one that put half of Farwan's people out of work, easy prey for raiders and the like. So now I've arrived in—and some would argue it's richly deserved—my personal hell.

"Give us a kiss." A guy nearby gets grabby, and his arms go 'round my waist.

I fight him back with an elbow to the sternum. "Hands off!"

My temper's barely in check at this point. With a hum, Dina's shockstick goes live, and the way she handles it clears a small circle around us. The music has stopped, and we're ringed in half-drunk nulls. I don't see a way for this to end well.

Until a tall man in black comes striding through the crowd.

He has long silver hair and a weathered, brown face, but he looks vital and vigorous. A goatee frames his mouth, which is compressed in a thin, angry line. Behind him come a couple of Peacemaker units, and the other patrons decide it's not worth the hassle. With a low rumble, they return to their business.

"Are you prescient, Ms. Jax?"

I raise my brows at the question. "Excuse me?"

"I just thought you might be, as you rang for assistance before the trouble started. Maybe you saw it coming." The stranger flashes me a white grin.

"With her around, it's not prescience," Dina mutters. "Just a simple matter of playing the odds."

"Let's retire to the VIP lounge, and you can tell me what you need." The tall man leads the way.

As long as it gets me out of here, I'm all for that. I glance back to make sure Dina and Loras are with me, then I pass through the automated door at the back of the bar. A short hallway connects to another area, one that's smaller and quieter. The music is cool rather than raucous. The VIP lounge is decorated in shades of silver and blue, with a lush carpet underfoot. There are only five other people present, and they don't look interested in our business. Excellent.

Our rescuer indicates we should have a seat. Once everyone is comfortable, he says, "I'm Erul McTavish Rafferty . . . but everyone calls me Mac. I own the place. I gather you're not here to enjoy the ambiance?"

"The liquor is good," I assure him. "But I'm looking for a friend." I'm not keen on lying to someone who pulled me out of a tight spot, but I figure Evelyn and I *would* be friends if she had any idea who I am. "We heard this is the place to get information."

He mulls that over. "Maybe I can help. What can you tell me about this person?"

"Her name is Evelyn Dasad, and she's with the Science Corps. She survived a Morgut attack, and a freighter picked her up. They dropped her off here. I came as soon as I could." All more or less true.

"Seems like someone as close as you purport to be would've heard from Evelyn, saying where she was, if she wanted you to know."

Crap, he's smart. I was hoping he wouldn't realize that. I'm not going to be able to lie to him, so I don't bother.

"We just want to talk to her, that's all."

Dina agrees, "If you could arrange a meet, it would be best. If you don't trust us, you can send your Peacemaker units along. We aren't going to hurt her."

"I am incapable of it," Loras adds.

That makes Mac take a closer look. "Mary's grace, you're La'hengrin. Good thing I got you out of there when I did. Spacers love to steal your kind."

The observation pains me, as I'm starting to see the universe from Loras's point of view. Things are stolen; people are kidnapped. I can't afford to alienate this man, unfortunately, so I don't correct him. But I'm still pissed on my friend's behalf.

"I'll send a message to Evelyn," Mac finally allows. "That's all I promise."

"Don't you want credits up front?" I ask. Most stations have a fixer—the man to see to get things done, and market gossip led us here to Rafferty's for that kind of business—but such men don't usually work for free.

"We'll talk about what I want later," he answers. "In the meantime, I suggest you three return to your ship and try to stay out of trouble."

I raise a brow. "Is Perlas dangerous these days?"

He shrugs. "No more than anywhere else in these uncertain times. But I will say, they've been demonstrating more. More fights to break up."

"Noted," Dina says.

I incline my head, pushing to my feet. "We'll head back to the *Dauntless*, then. Here's my personal comm code, whenever you have word for us." I beam the info to his handheld. "Is there a back exit? I'd rather not go out there and get them worked up again."

"This way."

In short order, we find ourselves on the other side of the promenade. Now all we can do is wait, and hope Hon stays out of trouble better than me.

.CLASSIFIED-TRANSMISSION.
.GOOD WORK.
.FROM-SUNI_TARN.
.TO-EDUN_LEVITER.
.ENCRYPT-DESTRUCT-ENABLED.

I collect we shall eschew salutations henceforth.

To business, then. First, let me commend you on that research. It was truly invaluable.

Even now, we have begun to manufacture the toxin. I call it Morfex. The way it works is truly ingenious. Our scientists have improved the delivery system. It's been upgraded into gaseous form, and the Morgut will theoretically absorb it through the membranes around their eyes. It eliminates the need for the poison to be ingested or applied to an open wound.

Unfortunately, we don't have any Morgut upon which to test it, and the weapon is harmless to us. Your first order of business is to procure a live specimen, which I know will be difficult, and deliver it to the following coordinates: attachment follows. The sooner we complete clinical trials, the sooner we can proceed and get our soldiers outfitted. Every advantage matters.

Your second order of business is to locate a Morgut vessel, relatively intact. We know that their weapons are better than ours. Now I want to analyze how and why, so we can compensate for it in the production of our ships and upgrade the ones already on patrol. Get me those results as quick as you can, in addition to the scans you performed on the salvage you retrieved. I want a complete itemized list of everything you find and what it does.

Finally, put some thought into those alternate revenue sources. We cannot assume we will win the war quickly, though I pray to Mary it is so.

Therefore, what kind of tariffs? On what goods? Bear in mind: The people cannot afford much in these difficult times. The last thing I want is for the Conglomerate to become a replacement for Farwan. We must do better, or they will think—rightfully so—that they have merely exchanged one boot on their necks for another.

Your name strikes terror into the hearts of common men, sir, but if they knew of your work on our behalf, I am sure they would sing your praises. I only wish they understood the truth.

```
.ATTACHMENT-COORDINATES-FOLLOWS.
.END-TRANSMISSION.

.COPY-ATTACHMENT.
.FILES-DOWNLOADED.
.ACTIVATE-WORM: Y/N?

.Y.
.TRANSMISSION-DESTROYED.
```

CHAPTER 21

Hon returns to the **Dauntless** *several hours later. He's* mussed, wearing a satisfied smile as he strides into the lounge. Loras and Dina have been gone for several hours, leaving me to wait for Hon or a message from Mac.

"How did your recon go?" I ask dryly.

"The cheese vendor can put both feet behind her head."

I had a feeling it was going to be something like that. "Been a long time since you had any shore leave?"

"That's a fact."

Belatedly I remember he's been lying low. If he's been holed up with the remnants of his raiders—who were always predominantly male—I can't blame him for his focus now. But I have no further interest in the cheese vendor, however flexible she may be.

"Did you learn anything else?"

"Certainly." His expression is mildly affronted as he settled into the chair opposite. "Dasad is in hiding. Since her arrival, there have been three failed kidnappings and two attempts on her life."

I offer a low whistle. "Sounds like we were right. She knows something valuable. Any intel on those responsible?"

"Syndicate, almost certainly. Hints that a rival crime family from Venice Minor may be in on the action."

"So whatever she knows, it's important enough that if they can't have it, they don't want anyone else to, either."

Hon nods. "That's how I see't."

"Thanks, that's helpful." I fill him in on what *we* accomplished.

By the time I finish, he's grinning. "See what a great team we make, Sirantha?"

I know where he's going with this, and I hold up a hand to forestall it. "March would kill you." There's no point in antagonizing him with the knowledge that I don't want him without the help of pheromones.

"He'd try." Luckily, the cheese vendor has left him too sated to make an issue of it. "So now we're waitin' for this Rafferty to get in touch?"

"That's the sum of it."

"Then I'm going to get some sleep."

Not a bad idea. I want to be sharp when it's time to move, so we head to our separate quarters. Before lying down, I bounce a message to March, knowing he won't see it for ages. In fact, depending on the efficiency of the satellites—and how long it takes here—I might wind up racing the data with another impossible jump. When we have a fleet of ships, we can utilize them to relay messages faster. That's what Farwan used to do, but I'm not putting this on open channels. Our best hopes lie in encryption and secrecy.

"We found her," I tell him through the uncaring lens of the terminal recorder. "At least, she's still here. With any luck, we'll be homeward bound soon. I miss you." That's all I can bear to commit to a message that anyone might see.

After I've sent it, I realize I didn't think to check my reflection or worry about taming my hair. Mary knows what I look like, after the near brawl at Rafferty's, but it probably doesn't matter. He's seen me at my worst and then some.

In my bunk, I muse on the fact that I didn't give in to the urge to start a fight in the bar. Once, I would've swung away without thinking about consequences. It seems I learned self-control on Ithiss-Tor, but I'm asleep before I can decide if that's good or bad.

It doesn't seem like I've been out very long before Dina's voice awakens me.

"Get moving, Jax. It's time."

I'm on my feet before my eyes are open all the way. "The meet's on?"

"No, I just *missed* you. Get your ass to the hatch."

I laugh softly and grab a cord. On the move, I weave my locks into a respectable twist. I don't want to make a bad first impression on Evelyn, and crazy hair won't help. When I arrive, Hon, Loras, and Dina are already waiting.

"What took you so long?" the mechanic gripes.

I grin at her. "Hearing your voice, well . . . You can imagine."

"Don't even joke about that." She feigns an elaborate shudder.

"You two finished?" Hon is all business now, his face stern with purpose.

"We don't want to be late," Loras adds.

Because I know they're right, I don't argue. I simply nod. "Let's do this."

It's after hours on station. The majority of humans on board are in the middle of their sleep cycle. A few aliens roam around at this hour, but none of them pay much attention to us. I'm not sure if that's luck or design.

We make for Rafferty's, but the place is closed up tight, a wide flex-steel gate drawn down to prevent unauthorized entry from the promenade. Since I didn't take the call and don't have instructions, I glance at the others for guidance. "What now?"

"Around back," Hon tells me.

"Why didn't you say so in the first place?"

Circling, we find a small door with a comm panel beside it.

"For deliveries," Loras notes.

Without further delay, I tap the screen, alerting them to our presence. It flashes red, telling us to wait. In a few seconds, Rafferty's face comes up as he peers through at us.

"Who's that?" he asks, gesturing at Hon. "I didn't agree to let *him* see Evelyn."

I see why he'd be alarmed. Even on a good day, Hon exudes a fair amount of scary. "He's harmless. But if his presence is a deal-breaker, we can send him back to the ship."

Mac decides swiftly. "Do it. The door doesn't open until he's gone. You better hope station security doesn't come by asking you what you're about before then. If that happens, the deal is off."

"Scuttle," I tell Hon briefly.

His face darkens—and I can tell I'm going to pay for that later—but he complies. Once he's left the narrow alley behind the bar, the lock disengages. "Come in. Quickly."

Maybe I'm just susceptible to other people's paranoia but I find myself gazing over my left shoulder as we slide inside. At this hour, the bar is dark and quiet. We're in a hallway between the regular area and the VIP lounge.

Mac leads us toward the latter, where we find Evelyn Dasad waiting, flanked by two Peacemaker units. Each has weapons out and on standby. Yeah, Rafferty's serious about us not taking her anywhere she doesn't want to go.

Dasad is smaller than I thought she'd be. Her presence and resolve on the vid made her seem larger than life, but in fact, she's a few centimeters shorter than I am. Her hair has grown a little since she sent the message we intercepted, a shaggy fringe down past her ears. She's a little thinner, too, and lines of strain are etched into her face, which bears the shadow of many sleepless nights.

This is a woman who lives in fear.

Only her eyes are the same, polished onyx that doesn't reflect the light. In one fashion, she's the negative reflection of the heterozygous genotype that heralds the J-gene. I wonder what unique gifts her appearance portends.

"I'm Sirantha Jax," I say, intending to make introductions first.

"I know who you are," she says. "And what you've done."

I can't determine if that's auspicious . . . or ominous.

Taking pity on me, she adds, "You set records with the Corp before going rogue and destabilizing the galactic economy with the truth of Farwan's misdeeds. Then you escaped the bounty hunter they set on you and went on to forge an alliance with Ithiss-Tor."

"Would you have done any different?" This, I decide, will help me take her measure.

"No. However much I regret our current predicament, Farwan was not the answer. They had gone from serving the people to serving themselves. And the alliance was the first good news I've heard in a while. I hope it will be enough."

"Absolute power corrupts absolutely," Loras murmurs.

"So it does," Evelyn responds tiredly. "Which is why I am not sure whether I can trust you."

"A fair question. How can we resolve the issue to your satisfaction?" In Dina's voice, I hear diplomacy and echoes of the princess she used to be. She would've made a far better ambassador than me, I think, but she wouldn't have had the job for any price.

"Not with words or promises," Dasad says.

"Are you all right to talk with them?" Mac asks from the doorway. His anxiety is palpable, even now.

Evelyn nods. "You can go, Uncle Mac. I don't think they mean me any harm, and if I'm wrong, your bots will make short work of them."

That explains a lot. On closer scrutiny, I see they have the same dark eyes. He turns to go with a final, narrow-eyed stare at the three of us, but without Hon, we're clearly no match for two fully equipped Peacemaker units. It would take heavy weapons to pierce their armor, and we're not carrying that kind of firepower.

I take a seat. "Shall we get down to business, then?"

CHAPTER 22

"What is it you want?" Evelyn asks without preamble.

"To take you with us to Emry Station." I hold up a hand to forestall her instinctive protest. "But unlike other factions, we won't attempt to do it against your will."

"You want the new nanite tech." She doesn't phrase it as a question.

I shrug. "We only suspected it was related to the nanite research. We were just sure it had to be important if the Morgut went to the trouble of trying to take you alive. They don't generally operate that way. We figured once word got around, there would be lots of people interested in you, and we don't want your knowledge in the hands of our enemies."

Among the three of us, we outline our mission as set down by Chancellor Tarn and the Conglomerate. Loras and Dina fill in technical bits, and she listens with great interest.

"So you're forging a central galactic regime," she says, once we've finished. "A true alliance of worlds, not a human authority, but one that governs all races with impartiality and wisdom."

"That's the goal." I may have my doubts that it can be accomplished, but I'm wise enough to hold them. She's seen enough to disillusion her. Leave the woman some hope. "And we're building an armada for the Conglomerate as part of that. I think you could be vital to our efforts."

Her plain face fills with disdain. "Of course I could. I *am*. My nanites will change the face of jump-travel forever."

Then there's no question we want her on our team. I see by the flare in Dina's eyes, she knows as much. As always, Loras is inscrutable, but on some level I sense his heightened interest.

Mary, I wish March were here. He could read her quietly, then tell her what she most wants to hear. Dishonest, perhaps, but effective. Without him, I'm left guessing. At lightning speed, I review what I know, then I realize we have a carrot to tempt her.

"Interesting," I say. "We, too, have some previously unknown scientific discoveries." Dina flashes me a look, but I'm too far out on this limb to second-guess it. "Though it's yet to be made public, I possess mutated DNA that permits me to regenerate grimspace damage. Right now, we have a geneticist working on an implant to regulate that function and, what's more, perfect a gene therapy to offer this ability to all jumpers. I imagine you and Doc have a lot to discuss. If your nanites are as revolutionary as you say, they might aid immeasurably in his work—and perhaps . . . vice versa."

Evelyn regards me with open skepticism. "That's impossible."

I grin. "I figure that's what they said about jump-travel when they first uncovered the tech in the pyramids. I can bounce a message to Emry and ask Doc to forward some of his findings, but the longer we linger here, the greater chance we'll run into trouble. Emry has been fortified against the Morgut—"

"You drove them out once before," she realizes aloud.

To be completely accurate, we killed them. "I had help."

"How do you envision my role in your endeavor?" she asks.

"We don't. That's up to you to decide. I suspect you'll want to work with Doc, but if you don't like him, we won't force the issue. If you decide you want to give up science altogether and learn to pilot, we have someone who can put in the shunt, and we'll do our best to protect you in the field."

I surprise her into a short burst of laughter, rusty and long unused. Her dark eyes actually shine, and I notice Dina giving her a second glance. I glare at her. *Oh, no, you don't.* She lifts her shoulders as if to say, *I can look, can't I?*

Evelyn says, "That scenario's quite unlikely, but good to know my decisions will remain squarely mine."

"That, I promise."

"If I am to consider your offer, I will need lab facilities and absolute access to all of your existing data."

"Done," Loras says at once, and I turn to him in surprise. He shrugs, adding, "Dr. Solaith gave me permission to make the offer on his behalf."

Dina bangs him on the shoulder gently. "Good on you."

I lean forward. "So now you know who we are and what we're doing. I understand you'll probably need time—"

She's shaking her head. "The longer I'm here, the greater risk someone will strike at Uncle Mac to try and break me. I don't want to wind up making the worst of choices because there are no alternatives left to me. If you'll give me ten minutes to gather my things, I'm ready to go with you now."

At that, I nod, and she rises, following after her uncle with the two bots beside her. That leaves Dina, me, and Loras in the VIP lounge. To my surprise, the mechanic slings an arm around my shoulders and gives me a squeeze.

"Well played, Jax. This calls for a drink."

She heads over to the limited kitchen-mate built into the wall. From here one can order just about any drink since we're hanging out in the VIP lounge. I expect her to need to use her credit spike first, but the machine hums to life. Naturally, Dina keys up something expensive.

"On the house," Rafferty says from behind us. "I've been

worried sick about that girl. My sister's kid, you know. I
never saw her much while she was growing up. Never had
much use for Farwan."

I offer a faint smile. "I'm hearing that a lot lately. Funny
how once the giant's dead, people grow brave enough to
speak."

"I wouldn't say dead," he returns gravely. "Wounded, but
they still have teeth enough to do some harm, particularly in
this climate. You'll look after her, won't you?"

On the surface it seems like a non sequitur, but it's not:
We live in dangerous times—take care of Evelyn for me.

"We'll do our best. I can honestly say she'll be safer with
us. We're farther off the beaten track, and the station has
been proofed against Morgut."

Mac inclines his head. "Good enough. You might want to
call that big fella back here. I can't send the bots out without
drawing more attention than it's worth, and you have some
ground to cover between here and the docks."

He's right. We don't want anyone to know she left with
us, and laser fire on the promenade deck would leave a trail
two light-years wide. This time, we need to be quick and
quiet.

"Good thinking." Dina gets on the comm and tells Hon
we need his escort back to the ship.

"Has the mission succeeded, then?" I applaud him for
being cagey.

"Confirmed," Dina tells him. "How long will it take you
to get here?"

"I'm nearby. I went to an all-night eatery on level two."

Rafferty says, "He's at Stuff-it. It's fully automated, so
there's no need to close." At my look, he adds, "No more
than three minutes out."

Excellent. For once, things seem to be falling into place.

By the time we finish our drinks, Hon has arrived, and
Mac buzzes him in via the side door. Unfortunately, he
brings bad news.

"There are four creeps watching the place, slicker than shit, they are. I make them for Syndicate goons."

Shit. So much for a quiet exit.

"You're sure?"

Hon flashes me a scathing look. "What do you take me for? They tightened up when we stopped by after hours."

"So they know something's going down," Dina surmises.

Rafferty paces. "I could let you use the bots. That should even the odds. I won't chance anything happening to Evie. She's all the family I've got left."

I smile a little over that unlikely nickname. "If we use reinforcements, so will they. We don't know what kind of manpower they have on station."

"Or firepower," Dina puts in.

No shit. I don't look forward to disruptor fire. "It could get ugly."

"What do we know about the four, you saw?" Rafferty asks Hon. "I don't suppose you got any footage?"

"As it happens . . ." He produces his handheld. "I got good images of three of the four—wasn't sure we'd be able to do anything with it, but it never hurts to be prepared."

"Brilliant," Rafferty breathes. "Can I see that for a moment?"

He synchs the handheld with the main terminal and I watch images run past at blinding speed. Soon we have names to go with the faces and all their known associates. It's a long list.

"Mother Mary," Dina curses. "I'm glad the promenade is quiet right now. Otherwise, we'd be looking at a serious body count."

The pirate includes his shorn head. "As it stands, we need to plan our strategy. We'll have to fight our way out."

"Or *think* our way around them."

We turn to Loras, waiting for more.

Ironically, he's gained confidence with Hon, devoid of any facsimile of friendship to shield him from the need to prove his worth. I don't say that's wholly a good thing, but he's more forceful than he used to be, less of a dreamy non-entity. Maybe that sojourn acted as a crucible.

"You have something in mind?" Hon asks.

"Yes." Without further delay, he tells us.

CHAPTER 23

The plan is brilliant in its simplicity.

We listen as Hon comms security. "I want to report suspicious activity on station."

The agent goes from bored to interested. "What's happened, sir?"

"There's four men scoping out Rafferty's right now. I think they might be planning on burgling the place." He lowers his voice. "They look like Syndicate."

Ah, what a lovely marriage of truth and untruth.

"What makes you think so?"

"I recognize one of them." Hon makes up some story about seeing one of the creeps in action on Venice Minor.

"And who are you?" The agent is logging the call, no doubt, keeping good records. Farwan no longer handles station security, so it's a private company, and they don't want to lose the contract. That means they'll check this out.

"I'm the night watchman at Rafferty's."

With his Peacemaker units, Mac doesn't need a humanoid guard on premises, but this rep doesn't know that. He advises Hon, "Stay inside. I'll deploy a team immediately."

"I must confess," Mac says, "this reassures me greatly. Some people look for the hammer-and-nail solution to every problem."

I know what to say. "We won't risk Evelyn that way as long as there's another choice."

"Good to know," she says coolly. "I'm packed and ready. I collect there's been some difficulty?"

"Security should handle it," Hon tells her.

We watch the external cameras as a full squadron appears on the promenade. They round up our four goons without a shot being fired. I wish I could hear what's being said, but Rafferty's cams don't offer audio. I could guess it goes something like this:

As security arrives: *Hey, we're not doing anything!*

We'll be the judges of that. The agent puts on the cuffs.

One of the Syndicate goons struggles, wearing an outraged look. *You can't do this. Do you know who I work for?*

The agent scowls at him. *We have questions about why you're loitering up here after hours. Loitering is a misdemeanor.*

Another security guard says, *Look, I found concealed weapons. That's more than a misdemeanor. Let's go, you.* And shoves the thugs toward the transport.

"Clear," Loras says with a faint smile. "Are we ready?"

Evelyn gives her uncle a hug, but he forestalls anything more with a raised hand. "Don't tell me where you're going or how to contact you. It'll be safer that way. I can't spill what I don't know."

"Do you have something to cover your head?" I ask Evelyn.

In answer, she produces a hat with a low, wide brim. It's not ideal, but anything larger would draw just as much attention. Mainly I want to cast some doubt as to her identity if any surveillance remains.

As we step out the side door, Hon contacts the *Dauntless*. "We're on the move. Keep watch for us."

Smart.

Dina scouts ahead, making sure the way is clear, as we pass from the promenade into the deserted corridors that connect to the lift, which will carry us to the docks. Though I'd never tell her so, there's another reason I have her roving ahead. Her limp flares up when she runs, so I want her ahead of us, no risk of her falling behind and being lost.

I don't like the way our footsteps echo. I don't like the dimmed lights overhead. Oh, I know it's standard, reducing energy usage during off-hours, but it gives the place a creepy air. Each time we pass a T in the hallway, I feel skittish and exposed. Loras and I keep Evelyn between us while Hon guards our backs. Once, I couldn't have imagined trusting him there, but he's proven true to his promise, and I believe he wants to earn back what he lost at Farwan's hands.

Sometimes I think I hear footsteps keeping pace with us. Finally, I slide a look at Loras, and whisper, "Can you hear that?"

"For the past three minutes," he confirms. "I can't tell yet if it's a threat."

"We should act as if it is," Evelyn says calmly. "You have a plan?"

Fight or die doesn't sound like much of a plan. So I simply nod.

Hon murmurs, "If we get to the lift, we can make a run for the docks. It's hard to hit a moving target."

Hard, but not impossible. It would be catastrophic if we got Evelyn this close to freedom, then some Syndicate sniper nailed her in the back. I have to make a quick decision. Mary grant it's a good one.

"Let's make for the lift. There's only one way to the docks, and if we get down there first, we'll lay in an ambush."

The others nod grimly, and we double our pace, catching up to Dina in no time. She's already at the lift. "Company?" she asks, brow lofting.

"Could be," I answer, as the door opens. "Any activity down this way?"

She shakes her head. "Dead quiet."

Loras mutters, "Wish you hadn't put it quite that way."

He has to be remembering the last time he fled a station with me, but I swear it's going to end a different way this time. The hallway is still clear as the lift doors begin to close, but I can hear their footsteps. They've started to run, abandoning subtlety for speed.

Shouts echo as we drop, but we don't get a glimpse of our pursuers, so I'm not sure if it's more Syndicate or independent raiders looking to sell Evelyn to the highest bidder. Her face is pale, but composed; for a scientist who's spent most of her time in a lab, she's amazingly courageous.

I'm considering asking her about the ill-starred voyage that left her stranded in the escape pod when the lift starts to open. A misplaced reflection catches the light, and I shout, "Get down!"

Instinct guides my reflexes. *Dive.* We hit the floor as a barrage of laser fire sears the wall behind us. I roll to my belly, weapon in hand, then shoot in a tight burst, singeing the wall, but they're around the corner toward the dock, popping out to fire, then spinning away before we can hit them. Hon comes up beside me, offering the next volley.

For an instant, I expect March to take command, make everything right, then I realize with a little spurt of horror: *I'm in charge here.*

"Loras, you've got to lock the lift down," I tell him quickly.

"Acknowledged." He sets to work immediately, understanding what's at stake.

"They herded us," Evelyn bites out.

Yes, she's a clever girl. Regardless, we couldn't have guessed they'd have men already in place down here, unless—

No. I won't say it aloud. A normal person wouldn't even consider it, but I have to wonder if Mac Rafferty put credits in his account tonight.

Another volley comes in, white-hot and so close it burns away the hair on my forearm. They're not interested in parley; I'd guess their instructions are simple. Kill us and take Evelyn. Beside me, Hon doesn't need to be told to stagger his fire, so that while my weapon is cooling down, he can cover me.

This time, when they duck out to take aim, he nails one in the chest. The stench of charred meat rises from the spasming corpse, and I know a fierce satisfaction. There's no telling how many there are, though, so we can't get cocky yet.

"Can you use a weapon?" I ask the scientist, firing with the weapon balanced on my forearm for better accuracy.

Evelyn manages a smile. "Give me one and find out."

I call to Dina, "Toss her your gun. I need you with Loras. Make sure we don't end up with enemies up our asses. I don't want that lift moving until next week."

There are other lifts to docking, of course, but this one leads directly to the bay where our ship is waiting. If they have to circle around, we'll be on board and greeting them with antipersonnel rail guns. I spare a smile at the thought.

Behind me, I hear the hiss and crackle of them severing electrical connections and expertly rerouting the controls. Evelyn wriggles up on the other side of me and mimics the way my pistol rests on my arm. She takes the next series of shots, and she nails one in the arm as he scrambles for cover, not a kill, but she got his gun arm. Unless he's ambidextrous, his aim will suffer.

I hear them arguing down the hall. They didn't expect organized resistance; whoever hired them didn't give them all the information. These thugs expected an easy snatch and grab. Clearly, they don't know us very well.

"We've got you pinned down," I call. "You've already lost two men. If you surrender now and beg nicely, I might let you walk away."

Hon flashes me a look that says it isn't going to happen, but they don't need to know that. I can't speak for everyone present, after all. I'm just promising not to kill them myself. Silence follows, unbroken by laser fire. They're talking among themselves.

"Maybe *you* better give up," someone finally calls. "We have reinforcements on the way. It's just going to get worse for you."

"Do you?" I ask brightly. "I wonder how that's possible

when we've got the lift tied up. They'll have to come in from the other side, won't they? Which doesn't offer you any tactical advantage at all."

Into the silence, Dina calls, "We're done. It'll take them *days* to figure out how to repair this lift."

Hon adds, "Whereas we have a crew full of trained raiders on the way from the ship. And they *can* come up behind you. Do you have a man watching the dock?"

"Maybe you want to walk away," I agree.

A curse comes in answer—then we're back to shooting. I take aim, and a man dies.

CHAPTER 24

Hon covers me while my weapon cools down.

A goon leans out, and the pirate captain takes him in the head. His face chars black in the center, the damage raying outward as he falls forward. From around the corner, his mates pull him back out of sight, like we're going to keep shooting his corpse.

I can hear the hushed discussion of what to do. I guess Hon got their leader. Nobody is surprised when they all pop out at once, slamming shots into the floor near us. I scramble back and take cover while Evelyn shoots. She nails one in the shoulder, and his scream echoes down the hallway. If they don't get him help soon, he'll die of shock.

They fall back and regroup. More whispering. The dying man groans his agony, wordless now. Laser pistols aren't as cruel as disruptors, but they're no less lethal. My weapon hums, telling me it's ready to discharge again. I use the sight and ease onto my stomach, waiting. Movement draws my fire. I miss, but this won't end until we kill them.

I didn't start this, but we'll finish it.

The fight turns into a slaughter. By the time we're done, Hon has killed four, I dropped two, and Evelyn accounted for the one she took in the shoulder. Though I'd have expected her to be troubled by it, she seems to want off this station too much to let shock take hold of her. Since she's been trapped here for a while, I don't blame her.

As it turns out, Hon wasn't bluffing about having alerted the crew, but they come in a little too late to join the battle. Instead, they work cleanup. We'll take the corpses with us, disperse their molecules, and space the dust. Harsh, I know, but it's better than leaving a trail this wide to follow. Better for their employers, whoever they are, to wonder what became of their thugs. We can't allow the wrong parties to follow us back to Emry before we're ready for battle.

Dina has wiped the cameras down, offering looped footage instead of a record of what actually happened. If we're lucky, nobody will have been watching the feed live, so we don't have to worry about security heading our way. But that's a hope, not a surety. We need to move fast now.

Doubtless they'll wonder about all the scorch marks, but we can't do anything about them. Dina leads the way back to the ship, and I don't relax fully until we're on board. She takes Evelyn to a vacant berth where she can settle; Loras goes with them.

That leaves Hon and me to make our way to the cockpit. My nerves flutter at the idea of doing this again. It hurt so damn much the first time that my whole body has tensed in anticipation of pain. Letting the phase drive use my body as a conduit isn't one of my more prudent notions, though I'm not exactly known for caution in any case.

Hon offers me a canny look. "You sure you can do this again? March'll kill me if I deliver you as an empty shell. Now we got Evelyn, we can afford to go back slow. Maybe."

I know what he means: mind gone, flesh intact. That's the worst part of burnout—it leaves your loved ones to clean up the mess. And to be honest, no, I'm not sure, but despite his attempt at kindness, we don't have the time for a long haul in straight space from the nearest beacon. We'd be sitting ducks the whole time, fair game for any Morgut ship able to come through wherever they choose. Unlike human ships, slow and limited in comparison.

Except for me, except for mine.

I tell myself again, *There's no distance in grimspace. It's all relative; therefore, I can jump from anywhere.*

Just because you can, it doesn't mean you should. I can almost hear March, saying the words. When did he become the voice inside my head?

"We don't have a lot of choice," I say gravely. "I'm not indispensable. Doc has my samples. In time, he can probably make more like me—and use Evelyn's nanites to do so. It's vital to get Evie to Emry, quick and safe; we can't afford another attempt on her."

This is more than me chasing adrenaline, more than me dancing on the razor's edge for the thrill of it. For the first time, it's not that I *want* to risk being sucked through the door on the far horizon. I want to live. I have people who care whether I come out sane and whole on the other side. For the first time, I'm *frightened* of what I'm about to do. At last, I have something too dear to lose.

He studies me for a long moment, dark eyes full of shadow. It's just as well March isn't here because he wouldn't let me do this again, knowing how much it hurt me before. There's no guarantee I'll survive it, but that's sort of the human condition, isn't it?

In the end, nobody gets out alive.

At last, Hon calls the docking officer. "We're ready for departure."

"Acknowledged, *Dauntless*. Did you enjoy your stay?"

Hon glances at me. "It was . . . memorable."

The docking officer offers the usual litany of questions. Are we departing with any new goods? Did we purchase livestock on station? We're able to answer no to the security questions. Stations like this don't much care about the hiring of new crew, so they only inquire about goods and services.

In all, it takes five minutes for the port authority to clear us. Thanks to Dina, they don't know anything about the gunplay in the docking corridors. Then Hon maneuvers us out of the bay in a smooth swoop. I remember when I flew the ship, leaving his kingdom; there was never a worse pilot in the history of starfaring.

He takes us a fair distance from the station. It's important that we get clear of the gravitational pull, if nothing else. I need a clean slate to work with—a standing jump is hard enough without detracting factors.

I take a deep breath and exhale slowly, knowing I'll need the fortification. Oxygen floods my bloodstream as I jack in. Blind now, shades of black and gray. My hearing sharpens. I can tell the instant Hon touches his shunt, then the phase drive starts to hum. *He's letting me do this.*

Then he's with me. This time it's different, and he's not guarding himself so tightly. I see him flooded with concern, edged in worry-red. If it was fear, I don't know how I'd gather my resolve to do what must be done, but he's not afraid.

He's raw and rough, full of hubris and ready laughter. Oh, he knows the danger of believing his own legend, and most times, he only pretends he does. I see a white-hot love of his sister, Shan, and a sad blue longing for what he's lost. For the first time, Hon seems wholly human to me, not a larger-than-life figure.

You set?

Yes.

The phase drive hits its height, seeking that connection, and it comes harder this time because there's more resistance in me. Oh, Mary, it's worse this time, a thousand times worse, as if my body boils from the inside out. A scream dies in my throat as the engine turns me inside out, twists through me, to carry the ship into a horrific birth in grimspace that blazes through every cell.

Moisture runs down my face once more. I can't tell if I'm still breathing, but I must be, because we're only halfway there. The pain prevents me from focusing for a moment. I'm still blind, even though I'm in grimspace—and that terrifies me more than anything ever has. It takes precious, precarious seconds for the colors to flare to life in my mind, for my brain to detect the pulses echoing through distance that is not distance and translate them into something more than agony.

From far away I hear something moaning pitiably, like an animal in pain, but I have to ignore the noise. Screen it out. *Emry Station. Emry Station. Emry Station—*

For endless moments, I'm lost. The damage is too great. I cannot do this. We are lost—grimspace will take us.

No. Fight through, Sirantha. We're counting on you. Hon, in my head. Can he feel how much this burns? My blood and bones are evaporating within me. I'm blazing like a chunk of cosmic rock hurtling through the atmosphere.

Not yet, he orders. *Where, Sirantha? Tell me where.*

There.

I *am* the beacon through which I must pass—and then another twist. I am the ship. I am the stars. There is no barrier between the building blocks of existence and me. Pure torment this time. There's no pleasure, no euphoria, only unceasing misery. Hon works furiously at the ship's controls. He's followed my insane directives once more, done his part to bring us safely through.

But I have nothing left to give.

My whole body locks in a rictus, but it's a blessing. I can't feel anything now.

"Sirantha?" I hear the voice, but it's too far, too far. Now there's pressure on me that might be hands, but there's no sensation of heat or warmth.

To my surprise, I realize I can see them all now: Hon, Dina, Evelyn. They're all in the cockpit, but their distress seems trivial. I have no connection with the broken thing in the nav chair, and I want none.

"Get Doc! Right now. I don't care if he's sleeping. Get him on board." Dina has her arms around my body.

On some level, I realize that means I did it. We reached Emry Station. Did Edaine—the jumper who gave her life to liberate me from Perlas—watch while they wept over her final jump? Did she whisper a farewell, unseen, unheard?

"There's no wound," Evelyn says. "These readings . . . the instruments must be off. How can she have lost so much blood if there's *no wound*."

Words tumble end over end, becoming sounds that make no sense, then even that goes quiet.

Peace. Peace, at last.

CHAPTER 25

Unfortunately, it's not forever.

I'm aware of someone forcibly raising my lids, and stinging light streams into my eyes. My body feels leaden, so I can't lift my hands to bat this annoyance away. All I can do is lie here, watching but unable to respond—trapped in my own flesh.

The sounds slowly coalesce into words. Doc's speaking, but not to anyone in particular. He's making notes. "At 2307, Jax appears to be catatonic. Vitals now stabilized. She was deceased for precisely one hundred and ninety-five seconds before resuscitation was successful. She has been transfused with one liter of synthesized blood, and the prognosis is positive. I am unable to determine whether her cognitive functions have been impaired, although initial tests indicate they are not. I posit that her unique physiological structure may be utilizing this near-comatose state to engender repairs to damage inflicted by direct jumps."

He stands over me for another moment or two, but since he's allowed my lids to close I can't see what he's doing anymore. Footfalls tell me someone else has entered the room. I recognize the way he moves, the way he smells. I don't need sight to tell me March is nearby. I wish I could reassure him, but I don't know what I've done to myself. I can think of few things more horrifying than to be trapped inside my own flesh.

"Any news, Doc?" His voice is raw, as if he's been crying.

"Her condition is unchanged, Commander. Perhaps she needs time to cycle through the healing trance, then she'll awaken naturally, as she did on the *Folly*. At that time, I'll assess her condition and see what secondary injury was inflicted by the neural repairs."

Though I can't speak up, that can't be right. I don't remember anything about those three days. I certainly wasn't conscious and able to listen in on other people's conversations. I want to scream, but I can only do so silently. My vocal cords don't work.

"You think she'll wake up on her own, then." With nothing else to focus on, I hear the request for reassurance in his tone. March takes one of my hands between two of his, and I feel the heat of his forehead against mine.

No matter what Doc says, I'm none too certain of that.

"I have no way of being sure," Doc returns quietly. "It is a hypothesis. Sirantha's physiology is suprahuman, so my knowledge base proves of relatively little use." He hesitates, and I hear uncertainty in his lengthy exhalation. "I feel I must prepare you for the worst," he goes on heavily. "It is possible she will never awaken at all. Though cerebral impairment does not normally occur until a patient has been deceased for greater than two hundred and forty seconds, this is only a guideline, not an absolute. The extremity of damage suffered in jump, compounded by duration of death—"

"There may be something permanently wrong with her brain," March snarls. "That's what you're getting at."

"It's possible. I'm saying I don't know."

"I should never have let her go." His lips brush my brow, then he moves back. March's hands remain wrapped around mine.

I wish I could give him so much as a twitch, a tiny return of pressure to let him know I'm still in here—not a sea cucumber—but I can't. Though the need to weep clots my throat, I can summon no tears. My eyes remain closed and dry as bone.

"With all due respect, I don't see how you could have stopped her."

"Doc, if I was to tell you something . . . a closely guarded secret . . ."

No. March, no. Don't tell him. The more people who know, the greater danger that someone will come after you. Psi-Corp is still up and running. They must still have enforcers on staff, hunters they send after rogue Psi. *Don't do this. You've kept your secret this long; don't do this for me.*

"I don't like the role of confidant," Doc says. "And I don't like being put in the position of telling people they're being foolish when my opinion will not change their minds. Perhaps you could handle this some other way."

He knows, I think, astonished. *But he doesn't want it confirmed. He wants to maintain plausible deniability.*

March laughs, but the sound is devoid of amusement. "Give me five minutes with her, please. Alone. Then get me Evelyn Dasad."

Heavy footsteps retreating tell me that Doc has gone. Mary, I hope March doesn't fall upon me and weep because I don't think I could bear it. But no, he touches his forehead to mine again, and there's a warm prickle at the nape of my neck. Doc should've warned him that there was a chance he could be trapped in my body, if I wasn't here to receive him. Despite the risk, despite the uncertainty, he's coming in after me.

Jax?

I'm here.

His relief drowns me in a golden wave. *Don't ever do this to me again.*

Amusement. *You know I can't promise that.*

He's too shaken to yell at me, and besides, I'm not out of the woods yet. Just because he can talk to me, it doesn't mean anyone else can. Doesn't mean anyone else ever will. At least, unlike most jumpers, I'll get to say good-bye, after a fashion.

A horrifying thought occurs to me. Maybe Farwan knew

about this. Maybe *this* is burnout, and all those lifeless shells actually have a person trapped inside them, unable to communicate. Did they ever bring anyone over from Psi-Corp to find out?

Even if they did, I doubt they would have told us about it. They made their fortune by spreading propaganda and half-truths to keep us trusting and compliant. There's no point in the revelation if they don't know how to fix it. The facts would just get us worked up, after all.

Do you know what's wrong?

No. I just came to a few minutes ago. I'm not sure why I'm stuck like this.

I'll keep Doc on it, he promises. *I won't let him give up on you. We'll get you well.* His arms go around me then, and I can feel his warmth, feel him holding me, but I can't respond to it. *You have no idea.* Grief blazes in him. *Right after we brought you back, I came inside, Jax. And you weren't here.*

Sorrow. Remorse. I'm sorry I put him through that—and since he's part of me, he knows—but I can't offer any explanation as to where I was. Maybe I was still roaming around outside my body, watching them, but I don't remember anything after the cockpit, after it all went dark. Maybe locked in the recesses of my poor, damaged brain, there's some record of what lurks beyond that door that's not a door, far on the grimspace horizon. Maybe that's where I've been.

Do me a favor, I beg of him. *If you can't fix me, if it comes down to me being stuck like this forever—*

No.

I don't have the heart to ask again. *Then keep me drugged so I don't realize I'm imprisoned. Something psychedelic would be nice.*

I'll see what I can do. I love you, Jax.

And I, you. Though in my mind I'm sobbing and begging him not to leave me, none of it manifests. He slips out, then he's only beside me, not part of me. I hope they'll believe him when he says I'm still salvageable. Right now, I'm not even sure I believe it.

Two sets of footsteps, one light and one heavy, come down the hall toward med bay. I know that's where I am from joining with March. This has to be Doc and Evelyn.

"You wanted to see me, Commander?"

I imagine March nodding. "Yes, have you had a chance to look at all the data?"

"I have."

"Your conclusions?" he asks.

"I posit that the blood loss can be attributed to Sirantha's using her body as a conduit for the phase drive. I think the device converted her erythrocytes directly to fuel needed to complete the jump, which offers an intriguing hypothesis as to how the ancients utilized this technology. Were they a fully integrated biomechanical race?" The enthusiasm in her voice reminds me that she's a specialist in the field.

"It's a sound theory," Doc offers.

Impatience colors March's voice. "I'm less interested in the *why* of the damage than in how to fix it. Can your nanites do the job?"

Evelyn points out frostily, "They've never been tested on human beings, Commander. That would controvert the fifteenth article of the Genevra Proclamation."

"I don't care," March snarls.

"If her catatonic state has been induced by some damage too minute to register on our scans, then yes, the nanites could repair the affected synapses. But I don't know for sure that she'll wake up. This is experimental technology, and something could go wrong."

There's a long silence. I can only guess he's weighing the pros and cons. At last, he says, "She wouldn't want to live like this. She's a gambler, so when the tech's ready, put her under and do it."

"She's already comatose," Evelyn points out. "What need has she of anesthesia? Even were she fully conscious, the introduction of nanites to her system would cause no pain, no more than receiving a dose of any medicine. That's how small they are."

"Microscopic," Doc agrees. I can tell he's vastly intrigued at what they're going to try with me, as soon as they finish the nanites.

For a moment, I think March is going to explain that I'm wide-awake inside this coma. But both Doc and Dasad are too clever to be fooled by anything less than the full truth, so March simply says, "Indulge me. And give her a shot now, please."

Muttering about emotional entanglements, Evelyn complies with his request.

Gratitude swells within me. Since he refused to kill me, at least he's doing the next best thing. Final thought: *I hope I don't wake up, unless the procedure succeeds.*

A hypo aligns against my neck, then, thankfully, my brain clicks off.

.CLASSIFIED-TRANSMISSION.
.FIELD INTEL AND CASUALTY REPORT.
.FROM-EDUN_LEVITER.
.TO-SUNI_TARN.
.ENCRYPT-DESTRUCT-ENABLED.

Truth is relative. I do not mind working in the shadows. In most situations it is preferable. People target the man upon the stage. I prefer standing where I cannot be seen. If it comes at the cost of glory, so be it. As to the power of my name, it will fade in time. In twenty turns, no one will remember. It is better that way. I wish I had better news to report.

Field Intel

The specimen should have arrived, and you ought to have had opportunities to test the toxin by now. The troops will appreciate this boost.

Our attempt to analyze the salvage failed. Once activated, the apparatus self-destructed, resulting in the loss of two key personnel. We will need to approach all Morgut technology with extreme caution henceforth.

To date, we have been unable to locate a downed Morgut ship for study. I am monitoring all satellite transmissions in the hope something will shake loose. If I locate a crash site, I'll dispatch my team at once to take control of the scene.

Casualty Report

Colonies destroyed: 4

Lives lost: 2458

Ships lost: 28

Damage to property: In excess of 34 million credits

I must also report that one of our satellite training facilities was attacked. Fortunately, the first recruitment class had already shipped off station and gone to join their assigned ships. Still, we lost nearly 250 volunteers in the raid. Intel indicates it was a Syndicate strike, looking to undermine our war efforts. I outline retaliatory action in the attached proposal. If it meets with your approval, I will set the plan in motion.

```
.ATTACHMENT-OPERATION_HYDRA-FOLLOWS.
.END-TRANSMISSION.

.COPY-ATTACHMENT.
.FILES-DOWNLOADED.
.ACTIVATE-WORM: Y/N?

.Y.
.TRANSMISSION-DESTROYED.
```

CHAPTER 26

Weeks pass.

During that time, I'm incapacitated, and it's galling to depend on machines to perform my bodily functions. Locked-in Syndrome, they used to call it. Anything I see, it's because someone opened my eyes for me. March told Doc I'm conscious, just trapped in my body due to brain damage. Anyone else would've asked how he knew, but Doc prefers to operate on a *don't ask, don't tell* policy, where unregistered Psi are concerned; after all, even with Farwan gone, it's still illegal. In an earlier period in history, my prognosis would have been grim, and though they try to be positive in my presence, nobody is sure I'm coming out of this.

Not even me.

Right now, I can blink—and that's all. We've devised a system that lets me answer yes or no if March isn't around to make my wishes known. But it still sucks beyond my ability to express. I want more than anything to climb out of this bed. And I *can't.*

My sole entertainment is being propped up to watch the vid and, let me tell you, the news is grim. Respect for the law has all but disintegrated, and raiders own all space close to New Terra while Morgut ships prey on outposts and colonies. As I stare at the screen across from my bed, a pretty, brunette presenter beams at the camera. I've seen her before, but I can't remember her name.

"The death toll rises. The fourth human colony went dark at Ibova two days ago. By the time Conglomerate officials sent a rescue team, it was too late." She leans forward. "What happened? What *has* been happening? The Morgut."

Ibova. I have—had—a friend there, one of the few I've made outside Farwan. I hadn't seen Sharine in a couple of years, not since before Kai died, but we'd always planned to get together later. Take a vacation and catch up. When her work slowed down or mine did. But that won't happen now. I almost can't process it. How can a whole colony be gone? But then, Ibova was small and struggling, out near the Outskirts, where patrols ran thin even in Farwan's day. Now we don't even have patrols.

And I am helpless to stop any of it. I can't even go to the bathroom on my own. Tears well up in my eyes and trickle down my face. Where they dry, salty on my cheeks, because I'm unable to wipe them away. Impotence stings.

A man joins the woman on the screen. She flashes him a dazzling smile. "Here to give an editorial opinion is Kevin Cavanaugh."

"Thanks, Lili."

Lili Lightman. Now I remember her.

Kevin dons a grave expression. "We've lost four human settlements in all. Who's going to help us? The alien-settled planets have powered up their Strategic Defense Installations, and they'll leave us to fend for ourselves."

No surprises there. Farwan did little to endear us to the others with whom we share the universe. Their policies were uniformly humanocentric, and they enforced their laws with a titanium fist. The days of human control have ended, and many alien races have taken the attitude: *Let them burn.*

The male presenter continues. "The answer is simple. We must defend ourselves. Our best hope lies with the Conglomerate Armada."

"Do you think they can build a significant force in so short a time?" Lili asks.

"If they cannot," Kevin intones, "then Mary help us all."

That about sums it up. I close my eyes and try to sleep. In a way, I wish they would keep me drugged while they work. Dozing the days away, I catch mumbled snatches as Doc and Evelyn program the nanites to repair my fried brain.

Though March is busy, he comes when he can to augment the electric-impulse therapy they provide my muscles, so they don't atrophy. He massages my arms and legs, and I can't feel it. Not the pressure, not the warmth, nothing. I feel disconnected from everything; I'm beyond broken. Despair lives in my heart as it never has before.

Vel visits as well, more than anyone else, in fact. Sometimes Vel takes one of my dead hands in both of his claws and leans his forehead to mine, and he offers a prayer to the Iglogth. I find it touching. Other times, he brings projects to my bedside and sits with me in silence, working. I find his company comforting because he doesn't burden me with talk I can't answer. There's nothing quite so awful as a one-sided conversation, where the person chatters to fill the void, unless it's when somebody tries too hard, and it becomes an interrogation.

Are you hungry? Thirsty? Hot? Cold? Tired?

I blink my response like a freak when I want to scream: *I'm not* anything *that you can fix—leave me alone already!* But I can only blink my *yes* and *no* like a good human wreck. I know I should be grateful I still have my life. I could have ended up like my friend from Ibova. But the truth is: I am *not* grateful. And I envy Sharine.

March keeps me updated on the progress. More ships have arrived. Classes have begun. He acts like he doesn't doubt I'll be out of this bed sooner or later. I wish I had his faith. But he doesn't come inside my mind much anymore, which makes me think he's putting on a good front.

Time is an anchor, and I wish it would drown me. I wish they'd let me go.

At last, Doc and Evelyn deem the nanites ready, pro-gramming complete. They've synched them with my DNA.

A quick injection, and they're off to work. As the nanites reconnect neurons that I shorted out, Evelyn takes samples of my blood to see how the nanites have adapted to a human host. She's used them on various primates but never seen these results before.

I imagine them as tiny robots, rebuilding all the broken bits. I'm told that's not completely accurate, and there's some fusion at the cellular level between biology and machine, but that parallel disturbs me. If they rewire me from the inside out, how long will I still be me? The very notion makes my flesh crawl, but the alternative is worse.

Gradually, movement is restored. I can wiggle my fingers, then my toes. Progress is excruciatingly slow, but before nanites, I would've been stuck like that forever. Never again. Swear to Mary, I will find someone who loves me enough to kill me if I ever find myself in this situation again.

But we hit a hitch.

I should be talking by now, but I can only make weird noises. Doc and Evelyn can't figure out what's wrong.

"Have you checked for anomalies?" Doc asks her.

"I've run all the tests and screens. Everything looks fine. The nanites are actually performing above expectations."

Good to know. But I still can't communicate. If it comes down to it, I suppose I could get a voice box, like Vel has. The intonations are pretty good. Not completely robotic like the old days. I ignore the arguing pair and continue with my physical therapy.

It takes another week before anyone works out the problem. As it turns out, Vel provides the missing piece of the puzzle. When he comes into my sickroom, I'm struggling to get out of bed on my own. My muscles are wobbly, and my coordination isn't what it should be. But the fact I can move again on my own? Heavenly.

He rushes over to catch me before I hit the floor, and then chides me in Ithtorian. "Brown bird cannot yet fly. Her wings are weak."

I try to answer, but only those damnable sounds come

out. The bounty hunter pulls back to gaze into my face in astonishment, then speaks in universal. "You cannot manage all of the vocalizations, Sirantha, but I believe you are attempting to speak Ithtorian. A few of those clicks had meaning."

While I'm processing that, he calls Doc and Evelyn. "I think your nanites may be trying to interface with Sirantha's linguistic chip."

"Of course," Evelyn says, her strong face brightening. "They're failing to repair her ability to speak that language because she lacks the vocal apparatus."

Doc nods. "We'll have to terminate this batch, alter the programming slightly, and try again."

That alarms me. I grab Vel's arm and mime writing. He gets me a datapad and a stylus at once. *Taking them out won't undo all the repairs? I won't be stuck again?* I don't even try to hide my panic.

Evelyn shakes her head. "Don't worry, Jax. It won't change your current level of ability. But if we don't try again, you'll never regain your ability to speak properly. Consider it a fundamental hardware conflict."

That makes me sound like a damned Pretty Robotics bot in need of an upgrade. But I give them the go-ahead to try again. Mary knows, I want to be normal. I'll never take certain things for granted again.

After they head back to the lab to start reprogramming, I touch Vel's arm to stay him. He sits down on the bed beside me, head cocked in inquiry. *Thank you,* I write. Vel rises and performs a lovely *wa*. *White wave will never forsake brown bird.*

Second time's the charm. They use a signal to tell the first batch of nanites to go inert and dissolve in my bloodstream. The next day, they inject me again, and I can tell a difference pretty soon thereafter. My words start coming back. I go on with physical therapy and see light at the end of the tunnel.

After she gets word I'm no longer a helpless lump, Dina

comes to visit me periodically. I don't blame her for staying away; I wouldn't have visited me, either. I respect her initiative. She wants me to look at modifications to the phase drive on the premise I'll be able to interpret mechanical bits since I was part of the device myself.

"How does this look? Is it like what you saw needed to be done?" She shows me a schematic on her handheld.

"I don't know. It looks close."

My memory is vague and blurry. At this point, I can only remember that there was some vital link missing. Live testing is the only way to tell if she's made the necessary connection between the phase drive and nav computer. I'm none too eager to try that again, but I know the Morgut can do this. More and more, we're receiving reports of their appearing beside their targets, not in known jump zones that could be more readily defended.

How do you defend against an enemy that can strike *anywhere*?

The station is full to bursting, and our Armada boasts fifteen ships. It's not much, but it's a beginning. Things have gotten worse; I've been listening to reports all afternoon. The Conglomerate is taking heavy hits for its lack of efficacy, and there's been no word from Ithiss-Tor as to when we can expect reinforcements.

CHAPTER 27

It's been fourteen days since I walked out of med bay,
grateful for my second chance. But I'm now arguing with
March over how I'm allowed to use it.

Currently, he's working on training pilots and jumpers in
the old style, making them combat-ready. And I want in. I'll
be damned if I let him go off to war with anyone else in the
cockpit beside him. I got enough of not knowing whether he
lived or died when we left him on Lachion. It's not happening again.

"Who would make a better combat jumper than me?" I
demand. "I have actual experience, unlike the rest you have
in there."

"Absolutely not," he says. "Who knows how the nanites
will interact with Doc's implant? He hasn't even perfected it
yet, so you shouldn't be jumping. Plus, you already have the
chip Vel put in you. If—"

Right now, I have more experimental technology in me
than any other human: Evelyn's nanites and Vel's linguistic chip. And I'll add more as soon as Doc gives me the
word that he's come up with an implant that can regulate my
grimspace repair system.

"Anything goes wrong, or they affect each other in unfore-
seen ways, I'm totally fragged. Thanks for the reminder. How
can you not see I can't let that dictate the way I live? If I stop
being who I am because of this, I may as well be dead."

I fold my arms, knowing I'm delaying the start of the class. Doc has undertaken the gene-therapy course to ready Argus for active duty, using *my* DNA, mingled with that of Baby-Z. If this works, Argus will be the next generation of jumper: my healing mutation, coupled with Baby-Z's resistance to burnout. He's since run extensive tests that confirm the theory he posited, based on preliminary Fugitive data.

That means the Dahlgren whelp has been accepted into the program already while I stand in the hall, arguing with Commander March, who doesn't feel like my lover right now. He's wearing his "in charge" face, and it looks like nothing I can say will sway him.

Except, maybe, this.

"Are you truly speaking as commander?" I ask him quietly. "Who puts the mission first? Because I don't think you can afford to turn away any able-bodied jumper at this point. If I jump with you, it frees someone else up. We need all the ships we can muster."

His jaw tightens. "Doc really thinks he has your implant ready to go?"

"It's untested . . . but when has that ever stopped me?" This will make my third piece of experimental tech. Soon I'll be adding laser cannons to my chest and upgrading to a shiny metal chassis.

Warmth indicates he's read me, and now March wears a look of abject horror. "Mary, I hope not. That's not funny."

"So I'm a go."

I don't wait for his answer, just push past him into the training room, where everyone else is gathered.

"You won't go out on patrol until you have the implant!" he calls after me. "I stand firm on that point."

Since I'm none too eager to repeat the experience of being held hostage in my own flesh, I'm fine with that condition. There are eleven other navigators in the training room, including Koratati. I can only imagine what Surge had to say about the mother of his child joining the Armada. Though he's a licensed pilot, he opted to stay on station with Siri, which I think makes sense. But it can't be easy to see his woman stride into danger without him. At least I'll be beside March every step of the way this time.

Constance is teaching the academic portion of the class. She's reviewed all the old manuals, all the subject matter that was once conveyed to combat jumpers as a matter of course, before the Axis Wars, before Farwan stepped into the void and assumed control. They, of course, disbanded the corps and stratified everything so the left hand never knew what the right was doing.

Unlike the rest of the jumpers, I'm not shocked to find a hologram giving our lessons. It makes sense from a time-allocation standpoint. Who can learn and present new information faster than an AI?

We spend weeks learning old patterns and formations. Drill myself on the information until I can recite it in my sleep. March pokes me awake some nights because apparently I'm doing precisely that. We have to be ready for anything: ready to assume command of the ship, ready to reroute weapons to the cockpit. Navigators used to be more versatile than we are now. Farwan turned us into one-trick wonders, content to rest upon our genetic laurels.

This includes a physical component, too. In addition to our classroom time, we spend hours in the workout room, practicing our hand-to-hand. In case our vessel is boarded, we're not just jumpers—we're soldiers, and this is war.

March comes to check up on us periodically. I'm sparring when he pops in this time, thankfully not with Koratati. We all draw lots on a daily basis to see who will go round with her; because of her greater size and strength, she beats the rest of us too easily for it to be a fair assessment of our skills. I'm up against a jumper named Sirius, who, despite what his name would imply, is quite a joker in the usual course.

I block one of his blows with my forearm. It's a solid hit, and it'll leave a mark, but I don't let the pain distract me. Since I know he leads with his right, I sweep his left leg and take him down, but I'm too slight to control him with my weight. My best hope lies in being faster and smarter. Since that's the way I fought even before I had this training, the experience benefits me considerably.

Instead of singling me out, he merely walks among us, inspecting the troops. March offers a comment or criticism here and there, telling a fighter where he can improve. When he stops at our mat, he says, "Keep yourself centered, Jax," then moves on.

What does that mean, exactly? Oh, yes. Women generally have a lower center of gravity than men. In a moment, I know how I can use that. I combine an arm twist with a sweep, and soon I have Sirius at my mercy. If he struggles, I'll pop his shoulder out of its socket; this is a lovely hold that offers excruciating pain in exchange for little harm.

Constance names the winners: "Jax, Michelin, Koratati, Wells, Jory, Finbar."

We each take a bow, knowing it'll come out different tomorrow. After we finish sparring, we begin our cooldown, light exercise designed to enhance stamina and overall fitness. I haven't felt this strong in ages. Constance watches over us, monitoring our vitals to make sure nobody is pushing too hard.

Later, there will be weapons practice. I had no idea the training would be so complex, but I'm glad for it. I'm starting to feel downright dangerous. All the drilling contributes to a sense of battle-readiness, of course, so we don't panic when our ship is being blown to bits around us.

I try not to think about that.

Evelyn has adapted well.

I stop by to check on her and find her in the lab. "How are things?"

She pauses in her work to smile at me. There are haunted depths in her dark eyes, but she looks better than she did when we found her on Perlas. "Good. I love working with Saul. He's brilliant."

"The way I hear it told, so are you."

"Well, we make a great team. We're working with Dina on a biomechanical matrix to make the connection between phase drive and nav com."

I perk up. "The one that lets the Morgut do direct jumps?"

She confirms with a nod. "That's the one."

"Are you close?" This could make the difference for the war effort. I hate that we've bumped it ahead of Loras in the queue, but it's vital.

"I think we might be. But close doesn't mean much in terms of research. Close could be two days or four years."

"I understand. There's no guarantee."

Evelyn sets her hands on the counter, perfectly at home in Doc's world. "I've never met anyone like him. He's a joy as a partner: clever, intuitive, methodical."

Oh, shit. She's . . . glowing. Listing his accolades like that, you'd think she was saying he's the man of her dreams. But maybe it's just the pleasure of working with someone who understands everything she says.

"He's a smart guy," I agree. "Keep me posted, will you? If you perfect the biomechanical matrix, we'll need it installed on all armada ships."

"Absolutely."

I step out into the hall. These days, I only have a little free time after my long day of training is done. I intended to find March and spend it with him. Though I don't yet have the same foreboding I knew on Lachion, I'm not altogether at ease with him going to war once more. The wounds are still fresh, and I'm afraid for him. Killing men up close and personal has been disastrous for him in the past, like on Nicuan, and again on Lachion. My one consolation is that we'll be engaged in space battles, which may safeguard him somewhat. Regardless, I want to curl up with him for a little while and pretend the rest of the universe doesn't exist.

On the way, I run into Dina, who's wearing a look that says she wants something. That never bodes well. I listen to her request with a raised brow, then I sigh. I don't want to look at more of her schematics. If I've told her once, I've told her a thousand times, I can't tell whether she's figured out the design flaw just by looking. Tiredly, I extend a hand for the blasted unit, but she shakes her head.

"I'm sure enough of this mod that I actually incorporated it into the *Triumph*," she tells me. "So I want you to come out with me and check it out."

She's less cautious than Doc and Evelyn. As scientists, they run countless simulations before they even think of creating a working prototype. Since Dina comes at this from a mechanical standpoint, she prefers trial and error, and so she's taken all the collective data and started building.

"There's no way March will approve that. I'm not cleared to leave the station."

"Then we won't tell him."

I sigh, regarding Dina with exasperation. "You're serious."

"Deadly," she confirms.

A jolt of horror runs through me. "You're asking me to field-test your design."

"Why not?" she asks blithely. "You've got enough experimental tech in you now to be designated as top-tier classified and hidden away from public sight forever."

She has me there. To my disgust, I find myself considering it. I should be able to validate her theory without jumping. Once I jack in, I'll be able to see if the necessary connection has been made.

But I made one final objection. "We need a pilot willing—"

"Hit's already on board."

Of course she is. Because March and Hon would confine both of us to quarters if they found out we were considering this. I know we need every advantage once we're on patrol, however. The Morgut can appear anywhere they like, and right now, we're limited to jumping through known zones, where the cations gather. That means they'll be faster and more mobile, and the fight may be over by the time we arrive to aid a ship in distress.

"Then let's go."

There's a faintly surreptitious air to our progress since we don't want to encounter anyone who might inquire what we're doing. As luck would have it, we reach the hangar quietly, and I board the *Triumph*. It's the biggest ship in our Armada currently, and Dina has been rigging the armaments accordingly. Though it was originally intended as a merchant's yacht, she's upgraded it considerably.

I find Hit waiting in the cockpit. She flashes me a white, toothy grin. "So she talked you into it? I swear you're crazier than she is."

"I'm not taking bets," I mutter. "Let's get this over with."

Sprawling in the nav chair, I admire her graceful way with the ship. Dina's in engineering, but connected via the comm. "Are we good? I can override the docking controls from here."

"You've been planning this," I note.

"Too right." I can hear the grin in her voice, but Surge won't be amused. Whatever she's done better not compromise station security, or there will be hell to pay.

"We're gone in thirty seconds," Hit cuts in. The tall pilot is all business, focused on her task. When we swoop out of the hangar, it's graceful as a bird in flight.

"We only need to go a short way out," I say then. "Make sure the station's gravitational field doesn't interfere with our instruments."

In a good, fast ship like this, that doesn't take long at all. The stars are so bright through the view screen, they almost blind me, constellations I could never have imagined from New Terra. I remember staring up at them from Wickville, lying in Sebastian's arms, and thinking, *One day* . . .

That day has come, and I can't regret the choices that brought me here within visual range of white-dwarf spirals and the variegated colors of cosmic clouds, older stars glowing gold and the newer ones gleaming blue-white. The loveliness here rivals grimspace.

"I'm powering up the phase drive," Hit tells Dina. Then to me: "Are you ready?"

Not by half, but this doesn't have to kill me or boil my blood inside my veins. We're not even going to jump. Mary, I never thought I'd need to give myself a pep talk before jacking in.

"Hold!" the mechanic shouts. "I've got a ship on sensors, and it's coming in hot."

Beside me, Hit scrambles, tapping a succession of panels until we, too, share the image. The crazy part is, it's not hauling fast toward us in straight space. The ship flickers, both here and not here. We couldn't fire on it if we wanted to right now. We've stumbled upon a jump in progress, and since we're as far from a known jump zone as we can possibly be, this can only be—

"Morgut." Hit bites off the word like a curse. "Dina, love, get our weapons up. Divert power from the phase drive and split it between cannons and shields."

"On it." There's a reason this ship has engineering adjacent to the gunnery.

Thanks to my combat training, I know what to do. Calm descends over me, and I lean in, daring what I never would've before. Coolly, I reroute the lasers to the cockpit, knowing Dina can't handle both at the same time. The targeting apparatus descends from a compartment in the ceiling, another excellent Dina-mod. Mentally, I thank her while the lasers cycle to readiness. With any luck, given that we came upon them before they were fully acclimated to straight space, we'll be battle-ready first.

"It's a scout ship," Hit reports.

She's left the comm open, so we can coordinate freely with Dina. I say, "We can't let them get away. They may not have bounced a message to their fleet yet. There's no telling whether they're investigating a rumor or looking for a place to nest."

"Regardless, we can't let them carry word about us," Dina says grimly.

She's right. If this vessel slips away to give warning, we'll wind up with more of them here than we can defend against.

If they take out our mustered ships, then the war's already lost before it's truly begun.

A new voice pops up on the comm, relayed from the station. March. "What the frag are you doing, *Triumph*? Who's at the helm? I didn't give clearance for a pleasure cruise."

"Can't talk, Commander," Hit answers smoothly. "We're busy saving your ass."

Oh, that'll go over smooth as s-silk, but I can't worry about him now. The Morgut vessel is coming about, readying to fire. Our sensors monitor their progress, and Mary help us, their weapons are faster, 65 percent and climbing. They must travel at half power all the time.

"Aim for their phase drive," Dina orders. "Relaying target coordinates to your apparatus, Jax." Her cannons let fly, fiercely red in the darkness.

At last, my lasers are ready to go, less impact, but I can fire more often. I adjust the targeting array more comfortably, take aim according to the location she's provided, and open up. Within the ship, even one this size, I hear the whine of the lasers as they heat up. Outside in vacuum, there will be nothing but silence.

We hit shields first, but they're weakening already with the way we're concentrating our fire. At this distance and on a ship so fast and sleek, the rail gun might do some good, but we don't have anyone to operate it. Unless—

"Dina, is there anyone on board who can—"

"Already on it," she answers briefly.

Then the antipersonnel weapons come online. Bless those crazy, savage clansmen. If there's one thing they know how to do, it's fight, and doing it in space probably just adds a little bit of spice.

"Argus Dahlgren, reporting for duty."

Bless the kid. He has my DNA running through his veins, and now he's about to become the second veteran combat jumper. "Welcome aboard. Blow a hole in those sons of bitches, will you?"

"Taking evasive action," Hit says suddenly, "so hold tight."

Oh, Mary, they're returning fire. There's something less magical about having weapons turned on you, but the exhilaration doesn't lessen. All of us must be crazy because I hear whooping from gunnery as Hit slings and rolls, performing impossible feats of reflex and agility.

And from that moment on, it's like nothing can touch us. Argus weights the fight in our favor. Their shields don't block projectiles and one of his shots goes clean through the hull. Once they have breach, their shields fall completely, and we first blow out their phase drive, then their engines; then Dina's cannons smash the ship to bits.

"No quarter," Hit says, studying the wreckage on-screen.

"None," I agree. "Do we have any power left to test your mod?"

Dina's answer comes slowly. "Just. We won't have enough to jump, but I think I can get it to cycle up."

"Go for it. I kind of doubt March is going to let us back out here anytime soon."

Hit laughs. "Yeah, we're in trouble, no doubt."

"If we hadn't been out there," Argus says, tentative, "they'd have succeeded in gathering intel if nothing else."

I nod. "We'd have been in deep shit. This was a lucky break for us."

"We were due one," Dina points out.

The phase drive hums as it powers up, not enough for a jump as Dina said, but I jack in, riding the adrenaline from the fight. Unfortunately, the phase drive and the nav computer still aren't linking just right; the web array isn't complete, so it's not a win for a direct jump. To access grimspace in this ship would still require me as conduit, and it nearly burned out my brain last time. The best analogy I can offer: The cations pass from my bloodstream through the shunt in my wrist and let the phase drive open a corridor to grimspace. But that carries too high a price. I won't be doing that again on purpose unless it's a life-or-death situation. Dina has to fix this.

"Sorry," I tell the mechanic. "Close, but not a go. Keep trying. We need that innovation to have any hope of keeping up with the Morgut ships."

"No pressure," she grumbles.

Then Hit takes us back to Emry, where the commander's waiting for us.

CHAPTER 28

March glares at us, pacing.

As the responsible parties, Hit, Dina, and I have been formally reprimanded. Let me just say—I don't much like having him in a position of authority over me. And he doesn't seem to care that it worked out for the best.

"If I am in charge here," he says in slow, measured tones, "then *I* am in charge. You don't so much as schedule a bowel movement without my clearance. Anyone who doesn't like the way I run things can get out. I mean it—pack your bags and get off Emry because I'm not putting up with this kind of insubordination from my officers."

Technically, I haven't accepted any field promotion, but I figure this isn't the time to argue with him. I've never seen him so angry.

He continues. "What do you think this does to my authority with the rank and file? If my trusted staff treats me like a fragging joke, then how do I enforce discipline here? In case you hadn't noticed, this is a military training installation, and we are *at war.*"

Well, yes. And we just won the first skirmish. I realize I shouldn't point that out.

"I'm sorry," Dina says. "I didn't think. I should have cleared the mission with you beforehand, however harmless I believed it to be."

Her humble tone doesn't fool me for a minute. She thought

he'd say no, deeming it too great a risk to me, and frankly, so did I. We intentionally went around his authority, which I suspect is why he's so pissed off. Listening to his tirade about how we're lower than slime, I try to look chastened. I don't think it works, however, because when his rant winds down, he dismisses the other two—having grounded them until further notice—but he asks me to stay. His expression cures me of the notion it's for personal reasons; I've seldom seen him so angry.

March stands before me, hands locked behind him. It's an intimidating pose, showing off his biceps and broad shoulders. "I need you to take this seriously, Jax. If you can't respect me as your commander, then I'm booting you off my team. You can stay here on Emry until you find some other ship to carry you, but it won't be one of mine."

That's when it sinks in—he means it. He has the power to ground me. Maybe up until now, I secretly thought the fact that we're lovers would protect me—that I could get around him—but it's not true. March is my lover only in our off-hours. Right now, he'll boot me if I smile at him wrong. Since it would kill me if he leaves me behind again, I can't let that happen. I have to prove I can be a good soldier, who respects chain of command, however much it chafes.

The old Jax would whine and insist it wasn't her fault. She'd blame Dina and offer a load of smart-mouthed excuses. I lower my head. "It won't happen again, sir."

His posture eases. "That said, you acquitted yourself admirably out there. It may make all the difference, buying us the time we need to finish up here."

"We need Dina to perfect that direct-jump mod."

"There's no guarantee she can get it done before we have to start patrols, and I can't factor it into the rotation."

My brows go up. "You're already working on the schedule?"

March nods. "I'm assigning sectors today. You want to help?"

"Trying to keep me out of trouble?"

"Partly," he admits. "But I could use a hand, and I feel like I've hardly seen you."

It's true. All the training and preparation has kept us from doing more than falling into each other's arms at the beginning of the sleep cycle. These days, we do little other than sleep together. Who has the energy for anything else? I keep my eyes fixed on the brightness that surely lies ahead. Our life together won't always be like this. We just have to stay strong and fight through. I don't like considering the alternative—that we were born for strife, and we will *never* clear the darkness.

"Lead the way."

March heads for the commander's ready room, a fancy way of saying "another converted conference room." We won't be interrupted unless more Morgut ships come calling. He brings up the array of data in 3-D, then Constance materializes. She's been helping him a great deal, I collect, and I suffer a small pang, knowing she's no longer just mine. But she seems to be thriving, pleased at being so useful, if such an emotional response can rightly be credited to an AI.

"Greetings, Sirantha Jax. You seem to be recovered from your incapacitation."

"Mostly," I answer. "I don't think I lost too many brain cells."

"Shall I scan you to determine the amount of retained cognitive function?"

I laugh softly. "Not necessary, but thanks. You like working with March?"

"I enjoy having access to station resources in addition to the facilities on the *Triumph*. I am able to complete my research in a miniscule amount of time."

"Speaking of which, did you place the order for the uniforms?" It seems like ages ago that she got those numbers for me. After endless scrutiny and committee action, we went with a manufacturer with a satellite factory orbiting a moon in the Outskirts. No planetary tariffs, and they deliver.

"Affirmative."

"Dahlgren," March barks into the comm. "I want two cups of hot choclate, and they better still be steaming."

That answers what price Argus paid for his collusion, though to be fair, the poor kid hardly had a choice. He just happened to be on the ship when we took it out. Still, he could've done a lot worse than serving as the commander's dogsbody.

Once we're settled, beverages to hand, we go over the information. March sums up his intentions, and I listen, thoughtful.

"Do they know?" I ask at last, referring to Dina and Hit.

He shakes his head. "Not yet. But we need her on the *Triumph*. With Surge staying with Siri, Koratati needs a pilot. So I've assigned Hit to the *Sweet Sensation*. They'll be responsible for patrolling the Gamma Omega galaxy."

I stifle a smirk. Some of the smugglers' vessels are former pleasure yachts, hijacked—and never renamed—out of some overdeveloped sense of irony or possibly . . . sheer laziness. You can never tell with pirates.

"That's a lot of ground to cover." I don't belabor our need for Dina's updated phase drive; we can't pin our hopes on an innovation when the technology hasn't been improved since we first discovered it. Sometimes you just have to make do and hope it's enough.

"Agreed."

"You assigned all the pilot jumper pairs, then?"

"I maintained the initial bonds whenever possible. Jory stays with Hon for instance. Hit and Kora are a rare case."

"How sensitive of you, Commander." I try for a light tone, but I don't pull it off.

Dina and Hit aren't going to be thrilled about splitting up, but I understand the logic behind the decision. Desolation prickles at the edges of my vision. It feels like everything is coming to an end; we're splitting into fragments, and there's nothing I can do about it.

His subsequent words only worsen my mood. "I wanted

to give you warning, as I know you're closest to him. Chancellor Tarn has a new assignment for Velith."

"You're joking." He has to be. My chest tightens at the idea of losing Vel.

I would never say this aloud, not even to March, but Vel has been there for me, ever since we holed up together in that icy cave on the Teresengi Basin. He's never wavered. Never faltered. Never doubted me. I've never had a friend like that—or known a devotion so deep it goes beyond species or sex. I don't even know what he is to me, really, but he's been my rock. And now I'm about to lose him; at least it feels that way.

"I wish I were. There's been a new ambassador appointed for Ithiss-Tor, a permanent one, and he pleads for his aid as cultural liaison."

"He won't go," I say. "He won't leave me."

March levels a grave look on me that says I'm being childish. "He would if you asked him to. We need to learn the status of their fleet . . . and if they have any intention of lending their aid, if the alliance is trade-only. When we fled the planet, we left a number of issues unresolved."

"Very well. I'll ask him." I can't promise more than that. Mary herself couldn't move Velith without his will.

Moving on, he indicates a spot on the 3-D star chart. "The *Dauntless* will take Delta Tau. Our ship, the *Triumph*, will rove between Sigma Psi and Pi Theta."

"The biggest ship gets the widest range?" I ask.

"Not only that." March leans forward, elbows on the table. "I have to preface this by saying, as the man who loves you, I'm unilaterally opposed to this. I'd rather you stay here with Siri and Surge." His gaze locks on mine, sparking gold with intensity. He means it.

"But as my commander?" I prompt.

"I accept that I can't change the woman you are," he answers heavily. "So if you're set on jumping, set on getting that experimental implant, then you may be able to perform direct jumps as a matter of course. Dr. Dasad told me that she thinks the nanites can be upgraded to interface with the regulator, assisting your mutation in regenerating you without the need for a healing trance."

A chill washes through me. "So we can ride to the rescue anywhere, jump like the Morgut do . . . without suffering an aneurysm each time?"

Will the pain remain, I wonder, if not the hard damage? Maybe they can install some neural blockers as well, so I can't feel it. At this rate, it won't be much longer before I cease being human at all. I try to contain my fear, knowing there's no place for it here.

I am a good soldier.

"That's the goal," he confirms. "You'll be our secret weapon."

Oh, dear Mary. I don't like the sound of that.

CHAPTER 29

Our training is complete, and the patrols have been divided up.

Only two things remain before we can all ship out, going our separate ways in a galaxy become so dangerous that Chancellor Tarn has declared a state of martial law, and he has a scruffy lot of former smugglers and thieves to enforce said law.

Over one task, I have no control. I can't say when Doc and Evelyn will have my implant ready to go, the one that'll turn the *Triumph* into the Conglomerate's secret weapon. Part of me thinks I already have enough alien tech in my head, but I won't say no. If there's any chance it'll give us the edge we need out there, I'd be a fool to refuse.

I'm about to take care of the other duty right now, as I promised March days ago that I'd speak to Vel. I don't look forward to the conversation. I don't want to lose my protector, my bounty hunter; I feel safer knowing he's nearby, but these times preclude self-indulgence.

I touch my communicator. "Constance, locate Vel for me."

"Searching." After a brief delay, she tells me, "He is assisting Dina in engineering."

"Thanks."

It takes a good ten minutes to make my way from the station back to the *Triumph*. For a moment, I stand in the doorway and watch them work. A week or so back, she brought

Vel into her efforts to make that missing connection between the phase drive and the nav computer, knowing he's a wizard with machines. In conjunction with Doc and Evelyn, maybe they'll succeed, though it seems like a long shot.

"How's it going?" I ask.

Dina sighs, straightening. Her fair hair clings to her forehead, sweat trailing down the right side of her face. "Slow. But I think we're on the right track. I'm integrating some data Ev and Doc put together. They've done some interesting work in linking nanoprotein strings to a biomechanical processor."

"I don't even know what that means."

Dina explains, "It's the first step toward connecting the nav com to the phase drive, so the phase drive fires outside known jump zones."

"That'll offer a way for the phase drive to detect grimspace from anywhere." That much I understand.

If I'm present, the cations in my blood make the connection because I have tiny bits of grimspace running through me. We need to find a way to make that happen through the ship, not the jumper. The course of gene therapy Doc designed for Argus imbues my regenerative mutation without the extras; we don't want to pass grimspace particles along without understanding their long-term effects. Argus was our first test subject, and it may be years before we know what we've done to him. Overall, I'd feel better if we could solve this through tech and not wholesale genetic manipulation.

"Can other mechanics learn to modify their ships once you perfect the design?"

"Sure," she answers, "but it won't do any good unless their jumpers have undergone extensive gene therapy."

I consider that. If—no, *when*—that happens, I won't be one in a million anymore. That prospect offers the promise of peace because what I do won't matter so much if others can do it, too.

"Good to know. Could I borrow Vel for a bit?" It's only

a courtesy to check with her. He's not her employee or her assistant.

She shrugs. "Ask him."

He pauses his work and comes toward me. I haven't seen him often during the course of my training, either. Not since I left the sickroom. Vel pauses to assess me. "You are harder," he says, after a brief inspection. "More fit. Stronger, too."

"Constance worked us to the bone."

"It was well-done. What did you want to discuss, Sirantha?"

"Walk with me," I tell him.

Our steps carry us out into the corridor and toward the quarters I share with March. He won't be there; he's in the commander's ready room, finalizing our strategies. No more than forty-eight hours remain before we ship out. My next and last stop will be med bay.

I make sure the door closes behind us before broaching the subject. It's not that I think he'll react badly to the request, but I'm afraid I might get emotional. It's not like me, I know, but this feels like a more permanent good-bye than I want.

"Commander March has asked me to speak with you on behalf of the Conglomerate. Chancellor Tarn has appointed a new ambassador, a permanent one, and he needs your help to finalize matters on Ithiss-Tor. They want you to serve as a cultural liaison, ensure that everything goes smoothly, and oversee the election of a representative, whom your vessel will transport to the summit on New Terra."

"Like before," he observes. "Except without you?"

"I'm not an ambassador anymore," I say softly. "Not that I was ever much of one."

"You were . . . perfect." Belatedly, I realize he's not using his vocalizer. Interpreting the sounds of his native language has become so instinctive that I didn't even notice the lack of human speech.

"It's very kind of you to say." I hasten on, knowing I won't be able to keep myself calm for much longer. I feel like I'm losing my best friend, as if I'll never see him again. "I can't force you to accept this assignment, of course. You're a free agent, here with us of your own volition."

That has to be the most mixed message I've ever delivered. The dutiful part of me knows he must go; the rest of me thinks something dreadful will happen to me if he does. Since he stopped hunting me and began protecting me, I've felt . . . safe.

"What do *you* think I should do?"

Oh, why did he ask me? If he were March, he'd have heard the immediate answer inside my head: *Stay*. But I manage not to say the word aloud. "I think the new ambassador will need you. The Conglomerate needs you."

I *need* you. But what do my needs matter? If we don't make use of every resource, every alliance, there will be nothing left. Humanity has engaged in the deadliest fight for our lives since we first stepped forth into the stars.

I remember how he promised he wouldn't serve another ambassador if I were fired. But times are different now, and I *wasn't* fired; I resigned. I don't want to return to that life. Here, now, I'm doing what I'm best suited for. So must he.

His clicks convey duty rather than desire. "Then I shall serve."

I coil dignity around myself like a cloak. If he were human, I'd long since have thrown myself into his arms and wept over the prospect of parting. Since he is not, I'm bewildered about how to deal with the impending loss.

"Chancellor Tarn will be relieved to hear it. Your ship is scheduled to depart tomorrow. You'll pick up the ambassador, then proceed directly to Ithiss-Tor."

"I thought never to return."

"I know. I hope it doesn't go badly for you."

He spreads his claws in a gesture that says it doesn't matter. "It always goes badly. I am a bitter reminder of profound failure."

"That's not true," I say at once.

"By their standard, it is. Fortunately I no longer measure myself by their standards."

"So it won't hurt you to return?" I'm glad of that if it's true.

The sight of his naked chitin offers *me* no offense. Vel is smooth, gleaming with high shine. In my opinion, the clean lines look better than the acid-etched markings his people wear as a sign of rank.

"Other things have the power to do me injury now," he answers obliquely.

To my surprise, Vel etches a particularly eloquent *wa*. Though it's been some while, the nuances don't escape me. The chip in my head offers his silent words, inflections that delve deep into my heart: *Brown bird glows with grace, and though flight carries her far, white wave waits, always, on the shore.*

Tears spring up in my eyes, but I hold myself with great ceremony, angling my body in reply. *White wave ebbs, his memory dearer than a diamond in a bed of sand. Brown bird watches, her wings stilled. Her song is silent until he returns.*

Did I get the gestures right? For an interminable moment, he studies me. Perhaps I am rusty, and my body language offered other meanings, nonsensical ones, and he doesn't know how to respond to my gibberish.

"You have an Ithtorian spirit," he says at last. "That was well-done. You make me feel at home, Sirantha."

How odd. I would've said he has a *human* soul. Perhaps between us, between his long exile and the alien chip in my head, we've met somewhere in the middle.

I manage a smile, though my eyes are stinging. "I'm glad. Because you always had the knack of that for me, even in a frozen cave on the Teresengi Basin."

I will not cry, I tell myself fiercely. *I will not.*

"I remember. You were never afraid of me, at least not after the first few moments. I will do my best to make you proud."

"I'm not going to say good-bye to you; but if it wouldn't bother you, I'd like a hug." Sometimes I can't help being human. He's been around us long enough that he should be used to our ways, even if he doesn't share the comfort in our customs.

"As would I, Sirantha."

Granted permission, I wind my arms around him and lay my cheek against the hard shell of his thorax. His limbs go around me in turn, and I feel his claws against my back. With one sharp movement, he could eviscerate me. His mandible rests against the top of my head for a long moment.

A human would offer warmth. I could listen to his heartbeat. Still, this is Vel, and there's solace in his proximity. I don't know how long we stand there, but I ease back first.

His final *wa* gains shadings of some significance I can't name. *There are no partings. White wave flows away. Brown bird is faithful to the sky. Where sea and sky cross, we meet again.*

It's a riddle, but the answer gives me a shiver of foreboding. *The horizon, the door that isn't a door.* Is he saying we'll meet again in death?

Sorrow has driven out any eloquence I might offer in answer. My *wa* is bare, a skeletal thing. My elbows won't do as I've asked, and I suspect I said something slightly impolite. He doesn't seem to mind.

Though these are my quarters, I flee first. He won't follow me. I won't see him again before he ships out. I'll be in med bay, sedated for minor surgery. It's time to get that third experimental implant. That's good; maybe it can take the edge off my inward ache. And maybe when I wake, I'll be resigned to being the Conglomerate's secret weapon, resigned to less humanity, more technology.

I touch my comm. "Doc? No more excuses on my end. If you and Evelyn are ready, I'm on my way."

CHAPTER 30

I wish I could say this is the first time I've awakened to too-bright lights and people peering into my face, but clearly, I've led that sort of life. It happened all too frequently on Perlas, generally in the middle of my sleep cycle.

Doc's voice comes from beyond my peripheral vision. "Patient is conscious, responding appropriately to stimuli."

"Vitals good." That's Evelyn.

Apparently, whatever they did to me, it was a success. My head still feels heavy, but I'm not aware of any pain. That's a plus.

"Jax? Can you hear me?" March is kneeling beside me, his face pulled into an anxious frown.

"Yeah." My voice comes out hoarse.

"How do you feel?"

I manage a joke. "Like I just fell out of the sky off a Skimmer."

"Good. That's good." He glances at Doc. "Can I take her out of here?"

"She may have questions," Evelyn says.

Do I? My brain isn't firing at full capacity right now. Oh wait, yes, I do have one. "Did you do anything to the nanites?"

Evelyn fields that one. "Yes, we . . . upgraded them, you might say. They're now configured to perform routine maintenance on the tech you have installed. That includes both your language chip and the prototype regulator we just installed. Your healing trances should be a thing of the past, as is your risk of burnout."

"Anything else I need to know?"

Doc makes a show of beaming some instructions to March's handheld. "Just this."

"So I'm discharged, then?"

"You might want to give yourself a few moments to—"

But March is already swinging me into his arms. "I'll take care of her, Doc."

Maybe it's just my general wooziness, but I like the sound of that. He carries me out of med bay, ignoring the half-articulated protests of scientists who doubtless want to poke and prod me some more. This behavior seems oddly unlike him, reckless, but then he taps his communicator.

"Constance, monitor Jax's life signs. Make sure she's not in any distress."

Ah, there's our fail-safe—and the cautious commander I know and love. He takes me back to our quarters and eases me gently into our bunk. Mildly disappointed, I expect him to leave me in Constance's "care," which is more palatable than staying in med bay. I spent enough time in there when I was recovering from catatonia.

Instead, he changes the setting, and our berth becomes a double. March lies down beside me, despite the fact that it's nowhere near the start of our sleep cycle. Propped on his elbow, he gazes at me in silence until I start to feel uneasy.

"You have bad news," I guess. "I'm permanently brain-damaged."

Still silent, he shakes his head.

"What, then? Don't you have work to do?"

"There's always something I could do, but right now, what I want, more than anything, is to be with you."

My heart, sore from losing Vel, swells inside me. Sometimes the man knows exactly what to say. It stands to reason, given that he's a mind reader and all. I curl into him, shivering at his warmth, and with a soft sigh, I tuck my head against his chest. The back has a residual soreness, so I'm guessing that's where they implanted the regulator.

"Good answer."

"It's the only answer." He hesitates. "Jax, I want you to know, this isn't my choice, any of it. I don't want this."

I answer gravely, "I know. Wishing I'd said yes back on New Terra, when you offered to become a homesteader?"

His hands skim down my spine, fingers playing each vertebra until I murmur in pleasure. "Not really. That life would've strangled you, so I'd have lost you anyway."

"Anyway," I repeat, "what are you talking about?"

Foreboding prickles over me, starting at the incision site. His heart races against me, indicating stress or arousal or both. I lift my face, studying his expression.

His eyes close. "I can't be both your lover and your commander, Jax. Not with so much at stake. I want you—no, I *need* you on my ship—but I can't multitask like that. I can't risk making bad decisions because I'm terrified of losing you."

"You have to consider the welfare of the whole crew." Maybe I'm dumb as a rock, but I didn't see this coming. I should have. "I can't be your primary concern."

"Exactly. We'll have separate quarters on the *Triumph*, and I expect you to behave professionally at all times. We can't let our history interfere with our mission."

So that's it? I'm "history"?

Intellectually, I understand the merit of what he's saying. Emotionally, I want to scream and hit him in the head. How am I supposed to jack in with him, jump after jump, knowing there will be no more contact between us? Mary curse the Morgut and this war.

I don't know how I sound so calm. "You're saying this is our last night together."

"For now. Until this is done."

"What then? You put me on a shelf until you can afford me again, then expect to pick up where we left off, as soon as it's convenient?"

He flinches, but a wounded soldier isn't afraid to attack.

"Isn't that what you wanted to do when you were afraid you were dying?"

"Are you punishing me for that?"

"No," he says wearily. "Strategically, I *must* do this. It will damage morale if your shipmates think you occupy a position higher than one granted by rank, by virtue of sleeping in my bed. They'll try to use you. Worse, some will try to supplant you, wanting that influence themselves. You have to trust me, Jax. I know how people think."

I suppose he would, privy to their innermost thoughts. One by one, I am losing everybody dear to me. Right now, I just want to see him bleed because all I know is that he's leaving me again. There's always a good reason for it, and I am fragging tired of loving a hero who always does the right thing. Except when he doesn't—and *I* have to fix him. My heart sizzles in my chest, and I lash out.

"By your statement, you can't show such favor to anyone aboard, so you have to be celibate. Do you think *I'm* going to act like a vestal virgin, too?"

His jaw clenches. I have that much satisfaction. At least I know he's hurting, too; that gives me back some sense of control over the situation. "It will kill me inside if you turn to someone else, but I have no right to forbid it, as long as that person is equal to you in rank."

"No," I say quietly. "You don't. Commander."

"We must leave it there. I cannot prevent you from looking elsewhere, and I'll not beg, either. Once this war is done, we'll see."

He says "once," as if we're guaranteed a victory, as if it's assured both of us will walk away. Right now I have no certainty of either, but that's why he's the commander, and I'm just a combat jumper. The soldiers will need his strength and his faith. My anger trickles away like water through curled fingers; I can't hold it.

I ask this of him more than is comfortable for me, but I need to hear it one last time before we set it aside for weapons and destruction. "Say you love me?"

His long fingers trail down my cheeks, shaping the sharp line, along the curve of my chin, and up to the swell of my lips. The warmth lingers like a phantom kiss. Tears slip from the corners of my eyes.

"More than the blood in my veins. More than the heart in my body."

I laugh softly, unsteadily. "A simple 'yes' would have sufficed."

"Nothing is simple between us. It never has been."

Oh, truer words were never spoken. "If we have only tonight . . ." I shift against him, my leg curling over his.

"I just want to be with you," he whispers. "One last night. But I didn't think—"

"It's only a bit tender at the base of my skull. You weren't planning on messing about back there, were you?"

His laughter cascades in luscious reverberation, his chest to mine. "Hardly."

"Then I'll tell you what I want." I press myself against him fully, whispering.

He listens, quietly avid. A shiver slides through him at my breath against his ear. "I've never done that."

"Then it's fitting that now should be the first time—and the last."

March skims away my clothes gently, and I offer him the same service in silence. There's no urgency yet, but our movements have purpose. We're consciously constructing a memory, for who knows how long it will need to last?

When skin touches skin, he comes into me, filling my head with his warmth, and oh, yes, that's what I want. Body to body, soul to soul—I want everything, and all of him, simultaneously. March rises up over me, bronze and strong. My hands skim down his sides. His pleasure is mine. His anguish and regret, also mine.

You're so lovely. There's utter heartbreak in him. I wish now I hadn't tormented him with the idea of someone else. I try to apologize in soft, silent kisses.

There can be nobody else for me.

He's hot and fierce, trembling against me. At my slightest touch he gives away, pulling me atop him. I tell myself it's better for my head, but the truth is, he likes it when I master him. He likes being the quiet recipient of my pleasure.

Easing down, I take him, his thoughts swirling wildly in my head. His moan pushes past my lips. The heat of my own body arouses me fiercely, his love and longing pouring through me in waves. With this intensity, his yearning spiking mine ever higher, we cannot hold it long.

We shake together, utterly one.

.CLASSIFIED-TRANSMISSION.
.OPERATION HYDRA.
.FROM-SUNI_TARN.
.TO-EDUN_LEVITER.
.ENCRYPT-DESTRUCT-ENABLED.

Apologies if I presumed too much, sir. I only spoke so because I know your reputation. Most people would say you earned it through brutality, but I wonder if that's entirely accurate. From what I have learned of you, it seems to me, you might have as easily earned that reputation via suggestion and misdirection. One whiff of your assistance in these matters would ruin me, toppling this administration, and yet I cannot regret bringing you on board. The past is past, but I would be a fool if I forgot its lessons. I think you understand this as well as me.

The statistics you report are grim indeed.

Your intel always arrives before any of my official sources. Thus, you advised me of the attack on the satellite training facility a full twelve hours before it came through channels. You will have seen my response on the bounce, but angry rhetoric can only carry us so far. If they are to believe I will strike when I curl my hand into a fist, I must deliver the first blow.

Therefore, I have reviewed your proposed offensive. Though there is some chance of harm to civilians, I judge it an acceptable risk in times of war and authorize you to proceed. You will, of course, be operating silent, and should your endeavor fail, I will deny everything.

Brighter news: the clinical trial went better than expected. The specimen reacted as predicted; there was no harm to the human control group. They were well compensated for their time. Thus, the first of our Armada ships have received the first shipment of Morfex. I look forward to hearing how it performs in battle.

Finally, I am still awaiting your input on the fiduciary issues.

Please send it at your earliest convenience, bearing in mind that matters discussed above take precedence. The wolf is not at the door just yet, but I fear I hear him howling in the trees.

.END-TRANSMISSION.

.ACTIVATE-WORM: Y/N?

.Y.
.TRANSMISSION-DESTROYED.

CHAPTER 31

So I'm a war widow.

Well, technically, we never married. And allegedly, after the war, we'll be together again as we were, but I'm afraid to hope for it. I can't dwell on it, either.

Like the other assembled soldiers, I'm in formation now and waiting for the commander's address. We're all in uniform, which gives us a sense of unity. The design came out better than I dared hope. In this midnight blue with our insignia sewn on the left shoulder in silver thread, we look confident; we look capable. We will become a force to be feared by our enemies.

March paces along, inspecting the troops. We hold ourselves to attention, shoulders back, eyes straight ahead. At last he seems satisfied, and he returns to his position at the center of the mess hall. It's the only room large enough to hold all of us at the same time.

"I will not lie," he says then. "The galaxy needs us desperately. In the months we've been training, two worlds have fallen. Our people are dying. But you're well trained and courageous, and I'm proud to serve with each and every one of you. It's imperative that you bounce messages quickly, ship to ship. The responsibility for that falls on the comm officers . . ." Though I can't pick them out of a crowd, March knows all their faces, and his gaze touches on them one by one. "Your diligence will mean the difference between victory and abject defeat.

"We face a cunning, merciless enemy, and our allies are few. I would not have it said that I glamorized our mission. And yet, if we succeed, we *will* make history. Your names will be remembered, your deeds sung. I believe we can defeat them with ingenuity, skill, and audacity. Now, troops, we have a war to fight. Are you with me?"

For long moments, there's only silence. His troops are not battle-hardened soldiers. Instead, we have smugglers and thieves, rebels and outlaws. They probably won't react well to hearing the odds given straight-out. Maybe he's erred, overestimating their nerve.

Then, from the back, I hear what sounds like a few feet stomping in unison. The cadence is rhythmic, intentional, and it gathers volume. I don't dare break formation, but I find myself joining in, becoming part of the whole. Soon, we're all doing it without knowing why; and then a lone voice sings:

> *To arms! To arms!*
> *Oh, heed the warrior's drum.*
> *Rise up! Rise up!*
> *Our enemies are come.*
> *They ask from us our blood and bone*
> *Next they look to steal our homes.*
> *But that we claim, we keep*
> *And all we want, we own.*
> *Fighting men, stand forth!*
> *Stand forth!*
> *Lachion tried and Lachion true,*
> *We will bring the war to you.*
> *Proud and tall, these Lachion men*
> *We fight until the bitter end.*
> *We have never known defeat*
> *In bitter cold or crushing heat.*

Now we fight among the stars
Soon the universe will be ours.
Sound off!

A different voice bawls out, "*Sweet Sensation*, ready, sir!"

Hon calls, "*Dauntless*, ready, sir!"

One by one, the captain of each ship shouts his affirmation of the mission. There's no telling if this display was arranged in advance, but I have no doubt it's effective. I can feel morale being buoyed up by show of solidarity and the comfort of marching in cadence. Even I can take solace in knowing I share the danger with like-minded individuals.

"You make me proud," March says quietly, when silence falls again. "You have your orders, men. Report to your ships. Patrols begin at once."

We snap a salute in unison and fall out, heading to the docking bays where our ships are waiting. I don't speak to anyone, too busy hoping I can be as professional as I need to be. It's hard when the relationship isn't over, nothing so clear-cut as an ending, but more of a hiatus. I don't do well with gray areas.

Before boarding the *Triumph*, I look up Surge, who's looking after the children. We still haven't heard from their parents, assuming they ever had any. They seem like normal kids, and they're happy enough on station. We've set up a small school, run by Constance. I'm going to miss her, but there's more for her to do here. She can coordinate communications faster than anyone else, so that's another private loss for me. I'm trying hard not to tally them, or I may fold.

"Will you be all right?" I ask Surge.

"I'll miss Kora," he answers, looking up from his work. "But I know better than to argue with her. I'll keep Siri safe and look after the other kids."

"Right. Constance, keep a sharp eye out."

"I always do, Sirantha Jax."

That's it, then. We're all going our separate ways. I leave without looking back.

The docking bays are pure chaos, full of people hugging and saying farewell. During our training friendships sprang up between people who are now assigned to different ships. Searching, I find Loras nearly ready to board the *Dauntless*. Mary, how I wish he were going with us.

"Loras!" I call. "Loras!"

He turns as I push through the press of bodies. "What is it?"

"Don't you dare leave without saying good-bye to me."

"I am La'hengrin," he says. "That is my lot."

"Not anymore. I haven't forgotten what you asked of me. I want you to know that."

"You spoke to Doc?" He seems afraid to believe in me, but I can understand that.

"I did."

"Thank you."

I hug him quickly, knowing we both have places to be. He's one of the comm officers responsible for quick deployment of ships.

"Take care."

My last farewell finished, I board the *Triumph*.

Dina's the first person I encounter in the corridor. She looks smart and skillful in her new uniform, but her eyes are red-rimmed. Without a word, I put my arms around her. It's a testament to her emotional state that she hugs me back.

"If anything happens to her . . ." Her words trail off in a shuddering sigh.

Unfortunately, I don't have any assurances to offer. We're at war, and the chances are good that we're going to lose some ships before winning this. The Morgut are too dangerous for it to be otherwise.

I can only offer my pain in answer. "March ended it. Said he can't be both my lover and my commanding officer. It would open him up to charges of nepotism and cause dissent among the ranks."

"He's right," she says quietly. "But, Jax . . . I'm sorry."

Now I have tears in my eyes, too. I didn't spend my last

night with him weeping, but I feel like I could now. Good thing I have more important things to do.

"We're a pair, aren't we?" I step back and swipe the heels of my hands across my eyes, just in case. "Is the ship fully prepped?"

Dina shakes her head and sighs. "I still haven't perfected the uplink between the phase drive and the nav computer. I have a feeling that's going to cost us."

Yeah, because without her technology, the *Triumph* is the only ship that can direct jump, courtesy of the new hardware in my head. There simply wasn't time to train *and* take the other combat jumpers through gene therapy, then fit them for their own versions of my implant. It took Doc and Evelyn months to configure one for me, based on DNA and brain waves. Though I don't understand all of it, apparently the brain emits a unique magnetic field, which must be imprinted successfully on the implant for the installation to occur without risk. Without the implant, there's no way I could conduct those cations safely. Frag, look what happened last time.

So that just leaves us as the cavalry, riding to the rescue.

"You did the best you could. Time's running against us. If we sat here on Emry until we were ready for the fight, there would be nothing left to defend."

"You got that right. I'll be in engineering if you need me."

"Dina." I touch her lightly on the arm. "Come see me after your shift."

She flashes me a grin that looks like it hurts—and it doesn't touch her eyes. "I hope you're not hitting on me. I already told you that you're not my type."

"I should be so lucky." I mean it. "I just thought . . . both of us are going to be lonely. We can play cards and drink. Watch vids. Whatever."

The mechanic inclines her blond head. "I could use a friend right now."

"Me, too," I say with feeling.

"And I guess I should stop pretending you're not the best I've got."

My heart clutches a little bit. If she's willing to drop the act, call it quits on the ribbing she offers as the main thrust of our relationship, then she's feeling worse than I am. I don't know if I can offer her any consolation, but I'll try.

"I'm right there with you," I answer, knowing she'll hate it if I make a big deal of it. "See you later."

Then it's time for me to head for the cockpit. Along the way I nod at a few folks who offer greetings. I've never served on a ship where everyone wears the same uniform before. There's something reassuring about it.

In my head, I run a list of the people who are gone beyond my reach now: Hon, Vel, Loras, Hit, Surge, and the children we saved. Mary grant that we can protect them. I've never been this scared before a jump; not even the promise of a grimspace rush can take the edge off.

So it takes all my courage to continue the last few meters and pass through the open doorway where March is waiting. On entry, I notice that Dina has installed the training chair I wanted with dual plugs; either a pilot or a novice jumper can use it.

Argus is already there, too. He's had the gene therapy, but he doesn't have the implant to control burnout yet, so he won't be performing any actual jumps until Doc and Evelyn finish working on him. But he'll share in the process through me. I hope he'll also prove a buffer between March and myself.

The kid greets me with an upraised hand. Our commander starts the procedure, checking his instruments without looking at me. I take my seat, professional and cool.

It's time to begin.

CHAPTER 32

Somehow I manage to sit quietly while we maneuver out of the docking bay.

As the Armada flagship, it's natural for us to take the lead. March proves himself worthy of his rank with his excellent flying. I think he puts a little flourish on his exit, giving those left behind something to cheer. Mary knows, they've had little enough in recent months. It will take the other ships several weeks to reach a hot point so they can jump to their assigned sectors. That means for the next several weeks, we'll be the lone soldiers in the wilderness.

"We'll begin our route in Sigma Psi," March tells me, bringing up the star charts for me to study. "Judging by the distress signals, it's pure killbox."

Which means we can expect a target-rich environment.

Luckily, I have time to map the route in my head. Since there's no single point we're trying to hit, as long as I deliver us anywhere in the Sigma Psi galaxy, I can call this run a success. I damp down my nerves, trying not to think about how much this could hurt. The good news is, now I have various mechanisms to help me cope with it.

"Is there any reason I can't use a hot zone for the second half of the jump?"

"It would be better if we came in quiet," March answers. "There's likely to be resistance near known jump sites."

"So we might be popping into an ambush."

Much like we had done to the Morgut. Since we can't jump with our weapons fully armed, they could blow us to bits before we got our cannons charged. I lean in and indicate a bit of nowhere space. "How about here? There's nothing around for thousands of klicks, not even an emergency station."

March studies the spot and nods. "If you think you can get us there, LC."

Lieutenant Commander. The man wasn't kidding about keeping things impersonal. He won't even say my name.

"I can," I say quietly.

Or die trying.

"This is . . . amazing," Argus breathes from behind me.

His awe fills the cockpit with an emotion bigger than my grief, reminding me that grimspace is more enduring and more faithful than any lover. Once we have sufficient distance from the station, I plug in. The kid follows my head, and look, there he is, sharing the nav com with March and me. As I'd hoped, he forms a certain buffer. In time I won't need it anymore, but for the time being, I need him here to keep me steady.

Phase drive cycling. March doesn't need to tell me that. In here, I can feel the ship, almost as if it's part of me. The cations in my blood fizz to life, reacting to the minute traces of grimspace still clinging to the engine.

Like last time, I reach for the phase drive as if extending a hand. With the other, I connect to the nav computer. Dina's close to a breakthrough in the magic of tubes and wires, but for now, they only touch through me. Doc and Evelyn are as good as their word, however, because it doesn't burn like before.

There's a faint stinging somewhere deep inside my head, but I imagine the tiny nanites patching up the damage before it becomes overwhelming. Other damage—regular grimspace damage—will be corrected via the regulator implant. I'm a Lila unit these days, practically self-maintaining.

Power blazes through me as the phase drive hits the peak

in its cycle. Deep down, I know this is wrong. I'm not supposed to be able to manage this. It's too much for one person to hold. If the Morgut can do *this*, no wonder they look on us as mindless animals.

Argus draws in a sharp breath, feeling what I do. Knowing it won't hurt him at secondary remove, I use the kid shamelessly to keep the bulk of it from March. I don't want him knowing precisely what he's asked of me. Only Hon has seen it firsthand, pre-mod, and he's too far away to tell.

This time, the jump begins at my will. I don't strain—I simply order it, and the universe obeys, folding so we can slip through. Our great ship shudders, then we wink out of straight space. It's an infinity of a moment, charged with all the colors of creation.

My blood sings at this sweet homecoming. I can almost hear the atoms that make up my existence humming with the eager need to join their brethren. As if I had not already suspected it, now I'm sure. I am not wholly human.

Because this seems as much home to me as any I've ever known.

Vel would understand better than anyone, I think, but he's not here.

Fiery scarlet, plowed through with a bitter amaranth heat. It is the light of an exploding star, cascading across our hull as March pilots us through. One day, I dream of launching myself out a hatch to see what will happen if I stay here. Is that death, or will it be merely the beginning of some glorious new adventure?

I cannot find out today. I have promises to keep.

Heartsick ecstasy careens through Argus at seeing the colors for the first time, and he lacks the experience to keep from sharing with us every nuance. That's good. I want his elation to drown out my heartache, like a loud, drunken chorus sung above a lone and mournful tune.

Using the beacons, I locate Sigma Psi, then visualize the nowhere space where we need to emerge. More stinging cuts slice into my mind like tiny knives, but it never blossoms to full pain. I feel as though my whole body is glowing with light, warmth that kindles without consuming the source.

Unexpectedly, Argus joins his focus to mine. I was right; there's good mettle in this one. I never expected him to do more on his initial jump than glory in grimspace, but maybe thanks to the long hours in the simulator, he's overcome his enthrallment and is holding the coordinates in his mind, like a local beacon for me to follow.

I am the ship.

I am the jump.

The mantra aids me as the phase drive powers up again. Relaxing into it, I let the current pass through me. It's easier this time, yielding my body to the ship's will. Because I don't fight it, it almost doesn't hurt when I birth the next jump, swirling through me and into Sigma Psi.

I'm still sweaty and shaky, but I don't feel in any danger when I unplug. Maybe it was Argus, maybe the implants—and maybe, just maybe, I needed both to make the difference. At least I can jump again without dread, and unlike any navigator who's come before me, if I survive the war, I stand a reasonable chance of succumbing to old age.

A vast field of stars greets me. I can't identify constellations like this, so I have no idea how I did. The stinging in my head recedes as I wait for the verdict as our commander taps various panels, checking our new location.

"Holy Mary," March breathes at last.

Running a hand through my damp hair, I glance back at Argus, who shrugs, wearing a huge grin. I don't think he cares *where* I jumped us. He just wants to do that again.

"How close did I come?"

"That's just it, LC. There's no drift at all."

"Excellent news," I say, pushing to my feet. Once, I would've made some joke about how I'm the best there's ever been, but I'm conscious of the need to be professional now. "Am I dismissed? I'd like to get something to eat."

March nods. "Enjoy a little R and R. I'll take first shift up here. If we need to jump, you'll be the first to know."

"I always am."

"Would you notify me as well?" Argus asks unexpectedly. "I can't imagine a better training opportunity."

"Will do, ensign." March turns from us then.

Clearly we're done, so I let Argus leave the cockpit first. Once we come to the first intersection, well out of earshot, he says, "If you don't have anything more important to do, LC, I'd like to deconstruct that jump. Based on what we've practiced in the sims, I don't understand what you did."

Nobody else does, either, kid. I'm the only non-Morgut who can. There's nothing like being the only one of your kind for job security. But I figure I can do a working dinner before joining Dina.

"I don't mind. How much do you know about Solaith and Dasad's experiments?"

"Only what they did to fix me, the gene therapy."

I clap him on the shoulder. "Then we have a lot to talk about. Once we get you fully trained, they're going to want to mess with your brain, too."

Following me with an uneasy smile, the poor kid obviously thinks I'm joking. We settle at a table, and I let him eat a bit before going into the details. "I told you once before that I was conceived in grimspace, right?"

He nods, listening.

"That means my blood is cation-rich, and I carry a jump zone with me. But using my body as a conduit to jump-start the phase drive nearly killed me. The human body isn't meant to do that unaided. Maybe Morgut physiology permits it—I don't know."

By his expression, he's following me. "So Doc's regulatory implant acts as a kind of filter, handling some of the overload."

"Exactly. It also regulates a natural ability I have." Quickly, I sum up how I recover from grimspace damage, unlike other jumpers. "This way, it won't ransack my heart, lungs, or brain. The nanites are also on board to help."

"Does it bother you?" he asks then. "Having so much tech inside you?"

I gaze at the screen for long moments. There are no windows in here, but screens in the lounge mirror the constellations outside. It's almost as good as the real thing.

"Yeah," I admit. "It does. Back at the Academy, I didn't even want the shunt."

"And look at you now."

There's a weight to his statement I don't enjoy. "If there's nothing further, I have plans with Dina. See you later."

CHAPTER 33

The vid plays some old film that neither of us has been watching.

I'm listening to Dina with full attention because it's unlikely she'll ever open up to me this way again. I've caught her in a weak moment, and I'm here, so that makes me the best choice to share what she's going through. On some level, I can empathize.

"There's never been anyone like her before," she concludes. "Nobody that mattered. Since I left Tarnus, I've tried not to get entangled in other people's lives. I just went ship to ship, job to job, never thinking about the future."

"Until you met March."

She nods. "He makes it hard to walk away."

Unless he's doing the walking. But this isn't about me.

"Are you worried?" It's a stupid question, but really I'm just a sounding board.

Dina hesitates, then admits, "Terrified. I was offhand in saying good-bye, like it didn't matter that she was assigned elsewhere. I . . . hurt her."

And then wept all night about it. The mechanic isn't as tough as she wants people to believe. Quite the contrary, she can be kind and tender, devoted to those she cares about but somewhat awkward in expressing it. I glimpse a little of myself in her.

"Maybe you could bounce her a message?"

"There's no privacy on these ships," she mutters. "If I do, the comm officer and no telling who else will see what I have to say."

"Can't you code it as personal to be passed along?"

"I can, but there's no guarantee they won't snoop. Loras used to do it all the time."

"Really?" For some reason, I'm surprised. I guess thinking him dead made me ascribe to him no bad habits, that sort of posthumous deification. After people have gone, you forget their faults, and you recall the ideal more than the person.

"He likes to gather information for sly little digs. You may not have known him long enough to notice, but he has quite a nasty sense of humor."

I consider. "That makes me like him better."

"Me, too." She manages a smile.

Whatever I might have said becomes irrelevant with the beep of my comm. "To the cockpit immediately, LC. We have our first fight."

"Alert Argus."

"Already done," March says.

"On my way." I glance at Dina on my way out. "You may want to get to gunnery."

She doesn't thank me for listening, just follows me out, and we go our separate ways in the hall. I make for the cockpit at a dead run. He didn't say if this fight will require a jump. It would be better if I'd gotten a little sleep before going again, but I knew when I signed on this wouldn't be an easy haul.

Thanks to my training, I'm not even out of breath when I arrive. Argus comes in close on my heels, eager to learn. March indicates two ships in the distance. I can see they're locked in battle, so we won't be jumping this time. That's good for me.

"Shortly after we arrived in Sigma Psi, I received a distress call from that merchantman. They noticed a ship on their sensors, tracking them and coming fast. This captain was smart and sent out a request for help before the raiders struck, allowing us to catch up. As soon as we're in range, I want you on lasers."

So that's why I'm here. It makes sense; I'm the only one besides Dina who has much live gunnery experience. When pirates take a ship, they usually do it with threat of force, and most freighters don't fight back.

But damn, I could've gone to the gun bay with her. If we aren't jumping, there's no need for me to be up here, even less for Argus. However, I've learned enough about chain of command that I don't question his decisions. Instead, I nod and take a seat. First I reroute the lasers, then I bring down the targeting array.

"Still out of range," I report, after peering through.

Regardless, I start powering up the lasers. They'll be ready by the time I can fire.

"ETA five minutes," he answers.

Argus stares out the view screen. "I hope they can hold out that long."

Though I don't say it aloud, I can tell that the merchant-man's shields are failing. Soon the raiders will be bombarding the hull itself, which means vacuum tearing through the ship unless someone's fast enough to lock the area down. I've never traveled on a freighter, so I don't know what kind of crew they carry or how skilled they'll be.

I tap my comm. "Dina, do you have the cannons ready to go?"

"Full power," she confirms.

"Can you get us a quick burst?" March asks her. "We need to knock a minute off our arrival time."

She swears, then says, "That's not good for the engines, but yeah."

The *Triumph* zips forward, reminiscent of a Silverfish, and soon the targeting array tells me I can blow them out of the sky. A chill washes over me, as I realize this pirate vessel is looking at an Armada ship for the first time. We have the authority here. They won't recognize the symbol painted on the side of the *Triumph* yet, but one day, the mere sight of it will send raiders running.

"They're flying a Pericles-class," March tells me, maneuvering closer. "That means it's weak here." He indicates the spot. "Concentrate your fire."

"Roger that." Dina will unload the cannons there, too.

Without speaking, I simply obey instructions and launch a volley of lasers at them, happy I don't have to worry about evasive action. With March at the helm, the flying is a lot smoother than the autopilot's programmed patterns. My shots disintegrate against their shields in a crackle of white-blue light, but by the accompanying ripple, I can tell March is right about the design fault.

"Enemy ship coming about," Argus warns, somewhat unnecessarily.

A thrill sparks through me. The pirates break off their attack on the merchantman and respond to the greater threat: us. If they had any sense, they'd try to flee—not that it would work. But maybe they don't know as much about ships as March, and they don't realize how outclassed they are.

Our shields take their shots without even a quiver. Unlike the *Folly*, we won't be dodging as much in the *Triumph*. It's a larger ship all the way around, which is why it requires more crew to maintain it.

Dina has fine-tuned the lasers, so they cycle back up faster. I could fire through, but there's always the risk of overheating if you ignore the recommended rate of fire. Since she'll break my head if I burn these out, I figure it's better to be careful.

I unload on them again, compensating for the drift of the ship automatically. This time, my shots go a little wide, slightly off the weakness March indicated; but Dina fires true, each cannon blast creating a tremor in the shields until they shimmer and wink out.

The comm beeps. "Commander, I have a request for ship-to-ship dialogue."

I recognize the voice of our communications officer—
Rose. With Evelyn on board, Doc doesn't need less-skilled
help, so it makes sense Rose would accept an assignment
that at least kept her on the ship. But I wonder if she's jealous
at the long hours Doc spends with Evelyn Dasad, working
on concepts too complex for her own understanding.

"From whom?" March asks.

"The pirate vessel."

"Hold fire," he tells Dina and me, then orders Rose,
"Patch them through, sound only."

In a few seconds, we have the voice of the enemy captain
in the cockpit. "Who the hell are you? Clear off. I saw this
take first."

He thinks we're pirates with a bigger ship.

"This is Commander March of the Armada ship *Triumph*. You have committed an act of war against the Conglomerate."

"Armada?" I hear scorn in the other man's voice. "There
ain't no bleedin' Armada. You're out of your mind, you
are."

"We're newly commissioned," March says tightly. "I can
understand your confusion. You have two choices here. You
can accept having your vessel commandeered by the fleet,
or I can blast you to atoms."

The raider captain laughs. "You are *not* taking my ship."

"So be it." After cutting comm signal, he says: "Resume
the assault."

Dina needs no further invitation, nor do I. With that short
break, the lasers are ready to go again, humming in readiness down in gunnery. I let fly and experience a little shiver
of pleasure as they sear into the hull, leaving charred black
streaks that signal loss of structural integrity. Dina's cannons come in behind, ripping our first breach.

Their return fire dissipates on our shields. Soon their
captain realizes he's overmatched, and they turn to run, but
the damage to their ship slows them. We continue the bom-
bardment, until the welded joints begin to break apart. After

that, it doesn't take long. Inertia and vacuum tear at the hull, wrenching the ship to pieces.

March keeps us firing long after it's reasonable, but atoms he promised, and that we deliver. Eventually, there's nothing larger than a meter left of this pirate vessel, just chunks of charred metal and ash. No survivors. We scan the wreckage to make sure there's nothing that could be a disguised escape pod, such as the one that preserved Evelyn Dasad.

At least in this, we're smarter than the Morgut.

CHAPTER 34

"Open a line to the merchantman," March tells Rose. "Full feed."

Within a few moments, a 3-D image appears in the cockpit. The freighter captain is an older man, heavyset, wearing full side whiskers. He looks sweaty and tired as he says, "I ask your intentions now, sir. Do you mean to take up where those ruffians left off?"

March repeats the introduction he spoke first to the pirate, and adds, "We will escort you to your port of call. How far are you from your destination?"

"Less than six hours," the other man answers. "Those rotten bastards had been tracking us since we came out of grimspace."

March nods. "They do lurk around known jump zones. On behalf of the Conglomerate, I apologize for the inconvenience."

"It's about time they took action. It's not safe for man or beast out here."

"We are at war," I say quietly.

"If you don't mind my asking," March continues. "What is your cargo?"

The captain harrumphs. "That's the devil of it, not gems or ore. We're carrying food and medicine to an outpost on Anzu. They're hard-hit. Word is, they're dying."

Anzu, a mixed-race colony in Sigma Psi—as I recall, there are humans, Rodeisians, and La'heng on world. The climate is somewhat extreme, but there are rich deposits available for mining. Like Lachion, it's a frontier world with lots of opportunity coupled with severe risk. But it's a new-ish settlement, not quite self-sufficient, and without regular deliveries, they *will* starve.

"All the more reason for us to get you there safely," March tells him, every bit the commander. "Please don't hesitate to comm if you need us further."

"Those pirates were Syndicate," I say aloud, once he's broken the connection.

March eyes me. "How can you be sure?"

No, it's not paranoia. I believe I've actually recovered from that tendency, more or less. At last, my head feels like my own again. Maybe I have Evelyn's nanites to thank, or perhaps I can credit the panacea that heals all wounds: time. Regardless, I have a theory, and it's a good one. The vessel we just blew up had distinctive markings on the hull. And I remember where I saw that last—on the yacht we stole before we decommissioned her for the Conglomerate fleet.

"Because it's a clever scheme. Take the settlement to the brink of starvation, then offer protection for their shipments. Who makes a fortune?" It's a theory, of course. I have no proof. But why else would the Syndicate hit a supply ship? Nothing else makes sense.

"That does sound like your mother," Dina says from gunnery.

My mother—Ramona—runs a large arm of the Syndicate; they're responsible for piracy, drugs, slavery, extortion, racketeering, black-market goods . . . you know, the usual. Not very maternal, but she wasn't even when I was a kid.

"Your mother?" Argus cuts in. "Mary, I thought *mine* was bad because she threw a fit about me going off world."

I mutter, "Long story. But it stands to reason."

"If Constance were here, we could put her on researching at-risk outposts," March says thoughtfully.

"And then find out where their supplies come from." Dina follows the idea to its next point.

"Once we know that," I conclude, "we can keep watch on those shipping routes."

"I'll do the research," Argus says.

I glance at him in surprise. "You will?"

"There's not a lot else for an apprentice jumper to do on board, you know. I wouldn't mind feeling halfway useful. I'll have a look at the news archives."

March nods. "Get me the information as soon as you can. This is top priority."

"Understood." Argus heads out of the cockpit with a renewed sense of purpose, which seems to be my cue to depart as well.

If I saw even a flicker that hinted March is having trouble with the distance between us, it might be harder for me. But this man isn't the one with whom I've shared so much. He's cool and formal, completely focused on the mission. That makes it easy for me to think of him as my commander and just partition off the emotions for which I have no outlet. Thank Mary I have years of practice.

"Am I dismissed, sir?"

"You are. Good work today, LC." He hesitates, then adds, "I called you up here in case we needed to give chase via grimspace. At first I wasn't sure whether this was a Morgut vessel."

"Aha. That explains it." Afterward, I realize I haven't asked him that question.

"I didn't touch your mind," he adds softly. "I won't do that now. But your face is as easy to read as it ever was."

If that's the case, I need to get out of here right now, before he sees how much I miss him. Maybe I should have asked to be assigned elsewhere, gone with Hon and Loras. I know the reasons behind keeping me on the *Triumph*, but they don't console me much.

"I'll try to work on my poker face." I etch a salute and escape into the corridor, feeling emotionally ravaged.

As I walk to my quarters, I reflect that Argus is a smart kid. Maybe I should offer him more training on guns. Based on his performance with the rail gun, he has a strong background, and ship lasers aren't so much different from pistols when you come down to it. I make a mental note to ask Dina if she can tweak the simulator.

Right now, I desperately need to sleep. Though I've lost track of where we are in the cycle, I feel like I've been up for days. Maybe I have been. At this point, it's all starting to run together. I miss Vel; I miss Constance. I miss Hit, Loras, and even Hon.

Today, we killed a shipful of people. I did it on orders, like a good soldier. They may have been corrupt and selfish, venal and mercenary; they may have been Syndicate thugs, but we killed them all. In my bunk, I feel very alone. Nothing could've prepared me for the reality, I think.

My door-bot alerts me as I'm getting ready for bed. "You have a visitor, Sirantha Jax. Allow entry?"

"Yes."

Hope sparks through me as the door swishes open. Maybe it's March. Maybe he sensed I could use a friend after that fight. I wasn't born to this. It means everything that he came, despite his edict about fraternization.

Except he didn't.

It's Dina waiting on the other side, looking no better than I feel. Her tough exterior is no more the truth of her than mine is. It's just what we show people we don't trust. I'm moved that she feels free to come to me with hell in her eyes: devastation from killing so many people and a longing for her lover.

"I didn't want to be alone tonight," she says softly.

I nod. "Come in. Stay."

She doesn't need to tell me she's come as a friend. We don't have to talk about what's eating at us right now. That's the beauty of a friendship like ours. Wordlessly, I tap the setting on my berth and make it a double. We lie down together, separate except for our linked hands. That warmth alone lets me sleep.

The ship is quiet when I awaken, which makes me think I'm off cycle somehow. But in a way that's good news because it means there's no crisis. Dina is gone already, so I beep her on the comm as I head for the mess hall for a meal. Once, I'd have called March, but it's out of the question now.

"You good?"

"Fine." Her tone says she'd rather not put last night's vulnerability on an open channel, so I follow her lead.

I change the subject. "Did we have any trouble on the way to Anzu?"

"None."

"So the shipment made it through."

Take that, Ramona. We're onto you.

"It did. Now we're heading back to the nearest hot zone."

"Has Argus come up with anything?"

"He has a preliminary list worked up and is now researching their shipping contracts and fulfillment routes. We'll use that intel to program our patrols."

"Already?" I arch my brows as I enter the mess hall.

"The kid's motivated. He feels like he needs to prove something to you."

"Me?" I repeat, shocked.

Her tone is disgusted. "Yeah, you. In case you hadn't noticed, he worships you. You're the goddess of navigators in his eyes, untouchable as the stars."

Well, it could be worse. At least there's no romantic component to the hero worship. He'll find out soon enough what a pain in the ass I am—although if the way I worked him on Emry hasn't put him off yet, maybe nothing will.

"If you say so. Have you eaten?"

"Yep, hours ago, you lazy ass." She sounds like her old self, and I smile. "Now, scuttle. I have work to do."

One thing I miss about the *Folly*—a kitchen-mate in my

quarters. Since the *Triumph* is so much bigger, that isn't practical, so instead we have shared units in a central space. The cafeteria is nearly empty at this hour, but to my surprise, I find Rose sitting alone, nursing a cup of something. She looks dispirited in a subtle way, lips slightly downturned. I know she doesn't much like me, but I hate to eat alone. Maybe I earned some credit with her by the way I helped with the kids?

Once I've ordered up a plate of pasta with plenty of peppers, I take my food over to her table. "Mind if I join you?"

She glances up, eyes bruised and tired. "No, of course not."

"You just got off shift?" I guess, sitting down and digging in.

"Yes, eight hours on the comm."

I feel guilty, as I was sleeping most of that time. But since I'm pretty much *always* on call, I shrug it off. "How do you like it?"

"It's boring," she answers. "But there was a slight thrill in being part of the action early on, however peripherally."

I wonder if that's how she feels, always left out, always on the fringes. I wonder if she knew it would be like that when she followed Doc into the stars. It's amazing what women will put up with for the sake of the men they love.

"How much time do you get to spend with Doc?"

At her sharp look, I'm sorry I asked. I brace myself for a verbal slap—*How is that any business of yours?*—but instead her shoulders slump as if she can't sustain the anger. "Not much."

"I'm sorry to hear it. I know he loves you a lot."

"Does he?" She doesn't sound convinced.

Being with a scientist must involve a lot of being forgotten for higher concerns. Sort of like March, come to think of it.

"Yes. When we were on Lachion, and he guided me through the tunnels, I saw his face when he realized you were alive and well. Though he may not be great about showing it, though he may seem distant and preoccupied sometimes, losing you would destroy him."

"Thank you," she says quietly. "I needed to hear that right now."

And there's my good deed for the day. As reward for it, I get to eat half my food before the Klaxon goes off.

CHAPTER 35

That sets the tone for the next week or so.

We scramble from fight to fight, living on the ragged edge of disaster. In that time, we haven't seen a single Morgut ship, which makes me uneasy because they might be mustering to stop this hit-and-run action. I can tell by March's preoccupation that he's worried, but if he wants my input, he'll let me know.

Instead, we eradicate Syndicate and smuggler ships from the Sigma Psi galaxy. We've defeated a total of seven ships. Five, we blasted to bits, and the lives weigh heavily on me. The other two accepted the press-gang-style recruitment and permitted our technicians to install a device to ensure they do nothing but proceed to Emry for training. There's crew enough to keep them in line while they complete the transition.

After I come off shift this time, I head to med bay. They want to test me, see how I'm reacting to all the new gear. The doors open silently, and at first Doc and Evelyn don't see me. Studying them together, I can see why Rose is bothered.

They're standing a little too close, peering at the same test results. Long hours, two people with a great deal in common—well, it's not an ideal situation for a woman who lacks the background to hold her own in the lab. Now she's been banished to comm instead of working alongside him. Wonder if he has any idea how much it bothers her.

"This is really brilliant," Doc says. "Groundbreaking. I've never seen work like this. You've advanced the scientific community by twenty turns. Dina will be thrilled. I think we can use this to mount her coupling."

"It was easier when I had the full resources of Farwan behind me. The discoveries came faster."

"But at what cost?" Doc asks gently.

She lowers her head. "I know. Have you taken a look at my hypothesis regarding improvement of the phase drive?"

I perk up. I didn't know they were still working on that; I thought they had given it over to Dina. They have so many different projects going, it astonishes me. Maybe that's the reason they spend so much time together, sheer volume and dedication.

"Though it's outside my field of expertise—and I wish Velith were here to evaluate your premise—I think it's feasible."

They're not going to explain, so I clear my throat delicately. "What is?"

"Jax!" Doc glances at me, smiling in welcome. "Evelyn theorizes that if we design an appropriate biological conduit, nanites could be adapted to work within the ship."

They were talking about the phase drive . . .

It doesn't take long for me to make the leap. "You'd use the nanites to monitor fuel efficiency or something? Can they work in a mechanical host?"

"There would need to be a biological component as well. It is all highly theoretical." Evelyn doesn't look thrilled that he's confided this much to me.

"Because you don't have a viable conduit."

Like, say, me.

"Among other challenges," she says. "Have a seat over there."

I comply, letting them gather their gadgets. They've promised nothing invasive this time. Watching them work, I see the bond even more: They've begun to anticipate each other's needs; words become unnecessary when a look suffices. I don't think they share a sexual relationship, but if

I learned anything as a jumper, proximity *can* spark an attraction.

Poor Rose. She might've been his rock on Lachion, but they're a long way from home now. Maybe she should've stayed on the station. Absence makes the heart grow fonder and all that.

"Now, just hold still." Evelyn leans down. "This won't hurt a bit."

It doesn't.

Once they have some readings, they act as if I'm not even here.

Doc indicates something on the display. "Oh, that's interesting. Were you expecting the nanites to reconfigure the regulator for greater efficiency?"

"I thought they might," Evelyn answers. "They're like physiological maintenance, making sure every aspect of Jax's body is running at peak efficiency. Now that we've installed other tech, they include that as part of the biological host."

"Fascinating," Doc breathes.

"Are we good?" I cut in.

Evelyn nods. "Yes, we have everything we need. You're the picture of health."

As I slide off the exam chair, it occurs to me to wonder: "How will this affect the aging process? If the nanites repair damage, does that include cellular decay?"

They exchange one of those speaking glances, then Evelyn says, "I am afraid I don't know. The trials I ran on the wood weasel offer limited insight as to how it may affect you, as your genetic structures are rather dissimilar."

Doc adds, "All your scans came up clear this time, which is good. Time will tell how the nanites impact your health in the long term. But that's why we've insisted you come in on a regular basis."

To make sure everything hasn't blown up inside me. Got it. I manage a smile. "Good to know you're on top of things."

Evelyn did warn me at the outset it was an experimental technology. I agreed to the fix at the promise of a whole life in grimspace—something a jumper never enjoys naturally.

In leaving, I offer a wave.

Mostly because I feel sorry for her, I go looking for Rose. As it turns out, she's on duty right now, so I head to comm, where she's monitoring distress calls and going through bounced reports from other Armada ships. Most of the calls we receive bounce in from other sectors, and we cannot do anything about them because by the time we hear it, the victims are long since dead. It's frustrating in the extreme and makes me miss Farwan's fleet, even as I loathe their ethics. But even I can't deny that they kept the peace.

She looks up from her work, mildly surprised to see me. "Something you need?"

I improvise. "Just came to see if you need a drink or anything."

"I wouldn't mind a cup of hot choclaste."

"An excellent choice. I'll be back."

On my return, she has a smile for me. "Look, I know I was rough on you early on. You're not . . . as I thought you were. Maybe we could start again?"

"Well, at that point, I probably *was* just like you thought," I answer easily. "But I can always use a friend. Dina and I have been playing Charm in our off-hours. You're welcome to join us if you'd like."

"That sounds lovely."

I'm just about to walk away when the comm beeps in the too-fast cadence that signals an incoming urgent transmission. Rose turns back to her station at once. I should go and leave her to it, but I'm nosy. It'll be nice to know something before the commander.

The *Dauntless* comm officer appears. Signal quality is poor, so the image is scored with diagonal lines. Sound has been corrupted as well, but I can make out his words:

"*Triumph*, it is with great regret that I inform you that the *Dark Tide* has been lost. We came upon their emergency beacon three days past"—no telling how long ago that was—"and found the ship in pieces. We salvaged enough to be sure it was, in fact, ours. There were no survivors. According to our tests, scoring on the metal indicates it was not a Morgut vessel. Their lasers leave a different burn pattern. I convey these tidings, knowing you will wish to relay the news to the bereaved families yourself."

I sink down on an empty chair. Comm is empty but for Rose and me. We're the first to hear this bleak news. Tears well in her eyes as it sinks in. People we trained with, people we ate with—they're gone. Finnegan, with his roguish grin and thunderous laugh: He's fallen quiet forevermore. War has a different meaning for me now.

"Shall I notify the commander?" she asks eventually.

"Yes. He needs to know."

.CLASSIFIED-TRANSMISSION.
.SUCCESSFUL EXECUTION.
.FROM-EDUN_LEVITER.
.TO-SUNI_TARN.
.ENCRYPT-DESTRUCT-ENABLED.

At this point, our business is sufficiently intertwined that I take no offense at your remarks. Indeed, you are compensating me for my efforts at such a level that I feel compelled to listen and consider, even if you wish me to direct my intellect toward self-analysis. Regardless, I am unsure whether you want a confirmation of your speculations, however inaccurate they may be, or the truth. Since despite your political bent, you seem inclined to the latter, that is what I shall offer, once and once only. I trust it will sate your curiosity.

My reputation was born in equal measures of terror, brutality, and threat of same. Let there be no misunderstandings: If I am employed to scorch a world, I shall do so. If I am employed to strike terror in the hearts of a native populace and make them worship their brethren from the stars as gods and offer great gifts, then I do that also. You have not hired a gentle, misunderstood soul, who thrives on information alone. I do whatever is required of me.

Thus, two days past, I executed Hydra. There were no survivors. In this strike, the Syndicate lost four hundred soldiers. The damage to property was considerable; we devastated the entire complex. Not a structure was standing by the time our ships left the atmosphere. For this operation, I used a mercenary company that cannot be directly linked to us, but I planted certain suspicions with Syndicate personnel. Soon they will be persuaded of Conglomerate culpability, but they will never be able to prove it, leaving them unable to spin it on the bounce. Unfortunately, they have redoubled their attacks on Armada ships. Such casualties are unavoidable. I recommend you send commendations to the families of all crew who served on the *Dark Tide*.

Of Ramona Jax, there was no sign. Unfortunately, she has since been sighted on New Terra engaged in high-profile pastimes. She is the new face of the Syndicate, and she is gaining in popularity. You will not win against them until she is removed from the equation. I am working on a way to accomplish this.

Finally, I have attached some possible tariffs. Of them all, I favor the luxury taxes on high-end food items, chem, and alcohol. It puts the burden of support on those who can best afford it. You can offer other compensations to assuage concerns, also detailed in the subsequent file.

.ATTACHMENT-TARIFFS-FOLLOWS.
.END-TRANSMISSION.

.COPY-ATTACHMENT.
.FILES-DOWNLOADED.
.ACTIVATE-WORM: Y/N?

.Y.
.TRANSMISSION-DESTROYED.

CHAPTER 36

I'm not there when March receives the news, so I can't comfort him when he feels personally responsible for what happened to his volunteers. There's no place for me at his side, except as LC. It's salt in the wound when people snap to attention as I pass by and call out my rank, as if it's somehow altered who I am inside.

"LC on deck!"

Jaw clenched, I return the salutes, and tell them, "Back to work."

I know the jargon, but I can't bring myself to use it. If I start talking like a real LC and barking orders, I'll lose something precious. That might not make a whole lot of sense outwardly, but I just know I can't give myself up to this, or maybe I'll wind up like March, after Lachion. Maybe it didn't happen because he was Psi; maybe it's the natural, inevitable result of too much killing.

Tonight, we hold a memorial service for them. Everyone assembles in the mess hall, and the commander wears his dress uniform, dark blue with a double row of silver buttons and extra silver thread. March has cut his hair; it is shorn with military precision. He looks untouchable now. In a gravelly bass voice, he reads off the list of our beloved dead. All around me, I see people with too-bright eyes, but straightening their shoulders to show they're not broken.

Afterward, the mood on ship is taut and dangerous. The crew wants more death to answer for our loss. We're all running on too little sleep and too much sorrow these days, and it's only going to get worse. I have that feeling in the pit of my belly.

That's borne out on our next call. I'm sitting in the nav chair, taking my turn on watch while the ship speeds along on autopilot, when Rose patches the message through.

"Armada ship *Triumph*, this is the mining colony from the asteroid Dobrinya." Ah, word's gotten around. They're asking for us by name now. They know we work this sector. "We have three Morgut ships circling our perimeter. Right now, they're working to disarm our minefield, and afterward, they'll go for our SDIs. We won't last long if they get through. Can you help us?" The man's naked terror strikes a chord in me; I remember how terrible the Morgut can be.

"How old is that bounce?"

A brief delay, then Rose answers, "Four hours, LC."

Shit. Mary help us, it's going to be tight. I hope they have good SDIs, the kind with weapons, shields, and titanium plating.

"Wake Commander March and get him up here."

"Yes, ma'am."

On my own, I start powering up the phase drive. I want to be ready for jump the minute he slides his ass into the pilot's chair. Then I bring up the star charts and start making the necessary translations, grimspace to straight space.

We're here. Need to be there. Got it.

By the time March arrives at a dead run, still buttoning up his shirt, I'm ready to go. His hair is standing on end, but I don't kill valuable time ribbing him about his dishevelment. As he sits down, I jack in.

His presence floods the nav com when he joins me. Since he just woke up, there are no partitions in place yet. He's tumbled, inside and out.

Miss you.

Want you.

Love you, Jax.

The feelings deluge me, evoking a shudder. Mary, his loneliness hurts. Surely this qualifies as cruel and unusual. Just when I think I can't bear to see any more of his quiet, private grief, he shuts it down. Iron curtain.

I expect him to acknowledge the lapse. Instead he offers, *Don't jump us right on top of Dobrinya. Put us out of sensor range.*

Ambush? I guess.

That—and we can't let them know we have a direct-jump-capable ship. If they find out, every Morgut vessel in the universe will receive our ion trail and come gunning for us.

I shiver again. *I'll take care of it.*

The phase drive is already humming at capacity, and we're good to go. This time, surrender comes easy. The drive roars through me, twisting into the nav com, and as one, we pull the ship into grimspace.

Heat pours through me, a volcanic mountain of it, but thanks to the neural blockers and the filter of the implant, I only experience a fraction of it, then I'm home. Magic. Chaos. Grimspace blazes to life inside my veins. Could be my imagination, but I swear each time I do a direct jump like this, using my body as the conduit, the magnetism in my blood gets a little stronger, like I could touch the view screen and alter the patterns swirling in such luscious, hypnotic hues.

But there's never time to experiment when we pass through. We're always on the way to somewhere else, where we're needed urgently. Nobody ever comes to sightsee in grimspace, for good reason.

Dobrinya asteroid. But not too close. Minute calculations. Then I find the nearest beacon and look through. For an infinitesimal moment, it's as though I can see in four dimensions, both where I am and where I need to be.

Easier, this time—practice really does make perfect.

The phase drive responds to my call, and March inputs the commands that result in our arrival at the spot in grimspace from which we need to jump. Once more, we pass through in fire burning white-hot beneath my skin. I feel as though I could shoot lightning from my eyes.

Despite my customary shakiness, I unplug quickly. I don't want him in my head any more than he has to be.

He's already checking our coordinates. "This is perfect. We'll be there in less than ten minutes, but they won't see us coming until it's too late. Will you be ready on lasers by the time we need you?"

I nod. "Ten minutes will do fine."

With trembling fingers, I route the lasers to the cockpit and engage the targeting array. My aim will be for shit if we're jumped right now, but I should steady up soon. To aid that, I breathe slowly and steadily, trying not to think about what lies before us.

Three Morgut ships.

Even if we take them by surprise, the odds don't look good. The asteroid Dobrinya seems to grow larger as we close the distance, an enormous dun rock with orange striations, and bits of ice on its extremities. Trenches scar the surface, deep, dark pits wherein bots labor to bring forth the ore.

This is all that remains of Dobrinya's moon.

Once, eons ago, it had a twin, but there was a collision, which caused a cataclysmic event. Life has not yet re-evolved to humanoid levels on planet, though Fugitive scientists found ruins with incredibly ancient technology. Some historians claim that the ones who seeded the galaxy, the ones who built the beacons, came first from Dobrinya. That's about all I recollect from my universal history at the Academy.

The outpost clings to the top of the asteroid like an ant colony, a scrabble of buildings and machinery. Why anyone would choose to live this way escapes me, but obviously there's money to be made. Someone has to sell the provisions and take care of cargo freighters that dock to carry away the ore. Someone has to provide goods and services to the maintenance crews who keep the place running.

"Computer, what do they mine here?" The question makes me miss Constance.

"Searching." The vast lack of personality in its monotone reply makes me miss her even more. "Uranium," it returns shortly.

Constance would've done a little thinking, tried to add that to what we know about the Morgut attacks and assimilate a pattern from it. Without her unusual autonomy, our ship can only offer exactly what we ask for, leaving us to connect the dots.

"Nanites and uranium," I say aloud.

March follows my train of thought. "That doesn't add up to anything good."

"Definitely not."

Nanites are used to perfect and improve biological organisms. Uranium is a high-powered fuel. The two together? I have the itchy feeling the Morgut are working on a hybrid; some kind of biomechanical intelligence that requires both. And if they succeed, it will go the worse for us. Because they're already kicking our asses without such an advantage. Otherwise, I wonder why they want Evelyn Dasad so bad. And why are they interested in stockpiling uranium?

The lasers are fully charged, but I need to make sure the targeting array is ready. Peering through to check its resolution, I spot trouble. A cold chill washes over me.

"On-screen, zoom in at 18.44." I name the angle I'm looking at. "Five times magnification."

"They're through the minefield," March says.

"And if I'm not mistaken, they've taken out at least one of the SDIs. It's hanging dead and blasted, clearing a narrow trajectory to the outpost. Based on the scrap, it looks like they still took heavy damage coming in." He nods, acknowledging my find. "If you angle a bit more . . ." I watch as he does. "You can see where they landed."

Three ships.

They look disabled. It'll take time to get them flight-worthy again. I know all about crash landings. If Mary is merciful and kind, there will have been Morgut casualties.

"Which means they've got no choice but to stay awhile, whatever they intended."

CHAPTER 37

Dina's voice breaks the silence. "What did I miss? The cannons are hot."

"I don't think that's going to do us any good," March answers.

I know as well as he does that it might be too late. Can we justify landing when that means risking the whole ship? March is the lynchpin of the war effort. If anything happens to him, the Conglomerate will never be able to replace him in time.

"Why not?"

"Check the settlement," I say.

She's clever; she'll see what I mean.

"Shit." Her dismay is palpable. "Are there any survivors?"

"We should try to find out before we put down."

That's new. Once, March would've landed without question, but he realizes what's at stake as well as I do. We can't rush to the rescue unless there's some surety we'll do more than expose ourselves to the Morgut for the dubious benefit of burying the dead.

I suggest, "We're close enough for direct comm link. Let's see if anyone answers."

March tries several frequencies, cycling through all available channels. Toward the high end, we receive a reply. "*Triumph*? Thank Mary! You got our message. The Morgut are inside the facility, and they're getting close."

So there are survivors. That's torn it, then. We'll be putting down on asteroid Dobrinya, whether it's wise or not.

"Give us your location," March instructs. "We're sending a team to help you."

"Transmitting coordinates. I can also program the SDIs to let you pass from here."

I study the terrain rising before us as the ship descends. "What kind of resistance can we expect?"

"Heavy. We didn't fight. When we saw they'd breached our defenses, we fell back immediately. The only thing saving us is the fact that our complex is a series of prefab tubular buildings, connected via a series of vacuum locks and pressure doors."

"In case of a breach," Dina guesses.

I surmise the rest. "So there's no atmosphere on the asteroid."

"Correct. You'll need to wear suits in passing from your ship to the facility."

March has been studying the coordinates. "You've taken shelter in underground storage?"

"Yes. There's machinery kept down here, but it was also dug to shield us from the worst of the tremors. The asteroid isn't entirely stable."

"Lovely," Dina mutters.

"We'll liberate you as soon as we can," March tells him. "Keep this channel open in case you need us while we're on the move."

There's no conversation while he lands. March needs all his concentration because there isn't a nav com on the other end, assisting and providing trajectory. I remember all too well another crash on Marakeq, but he doesn't repeat the mishap. We land as smooth as can be expected on a rock like Dobrinya.

"I'll meet you at the hatch," Dina says.

Normally, the captain would stay on the ship, but March has the most ground-combat experience. He won't remain safely on board while his men take all the risks. If I know anything about him, I know this.

"Squad one, report to the disembarkation chamber." Turning to me, he adds, "You have the ship, LC."

My brows go up. "Excuse me? Sir."

"You're not going with us. We can't afford to lose you."

Is he being professional here? If I stay behind, he'll give me the satisfaction of the *real* reason why.

"Any navigator can be upgraded if they're willing to sign off on the risk," I say coolly. "You have Argus on board. I'm sure he'd agree to more gene therapy to deliver the cations, so even were I killed in action, the fleet would not lose its advantage permanently. The same cannot be said of you, sir."

"Are you refusing a direct order?"

"I'm merely pointing out the fallacy in your logic, Commander. Through technology and gene therapy, I am expendable. Your combat experience and your leadership abilities cannot so easily be replaced. Therefore, by your logic, you should remain on ship, and *I* should lead this mission as next ranking officer."

Unless you're speaking of yourself as the royal collective, unless it's you *who can't bear to lose me. Break your rule. Say it out loud, and I'll stay behind.*

There's nobody here. Nobody listening.

His eyes narrow, his lashes a dark tangle. "You sound like Velith."

"My time as ambassador taught me to argue my points well."

"To hell with protocol," he mutters at last. "We'll both go. We're taking a full squadron with us, so the risk should be minimal."

Ah, well. If I had to choose between making him admit his feelings and being left behind, I'm glad it fell out this way. Despite my slight disappointment, I smother a smile. Faced with the inarguable point that I'm right, he'll be damned if he sits and waits to find out what happened down there. I've done my share of sitting and waiting, so I understand his reluctance. Authority doesn't come easily to either of us; we aren't the sort who delegate tasks, then expect other people to do the work for us.

He makes one last comm. "Lieutenant, you have the ship in our absence."

The first lieutenant is a capable clansman who will keep things together while we're gone. That settled, March leads the way to disembarkation, where squad one is already assembled. They've gathered the need for protective gear and are suiting up. I pull a small one out of the nearest locker and start my preparations as well.

The mood is somber. Everyone knows what we face today. Our first fight against the Morgut in this war isn't occurring out among the stars, behind the protection of shields and reinforced hulls. Instead, we oppose them in our fragile flesh, eighteen brave Armada soldiers. If I were a poet, I'd construct a verse in honor of the occasion, but I have nothing like that to offer.

Once everyone is ready to go, suits on and weapon packs to hand, March studies us lined up beside the hatch. "You are the best this ship has to offer. If you've never fought Morgut before, beware their bite for its paralyzing effect. It's better to take them from a distance. Use your Morfex grenades."

Damn, we have heavy artillery, then. Good to know. I received a memo from March earlier in the week about a new toxin Tarn has commissioned. It's a synthesized poison gas based on Ithtorian physiology. The Morgut absorb it through their pores and mucous membranes; they die within ten minutes of exposure.

March lists off a few more issues to beware, like web traps and their spiky limbs. To their credit, none of the soldiers around me stir. They're listening. They're ready.

"Moving out."

Outside the ship, rock crunches beneath my boots. The horizon is dun and gray, no sky to liven our progress. There's rock, more rock, and a pit so vast it seems it must extend straight to hell. Within the crevasse, I can hear the distant hum of machinery.

We pass by the three dead Morgut ships. At this range I can see the scoring along the hull, see where chunks have been torn away by the stress of landing. It doesn't look like a hatch opened so much as they crawled out of the remaining pieces. Only one of them looks like it could be repaired.

"Tracks in the dust, Commander." The scout's mouthpiece distorts his voice slightly, adding an edge of reverb. He kneels briefly, then indicates a path so wide I could've followed it. "Based on the size of the ships and the prints here, it looks like they lost a good portion of their number."

Dina says, "Unless they were running a skeleton crew."

I'd rather believe that a bunch of them died on impact, at least until that becomes impossible, like when we're staring at way more than we expected. Without further discussion, we continue toward the facility.

To me it looks like a train made into living quarters. The buildings are strung together like cars, connected as the man said, by a series of locks. It stretches an incredible distance, forming a semicircle around the open pit out of which they bring the uranium. On the other side of the complex, there's a proper landing area, but if we want to come in quietly and have a chance at taking the Morgut by surprise inside, we need to sneak up behind them.

"I don't think they've had time to nest," March says.

That's in our favor.

Each step feels slow and heavy in these weighted boots. There's not much gravity out here, just a tiny residual, and if I wasn't wearing the suit, I'd go floating off this rock. But even in the protective gear, I notice that the squadron marches in cadence. They keep pace to the song I can still hear in my head.

Lachion tried and Lachion true,
We will bring the war to you.

We reach the outer door without incident. My nerves string tight, adrenaline pumping in anticipation of the coming fight. One of the soldiers steps forward to examine the door.

"The Morgut came this way," he confirms after a moment. "See the scoring here and here?"

March nods. "Then we must follow. All comms off but mine, please."

The soldier disengages the lock and slides from sight. One by one I watch them go. I'm among the last. Taking a deep breath, I, too, pass into the dark.

CHAPTER 38

"Welcome to Dobrinya mining colony," the computer tells us, as the door seals. "Please do not remove your gear until decontamination and pressurization has completed. This process will take approximately four minutes."

That leaves us standing while yellow rays beam out all around us. I don't think we came across anything radioactive in our trek, but I understand their caution. Radiation sickness, or Bluerot, as miners fondly call it, isn't anything to trifle with, particularly so far from real medical care.

The interior is almost anticlimactic.

It's a locker room in dingy gray-green, that industrial shade you find all over places like this. The floors have been tracked with dust and dried Morgut blood. So they came bearing injured. That'll help.

Mary, I wish we had Vel with us. He's poisonous to them, whereas we're a sought-after delicacy. I didn't really expect Morgut to be lying in wait just inside the door, but once your muscles coil, nothing but a battle will do to ease your nerves. Still, it's a relief that we have a place to put our suits.

"No contaminants found," the computer announces. "Atmosphere now habitable for most humanoid species. Unlocking inner doors. Please enjoy your visit."

Following March's lead, I begin stripping out of the environmental gear. Nobody would choose to fight in these; they limit mobility and peripheral vision. Not to mention, if we need to retreat and run for the ship, we can lock these doors behind us, but we can't repair a suit if it tears on the fly. Better to secure our safety net.

I choose a locker at random and stow my suit. It has a thumb lock, which means only I can retrieve my suit when I'm finished here. The device codes itself to the last user in a onetime pattern, so that once unlocked, it becomes cleared for use. Very convenient for a mining colony where freighters are always passing in and out.

The commander lets our scout take point, which surprises me faintly. I know how tough it is for him to hang back. Overhead, the lights gutter in staccato fashion, indicating some fault in the electrical system.

Weapon at the ready, Dina tips her head back. "That's going to get old. If I could find the maintenance area, I could fix that."

March agrees, "It's annoying, but not a high priority. We're here to exterminate some pests and rescue civilians."

For my part, I'm just glad the lights aren't out and the place isn't dripping with human blood. That would offer echoes of Emry Station, where we failed to save anyone but that little girl. Here, I have some hope that we're not too late.

The first body scares the shit out of me.

I barely manage to stop myself from recoiling in terror, shaming myself in front of the men. Too late, I notice that it's not moving. This is proof that not all the Morgut made it. Its blood stinks like hell, and it's smeared all over the floor.

Drake, our medic, kneels to investigate. He's not much older than Argus, and I think they might be related because they share bone structure and the line of the jaw. However, he has deep brown eyes, marking him as unsuitable for a jumper. Half the ship bears the last name of Dahlgren, so March has instigated a policy of differentiating them via rank and first name.

"Not combat wounds," he determines, after scanning the body. "Cause of death appears to be the result of impalement here—" He gestures. "And here."

Dina nods. "During the crash. The skull's damaged, too."

Despite myself, I lean in, fascinated by this close look at our dire foe. In death it looks no less monstrous, that paralyzing saliva crusted like brown rot on its fangs. The triangular head looks even more arachnid in the pulsing light. Its forelimbs still look like spears, and the hairy, segmented body makes bile rise in my throat, so I take a step back.

"Interesting they didn't leave it on the ship to die," the medic says. "They tried to save their comrade."

But that makes them less horrible. Less loathsome. Even monsters love their own.

"Search it for any tech that might help us." March toes the corpse.

Drake checks it over and comes up with a device that slightly resembles Vel's handheld, but when we touch it, the thing begins to emit blue sparks. The medic drops it on the body and scrambles backward. The glow intensifies, filling the hallway with a searing electrical field.

"Shit. Fall back. Fall back!"

As one, the squadron retreats at a run. I'm near the back, but I don't look behind me. I have to keep up. If that light touches us—

Someone moans behind me, and the world narrows to the stink of cooking meat. Despite my terror, I keep moving. Eventually, the light dims, giving us one smoking, dead soldier to abandon like that Morgut corpse.

"They trap their dead," March says grimly. "Even if they have no reason to suspect pursuit. Noted."

A costly mistake. So maybe it wasn't that they wanted to save him. Instead, they use his meat. Staring down at the first casualty, I feel sick to my stomach. His face is burned almost beyond recognition, and the smell leaves me reeling. I fight not to remember what it was like trapped in the wreckage of the *Sargasso*. Damn. I thought I'd conquered this.

Drake squats and pulls the name patch off the shirt. "His mother will want it, back on Lachion."

March nods. "I'll see that she receives his death benefits."

Everyone knows we can't take the body with us, so we spend a moment in silence. Then there's nothing left but to move on. But I must wonder: How many good soldiers will die, saving these civilians? And how many people will shrug later and say: *That's their job.*

Our scout goes out into the dark alone to check the facility ahead of us. He's quick and quiet, the best hope we have of staying unnoticed, assuming they didn't have sensors on that dead one. I'm none too sure they aren't watching us already. Then again, they may have left the trap to slow down pursuit while they patch up their wounded. It's just impossible to guess why Morgut do anything. They're simply not like us.

Eventually, the scout—I believe his name is Torrance— loops back to us silently. "There are five heat signatures up ahead, Commander."

"Moving away from us, toward the storage areas?"

Torrance shakes his head. "No, sir. Stationary. Vitals indicate nonhuman."

"Look before you kill, men, but we're going in san-bot, got me?" March glances at all our faces, making sure we understand.

Though the slang is foreign to me, I get the gist. He means we're cleaning this place out; no Morgut gets away, no quarter granted. I have no problem with that. It's not like they've ever shown our people mercy. Hatred is new to me, but a surge of it spikes through me, considering the monsters who don't even respect us enough to consider us a worthy foe. We're not an enemy to them; we're food.

"They're clustered fairly close," Torrance says. "I think I can get near enough to soften them up with a grenade if you lot can cover my return."

We don't know much about the exact speed of incapacitation. They'll most likely be weakened, but they'll give chase. It's a risk.

March considers the question for a moment. "Are you fast?"

"I can go a kilometer in two minutes, forty seconds."

Damn. His record speed aside, one man can move quicker through these halls than the whole team. It's a baiting maneuver, drawing the enemy into your terrain to close the trap. That sounds like a good idea to me because once the laser fire commences, there will be no hiding our location from the rest of the monsters.

Apparently March has the same thought because he says, "Then we need to pick our spot, somewhere we can readily defend."

That's when I realize this won't be hide-and-seek like Emry. It's going to be a great big bloody free-for-all, and most likely we won't all walk away.

Another soldier says, "There's a dead end around the corner. Looks like it leads to a small storage area, no life signs."

"Then that's where we're headed." March leads the way while Torrance heads off to bring us some Morgut to play with.

On their own, the men draw their weapons. The quiet click announces they're powering up. I fall in and do the same. Since I'm small, I assume a position near the front. Others will be able to shoot over me. On either side of me stand burly clansmen, shorter than the rest. They'll go hand-to-hand to protect me, if necessary.

The boom tells us that Torrance has delivered his invitation. Impossibly quick footfalls pound down the hall toward us. The scout shouts, "Two died instantly, three on me, and I'm coming in hot!"

As he bursts around the corner, I raise my weapon. Red targeting dots skim along the dark wall, making patterns that almost form into lines. Around me, nobody speaks. Total focus now, total concentration. This is a different kind of combat, something I've never experienced before—skilled, planned, professional.

Today, I learn what it means to be a soldier.

CHAPTER 39

The clatter of spiky, jointed limbs gives me the creeps.
They're clicking toward us fast. I tense, fingers sweaty on
the pistol. Logically, I know we'll be fine this time. We outnumber them. We chose our ground carefully, so we have a
long corridor between them and us, lots of firing room.

By the stench of the ichor, some of them are wounded.
I confirm that with a glance as the Morgut round the corner; one is missing a forelimb. Saliva runs in yellow rivulets
from their fangs. They have our scent now, and they want
more. As we open fire, Torrance dives between Drake's legs
and rolls to his feet, weapon in hand.

The corridor becomes a wilderness of laser fire, and the
monsters keen at the searing of their flesh. It bubbles and
blackens, adding to the stink. I lose track of whose shots hit
where. The lead beast falters, its chest laid open. Blood spat-
ters the walls and slicks the floor beneath our feet.

At last it falls, but the other two skitter over the top of the
body, urged on by fury and hunger. Despite my hatred, such
butchery bothers me, but I tell myself they started it. They're
inside one of *our* settlements, and they didn't come to talk.

My pistol reaches the hot point, so I have to fall back.
Another soldier takes my place on the front line, his weapon
sparking in the dark. The Morgut bodies jerk with each hit,
more burning flesh, and another one drops.

There's only one left, and it's nearly on us, but it's outnumbered and wounded. It has assimilated the threat we pose, so it turns, far too late, and attempts to flee. *No quarter.* Our squad continues to fire, burning a hole its back. Its entrails spill out, dangling as it tries to run. From *us*, as though *we're* the monsters. The thing emits a high-frequency whine as it dies, and the noise reminds me of a crying child.

"Rest up," March says. "We'll have more incoming soon."

I daresay he's right. While my pistol cools down, I focus on breathing through my mouth. It cuts down on the smell while I rummage in my pack for the dry-acid chem-burner Vel used on Ithiss-Tor. Our packs are outfitted with it; makes for efficient cleanup.

There, got it.

"Stay back," I warn.

The powder looks so harmless, but when I sprinkle it on the corpses, they immediately begin to smoke, drying inward into a fine gray ash. Instant decomposition. It'll make it easier for the san-bots, less trauma for the humans we save. On a more practical note, it helps with the slickness of the spilled blood. If we're fighting in here again, we need better traction.

"Let me scout ahead, sir." Torrance is already chafing.

March considers for a moment, then nods. "Be careful."

The rest of us remain battle-ready in case he brings more back to us. Squadron one has tight discipline. Nobody chatters or fidgets. They're all hard-eyed and ready for round two.

I've had some time to think about the problems facing us, but this is the first opportunity I've had to talk to March, as I've been avoiding him. I may never have a better chance, so I make my way to his side, and he glances down at me, eyes shadowed in the uncertain light. Might as well make some use of the downtime.

"Did you need something, LC?"

I don't let the formal address discourage me. "I was just thinking about why we're at a disadvantage in our patrols."

"Oh?" His voice gains interest when he realizes I don't intend to get personal.

"Farwan policed the galaxy using their reputation. We don't have a reputation yet to act as a deterrent."

"What are you getting at?" March asks.

"Well, fear of reprisal kept most of the worst elements at bay because if they harmed another ship, the gray men would chase them to the ends of the universe."

Gray men had worked security for Farwan once upon a time, and nobody knew much about them, except they weren't human. They lived for the thrill of the hunt, and they made excellent enforcers. I remembered reading they had come from a dead world. Their sun had gone nova at some point after they went interstellar; it was nothing but dust now, but they'd carried their love of stalking prey out to the stars. I have no idea what they've been doing since Farwan's fall; in fact, I shudder to think.

March says, "They didn't worry about prevention of crime, or safeguarding human life, that's for sure."

"They depended on people's fear of punishment whereas we're coming at it from the other side," I conclude.

"There's no fear in our regime," he agrees.

Which is exactly my point. Without a deterrent like the gray men, how are we to get the raiders and pirates to take us seriously? We can't blow them all up; we can't be everywhere at once. We either need a stick or a carrot.

"Not yet. But is it possible to govern wholly without it?"

"She's right," Drake says then. I hadn't realized anyone else was listening to the conversation. "If you don't smack a kid's hand the first time he steals a biscuit, he thinks he can get away with more."

Dina nods. "Always more."

I forget, she had little sisters once.

"So what are you suggesting?" March asks.

"That we find out what happened to the gray men. They lived to punish the guilty, right? Well, what are they doing now? They should be willing to work for the Conglomerate, accepting their determinations of guilt. The gray men were never judges. They didn't give the orders. They're a race of hunters, pure and simple."

"In addition to the Armada," Dina says thoughtfully, "we could use a police force to punish the guilty for those crimes we're unable to prevent. The Conglomerate doesn't want to rule by fear, as Farwan did, or we've only traded one tyrant for another; but neither can it be seen as weak."

"I'll see if Tarn can find out what happened to the gray men," March says, as if he's come to a decision. "The Conglomerate seized ships from Farwan that won't operate for a human crew, so if the gray men come to work for us, those resources can be restored."

He bounces a message to Rose on the ship right then. She'll forward it to Tarn.

"They weren't imprisoned?" I ask.

March shakes his head. "Only the top-level executives were held accountable and are now standing trial for their crimes on New Terra. The rest of Farwan simply found itself unemployed as the company collapsed."

Ah. Well, if the gray men have been at loose ends, they may look kindly on another offer. Hunting is in their blood. They look human, apart from their coloration, but their hearts and minds are dark to us.

Another boom warns us that we're about to greet the second wave. I wonder how many Torrance blew up, then I hear footfalls signaling his return. He's out of breath this time, bracing his hands on his knees for a few seconds before he can speak.

"Found another group at rest," he pants out. "Bigger. Killed five. Eight incoming this time. I—"

But whatever he might've said, there's no time, because I hear the clatter of their limbs against the floor. They're rounding the corner, a vast wave of monsters with spears for arms and the bodies of fat, bloated spiders. They don't pause at our numbers; they're used to devouring humans en masse.

But they've never faced our like before. Calmness descends upon me. Long hallway—they're almost in range.

"Grenades, this time," March calls out. "Don't spare them."

I draw one from a pouch on my belt, arm it, and let fly. The men to either side of me do the same. Training tells us not to aim for a moving target because by the time it lands, they'll be somewhere else. Instead, you throw toward where they're about to be, and as they pass by—

Red light flares in the darkness, and the gas hisses out. I'd wondered about the noise. What a fantastic idea—the scientists have disguised the real product beneath a harmless flash-bang charge. The Morgut don't realize until it's too late. Our aim is good, and the grenades hit in a near-perfect spread to encompass them all.

Almost immediately, a bloody foam gushes from their mouths, and their flesh roils.

March takes aim and shoots one between the eyes. You could call what comes next mercy killing, but it's not, really. There's no mercy in any of us. I just want them to stop twitching. There's nothing heroic about what we're doing.

I fire the pistol again and again. Some of them don't seem to be driven by intelligence. It's as if the hunger permeates to a cellular level, and the things can't stop moving toward their prey until they're completely incapacitated, charred into useless lumps of stinking flesh. And at last, we drop them all. To live through this and not lose my mind in the horror, I have to focus on our goal: clearing this place out and saving the humans who call Dobrinya home.

One of the youngest among us, Drake, staggers to the far end of the corridor and hunches over. My stomach lurches in sympathy when I hear him puking. I give him a minute, then walk over to touch his shoulder. He's leaned his head against the wall, trembling from head to toe. Like Doc, he's not born to fight, but the team needs a medic.

"You all right?"

He glances back at me like it's a stupid question. "Not even close."

"Use the chem-burner," I tell him. "It'll help with the gore."

Straightening his shoulders, he seems pleased to have a task, which is why I assigned it to him. I'm not surprised by his reaction, but it alarms me a little to see the other squad members totally unmoved by the carnage. It gives me too clear a picture of what they went through in those tunnels on Lachion, and it breaks my heart that this is not the worst thing these men have ever seen.

"Facility is now half-cleared," Torrance reports.

March nods. "Then we need to push onward and find another defensible location. They aren't coming this way again. We also have to expect them to adapt to our tactics and ordnance. The Morgut aren't stupid."

"Yes," I agree quietly. "It gets worse from here."

CHAPTER 40

Torrance breaks the silence. "I'm tracking heat signa-
tures, Commander."

We've been moving toward the storage areas for a while
with no sign of further Morgut, but I know they're here.
We're not done yet. It's a crawling of my flesh, prickling
in my skin, just like when I was a kid and nobody would
believe there were monsters in my room. There weren't, of
course. I have a vivid imagination.

But I'm not a child anymore, and there really are monsters here.

"Where are they?" March demands.

I understand his impatience; it's about time they showed
up on our instruments. I was starting to think they had their
own version of Thermud—a dark paste that offers visual
and heat signature camouflage—and wouldn't that be a terrifying prospect?

"Outside the pressure door that leads to the storage area."

"They're trying to rest up and feed before facing us,"
Dina realizes aloud.

That means they're not going to turn and fight, as we
thought. They came to eat, and they intend to. If they succeed, we will have landed for nothing. We will have lost a
good soldier for *nothing*. I shake my head, jaw locked.

"Double-time," March orders. "Quiet is no longer our
concern."

Our boots thud in cadence as we tear through the halls: left, right, and a long straightaway. Only two more turns until we'll be there. A distant boom scares the shit out of me, as Torrance is running alongside me.

The comm crackles; the mine manager's voice is tight with terror. "They've blown the upper doors, only one more to go. They'll be on us soon."

This is the first time we've heard from him since we landed, and I admire his fortitude. I know what it's like to huddle in the dark, wondering if your next breath will be your last. But not this time. Not these people. This time, we save them. This time, we make a difference. I never thought I'd say this, but—

I wanna be a hero, dammit. No matter the cost.

"Don't panic," March tells him. "We're almost there."

The floor slopes beneath our feet. That means we're close, thank Mary. As we pound down the ramp toward the blown access doors, web traps explode all around us. They're not the same as the ones we faced on Emry; they don't draw us up and away from the group, but most of us are immobilized. I can't get my fingers on a blade to cut my way out, and the more I struggle, the tighter this stuff gets.

I call out, "Don't fight it! I think it might strangle you."

You'd think we'd have learned this by now; we simply can't plan for the Morgut because we don't think like they do. Our attempts to predict their behaviors will always, always fail because we're operating without insight, without context. We don't know enough of them to be considered their enemies. We're only victims. Or we have been. If Vel were here, I'm sure he'd know a way out of this, but . . . he's not.

"They're doubling back, sir." Torrance's voice sounds muffled.

"A ruse," March bites out. "And I fell for it. They guessed threatening our civilians would flush us out."

"And now the dangerous food isn't so risky," Dina mutters.

"Can anyone get free?"

"I am, Commander." Drake steps forward, tearing the last of the webs from his body. "I fell behind. I'm sorry."

So he's the one I heard throwing up in the hall. Poor kid—but his weak stomach may save us all.

"Cut us loose!"

"Do me first," Dina demands. "I have an idea."

Quickly, he cuts her free and she heads for the blown access doors in a slightly uneven sprint. Dina fiddles with the loose wires, muttering to herself, while Drake slices through the filaments holding March. They redouble their efforts, vibroblades humming. The commander frees Torrance first, probably hoping his speed extends to knives.

I hear the monsters coming. There are a lot more of them this time. Intellectually I already knew that from looking at the heat signatures on Torrance's display, but it feels different when you can hear their weight drumming against the floor. Noise echoes down the hall toward us, eerie in its cacophony, but by the rise and fall of it, the chip in my head interprets the significance, even if it can't offer meaning.

They're *singing*.

It's the most terrifying thing I've ever heard.

My heart pounds while I wait, captive. To his credit, March slices three random soldiers free before coming for me. He's controlling his personal feelings. Good for him. It doesn't slow the panic careening through me.

"How many are there?" I ask Torrance, as he frees the last squad member.

"Thirty," he answers quietly. "Maybe more. They just keep coming."

Shit. Bad odds. Really bad.

I see them now, but the sloping corridor is too short to use regular grenades. The blast would catch all of us, and there's no differentiating our meat from theirs. I raise my weapon, but Dina stands in my line of fire.

"Clear out of there!" March shouts.

She ignores him. "Almost got it . . ."

Sparks shower down atop her, and she scrambles back as a pale, shimmering field springs to life. My eyes widen. "What did you do?"

She grins and checks her weapon. "Electrified the metal plates by rerouting the wires into the . . . Ah, here they come!"

Their eyes must not be designed like ours because they pay the danger no heed. One by one they push through, screaming and shuddering as electricity jolts through their nervous systems. Unfortunately, it's not strong enough to take them down; it just scrambles their brains for a few seconds.

We take advantage of the time. We saturate the air with Morfex grenades, trusting it won't cause us any harm. The Morgut go mad with pain, and it's hideous to watch. I stand with the gunners, shooting away, while our best hand-to-hand fighters wait for the first monster to make it into range. Morgut fall to our onslaught, but they outnumber us. March wheels into the fight like a berserk dervish; he's fighting two, but I can't focus on him.

Fire. A wound blossoms on its chest, a dark stain of burning flesh. The smell doesn't touch me. I've found my center. Beside me, Drake stands firm. His face is sickly pale, beaded with sweat, but he doesn't falter.

We are squadron one.

Someone is screaming, a distinctly human cry. One of the clansmen staggers, a spiked forelimb through his gut. The monster raises him up and delivers the bite, and he's done. I can't grieve. If we survive this, we will pull his name patch from his chest and send it home to his mother on Lachion. There's a fire in my heart that burns too bright for tears; it could power a whole world if someone harnessed it.

Being careful not to injure with friendly fire, I hold the line. Near the access door, a soldier stumbled into the shock field Dina rigged. He shudders and screams; we are not so robust as the Morgut. She flinches but she doesn't falter in her own attack. *Collateral damage,* I can almost hear March say.

He kills two at once in a smooth, outward sweep of his blades. He's strong enough, skilled enough, to dual wield. It's almost lovely to watch, if I could ignore the spattering blood and the chunks of meat that spatter in his wake. The others fight with grim competence, staying away from those deadly teeth. Another clansman screams.

After twenty shots, my pistol delivers a mild shock to my palm as warning and goes inert. If I try to override the safety, it may explode. I toss it at the head of a Morgut stalking toward me, then smoothly draw my vibroblade. I'm not the best on the squad by any means, but I'm no longer the girl who fights with more bravado than skill. I plant my feet and wait for it, while my brothers in arms flow in battle all around me.

The noise of it recedes.

As I've been taught, I retreat into a circle where there's only my enemy and me. If another threat emerges, I'll respond to it, but I can't afford distractions. It's focused on me, thinking I'm small and weak. Easy prey.

Think again, monster. Your kind had a taste of me, but you'll never have the whole.

My blade swoops before me in tight circles, forming a dangerous barrier to attack. If it lashes out—

Oh, you stupid beast.

I lop off its left forelimb, and it keens, the pain echoing from the walls. The Morgut face looks much the same to me, monstrous and fanged, regardless of expression. Smiling, I beckon it forward with a lift of my chin. My back is to the wall; I'm well defended.

Feint. Dance forward, slide left, all while spinning my blade with both hands. It's a deceptive movement that makes me look as though I'm uncertain, barely able to lift the weapon. Even as it's dying of a poison it cannot comprehend, the monster lunges, confident it can handle me.

So. Not. True.

In a graceful loop, I take its head.

The battle rushes back at me with the weight of an

avalanche. I'm drowning in sound as the body falls, but another rushes to take its place. One, then another. I'm flanked. The others hold their own all around me, but they have no eyes for me. Why should they? I'm not a damsel in distress. After all—

I'm Sirantha Jax, and I have had *enough*.

CHAPTER 41

The monster on my right lunges, teeth snapping, and I duck low, spinning into a fighting squat. I sweep with my blade and take it at the joints. My weapon slices clean through. It's down, but not dead. I'll worry about it after I take out its partner.

Spilled blood lubricates my spin, though it looks as if I've fallen. On the ground, I mimic injured prey. I lure the other one closer, a calculated risk since one brush of its fangs will immobilize me. A spiked forelimb drives into the floor where I used to be, a hard blow as I roll sideways, and it's caught momentarily, a victim of its own strength.

Using my blade to vault, I push into a kick, using my weight to increase the velocity. Impact, feet first. The Morgut staggers back, and its limb snaps. While it's still off balance, I press the attack, but I'm not quite fast enough. It lashes out with a sideways, glancing blow, and if my uniform didn't contain light armor woven in the filaments, I'd have a spear through my chest instead of a stab wound.

The pain takes my breath. I twist away, resuming a centered stance, and try to ignore the blood trickling down my belly. I can't tell how bad it is, but I know it didn't pierce my sternum. Thank Mary for the Armada dress code.

To my surprise, the Morgut makes a sound that the chip in my head interprets as conversational. Unfortunately—

My head fills with cascading whiteness, superimposed

over my eyes. I can't see. Panic spills through me. It's no more than a microsecond, but my blade wavers. I'll die, right now, because I can't defend myself.

But no, it doesn't move. Its limb drips blood, pooling at our feet. The Morgut speaks again, and this time, the clicks and hisses that sound so unnatural to my ears coalesce into meaning.

Why does the meat fight?

It worked. I can't believe it fragging worked. I remember the conversation on Ithiss-Tor with Vel as if it were yesterday.

"Are there any other languages you would like while we are doing this?" he'd asked, just before injecting me with the translator chip. *"We will not be able to modify the chip once it is in your body."*

"Is there anything that would help me understand the Marakeq natives?"

"They are class-P, so no translation programs have been written—and the only available research comes from Fugitive scientists."

"I suspected as much." I shook my head. *"Never mind, then. What about the Morgut?"* It seemed like it would be an advantage to understand my enemies.

"I can offer you a partial vocabulary, I think, but I do not know how it would interface with your brain stem. I can't offer any guarantee of complete comprehension. The Morgut language is alien, even to me."

"Give it a whirl."

Revulsion coils inside me now. Obviously I can't answer, but it sees comprehension in me. The Morgut takes a step back, and its eyes widen. In a human I would interpret that look as shock or horror. Froth dribbles out of its maw, tinged with ichor. Its limbs twitch uncontrollably now, poison devouring it from the inside out.

It understands me?

Driven by some instinct, I offer a *wa* in answer: *Brown bird sees the fierce hunter.* The Morgut respect the Ithtorians as fellow predators. If the Morgut are long-lived as well, then this one may remember the silent language, though it has been many turns since the Ithtorians passed among the stars.

The monster takes another step back, as if I'm something beyond its experience. I can see that it knows what I said, but it is having trouble parsing my facility with civilized conversation. Slowly, it returns the honorific: *Yellow dog greets brown bird.* Its gestures are simple, without grace or eloquence; but I cannot be sure if it thinks it needs to speak to me as if I am slow, or it simply does not know the nuances.

Out of respect for its possible limitations, I keep my response plain as well: *The house of yellow dog steals from brown bird.*

Brown bird has no tongue and cannot speak. The Morgut does not offer *wa* this time; it has decided I am not worthy, but I understand its vocalizations. *The house of yellow dog claims all.*

I shake my head, my *wa* clear and emphatic. This is not respect; I am interrogating it. I don't know of any human who has ever done so before. *Yellow dog loses all. What seek you here?*

Power, it spits.

Belatedly, I notice the battle has ended around me. This creature is the only one left. The others have gathered, watching with disbelief. Their blood-spattered faces reflect the same horror I saw in the Morgut: *What the hell* are *you?* No human has ever been able to do this, and it doesn't seem like the time to explain about the experimental chip and Vel. No, they just see what I am feeling: that I'm a freak with a head full of unnatural tech.

Perhaps I should rename myself *talks-to-monsters*, instead of *brown bird*.

Brown bird takes yellow dog, I tell it with my final *wa*.

It sees. It knows.

The monster doesn't fight when I run it through. While I stood talking, someone gutted the one whose lower limbs

I severed. We lost five men here. Torrance passes among the Morgut, covering the corpses with chem-burner. Soon there will be nothing left but ash.

I stand there, blood trickling down my belly, wondering what I've become. Eventually, I gather myself enough to clean my blade and return it to its sheath. That was drilled into me in training; if I don't take proper care of my gear, it will let me down at the worst possible time.

"Were you talking to it?" Dina asks.

She's the first one brave enough to approach me, although that's not entirely fair. Bravery doesn't factor into March's decisions. He can't come to my side anymore; he can't treat me differently from the other soldiers beneath his command.

"Yes. I think I was."

She nudges me. *"How?"*

"I'd guess the nanites upgraded me, including the chip Vel put in. He put the rudimentary vocabulary in place on Ithiss-Tor, but said he couldn't guarantee results. And the first batch of nanites was trying to configure me to speak Ithtorian or Morgut or maybe even a hybrid. There's no telling exactly what they did to the language centers of my brain before being terminated."

Dina hesitates. "Did you know that would happen?"

"I've got three pieces of experimental tech in me now. I'll be surprised if all my hair doesn't fall out." Fingering my coarse curls, I consider their loss grimly.

"You might also glow in the dark," she offers, helpful.

"Thanks." I give her a sour smile.

"No problem."

"Everyone ready to move?" March asks.

"I could use a patch." I tap Drake on the arm to get his attention.

The medic parts the lapels of my jacket and cuts through my undershirt to expose the wound. His touch is warm and gentle, but his eyes are wary. I'm something beyond his comprehension, too. I feel more alien now than I did on Ithiss-Tor.

"It's deep, but not dangerous," he tells me. "No bone fragments. I just need to clean it and cover it with some Nu-Skin. That should hold you until Doc can take a look."

"Do you have a local for the pain? Nothing that'll mess with my head?"

Drake nods. "Sure."

"You hurt, LC?" March comes up beside us, watching the younger man's hands on my skin. There's nothing proprietary in his manner, but I wish there were.

"Nothing major. I'll be good to go in a minute."

Actually it takes nearly five for Drake to finish with me, but once he's done, I feel almost good as new. I tug my jacket in place and look at the faces of those who survived. We have six name patches to send back to Lachion. I wonder how many civilians we saved.

"Let's finish this," March says.

He leads the way down the ramp to the last set of doors and taps the comm. "The area is secure. Your people can come out now."

Within a few moments, the denizens of mining colony Dobrinya venture out from behind the seal. There are almost a hundred in all, including women and children. Despite my grief at losing good men, I know we did the right thing. Their grimy faces and too-fierce handshakes tell us so.

I've never had this feeling before. Sure, I've waved to the gutter press and celebrated a jump, but it's a different kind of triumph. This is raw, gritty, and personal. This little girl with the dirty blond hair and the heaven blue eyes is alive because of us. By her tentative, awed smile, she knows it, too. She takes a step forward, extending a hand.

Since nobody else is paying her any attention, I offer mine. "What's your name?"

"Calesta."

"You live here?"

A wide-eyed nod.

"How do you like it?"

"It was okay until the monsters came." She beams then,

showing me she's missing her front teeth. "But you guys got them all. We heard the shooting. Pew, pew, pew! Did you use your sword? Can I see it?"

I start to tell her it's called a vibroblade, but what the hell, she's all of six. Instead, I draw the thing from my back and pose with it, delighting her. I smile back. This isn't the sort of thing the old Jax would do at all. The old Jax didn't even *see* little kids.

"Thanks," she whispers.

I don't know if she means for saving them, or for the little show, but I etch her a salute before turning back to the larger group.

"We won't forget," the mine manager is saying to him. "We will *never* forget that the Armada came when we called. Thank you."

March inclines his head. "Before we go, we'll sweep the place one last time, just to make sure we didn't miss any of them."

"Let me go, sir." Torrance steps forward. "I'll make sure the whole complex is secure before we call it clear for civilians."

March says, "Do it."

"If there's time, I'd also like a look at their ships," Dina adds.

Her face is incandescent at the prospect of checking out their alien tech. Like anyone who's worked salvage, she loves to scavenge and adapt. Who knows, maybe she'll even figure out their secret for making direct jumps.

I nod. "That's a good idea."

Looks like this is a day for firsts.

.CLASSIFIED-TRANSMISSION.
.INSTRUCTIONS.
.FROM-SUNI_TARN.
.TO-EDUN_LEVITER.
.ENCRYPT-DESTRUCT-ENABLED.

Your honesty is appreciated. Perhaps I can be forgiven for wanting to see the best in my colleagues, but I begin to think I have romanticized the idea of what your best may be. It occurs to me that you are discouraging me from viewing you in any heroic light. I shall let that stand, as it does not impinge upon our business.

I'm pleased to hear of your success with Hydra. I followed your recommendation and sent medals to the families of soldiers who died aboard the *Dark Tide.* Unfortunately, I have more lost ships to mourn and more families to commend. I am tired, and I wonder where it all ends.

For now, take no overt action against Ramona Jax. Market shares indicate she is too popular to be removed at this time. Instead, focus your energies on a smear campaign. If the Syndicate can use the media, so can we, and I expect you will be better at it than any of their people.

After looking over your proposed tariffs, I can only say: If you had chosen politics, you'd have my job. I am a little afraid of your ingenuity; this is nothing short of brilliant. I like the indulgences to offset the luxury tariffs. I am bringing this matter to a vote at the summit, quietly attached to another proposition. If all goes well, the measure will pass without notice.

For a change, I have intel before you do. I've heard from one of my commanders. His message leads me to believe there are not one but *three* vessels waiting our salvage efforts on Dobrinya asteroid. When you dispatch your team, please take every precaution in retrieving the technology and make sure no lives are lost this time. I also want your people to oversee distribution of aid and medical supplies on the mining colony. Take a news crew. I realize you can't be there in person because it wouldn't make sense, given your ostensible position, but make sure you put your best agents on this. I'm including some media contacts.

Bonus: My commander suggests in that same message that we may want to contact the gray men and see if they'd be willing to contract with us as our police force. Given your past contacts with Farwan, it seems you would be ideally suited to locating them and cutting a deal. We must be perceived in a position of strength, but don't do anything to compromise our integrity. At this point, that's all we can offer to differentiate ourselves from the Corp.

.ATTACHMENT-CONTACTS-FOLLOWS.
.END-TRANSMISSION.

.COPY-ATTACHMENT.
.FILES-DOWNLOADED.
.ACTIVATE-WORM: Y/N?

.Y.
.TRANSMISSION-DESTROYED.

CHAPTER 42

Back outside the facility, my weighted boots seem heavier than before.

Now that the threat has passed, I'm feeling every year of my age. Most likely, nobody would stop me if I wanted to head back to the *Triumph*, but I'm curious what we'll find on board. The other two vessels are completely wrecked; it wouldn't be safe to explore the debris.

This third one is more or less in one piece, though the breaks in the hull mean we can't remove our suits once we get inside. I'm not sure I would do so in any case, despite being sure that the Morgut do breathe oxygen, just as we do.

March comes up, nudging my arm to get my attention. I glance up. "Aren't you afraid they'll gossip about your familiarity, sir?"

Color stains his cheeks. "I need to talk to you."

"I'm at your disposal, sir." Oh, Mary, I hope this perfect formality bothers him half as much as it does me.

"Did you think they died too easily?"

Come to think of it, they didn't seem as ferocious as the ones we fought on Emry. Slower, less certain, less skilled. "Yeah. But I thought it was because there were more of us, better trained, better gear, and we knew what we were getting into."

"So preparation made the difference?" he asks.

I shrug. "I thought so, but now you've got me wondering. What are you thinking?"

He hesitates too long before offering, "What if there are different types of Morgut?"

"You mean ones who don't eat humans?" I'm not sure I buy it. Not sure I want to.

What if we just slaughtered three ships of tourists? But no, that doesn't track.

"I don't know," he says finally. "Just . . . there was something off about them. They weren't like the ones on Emry."

"They died faster," I answer. "So maybe they weren't soldiers. That doesn't make them *nice*. They might've still eaten us—and the colonists. But maybe they're not the elite shock troops, just your average fanged monsters."

"But we didn't know there were castes. Did we?"

I shake my head. "Clearly we need to learn more about them if we're going to fight them effectively. Anything else, Commander?"

His face quiets, as if I've hurt him. "No, dismissed, LC."

I step toward the ship to see how we're coming on gaining entry to it.

Torrance has been working on the locking mechanism, trying to get us inside. Watching him, I can't help but think Vel would've gotten us past long before now. I miss him. It feels like I haven't seen him in ages, but the time I spent in training factors into that. Even before he left, we went weeks without contact due to our conflicting schedules.

I'm not used to that, after Ithiss-Tor.

"It's using some kind of sequenced algorithm," Torrance says eventually.

"Can you crack it?" March asks.

He's already wasted a code-breaker charge on the ship. The slender filaments twitched against the impermeable device, then shuddered and broke into slivers of dust. Which leaves all of us watching our scout, hoping he can achieve a miracle.

"Less than an hour of air left," I say quietly.

We don't have a huge amount of ground to cover, but we don't want to leave it too long, either. The scout swears as the panel flashes yellow again. We've figured out that means a reset, so anything he accomplished toward opening the door has been wiped.

"Over here!" Dina calls. When I jog up, she points at the hull breach and hefts her cutting torch. "Who needs to crack their code when you can make a door?"

I grin through my helmet at her. "Works for me."

Drawing my blade, though I don't activate it, I step through the narrow break, avoiding jagged metal that would tear my suit and leaving me to choke out my last few seconds on this barren rock. I hear footsteps that say the others are right behind me.

The Morgut ship is unlike anything I've ever seen.

This dark metal shines like diamond chips ground into obsidian. I reach into my pack. After snapping the torch-tube, a wan glow kindles in my hand. I shine it around, marveling at the layered, tubular design. The floor has a faint slope in the middle, almost like a channel of some kind. With gloves on, I can't assess how the strange material feels, but Torrance gets out his field kit and starts trying to chip off a sample of it.

Dina peers at the blade and shakes her head. "It won't work. Can't you tell by the way it's warping our metal?"

I lean closer, eyes narrowed. Weird. The silver bends *away* from the surface, not as a result of too much pressure. "Like it's trying to get away from it."

"Magnetized," Torrance guesses aloud.

March comes up behind us and puts a hand on Dina's arm. "Let's move on. If you want to see the whole ship, we'll have to be fast."

She agrees, "I'd like to see the engine rooms, learn what they're working with. Maybe I'll find something that lets me perfect the pattern for the phase drive."

"Torrance, you're with me. And you three." He points at a trio of sturdy clansmen, grim-faced, implacable, and covered in gore. "The rest of you, follow the LC."

They head off in the opposite direction. For a brief moment I watch them go. Once, it would've been me at his side. Not Dina. And it hurts, no matter how often I tell myself it's not because he doesn't care. It's not because he doesn't love me.

But hearing it in the silence of my own head isn't the same as feeling his warmth wash through me, feeling him inside my head. It's definitely not the same as feeling his arms around me.

But the air is ticking out of my gear while I stand around. Time to check this place out. I glance around at my men, not recognizing the faces at first, then I place them. Figures, he left me with the smugglers, except for our medic.

"Any of you have vid?"

"I do." Drake lofts the device, smiling at me.

"You four follow in pairs and keep a sharp eye out. I don't expect trouble, but . . ." A shrug finishes that sentence. Then I turn to Drake. "Come on, kid. You're up front with me."

"Do you have any idea how old I am? Ma'am." By his tone, I've pissed him off.

It's always the young ones who mind.

"Not a clue," I answer, moving along. "Would you like to tell me?"

At least he turns the vid, following the way I shine the light. "Twenty-five turns."

How depressing. I'm nearly ten turns older than him— and it feels like twice that. Jumping takes a toll on the body and the mind. Each time I look in the mirror, I'm mildly surprised not to be looking at some withered old crone.

"Coming up on a door to the right." I hope it's not locked, but it doesn't make sense that interior doors would be.

"Motion activated," Drake notes.

I beckon them all forward as I step inside. At first glance, the room seems to be empty, but as I step to the center, a series of sigils lights up on the fall wall. I've seen them before; unfortunately, I can't remember where.

"It's a menu," one of the smugglers volunteers.

"Like, to order food?" another asks.

The first guy shakes his head. "Don't be an idiot. An interface, not dinner."

That's where I've seen it: in the cockpit of the Silverfish back on New Terra. It must have been adapted for use by a Morgut pilot. The language chip doesn't seem to guide me on written linguistics, as I'm staring at these without a clue what they mean.

I cock a brow. "Think I should activate one?"

"I don't know if that's good idea." Drake focuses the vid on the wall, however, just in case I decide to be stupid.

The tallest—Benhamin—takes a discreet step back. "If you do decide to play with that thing, ma'am, I hope you won't mind if we wait in the hall."

"Of course not." I grin. "Go on, all of you."

They accept with alacrity, then it's just Drake and me.

"I'll stay," he says. "We need something to show the commander, so he knows it's not our fault. You know. If something horrible happens to you."

Ignoring that, though he's most likely right, I approach the citrine symbols pulsing on the onyx wall. Tentatively, I tap the one on the far left. It's a little like an S with a slash through it, a squiggly line under it, and a trill going off toward the ceiling. At first nothing happens, then it slides out of sight, and appears on the far right, now flashing twice as fast. The other symbols blink slowly at me.

"Hm." I glance back at Drake. "Do you think I should quit while I'm ahead?"

He points the vid at me, and from long experience, I can tell he's zoomed in on my face within the helmet. "Do you know what you're doing?"

"Nope."

"At least you're honest. I wouldn't presume to advise you, LC. Even though I think you're nuts." He adds the last sentence in a low mutter.

Well, he may be right. I tap the circular thing next to the quick-blinking one. and it flashes bright green. A low hum seems to come from the very wall itself, the obsidian lightening to pale gray, then an image appears. It's a giant display screen, except I can't see where the display ends and the wall begins. There are no mechanical bits at all.

The dark silhouette resolves into a hissing, clicking Morgut. This appears to be a transmission of some kind. I can't tell if it's live. I can't tell if there are sensors in the dark, telling it that we're here. Shit, I hope it's not coming from within the ship.

14.54.66.78.94.33.0

Numbers. It's listing numbers. Streams of them. Before long, I realize they're coordinates. I'm not sure I'll be able to memorize all of this, so it's good thing he's recording. I'll play it back later and note each location on the star charts.

"Are you getting this?" I ask Drake.

"Sure am," he breathes. "What does it mean?"

I shush him because there's more, and when I understand the rest of the message, courtesy of the chip, my blood runs cold.

CHAPTER 43

We're back on our ship, assembled in the officers' lounge.

Though he's not of appropriate rank, Drake has been allowed to stay, courtesy of being present when I made the discovery. He takes the chip from the vid and pops it into the terminal while the others get comfortable. Our team is small: March, Doc, Dina, a clansman named Birrick, and me. Doc studies my grim-faced expression as I stand, fingers laced behind my back.

"Start it," I tell Drake.

The image is no better at one remove, but the sound is clear enough. I let it play through all the way. I've watched the thing so many times—wanting to be sure my chip always offers the same meaning—that I can recite the translation from memory.

"Is it a message of some kind?" Doc asks. "How does this help us?"

"Because I understand it." I hold up a hand, forestalling questions. "Among other things, this message provides coordinates, listing the sites scheduled for attack."

Dina breathes, "So it's not random."

"LC, I want those locations pinned down at once. We need to get the information out to the rest of the fleet."

Fleet. That word is laughable to describe the number of

ships we can bring to bear, now that I know what we're up against. I feel sick. I don't want to be the bearer of these tidings, not when we seemed to be doing so well. But it's deceptive; the bad news just hadn't caught up with us yet.

"What's wrong?" Drake asks.

Perceptive kid. I didn't even tell him the worst of it.

"There's more," I say, reluctantly. "It speaks of mustering the red cloud. I don't think that's the right word, but it's the equivalent my chip offered. It doesn't always find a synonym, so it does the best it can."

March stills, studying my face. He's no longer distracted by the apparent good news of those coordinates. "Do you have any idea what the 'red cloud' is?"

I close my eyes. "Based on context, I'd have to say it's their battle fleet. They're mobilizing at last, no more scout ships."

"How many are we talking about?" Dina asks.

It hurts me to give this answer. "Three thousand."

Shaken, Doc breathes, "Mary's grace."

"In what context did they refer to this red cloud?" March asks, his face closed and cold.

"Protecting the colonists, who were to secure the power source."

Dina nods. "The uranium, of course."

"Yes, that's what I thought. It spoke of the final phase of a mass migration, too. This red cloud will carry *all* the Morgut from their homeworld. It didn't say why."

"A cataclysmic event," Doc offers.

March shakes his head. "I don't care why. We have to deal with the what."

There's nothing for it, except that I must relay the rest. "One more thing. It reassured the colonists they would be safe, reporting the destruction of six Armada ships."

I don't have to point out the calamity of that. On the brink of the worst war in human history, we now have nine ships left to us. *Nine*. And that's assuming the *Dark Tide* is factored into that six; otherwise, we're down to eight. Eight, against three thousand. It's laughable and hopeless.

Though Tarn has the shipyards going and he's training volunteers, they can't make up the difference. Not in time.

"We need to muster," March says. "I'll bounce an order for a meet. We have to pool our resources and our strategy. I'll also ask Tarn to push to finalize the contract with the gray men. We need them."

I shiver. It's true; we do. But I don't like what it portends.

"And I need to work on the other ships," Dina adds. "I took something from the Morgut engine room. I've never seen the like before, but I have a feeling the design lets the nav com interface with the phase drive, permitting a direct jump."

"You'll test it on ours first?" I ask.

They don't seem to be feeling the same weight I am. They want to pretend we have a chance. But what choice do we have? The alternative is to cede our lands and our lives to the Morgut without a fight.

She nods. "As soon as we're finished here, I'm going to work on it."

I glance at March. "Are we done?"

"Dismissed. LC, if I could have a moment?"

Great, he wants a private chat. That's the last thing I want or need. But I nod as the rest file out of the lounge. Once the door has closed, he closes the distance between us.

"How can you talk to the Morgut? What's going on with you?"

In cool tones, I explain, just as I did with Dina, and conclude, "At least, that's my theory. When you're chock-full of experimental tech, there are no absolutes. Who knows what Dasad's nanites are doing to my brain? I might not even be myself this time tomorrow."

"Jax." His dark eyes reflect pure torment because he doesn't have the right to comfort me.

"Is there anything else, Commander? I need to bounce a message before we jump."

We're abandoning the people of Sigma Psi. Guilt stings me, but if we don't regroup, we'll be the only Armada ship left, with three thousand Morgut vessels gunning for us. March knows what he's doing in this regard. If anyone knows about fighting impossible wars, it's him. Maybe he can win this one, too.

But I don't have any hope. Even in that cell on Perlas, despair didn't own me so fully. Now I see humanity caught amid endless night with no promise of sunrise.

"I'll expect you in the cockpit in a quarter turn. Dismissed, LC." He faces away, but not before I glimpse the pain thrumming through him. The need to touch forces me to curl my fingers into fists, so I won't reach out.

I wonder whether I'm going to die—this time forever—without ever hearing him say my name again. Is this how it ends? Marshaling my strength, I go from the officers' lounge, my tears frozen into a hard knot inside me. To my surprise, Argus is waiting, and he falls in step beside me.

"Are you all right?"

I'd forgotten how well he knows me, courtesy of sharing mind-space in the simulator and the nav com. There comes a point when familiarity crosses into empathy. I used to know when Kai was sad, even if he was somewhere else. At the moment, March is actively blocking me—a kindness—or I'd feel too much of his pain.

I shake my head. "Nobody is."

"They won't tell me what's going on."

"It would start a panic," I say quietly. "You'll get the bad news soon enough. I recommend you spend some time with that cute blond cadet."

"Now I'm really worried."

I stop outside my quarters and eye him. And I decide to be straight with him. "You should be. Go."

The apprentice jumper does as I ask, but not without a

last, speaking glance. He wanted me to tell him, but I've carried enough bad news for one day. Now I'm about to do something I swore I never would, but it looks like hell has frozen.

Recognizing me, my door swishes open. My quarters are beige and impersonal, but it's a place to rest. More important, it offers some privacy. If Rose checks the outgoing messages, I'll have some explaining to do, but by then it will be too late.

I sit down at the terminal. "Computer, record on."

"Acknowledged."

I still have her private comm code, though I knew her by another name when I received it. So I speak the numbers aloud, encrypting it for her eyes only. "It's time to set aside our differences," I say, gazing directly into the vid as if it were my mother's eyes. "I do not believe even you will wish to persist in profiteering in the face of a threat this vast."

In even tones, I summarize what we face in the red cloud and the mass Morgut migration. "You can attempt to validate this information, but in the end, you know what this means. No world is safe. To have any hope of preserving your empire, you must commit your resources to the defense of humanity. *All* Syndicate attacks must cease. You must turn your eyes to the true enemy, our shared enemy. If you agree, contact me on this code, and I will provide you information as to where we can meet."

She might think it's a trap, at first, but in truth it's nothing so cunning. Only desperation would have driven me to speak those words and ask her help. Only that.

It takes me a few moments to get myself together enough to face March again, but within the allotted time, I report to the cockpit. That's when I learn the location of what may be the last human summit.

It's New Terra, of course. That planet represents every proud and shining moment in human history: how we came from a dying world, one choked with pollution, global warming, and acid rain. After one hundred years of voyaging, the generation ship delivered our forefathers safely to New Terra, where we built things anew with no help from anyone. It's an inspiring story—and so, of course, it is there we must go, carrying precious little hope.

Without speaking, I settle into the nav chair.

CHAPTER 44

Dina's done it, finally.

I can tell as soon as we jack in. There's a clear connection between the nav com and phase drive, a silver thread of pure grimspace. After examining the Morgut model, she used a biomechanical matrix linked through the nanoprotein strings. To me, it feels like we're carrying a pocket wormhole on board, though that's an imprecise analogy at best.

Feels that way to me, too, Argus says.

Now the ship isn't inanimate anymore. In a very basic sense, the *Triumph* is alive. Doc and Evelyn asked my permission before they did it because they based the biological components on my DNA. It's weird knowing I'm woven through this ship in minute particles, allowing the direct-jump process. They can—and will—do this to every Armada ship, and any navigator could make it work.

I glance at my apprentice. It's an easy jump from Sigma Psi to New Terra. Why not let him make it? We need another trained jumper who's familiar with the direct-jump process. It has to be Argus; there's just nobody else. With the ship technology in place, maybe he doesn't need nanites. Like me, he has the regulator. Doc and Evelyn have done their best to get him ready.

Maybe it's time.

You handle this one. I'll be here if you get in trouble.

Joy cascades through him, through me. *Are you sure?*

Positive. You're ready.

We don't need to switch seats. As long as I ease back into observational mode, he can take control of the jump from his training chair. I'm going to let him.

March seems startled to find Argus in charge when he jacks in, but he doesn't protest. Most likely he could track my train of thought in coming to this conclusion. So he'll know why I'm letting Argus do this here, now.

I've notified the rest of the Armada. They'll meet us on New Terra.

Ready? Argus asks.

But he's not talking to me, so I keep silent. This is his show. I'm just along for the ride and to bail him out if things go wrong. I keep that thought to myself, behind my walls. He doesn't need outside anxiety added to his first jump.

Ready. March offers the kid steady confidence and nothing more.

The phase drive powers up, but there's a different feel to it now, darker and more dangerous. In my blood, the cations fire to life, and I shudder at the pull of the grimspace link. Whatever Dina did, it changed things profoundly. The nav com knows what's expected of it now.

How strange, I haven't felt anyone else do this since we shared time in the sim, back at the Academy, but today, I piggyback on Argus. He's calm and cautious, exploring the new component to the phase drive. Soon he realizes he can direct it. Perhaps someone who wasn't subject to my genes could do so as well, but it wouldn't be as natural. Since we don't know how the Morgut interface with it, my mutation is grease to the gears.

Smooth as s-silk, he opens the way for us. I ride his elation all the way into grimspace. The kid can't shield himself; he isn't experienced enough to manage that along with navigation, but I don't mind sharing his delight. It's fresh and clean, wonderfully untainted by ambition or self-interest.

Grimspace, filtered through his mind's eye, is glorious. Because they're new to him in this perspective, they seem different to me as well, jewel-bright and fluid as fire. He wants to sing; he wants to dance amid the souls of the stars, for that's surely what we find here: the beginning of every galaxy, scintillating and refracting light into poetry.

Ah, he has an artistic soul, this one. This is good for me, pleasure without pain. I share it with him gladly, and the feeling redoubles between us. It's oddly like the pilot-jumper bond, but I've never had it with a fellow navigator before because they didn't train this way in the Academy.

But he's not lost in it. After a few jubilant seconds, he sets himself to finding the beacons. Like any good navigator, he locates the right ones quickly and relays that information to March. Then Argus gives himself over to the beacons; I don't have to teach how to use them to twist. For him, it's instinctual. His first solo jump—a direct jump. Truly, the kid's making history today.

And for these moments, I am free. Home and . . . *free*. I savor them. Nothing can touch us here.

I sense my apprentice's reluctance to bring us out, but I've hammered home the danger of lingering. He knows the stories of ships lost forever because their jumpers fell prey to the seductive pull. Argus focuses his thoughts, then the phase drive powers up again. When we push through, we'll be a few thousand klicks from New Terra.

He does it perfectly. There's no fear or uncertainty in him, only enjoyment. This young man was born to jump, just as I was. I take a certain bittersweet satisfaction in realizing I've trained my successor. If something happens to me, my gifts will not be lost. Argus can carry them on.

Smiling, but with a heart full of melancholy, I unplug. I'm not surprised at all to find New Terra rising before us. From this distance, the world shines aquamarine, with paler hues indicating land. This is the jewel in the crown of human achievement. When we set off from our wrecked and wretched homeworld, we didn't even have faster-than-light travel.

That, we found along the way.

"Good jump," March says.

Argus flushes, practically glowing with his achievement. In another ten minutes, March interfaces with their SDIs and receives clearance to proceed into the atmosphere. I'm not needed here any longer, so I push out of the chair. The commander is busy talking to the port authority, receiving landing vectors, but he dismisses me with a gesture, making it official. I can go.

To my surprise, Argus follows. He stops me with a hand on my shoulder, practically vibrating his pleasure. He's so jacked, it's not even funny. "Thank you, Jax. I never felt whole before now."

I know the feeling, but I don't tell him the pleasure also comes with an ache that only gets worse, the longer he jumps. Grimspace is a bitch mistress who carries unearthly delight in one hand and a crop in the other. We bear the latter to receive the former. He'll learn that soon enough—and maybe he'll hate me for the subterfuge. Maybe he'll judge me no better than Farwan, who parceled out their truths like niggardly coin.

"I had to train you," I tell him honestly. "You have the genotype and the drive. Otherwise, that inexplicable need would've driven you mad."

Then he surprises me by kissing me on the mouth. His lips are firm and knowing, still charged with the thrill of grimspace. Shock holds me still, but it's over too fast for me to protest. The heat of it lingers after he raises his head.

"That's for letting me jump on my own." Argus flashes me a roguish grin.

I try for a severe expression. "That was inappropriate. I didn't do it for sexual favors. You were ready."

"You're ready, too, Jax. You were wide open in there." He tilts his head toward the cockpit suggestively.

I don't feel threatened, but for the first time, I'm aware of him as a young, healthy male animal. Like the majority of the Dahlgren clansmen, he's tall and fit, more than moderately handsome. I shouldn't be remotely tempted because he's too young, and I'm his superior. I can't have him for the same reasons March can't have me. Yet there's a spark of the old Jax in me, who wants to be touched. She wants the uncomplicated pleasure he offers. It's been a long damn time since I had sex, and my body is hungry.

I also know he's not looking for an emotional connection. For him, this is about burning off the high he got in grimspace, and sharing it with someone who knows exactly how it feels. That's the danger of the pilot-jumper bond, extended through the training capacity of our dual nav chair. So I get where he's coming from. This won't be a big deal: total wham-bam-thank-you-ma'am, and honestly, I'm a little flattered that he'd look my way even in passing.

But things will never be the same between March and me if I do this. I know that.

"Go find your blonde," I manage to say. "I know you have excess energy. I remember my first jump well enough."

As a matter of fact, I stayed in bed for three days. The idea of doing that with Argus—forgetting the world and all its troubles—kindles a knot of pure desire in my belly. Mary, how I'd love to be young and carefree, but I'm not, and I never will be again. For good or ill, I've moved beyond such simplicity.

He flashes a smile. "She won't understand how I feel right now, but Esme will do."

So that's her name. I watch him go, knowing I've done the right thing. Argus offered oblivion, but I couldn't stop thinking of the consequences. I really *have* changed.

"Jax." March's voice comes gravel-rough from the cockpit, calling me back.

He's not calling me LC now. I don't know what that means. How much did he hear?

Nervous, I retrace my steps. I thought he was too busy with the port authority to pay us any attention. Over the past months, he's given a fair approximation of being indifferent to me. Deep down, I'd begun to wonder how much of it is true.

And yet I turned away days of pleasure for the mere hope of him. I don't know whether that's lovely or pathetic.

"I always know exactly where you are in a room," he tells me without looking round. "I know how many times you run your fingers through your hair. I know when you look at me as well as the precise instant you look at anyone else. So I *certainly* know when one of my crew propositions you six meters away."

"I turned him down."

"I know," he says softly. "That's why I called you in here, against my better judgment." At that he stands, the ship on autopilot. We're still waiting for the final clearance before we can make our approach.

Something tells me to close the door.

CHAPTER 45

His eyes are molten. I let myself look my fill for the first time in months, and I note he's thinner, cheekbones jutting like jagged rocks, and his face holds a weariness that no sleep can assuage. He's *letting* me see it. The shields are down. No longer does he play the role of commander with me.

I take a step toward him. Suddenly it doesn't matter that he put the good of the ship ahead of us. Would he be the man I love if he had chosen differently?

His arms go around me, and he buries his face in my hair. I can hear his heartbeat, thumping too fast beneath my ear. I wind my arms around his waist.

"I love you," I whisper. "It won't go away because I can't have you in my bed."

Maybe he had a flicker of doubt. Maybe he thought because I fell for him—though I didn't want to—after Kai died, that I'm still the woman who loves the one she's with. But it was never like that between us. It's more that March proved himself the man I didn't know I wanted but always needed.

He breathes, "I need you. It's killing me."

The ache blazes to life in me as well when I remember how he took me in here on this very ship. We could do it again. Nobody would know.

Against the door, in his pilot's chair. I don't care where.

Long tremors shake through me. It's too much, being

this close to him. No wonder he's been avoiding me. I didn't know until this second just how much I had shoved back and compartmentalized, and it's threatening to break me in two.

"Me, too," I whisper.

March lifts me, as if he can't control himself. We're not supposed to, bad for morale, but I don't have any self-denial left. He rocks against me through our clothes, and I'm utterly undone.

"We're not going to," he murmurs. I don't know if he's trying to convince himself or me. "I just need to feel you."

I guess he hasn't noticed; I'm not exactly fighting him off. Instead I curl my fingers into his waist, pulling him closer. Searching under his jacket I find a strip of hot, silky skin. He shudders at my touch.

Helpless, he mirrors the movement, his fingers skimming my bare belly. These touches are tiny, almost innocent, but I'm so hungry for him, the contact leaves me reeling.

"I'm sorry for the delay," the docking officer says over the comm. "We're working on some things with Chancellor Tarn on our end. We want everything to be perfect when you arrive, Commander."

With little sigh of loss, he pulls away and goes to answer. "It's not a problem. Just keep me posted."

When he returns to me, I sense he's taken a step back from completely unprofessional behavior. But he puts his arms around me again, and I take comfort in it.

He rubs his cheek slowly back and forth across the top of my head. "I just keep pushing you. *Testing* you. I'm not doing it on purpose . . . Circumstances dictate my choices, but deep down, I'm afraid I'll hit your breaking point. That you'll decide it's more trouble than it's worth—and I'm not worth waiting for."

It's time for me to say something I should have, ages ago. "You're worth *everything*. I've changed because of you. You inspire people, make them want to be better and stronger than they ever thought they could be. Who else could've cobbled together an armada from the dregs of society?"

"And yet, it's not enough."

"It will be," I say firmly. "It must be. We haven't seen the endgame. There may yet be some surprises."

He raises his head then, his face stark. "We're at the wall, Jax, and I cannot see the door from here."

I understand his despair. Somewhere in the silence of space, three thousand Morgut ships muster against us. The idea of fighting such a force seems laughable.

"These are the worst odds yet," I agree.

"I can bear anything, as long as I know you're with me."

I reach up and touch his face, tracing his features with my fingertips. March closes his eyes as if I offer a pleasure too sharp to be borne. At length he turns into my caress, sealing his lips against my palm.

"I *am* with you. You are my captain, my commander, and my love. Neither war nor death will change it."

His hands curve around my back, holding me tighter. "I couldn't survive losing you. It nearly destroyed me, thinking I had."

I shake my head. "You can't consider that. You were wise in saying we had to put distance between us. This is not the time for personal concerns."

"When will it ever be?" he demands.

"I can't answer that."

Responsibility weighs on him today. He's feeling the burden of all the lives resting on his shoulders, and there's nothing I can do. My one consolation is that I don't see the cold detachment building in him. This is a different kind of war from the one he fought against humans in tunnels.

"Do you ever wish you'd answered differently?"

I tilt my head, puzzled. "When?"

"Back on New Terra, when I asked you to come away with me."

"You suggested we grow rutabagas." Much as I love him, I can't regret not becoming a farmer. That would've meant sacrificing one great love for another.

"You didn't think that was your only option, did you?"

To be honest, I hadn't thought about it too much. Back then, I didn't realize he was seriously asking me something. He's the mind reader, not me.

"I didn't want a life where I had to stay in one place," I tell him gently.

"So you're not sorry."

Warmth surges through me. He's touched my mind at last, trying to get a sense of how I feel. "Here, as we teeter on the brink, I'm in your arms. So no, I'm not sorry."

March draws back, incredulous. "You think we'll figure some way out of this."

"We always have before."

"If I didn't know better, Jax, I'd call that faith."

I nod. "In you, not indifferent gods."

He kisses me then, his hands in my hair. For one glorious moment, I'm overflowing with him. The loneliness recedes, and I'm reminded why I wait for him, why nobody else will do.

A crackle from the comm pulls him from me. With an apologetic look, he takes his seat. "This is the *Triumph*."

"You're cleared to enter our airspace," the docking officer tells him. "And landing vectors have been transmitted and received."

Like any good pilot, March double-checks before initiating the landing sequence. "Acknowledged, control. We'll see you shortly." He glances at me. "You should probably take a seat in case there's turbulence."

"Is that code for 'please, stay'?" I raise a brow as I settle into the nav chair.

He shakes his head. "No code. I'll say it straight-out— please stay. You have no idea how much I've missed you."

"Sure I do."

March taps the comm. "We're landing shortly. All crew should be prepared."

New Terra swells before us: Patchwork land deepens into

contour and texture, then I can begin to make out details as the *Triumph* angles downward. We won't be visiting Ankaraj this time. Since we left, Tarn has seen to the construction of a new capital complex in a more hospitable city.

We put down in Ocklind, a more temperate locale. Since we're VIPs instead of fugitives, disembarkation doesn't take long. Long lines of people snake all the way to the far doors, and they offer us ugly looks when they see we're not joining the queue. Instead, officials wave us through the checkpoints, manned by an embarrassment of Peacemaker units. These bots wear enough ordnance to pacify a small country.

But it's not the droids that cool the heat of resentment in these folks. "Mary's grace! That's the Armada commander. Something big must be brewing."

"They saved a bunch of colonists out on Dobrinya aster-oid," someone else says. "Saw it on the midnight bounce."

Unlike Perlas, they recognize *him*, not me. That makes me so proud.

On the other side, we find the docking officer. "Welcome back to New Terra."

"Thanks. The rest of our crew will arrive shortly." March glances back as if looking for them.

I spot Doc and Evelyn heading our way. Nearly joined at the hip, they are. Even if it's a strictly working relationship, I can't help feeling sorry for Rose. It's five minutes before she arrives, and Doc looks surprised, as if he thought she'd stay on ship. Which makes no sense, considering we're on New Terra and not some Podunk outpost.

Dina ambles up, the slow stride camouflaging her limp. Her expression is brighter than I've seen it for a while, though, and I'm positive I know why.

I grin. "She'll be here soon, I'm sure."

"They were near a jump zone when our message came in. So, yeah, she will."

That means they made it. I hadn't realized how afraid I was that Kora and Hit might've been among those six vessels reported lost. Since we jumped from Dobrinya, I haven't heard from comms whether they've determined what ships we have left.

While I'm thinking of Kora—

"Are we going to have trouble?" I ask March, low. "Some of our ships have nonhuman crew." And the new immigration laws are harsh.

"I'll leave word. If they want us to keep fighting out there, they can't afford to limit the pool from which we can draw our soldiers."

At length, Tarn sends an honor guard to escort us to the quarters he's arranged for the *Triumph* officers. The crew just seems happy to get some R&R in a decent human settlement. Ocklind is the capital city on a large island, highly defensible. In addition, there are white-sand beaches here and crystal blue water.

They, at least, can expect a little joy while we're here.

.CLASSIFIED-TRANSMISSION.
.CONTACT.
.FROM-EDUN_LEVITER.
.TO-SUNI_TARN.
.ENCRYPT-DESTRUCT-ENABLED.

The team arrived shortly after the departure of the *Triumph*. Everything you requested came to pass. Mining-colony residents were appropriately thankful, and they told the media of their great love and appreciation for the Conglomerate. Several suitable sound bites resulted and have been since bounced to every major satellite.

Your requested smear campaign proceeds apace. We have uncovered several little-known facts about Ramona Jax. Cruelty can be quite delicious when deployed against one's enemies, don't you agree? In any event, the people will be hard-pressed to overlook these atrocities, should they become public. Henceforth, she may smile for the vids all she likes, but those voice files are unmistakable. Even I am shocked at the sins she has committed against her fellow man, and I believe I may be acquitted of naïveté. She will either bend to my will, or I shall see her broken before I'm done. I should have some response from her shortly regarding how she intends to proceed.

If you review the market shares, you'll see that the Conglomerate has gained more than twenty points while Syndicate approval ratings are falling. Polls indicate the general public sees the Syndicate not as security, but as brutal, heartless thugs. We're winning the media war on New Terra, at least. The rest will follow. After all, you have employed me to make it so.

Though you had not directly asked me to do so, I have taken the liberty of destroying a Syndicate weapons cache on New Terra. If their people are poorly supplied, they will find it harder to fight. Hired hands lose morale faster than those who fight for higher ideals.

Lastly, I successfully made contact with the gray men and they have agreed to meet. I will need to travel to them in person, so they can scan my DNA to ascertain I am who I claim to be. I cannot avoid this circumstance, but I will take all precautions to prevent any whisper of my identity leaving that locale. The gray men can be trusted, absolutely, because they have no interest in anything but hunting, not for the kill but for the chase. They are lawful in the extreme and if we reach an agreement with them, you can rely on their keeping the contract, though sometimes in annoyingly literal fashion. They will do business only with me because I am a known factor, and they understand that I, too, am bound by my word. Once we have established tentative terms, I will forward the facts and figures, as relate to their hire, including salary and benefits. Do not fear. In these negotiations, I will not compromise you or the Conglomerate in any fashion.

.END-TRANSMISSION.

.ACTIVATE-WORM: Y/N?

.Y.
.TRANSMISSION-DESTROYED.

CHAPTER 46

Chancellor Tarn greets us before the summit. His clothing is a little rumpled, and his hair shows evidence of nervous hands. I can tell he hasn't slept in a while. Oddly, that reassures me. You don't want your people led by someone who can rest well while they're dying. That's too much like Farwan at the helm.

He extends a hand to me. "Lieutenant Commander Jax, you're looking well."

For the first time, the rank feels real to me, one I've earned and not an arbitrary title hung on me by someone else. "I wish I could say the same, sir."

His eyes actually twinkle at me a little. "I was being polite."

So I *do* look like hell. Well, I'm not surprised. The constant patrols have worn us all down, and it doesn't help to feel like we're fighting a losing battle out there. We talk on the move, heading toward the formal senate chamber built to house the representatives for all tier worlds.

March shakes the Chancellor's hand in turn. "What time is the summit?"

Tarn answers, "A little less than an hour now. You cut it close."

"We weren't expecting to attend," March says wryly.

I follow along, listening. The rest of our crew has been cleared for whatever amusement suits them best. Dina is still camped out in the docking area, waiting for Hit's ship to come in. Imagining their reunion puts a smile on my face for all of thirty seconds.

Tarn inclines his head. "In a very interesting development, there is another faction recently arrived on New Terra. They're rebels, refugees from Tarnus: a militia as I understand it, fragments of the palace guard. All this time, they thought the royal line had died out, so they kept their counsel and lived quietly on world. They've since learned that your ship's mechanic is a princess of the blood. They've come to fight for her."

Dina has her own soldiers? I can't wait to see her face when she finds out.

"Let me guess. They sign with the slogan: 'The Oppressed Shall Rise.'"

Tarn seems surprised. "How did you know?"

"I came across their handiwork on Perlas Station, but I didn't know what it meant until now."

It's amusing to think of a royalist party as oppressed; but history teaches us that any government, however egalitarian it purports to be, can swiftly become more brutal and corrupt than the one it supplants. That thought leaves me uneasy as I study the face of the Conglomerate. Will Tarn one day be worse than the Farwan execs?

"What news from Emry?" March asks.

We left Surge in charge of liaising with New Terra. Time to see if he's reported anything of note, as his messages may not have caught up with us. That's the danger of frequent jumps. By the time the satellite relays catch up, your ship is somewhere else.

"Varied," Tarn returns. "He reports that ships have arrived from seven different nontier worlds, Outskirts rabble mostly."

I grit my teeth because that *rabble* is fighting and dying bravely on his behalf.

Tarn goes on. "They were private vessels, come to collect some missing children."

Finally, some good news.

"But after hearing what the Armada did on their behalf, their leadership contacted me, requesting to join the Conglomerate. They've since pledged ships and trained soldiers to our cause," the Chancellor concludes.

The Armada, my ass. It was us, plain and simple. But I'm thrilled to learn those kids are going home, and even happier to hear we can count on the support of seven more worlds. We're going to need that strength of numbers real soon.

March pauses behind Tarn, who has drawn up outside the senate chamber. "Nice to know what we do out there makes a difference."

I peer inside, taking in the vast room with stadium seats. The magnitude steals my breath, though part of me wonders if the credits that went toward this construction might've been better spent on ships and soldiers. Still, I must admit it's impressive. In a few moments, this ivory-and-gilt chamber will be filled with representatives who will decide the fate of the galaxy.

Tarn levels his gaze on both of us, for once devoid of his politician's charm. "You are the last dam holding back a very dark tide. Never doubt what you do matters."

March inclines his head. "Thank you. But you may feel less grateful when you hear the news we carry. It's grim intelligence, Chancellor."

"Do I need preparation or can it be presented with the rest at the summit?"

March slides me a look, touches my mind with his. The warm prickle warns me. He's taking a quick census as only he can.

Thus assured of my position, he says, "I think we'd better talk first."

Alarm registers on Tarn's mobile features. "Then let's step into my private office. It's not far."

Once the door slides shut behind us, and we've all seated ourselves, March summarizes what I learned from the downed Morgut ship. Though he levels a sharp look at me,

Tarn doesn't ask how I understand them. Just as well—we're short on time.

"Such tidings are . . ." For once, he seems at a loss for words.

"Catastrophic?" I offer.

"That will do. I haven't been idle," Tarn says. "Each tier world has complied with the decree that they levy at least one ship and crew toward defense of the Conglomerate." Seeing my surprise at the paucity of the offering, he explains, "Some tier worlds are colonies barely starting out. Even this will prove a hardship. But I've received promises of aid from Tarnus, Rodeisia, and the Nicuan Empire, well beyond that single ship."

That astonishes me. By March's expression, he shares the feeling. "They've agreed to put aside their own differences long enough to commit resources to a galactic conflict?"

Tarn nods. "The enemy of my enemy is my friend."

"It's wise of them to be concerned," I say softly. "The Morgut are not just attacking. They're colonizing. Conquering. One world will never be enough."

"So reinforcements are coming." March threads his fingers together, looking weary but thoughtful.

"That means we need enough time to let our allies get their ships in place."

"Having the coordinates will help," Tarn says. "But I fear many colonies will be lost."

No shit. I share that fear. He's never seen the Morgut close up. New Terra has never seen what they can do. If we do our jobs here and now, it never will.

Secretly, I'd hoped to hear from my mother by now, but it's not like she ever helped me before. It's kind of a long shot. Her goons will most likely go about ransacking the galaxy until the very end.

"Not having their timetable as well as the locations will cost us," March agrees.

"Any news from Ithiss-Tor?" I'm curious what the new,

permanent ambassador is like, and how he or she is getting on with Vel.

"Yes, as a matter of fact. Computer, play message 49781-B."

"Certainly, Chancellor Tarn."

Hearing the voice I chose for Constance come out of Tarn's terminal gives me a little start, but that's forgotten when Vel's image resolves on the display. How like him that he omits a greeting and begins the report immediately. "The opposition party has been defeated and manufacture of new vessels has commenced. I cannot say how soon the fleet will be ready, but a number of lower-caste kinsmen have entered training to crew them." He etches a *wa* in closing, though the meaning is lost on Tarn: *At last we hunt again.*

A woman steps forward then. She is slim and fair, every hair in place. Instead of my haphazard burns, she has ritual scars etched into her shoulders and elegant patterns notched into her cheeks. Once, I would have found the effect akin to self-mutilation, but my perception of beauty has expanded considerably since my callow youth. Loveliness is not just smooth skin and bright eyes. It comes in all hues and aspects.

"Chancellor Tarn." She pauses as if giving him a chance to respond. Her smile reflects that she knows the impact of her manner. "As my cultural liaison notes—" There's warmth in her gaze as she glances at Vel. "Things proceed apace. I am confident not only that the trade agreements will hold, but that I shall forge some new pacts as well. There is a hungry merchant faction that will permit me to leverage the issues we discussed."

She must be talking about the war. When I was there, the Ithtorians were wary of being dragged into our conflict; but once a hunter scents the blood of an old foe, they find it hard to reject a new contest. The ambassador's gold robe shines as she closes the vid letter.

There's an unwelcome hole in my gut because Vel's there with her. If I didn't know better, I'd call the feeling jealousy.

He's supposed to be here with me. Because I must, I set the sensation aside to consider later.

"Who is she?"

"Catrin Jocasta," Tarn tells me.

"Jocasta," March repeats.

"You know the name. She is Miriam Jocasta's daughter, a diplomat trained at her mother's knee. It took months of begging before she would leave her seclusion." His expression says he'd have sent her instead of me if she hadn't been grieving, and Vel would've consented to escort her.

That explains it. Miriam Jocasta died on the *Sargasso*, the most famous of Farwan's victims. New Terra itself spent a whole day in mourning for her when we revealed the truth of her murder. If Catrin is truly her mother's daughter, she will bring an exquisite gravity to her role as ambassador, and Vel will cherish the time he spends with her. I wish that prospect didn't fill me with such ambivalence.

"I'm glad they're in good hands."

"Technically," Tarn says, "that was old news. They arrived on world for the summit, just yesterday."

"So there's an Ithtorian delegation present?" The pomp and circumstance must've been enormous. But I need to see Vel—Mary, how I've missed him.

Tarn rises then. "Yes, Catrin handled things beautifully from start to finish. I'll think on how best to present this information to the summit. I don't want to start a panic."

"Will you need us to speak?" I ask.

"Commander March, if *you* would stand by in case you're needed, I'd appreciate that very much."

"Can I watch?" Everyone else will see only snippets of history being made, after it's all done. I hope to have a front-row seat.

The Chancellor says, "Of course. If you'll excuse me?"

The show is about to begin.

CHAPTER 47

I'm watching the summit.

I can see everything through the windows of a small room off the senate chamber. The tiered seats are now full. So many representatives have come from so many worlds. It's mind-boggling. Searching the vast hall, I find Vel standing beside the Ithtorian representative—of course, they need him to interpret the proceedings and speak for Ithiss-Tor. From where I stand, I can't make out who has been elected.

March waits with me in case he's needed. He shoots me a quiet glance, but even when we're alone he doesn't get personal. His self-discipline kills me.

Into the silence steps a slim, lovely woman. I recognize Catrin immediately from the vid message Tarn played for us. As a VIP, she's joined us for the up-close view. I wonder how well she knows Vel.

Dismissing the thought as jealous and petty, I extend a hand. "Sirantha Jax."

"I know your work," she says, shaking it.

I don't know if that's a good thing or a bad one. Her expression gives me nothing. The summit commences, sparing me from further social intercourse.

Tarn completes his opening remarks, greeting his fellow representatives. I can't think when so many dignitaries have been gathered on New Terra, and part of me thinks this would be an excellent time for an attack. Farwan used just such an occasion, after all, but the Conglomerate has learned from their mistakes, at least; the representatives arrived on different ships, preventing such a great and collective loss.

There are chairs, but I don't want to sit. This seems like an occasion I ought to face on my feet. Tarn wades through a number of less weighty issues first, and votes are taken. It makes sense to organize the docket that way. But at last, he has no choice but to broach the news we've given him.

"One final order of business, ladies and gentlemen."

A restive hum sweeps over the assembly. If I were watching this on the bounce, where the general populace will catch only a glimpse later, the camera would zoom in for some strategic close-ups. Instead, I make my own observations. That one is bored and needs to use the san facility. This one has some idea what's coming, a wreath of worry crowning her brow. I can identify them by the symbols set before them.

"We have long known this day was approaching, but I am afraid it has now arrived. We are at war."

"You speak of nothing *but* war," says the representative from Geyahu. "Yet we have seen little evidence of it."

"That's because you stay on world," I mutter.

"Do you not think there's a *reason* for that?" Tarn thunders. "I've been trying to avoid a panic, which would lead to a recession. But by all means, sir, let me show you the reality. The whole Conglomerate shall see it now, for this conflict has become inevitable."

At some unseen cue, a three-dimensional representation of a planet springs to life behind Chancellor Tarn. I don't recognize it off the top of my head. It's not a particularly lovely world, all dun and green, but his expression holds immense gravity.

"This is the Inabeni colony. Lost. No survivors." He doesn't need to elaborate. The subsequent images do it for him. "It is occupied territory now."

A low moan fills the senate chambers. Even if they're politicians, they can still be shocked by such carnage. To some degree, I'm inured to it by virtue of having waded through the bodies in person, but by the fourth still frame, I have to turn my face away.

"Occupied?" A man asks. "What do you mean?"

"It means you should remove it from all trade ships and cargo manifests, unless you care to do business with the Morgut."

Doubtless my mother is working out a way to do precisely that. Shame coils through me, fierce and sharp. Not only is she heartless; she's a traitor as well.

"They have a foothold in this galaxy, then, if they've taken Inabeni." The squat, dark representative from Tarnus bears no resemblance to Dina, but then, why would she? Dina is a remnant of the royal family, who fell twenty turns ago. This representative will be furious when she learns about the recruitment of the old guard.

Tarn nods. "I am afraid so."

The room falls into such an uproar that it takes a good five minutes to restore order. The Chancellor manages it by pitching his voice above the furor of conflicting ideas. "Ladies and gentlemen, steel yourselves. There is more." Another planet follows. "Outpost 9. Lost. No survivors." More horrific images appear, but they're not still or quiet. They carry the screams of the dying into the room with us, courtesy of a security droid.

This is what Evelyn Dasad faced, alone on a dead ship. This is what she survived. No wonder Doc admires her, beyond their working partnership. She is a woman of fierce intelligence and indomitable spirit.

"Gerilo colony. Lost. No survivors. Ibova colony. Lost. No survivors."

By the time he finishes, I am numb with grief. Even with my position in the Armada, I hadn't known our losses were so severe. It makes our small victories seem futile. Seeing my mood in my face, March sets his hand gently on my shoulder. I try to take heart from it, but there's worse to come.

Our news.

"What do they *want*?" a female representative demands. By her tone, she hovers on the verge of tears.

In the center of the chamber, Tarn stands commanding and tall—a fit chief to steer us through the wreckage. "Our resources, our lives, our worlds. Nothing less."

"What can we do?" It is the man from Geyahu, humbled by what he's seen.

"Fight. We can dance along the fringes of it no longer. We must commit all our resources now, before it's too late." Swiftly, Tarn outlines the preparations he's made, and promises of aid received. "But all hope is not lost."

Near enough, I think.

But Tarn is a skilled showman. First he showed them those images to establish the worst, and now he will offer them an alternative. He knows how to motivate a room.

He continues. "We've received reliable intelligence of where the Morgut intend to attack. I will not reveal that information here, but we'll use it to plan our defense."

"How did you come by this information? Can we be sure it's not a trap?"

That must be March's cue because he steps past and strides into the senate chamber. He cuts an imposing figure in his uniform, hair cut severely, and the marks of battle on his face. March stands for a moment at attention, waiting for Tarn to acknowledge him. Did he use his gift to know he was needed *before* any summons? There's no question that this way is more effective. Tarn yields the floor with a graceful gesture.

"We pulled the data from a damaged Morgut vessel after we had defeated its crew," he says. "I don't see how it could be a trap. They had little reason to believe the message in its archives would ever be seen by human eyes."

And no reason to think we'd understand, even if we did see it. The collection of odd technology rattling around inside has turned me into something other than human. If it becomes general knowledge, people will see me differently. I can already see distance in some of the crew.

"Thank you, Commander March."

Nobody in the assembly seems inclined to argue, so March returns to the viewing room. I smile at him, but it's distracted at best. I want to know what they decide.

"How many do we face?"

To his credit, Tarn doesn't hesitate or flinch. "Three thousand Morgut ships."

"It is impossible," someone cries out.

"I could say we have faced worse odds, but I would be lying. Even during the Axis Wars, our outlook was not so grim. At least we had a standing armada back in those days."

"Farwan has destroyed us," the representative from Geyahu says bitterly.

Tarn shakes his head, grave and tired. "We *let* them."

It's true. After the Axis Wars, the Conglomerate was so broken that it had all but ceased to function. Humanity wanted another authority—an impartial one that would absolve us of bad decisions, like the one that led to the deployment of Karl Fitzwilliam to Rodeisia, despite the fact that he had little aptitude and less training. Because he was married to the right woman, he went.

And the whole galaxy paid.

Then Farwan stepped in. *Trust us,* they said to the Conglomerate. *We'll help you rebuild. We'll negotiate treaties. Don't worry about a thing.* And we didn't, not for hundreds of turns.

Small wonder we're no good at it now.

"They will hide like insects, then pick up the pieces after the Morgut have all but annihilated us, just as they did during the Axis Wars. We will die for nothing."

"You would prefer to surrender and *still* be slaughtered?" Tarn gazes around the assembly, waiting for dissent.

No one speaks.

A short man with a balding pate and a round build gets slowly to his feet. "I own a controlling interest in a manufacturing concern on Arkady. We will convert immediately to the production of warships."

"I have a legion." By the cut of his hair and the purple garments, this can be none other than the current emperor of Nicu Tertius. "They are brave men, but they've never fought off world. But if I order it, they will serve."

The Ithtorian representative stands. Through Vel, he says, "I can see that the Morgut are more dangerous than we wished to imagine. If they are allowed to devour humanity, they will turn their eyes on greater enemies." The room rumbles a bit at hearing Ithtorians called "greater," but nobody protests. "We will commit our resources to updating our fleet and becoming a force to be reckoned with. We name Velith Il-Nok the general of our forces. He will lead our ships when we go to war."

It is the only decision that makes sense, whether they respect him or not. No one else has been off world in two hundred turns. His knowledge makes him the natural choice, whatever their personal feelings.

As we watch, the rest of the Armada takes shape. They will buoy up our numbers. They'll need training in our methods, but from so few ships, we leap to the promise of hundreds, possibly thousands.

I just don't know whether the help will come in time.

CHAPTER 48

After the summit, I find Vel alone.

"You did it," I say softly. "General."

He turns from the window in his quarters. His carapace is still bare; he will not wear their stripes now, even if he leads them in war. I think that nakedness comes of pride—I don't think he would accept their honors. The light catches his faceted eyes, gilding the darkness. He is inexpressibly dear to me. I hold out my hands, and he takes them.

"It is not a title to which I aspired. It carries too much death."

"I know. Regardless, I'm proud of you. How was it, working with the famous Miriam Jocasta's daughter?"

"Catrin is a calm pool," he tells me. "She is . . . restful."

I manage a smile. "That's probably nice, after being stuck with me."

"Not better. Just different."

I miss you. It's all I can do not to speak the words aloud because clearly we're going separate ways. From here his work lies on Ithiss-Tor, then he'll have his own ship, his own crew. Like Constance, he can best serve away from me. That doesn't mean I have to like it.

"Are you all right?" I ask, a pale facsimile of what I'd rather say.

"I am lonely."

His fearless honesty humbles me, and I fight the rising

tears. "Me, too. Oh, Vel. This is so fragging *hard* without you."

One step each, and the space between us vanishes. He releases my left hand, then, with odd reverence, touches his claw to the tattoo on my throat. I hold still, unsure what he intends.

"I have not cared so much since I left Adele."

She was my mentor, and she was kind to me during the weeks on Gehenna in which I tried to make my own way. A memory comes to me: Vel wore Doc's skin, and when we said farewell to her, Adele answered, *I'll be seeing you again, I think.* At the time, I guessed she meant the words for me, but he just admitted caring for her. *She must be the human lover he mentioned on Ithiss-Tor.* If so, then she was talking to *him.* And that implies she recognized him, even in a stranger's skin. What a deep bond; I'm not sure I'd sense the heart of him if he came to me in disguise. I like to think I would.

"She was special to you?"

"Yes," he answers. "But I would wear your colors, if you asked."

"I don't know what that means." I remember the merchants talking about such pattern exchanges, enough for me to know it's significant.

"If we both survive," he says softly in Ithtorian, "we will speak of this again."

He winds his arms around me, more adept at comfort than I could've ever imagined. No longer awkward, no longer uncertain. He knows what I need, sometimes better than I do. The wire twined about my heart tightens to painful resonance. For an endless, wonderful moment, he tilts his head against mine. I remember he once said to me: *White wave will never forsake brown bird.* No one has ever made me feel as safe. Not even March.

For the first time—and perhaps the last—I lift a hand to his face. The chitin is cool and smooth, ridged where it joins the mandible. I don't know how much he can feel it, or if he takes solace in the contact. For me, it's an embrace within the embrace, another connection to ward impending loss. As if in answer to my unspoken question, he turns his head, leaning infinitesimally into my touch. *Yes,* the gesture says. *I can feel this. It matters.*

Then I steel myself, though the weight of necessity threatens to drown me.

"I can't stay." I step back, reluctant to my bones. And he lets me go. "We're shipping out tonight. March has orders from Tarn. Very hush-hush. He won't talk about them even with me."

Not like he talks about anything with me, these days.

Mary curse it, I hate good-byes. My eyes are damp when I part from Vel. The hug wasn't enough, but I have no words for what he is to me. I permit a final *wa* to speak my heart, and I don't even know what it said.

His reply offers infinite solace in a single word. *Always.*

Clutching that promise close, I turn and stride away without looking back.

The spaceport is quiet, unlike our departure on Emry. Most of our ships haven't made it back yet, but that's all right. Dina will take it from here. She has all the components needed to upgrade our fleet with direct-jump technology. I glimpse the mechanic from across the floor and angle my path toward her, dodging bots and the occasional human.

With the quiet hum of the lights and the droids going about their work, it's hard to imagine that the Morgut are still attacking our settlements. People are dying. I want to believe this is the truth, not what lies beyond the stars.

But I know better.

Our R&R is over. For most of the crew it was too brief. I never thought of it as a vacation, though. We had too much work to do.

I reach her side, and she straightens from her work. Dina looks like she might lose it, and I'm not doing much better. That feeling I had a while back—as if I'm losing everyone dear to me—well, it's back in force. Knowing she's not coming with us, I feel completely alone. Tears trickle out the corners of my eyes.

"I understand why," she chokes out, "but I don't like it."

They need her to train the other mechanics and quickly, so they can install the coupling that permits direct jumps without the need for the navigator to channel the power as I do. Never mind the fact that only Argus could survive it. There's just no way they'd get enough volunteers for the gene therapy, because they can't guarantee it's safe. It has to be this way, and that makes Dina indispensable. She has to stay on the ground, get the other techs up to speed, and make sure the other ships catch up to the *Triumph*. It's a bizarre fusion of biomechanics and alien tech.

I manage a smile. "You're key personnel, one hundred percent irreplaceable."

"So are you," she says fiercely.

"Not anymore."

For direct jumps, they have Argus. What he lacks in experience, he makes up in good mettle. Most people might think I'd mind that I'm no longer unique, no longer the sole warden of this strange gift. Instead I feel free. In the grand scheme, it matters less what I do now, and so, conversely, my choices matter more.

Our mission is clear: Wreak as much havoc as we can, disrupt the Morgut plans wherever possible, and draw them away from *our* preparations. We're bait—the Conglomerate doesn't want to tip its hand too soon. It's better if the Morgut are hunting one ship—annoying but not worrisome on their end.

On our end . . . well, there's a reason I'm saying good-bye to her.

She reaches for me then, angry in her tenderness as only Dina can be. "Not as a navigator, you dumb bitch."

I hug her back, resting my head on her shoulder. She's warm and solid, pure muscle from wrestling the myriad parts in engineering and cut from the hours in gunnery. As always, she smells of flowers.

There may never be another opportunity, so I ask, "I never took you for the perfume type. How come—"

"A gift to the royal family at birth," she answers, anticipating the question. "A minor tweak to my apocrine glands."

"So you sweat *flowers*?" Well, that explains a few things. I'd always wondered how she came out of a hot workout daisy fresh.

She steps back, ending the embrace. "Great joke, right?"

"Seems like it might come in handy."

"It was supposed to be make me more majestic, more . . . pristine." She shrugs, dismissing that. "I've trained Torrance. He'll be my replacement in gunnery."

"Can he patch the ship up, too?"

"Not as well as me," she answers without false modesty. "But he'll serve."

Dina cups my face in her hands then. Her eyes search mine for a long moment, and then she kisses my lips. This is a tradition on Tarnus, so I keep still; she's honoring me with a custom she has long since abandoned, sharing part of her past. There's sorrow in the caress, not desire, but friendship and love, too. She whispers something against my mouth, too faint for me to make out, but I call it a royal blessing. I'll carry it into battle proudly, no matter that she's a queen in exile and always shall be.

When she steps back, tears spill freely down her cheeks. Mine, too. I don't wipe them away. The salt should linger; it would be unworthy to act otherwise.

"Thank you."

"I always secretly knew you wanted me," she jokes.

I smile wanly. "Maybe I did."

"I love you, y'know." She doesn't need to qualify it—I understand Hit is the great love of her life, but there's always room in the heart for others, too.

There are shades of warmth from the sweet ember of possibility to the roaring fire that fills your soul. I've never loved any woman more. I remember how she dove from the top of the rover to save my ass, back on Lachion, when she didn't even like me. In the bunker, I prayed to a goddess in whom I don't entirely believe for her health and happiness. Parting ways from her is one of the hardest things I've ever done.

"And I, you," I say softly.

"You're not the woman we saw on the vids at all."

My false, tremulous smile shifts, but I answer as I did before: "Not anymore."

I turn and go up the ramp to the *Triumph* then, leaving her behind. Over the years, I've left so *many* people behind. It weighs on me, but there's some small comfort that Doc will remain on board, and that I'll serve with March until the end.

"LC Jax to the cockpit," the computer announces as I come down the corridor.

I already had my orders, though. No need for repetition. I know we're taking off at once, now that March has verified our intel to the summit's satisfaction. Tarn will handle the muster of our ships from here.

Fortunately, I'm not permitted time to consider my losses. In the nav chair, the wider world goes away. New Terra is lovely, receding through the view screen. As the fields fade into gilt patches surrounded by cerulean seas, I regain my self-possession.

Argus isn't here, I realize belatedly. It's just March and me.

"I asked him to sit this one out."

I glance over at him. There was no telltale warmth to indicate he read me.

"Your face," he reminds me, glancing away from the controls.

Yes, he knows me that well by now. "You wanted to speak to me in private?"

He nods. "I made inquiries while we were on New Terra."

It takes me only an instant to track the seeming non sequitur. I know him that well, too. "Did you find your nephew?"

"I found his trail. He's not there anymore."

My heart sinks. This is a bad time for a kid to be out in the galaxy. "What happened?"

This has to be killing him. His nephew is the last link to Svetlana, and he may need rescuing. I doubt duty has ever carried such a high price for March.

"He tested as level-eight Psi," he tells me, as the ship pulls away from the planet's gravitational field. "There was no facility on New Terra adequate for his training."

"What does that mean?" I'm not familiar with Psi-Corp. Unless they've had a relative tested and placed, few people are.

"Level one means a minimal gift. They often skate unnoticed. It can be explained as intuition, so I suspect many people have at least that much."

"What's the highest rank, then?"

"Ten."

"Sounds powerful."

"You have no idea." At my inquiring glance, he adds, "A person with TK 10 could start an earthquake that would level an entire city."

"Mother Mary, and he's an eight? What ability does he have?"

March looks uneasy. "I don't know. The documentation in the file Tarn found was sketchy at best."

"But you know where he is."

"He's on Nicu Tertius, where Farwan trained its most powerful Psi agents. The corruption on world made it perfect, as any official can be bought."

It's also where March went through hell. He's bound to think it's worse for the kid, based on his unpleasant associations.

"Do you plan to combine the search for him with causing trouble for the Morgut?"

He parries my question with another. "Would that be wrong of me?"

"That depends on whether you can do both effectively."

"Now, that's the question, isn't it? I can't in good conscience jeopardize on our mission for the sake of one child."

I know that; we've covered this ground before. If he wants me to give him permission, that's not going to happen. We all have things we'd rather be doing.

"You're the commander," I say. "You'll have to make that decision."

He sighs. "I knew you wouldn't offer me the easy answer. If I see a chance to combine the two tasks, I'll take it. Otherwise, our assignment stands."

I hide a smile. His decision doesn't surprise me in the least. "Yes, sir."

He barely manages to control his flinch. "Don't call me that. Not you. Not when we're alone." For a moment, he closes his eyes. "That's all I ever am."

Uneasy lies the head that wears a crown. The line comes to my head from somewhere, but I don't speak it aloud. Part of me wants to yell at him because the distance between us, the separation, was his idea. I can't bring myself to chide him for it because I understand the reasons. He won't put his own needs first. March never does. And if his nephew dies in the hands of strangers while we're fighting this war, he won't rebound from that. Some losses even I can't heal.

Rose interrupts, sparing me the need to reply. "I have a message for you, Commander. Shall I patch it through?"

"Please."

It's Tarn, and the significance is clear. "It's begun. You have the coordinates."

Ah, Mary. The Morgut have initiated the first phase of their attack. If the sequence of the numbers means anything, New Terra will be hit last.

March accesses the terminal. "Another mining outpost."

"Uranium?"

He checks that quickly. "Looks like it."

They must need it bad. I wish we knew for sure why, but

we have only my best guess. While I ponder, Rose adds, "There's a message for you as well, LC."

"Go."

To my surprise, Ramona pops up on the holo. It's brief, just one sentence: "I will do whatever's necessary to protect what's mine, Sirantha."

Cryptic, as always. I sigh. Not the promise of help I'd hoped for, but we have more important matters to attend right now.

He eyes me, one brow raised. "You want to tell me what that's about?"

Even if he's furious with me, like when we took the ship out at Emry, I can't lie to him. That's the one thing I'll never do, even if the truth paints me in shades of treachery or cuts him to the bone. "I asked her for help. Appealed to her higher nature."

A long silence as he considers the implications. Then he shrugs. "Tarn probably won't like it, but in desperate times, we'll take any allies we can muster. Keep me posted."

I nod. "Shall we go raise some hell?"

March grins at me, looking more like himself than he has for months. "I thought you'd never ask."

CHAPTER 49

The Triumph *comes in hot.*

We jump a few thousand klicks out and hit the Morgut from behind. Their ships are sharper than ours. To my eyes, they look like dark stars, and they wheel at unlikely angles. Each prong of the ship represents a different function: engines, navigation, communications, and medical. The power grid lies in the middle, I think. These aren't like the ones that crashed on Dobrinya.

"They're starshredders," March tells me. "Fast and powerful, but not durable. That's good for us."

They've focused their assault on the SDIs, which means our timing is good. On the downside, we're facing six, twice as many as before. Whatever they need the uranium for, they're determined to get it. I'm just as determined to blow them out of the sky.

Six Morgut ships ring the SDI. Unless they take all of them off-line, passing through the shields will prove impossible without frying their nav coms. This mining colony spent more credits on defense.

I open a channel to gunnery. "You set, Torrance?"

"Loud and proud, ma'am. You've got lasers, yeah?"

Pulling down the targeting array, I answer with the first volley. The Morgut ship's shields take the first hit, not even a glimmer of weakness. They're caught between the SDI and us, but even with the assist, we're outnumbered. March swoops, spinning us through a graceful arc that dodges most of their return fire. A few hits glance off our shields, but nothing solid.

March says, "Looks like they've configured their shields against our weapons. Change the pulse."

While Torrance shoots away in gunnery, I do as March has asked. Before we left, Dina optimized my lasers so they cycle back much faster now. I let fly again, targeting the lead Morgut vessel, but once more the shields hold firm.

"It's not working," I growl.

The whole ship rocks. Since we're soaking hits from six different sources, our shields will go down first unless we get creative. March takes evasive action, rolling us beneath them. Their pilots seem less skilled, as one ship goes into a hard spin, trying to avoid what must look like an imminent collision.

March laughs softly, pleasure blazing in his face. "They felt the draft from that one." He taps the comm. "Doc, Evelyn, what can you tell me about Morgut shields?"

"This doesn't seem like time to chat," Doc says wryly. "But I presume you need a weakness?"

"That would be nice," March grits out.

The *Triumph* shudders again, and I hear a distant boom.

"Aft shields down," Torrance reports. "I've got an ensign working on the problem. I can't stay on cannons and repair the ship at the same time."

"There's too many of them." I launch another round, only to see it dissipate.

"Going on defense," March says. "Maybe we can lead them away from the colony."

I spin the targeting array, covering our retreat. My shots do nothing that I can see, but the Morgut definitely give chase. With our weakness aft, only March's preternatural skill at the helm keeps us in one piece. Several more hits rock us, even so.

"We've got power leakage," the ensign says. "And a fire smoldering on deck two."

Mary, I wish Dina were here.

"Patch it up," March orders. "Send bots to deal with the fire, and get those shields back up. Doc, how we coming on your end?"

"We're working. It's not instant soup," he answers with asperity.

Evelyn's voice comes over the comm. "I may be able to reconfigure the lasers to emit a pulse that will temporarily disrupt their shields."

"I'll be ready on cannons," Torrance says.

"Do it. Quickly."

"We need control of lasers back in gunnery for me to work on our end," Evelyn says. "I'll send them back up when I've finished."

March grunts an acknowledgment, opening the ship's engines to full speed. He loops back around, no doubt hoping to drag the Morgut ships back into SDI range. Maybe they'll do some damage when our lasers take their shields down.

As we skim around the planet, I notice they've destroyed half the SDIs. When the last one goes down, the colony will be defenseless. For the next terrifying moments, I'm a passenger. Sure, I could jump us out of here, but that wouldn't help the colony. If we leave them undefended, the Morgut will sack and pillage the place, stealing the uranium for their use. No matter their purpose, that won't be good for us. Uranium can be used for fuel, so maybe they need it to power the fleet.

Beside me, March flies like a man possessed. He's successfully drawn them back to the SDIs, and through his swift reflexes, we're avoiding the worst of the hits. But unless Evelyn can do as she suggested, we're outclassed.

"I think I've got it," she says at last.

March tells Torrance, "Focus on their power grid."

My lasers come back online, and I take aim. The blue beams soar away, striking true, but at first it seems like Evelyn's trick didn't work. Then the blue light spreads, sparking through the shields, and Torrance follows it up immediately. His shots scorch the side of the ship. I imagine the stink of ozone and burnt metal.

"You got the power grid. Shields are down!" March whoops.

Without being told, I know to target the other five ships in quick succession. If Torrance can take their power off-line, it will take them longer to get the shields back up. More chance for the SDIs to inflict damage.

He follows my lead, switching targets with a speed that speaks both for his reflexes and Dina's training. Four out of six lose power. As if scanning for vulnerabilities, the SDI switches targets. The first Morgut ship takes a barrage of minilaser fire. The SDI lasers impact on the hull, creating a fissure visible through the targeting array.

"We have breach!" I dance in my seat while continuing to fire on the last two ships that still have shields.

We take two more solid hits, and the Klaxons go off. Red light fills the cockpit. Mother Mary, that means we have breach, too.

"Seal it off!" March shouts.

The rest of us stay on target. I lock on the weaving Morgut starshredder and let go.

Got you. Its shields flicker and go out, leaving them vulnerable. The SDI rains constant fire in a ninety-degree arc. It will go this way until we win, or it runs out of power, whichever comes first.

Rose beeps us. "Comm request from the colony, sir. Do you want it?"

Though he grumbles about the timing, March answers, "Send it. Voice only."

An unfamiliar female voice speaks: "You're just in time, *Triumph*. I'm sending long-range missiles from other SDIs. You'll have more support soon, if you can hold out."

"Roger that. If you don't mind, though, we're kind of busy up here."

Unlike the other colony manager, she doesn't sound

frightened. She laughs. "Understood. Call me when it's done."

We evade their fire as best we can. They haven't pulled off because they can't imagine losing this fight to one ship and planetary defenses. But they don't know our crew, and they haven't seen our mods.

Proton missiles come zooming past us, blowing one of the Morgut starshredders all to hell. Lucky break for us, that was the one whose shields I hadn't managed to disable. Now I can just shoot away.

Like hive-minded creatures, the five remaining Morgut ships focus their fire on our weapons array. Only March's skill in the pilot chair keeps us from utter destruction, constantly twirling us away, which makes my job a little harder. Not that I'm complaining. I can't worry about the fires or the breach, as long as I have weapons.

My lasers sing, slamming into their hulls again and again. I look for a weak point but find none. Torrance supports on cannons; he fires less often, but he can do a lot more damage. Soon, another round of proton missiles come screaming past, blowing another ship to dust. Two down, four to go.

"Target medical," Doc says. "I think life support may operate from there."

Without life support, they can't shoot back. *Good thinking, Doc.*

Torrance and I switch targets, aiming for the medical prong. Our concentrated fire bites deep into the hull, and vacuum does the rest, pulling the prong off in a ragged break. That becomes our new strategy: We whittle them down, then the incoming missiles do the rest. Though our ship stinks of burning metal and hot wiring, we're still flying when the last Morgut ship dissolves into scrap.

"Status," March demands.

"Aft shields back online!" The ensign says finally. "All fires out."

An eternity later, Doc answers, "Ten wounded, none critical. No fatalities."

We open the comm shipwide and listen to our people cheering. A trickle of something drips into my eyes. I touch my brow, surprised to find I'm sweaty as hell, but unlike Dina, I don't smell of flowers.

I tap the comm and ask Evelyn, "How did you work that trick with the lasers? Not that I'm ungrateful. Just amazed."

"I noticed that certain radiation frequencies disrupt the guidance fields of my nanites, and I thought it might work on shields on a larger scale. I figured we had nothing to lose."

That was certainly true. The Morgut were kicking our asses before her brainstorm. "Way to go, egghead. We'll make a soldier of you yet."

"Unfortunately, the alteration burned out our lasers."

On the grand scale, the ship has bigger problems. At least we're in once piece. More or less. "We should put down to make repairs," I suggest to March.

March shakes his head. "We can't stay in one place long. Don't know how long it'll be before the next site is hit. It might be a simultaneous attack for all we know."

"Can Torrance fix things en route?" Dina could, no question. But I don't know how good her replacement is.

"He'll have to."

CHAPTER 50

I never thought I'd say this, but—

I'm tired of jumping.

Even when Argus takes the lead, I have to be on-site in case something goes wrong. So far nothing has, but you know the one time I refuse the call and sleep ten minutes longer, well, that's when we'd wind up lost in grimspace.

So I drag myself to the cockpit, time and again. For the last ten days, we've gone from fight to fight, and the ship is limping. The constant repairs have been hard on her, and we don't have Dina on board to work her usual magic. Torrance is doing his best, but he doesn't have the skill or experience to keep up long term.

The good news is, more Armada ships have joined us on patrol, fully upgraded. The *Dauntless* arrived first, and Hon's jumper, Jory, handles the new direct-jump technology like a pro. She stays with me every step of the way. It gives me strength to glance out the view screen and see them pacing us. We're not in this alone anymore.

We try to stay within one satellite bounce of our next target, however, which means raiders can wreak havoc in other parts of the universe. Unfortunately, we can't worry about smugglers and pirates anymore. My mother must be thrilled.

During one of my rare down moments, I'm lying on my bunk, arms beneath my head, when the door bot announces: "You have a visitor, LC Jax."

No nap, I guess. "Allow entry."

To my surprise, it's Rose. She steps inside, looking hesitant, but I can see grief shadowing her gaze. The time on the *Triumph* has aged her, put new lines on her face.

"Sorry to bother you," she says. "But I don't have anyone else."

Her stark tone makes me sit up at once. "Everything all right?"

She shakes her head, sinking into a chair near my terminal. "No. And it hasn't been for the longest time."

"What happened?" I fold myself in the lotus position, preparing to listen.

It takes her a moment to compose herself. "I went to the med lab, intending to bring Saul some food. I hadn't seen him at meals for days."

Uh-oh. I keep my face impassive. "Maybe he was working?"

Mary knows, between finding a cure for Loras and postulating long-term effects of my various implants could keep him busy for turns. Somehow, I don't think competing with genetic data has her so upset, though.

"Not so that I could see."

"What *did* you see?"

"He was holding her." Anguish bleeds through her flat tone and finds an echo in her trembling chin.

I can see she wants to cry, but I don't want her to get started because then I won't know what to do with her. We're not close enough for me to comfort her, not that I'm generally any good at it even when such emotional ties are present. I picture myself thumping her on the shoulder while saying, "It will be all right." No, we have to avoid that scenario. No tears; therefore, I need to keep her talking.

"Were they celebrating some accomplishment?" I ask lamely.

She raises a bleak gaze to mine. "Would you do that by nestling someone close and stroking her hair?"

I have to admit, "That doesn't sound like a happy, way-to-go hug."

"It wasn't. He was comforting her, I think."

"Maybe that's all it was. You should talk to him about it. Tell him how you feel." Unfortunately, that's all I can offer her.

I don't think Doc is the kind of guy who'd play fast and loose, but sometimes the heart can surprise us. Maybe he loves them both. Or maybe he doesn't realize how this looks; he suffers from tunnel vision sometimes.

"You're right," she murmurs. "I know you're right. But I'm afraid of hearing how he feels in return."

"You think his feelings have changed."

"Maybe." A jerky nod. "Yes. She's perfect for him, after all. They can share everything. She's young and clever, educated and—"

"Not you. The two of you have weathered worse, right? Don't write him off without letting him explain."

Giving relationship advice when I'm not even allowed to touch the man I love strikes me as rather backward, but I do want to help her. She has no close friends on board, just acquaintances from Lachion who were mad to get off world, and I have the feeling she never would've left home if not for Doc.

"If by 'weather' you mean his going away and my waiting, then yes. We have."

"Talk to him? Please?"

She seems reluctant, but by the time we've sipped through two cups of hot choclate, she agrees it's the best course. When Rose leaves, she is dry-eyed and full of resolve. I don't envy her the coming conversation.

Thus denied my nap, I gaze at the comm, tempted. As lieutenant commander, I can access any public vid com and listen in. Generally, I don't because it's boring and banal. March can as well, but hell, he can do it without technology. I'm sure he skims now and then, making sure morale is high without intruding on personal privacy.

It takes me all of two minutes to lose the fight. This has personal bearing on me, I tell myself. Rose brought the concern to me. I should follow up.

Feeling guilty, I input my command codes and hijack the vid com in med bay. I won't follow them elsewhere if they seek greater privacy. That's a reasonable compromise, right? The fact is, I'm dead nosy, and now I have the power to indulge myself.

For a few moments, it just shows me Doc and Evelyn working at various stations. I don't see any evidence of intimacy; but they can't go around canoodling all the time, or they wouldn't ever get any work done. Then the door swishes open, showing Rose on the other side.

She went straight to him. Good for her.

Doc turns to greet her with an absent smile. No kiss. *There's strike one. Stupid man.* I narrow my eyes at the screen.

"May I speak to you in private?" she asks without preamble.

To her credit, Evelyn straightens from her work, taking the cue at once. "I'll head down to the mess for a bite to eat."

Then it's just Doc and Rose. He looks perplexed, setting aside some samples with a faint crease of his brow. "Is something wrong? Are you ill?"

And there's strike two, implying she needs to be sick to come see you.

"No. I just think we need to talk."

"Can it wait?" I wince. That was beyond clumsy. Sometimes there's so much scientist in him, I'm surprised it left any room for Rose at all. "I'm on the verge of—"

"No, it can't," she says firmly.

He folds his arms. Defensive posture, not good. It hints at a guilty conscience at worst, or impatience, at best. "You have my complete attention."

"I'm going to ask straight-out, Saul. Is there something

between you and Evelyn?" Rose fixes her gaze on his, and I can see her intensity from here.

"Why in Mary's name would you think that? I'm sorry if you feel neglected, but we're at war, Rose. Certain sacrifices must be made."

Wrong. That was the wrong answer in so many ways that I can't even list them all. She needed an immediate, emphatic denial. Maybe he's legitimately bewildered by the suggestion, but answering a question with a question smacks of prevarication. As for the rest, well, he dismissed her feelings as minor pique. Funny how such a smart man can act like such an idiot.

"It's not about my feelings, at least not entirely. Because I saw you with her, two days past."

If I wasn't watching closely, I might have missed the way he stiffens. "What did you see?"

Son of a bitch. You just broke her heart, Doc.

She deflates, her bravado replaced with defeat. "Ah. I won't keep you further."

"Rose, wait!" But he's too late. She's out of med bay and running. Doc lingers in the doorway for a moment, as if pondering whether to chase her.

Yes, go, I urge him silently.

I see the moment he decides it will be better to let her cool off before he pleads his case, offering his excuse for that embrace. Certainly, that's the logical course. He goes back into med bay and returns to work. Mary, but I'd like to smack him.

That's not my purview, though, and I've snooped enough. I don't want to know what he says to Evelyn when she returns. I don't want to see what comes next. So I turn off the feed.

Before I settle back on my bunk, the comm beeps, delivering March's voice. "LC to the cockpit."

Stifling a curse, I head off to another fight.

.CLASSIFIED-TRANSMISSION.
.UNREST.
.FROM-SUNI_TARN.
.TO-EDUN_LEVITER.
.ENCRYPT-DESTRUCT-ENABLED.

It has been too long since I heard from you.

Worry eats at me. I fear that all we have done, for all your great craft, is not enough. The Syndicate vanquished is a great boon, but they were not the true threat. We move too slowly, weighted with a history of error and indecision.

A dark army gathers overhead, and I do not know if I have the wherewithal to drive it back. What right have I to ask other men to die for me while I *talk*? Such endless talk.

So many futures hang in the balance. I am not worthy of this charge.

Where are you? What news of the gray men?

My intel from other sources indicates there is a new threat rising. The Morgut come in great swarms, and there are rumors— well, they are too dreadful to contemplate. We are not ready. Dear Leviter, we are not ready. We need the gray men. We need the promised ships from our allies. You own the grease that makes such colossal wheels turn at your whim.

What can we do? You say you always keep your word, and I pray that is so. Mary grant that you have not abandoned us, finding another face and another shadow from which to weave your webs. Would you be a hero in our darkest hour? Come, if you are alive and able, I beg you. You are needed.

.END-TRANSMISSION.

CHAPTER 51

Putting Doc and Rose out of my mind, I go at a run.
Crisis mode is normal these days. On the way, I pass crew members who salute when they recognize me. I spot Drake among them, so I call, "Head for medical. Doc might need a hand before we're through."

"Are we headed for action, then?"

"Think so," I answer over my shoulder.

March looks tired. I notice that much in his eyes before the walls come up between us. The expression I caught on him beforehand will have to hold me for a while—that and the feel of his fingers brushing over my bare skin.

Miss you. I whisper it in the silence of my own head, knowing he won't hear me. He's promised not to touch while we're thus separated, and for the most part, he's kept his word. I'm trying not to mind that he *can*.

The cockpit is positively commodious, compared to some we've shared. Before we left, Dina overhauled everything, and the instruments positively shine. At this point, I've spent so much time in here, I could do this in my sleep.

I slide into the nav chair and glance at March. "What's our target?" I could check the coordinates myself, but I figure he's already done so.

"Venice Minor."

Shock spikes through me. The last time I was there, my mother was holding me hostage, trying to destroy any chance of alliance with Ithiss-Tor. It's a beautiful planet, rich in natural resources and with a lush ecosystem. I hate the thought of a Morgut occupation, but there's plenty to eat on world, not just humans. As ultimate carnivores, they don't subsist solely on us; they just like how we taste.

Argus slides in as I'm checking the star charts. "Did I miss anything?"

You'd expect there to be awkwardness between us after I turned down his offer to celebrate together; but like all young animals, he has a short memory. And if it doesn't bother him, I'm not going to let it make things weird. I know it wasn't personal; under the circumstances, any warm body would do, and mine was improved by the prospect of understanding his elation.

"Nope. How's Esme?"

"She says you don't know what you're missing," he answers without missing a beat.

I grin. "Sure I do, and it's best left to nineteen-year-old girls."

March glances at us in amusement, the first real smile I've seen from him in a while. I'm glad he's not seething with unreasonable jealousy. "You two ready? Who's taking the lead?"

Though I sense Argus wants to, I say, "I am."

He's done the last two jumps, and he needs a rest, whether he admits it or not. Argus sighs faintly, but he doesn't argue.

Shortly, Hon's voice comes through the comm. Our sister ship doesn't require a patch via Rose; they can contact us directly. "Anybody else feel like a fight?"

"I was getting tired of playing Charm," March answers.

That gives me a little pang. I mean, I didn't think he spent all his time alone, but I hate being left out. It hurts that I can't even socialize with him casually these days, but other people can. I understand why he doesn't invite me; spending time together would just make the hiatus harder. Putting that aside, I don a professional mien. March powers up the phase drive, and I jack in.

The ship thrums with readiness. I'm accustomed to the speed of it, so we push through with hardly a moment's delay. On the other side, grimspace bathes me in primeval splendor. Oscillations in rainbow hues cascade through my mind, better and brighter than anything my eyes can offer. Pleasure shimmers through me. I'm wide open, letting the universe flood through me.

Reverberations echo in my blood, filling my head. The beacons pulse in answer, and they sound almost like a heartbeat. Excitement makes my heart race, and the beacons answer. I can almost slide free of my skin and skate along the liquid sun that connects them in a fierce, glowing skein. For a moment, I forget that we're supposed to jump. *Such a rush.*

I receive a nudge from March or Argus. Intertwined as we are, I've lost my sense of separation. Reminded of our task, I find the proper beacons and use them to guide my way. Distant beacons call to me, as if my frequent passage has created ghosts, or echoes of old intentions. I'm not sure what it means, and I have no time to parse it.

I just know something has changed here, including the way the beacons feel. They're more responsive. When I reach out for them, it feels like they're reaching back. They want to take me, carry me wherever I want to go. But it doesn't alarm me, and I wish we had more chance for study. Unfortunately, we have a world to defend.

March guides us smoothly, following my directives. The phase drive hums, telling me it's ready for the shift back. We emerge near Venice Minor, just outside the gravitational field. I feel strong and capable as I unplug.

And I immediately want to run.

The hovering ship is immense, a black stain amid the stars. With its strange shape and tentacle-like appendages, it almost resembles an enormous sea monster set free in space. I shudder in horror, not wholly understanding the cause.

"What in Mary's name is that thing?" Argus breathes.

March scrambles at the controls, trying to pull us out of range before we're spotted. "That can't be right."

His reaction unnerves me. "What is it? Have you ever seen anything like it?"

"Only in vids," he answers grimly. Once we've retreated a thousand klicks, he turns to me. "It's a dreadnaught. And we don't have a weapon on board that can touch it."

Argus leans forward. "What's a dreadnaught?"

I'm glad *he* asked, so I don't have to.

"An ancient ship-race. The Rodeisians think dreadnaughts date back to the Makers." He refers to the ones who seeded the galaxy with technology eons ago.

"Wait, you're saying that thing's alive?" Argus asks.

"It shouldn't be. They were allegedly hunted to extinction four hundred turns ago."

"Holy Mary." Argus shakes his head, gazing at the image frozen on the view screen.

We're out of range, but the sheer alien wrongness of it raises the hair on my arms. "What else do we know about it?"

March doesn't look at me. "Other species called them suneaters . . . starkillers. Wherever they went, they left carnage in their wake. I'm talking about worlds ravaged, stripped entirely of life. They were symbionts, bonded with a species called the Vermis, also believed now to be extinct."

"So who's driving this one?" Argus asks.

As if in answer, Rose pings us from comms. "I have an incoming message."

"Forward it, full display."

A holo pops up. At first it's a prerecorded warning, although I don't know what the creature is that's hissing and gargling because I've never seen one; it looks like a fish on three tentacles with a thin, hammer-shaped head. I'd guess it's a Vermis. Then a new verbal track cuts into the feed, and I recognize the sounds. *The red cloud claims this world.* That's all; communication cuts off before we can respond. It's a statement of ownership for Venice Minor.

I glance at March. "You think the Morgut found a derelict, revived it somehow, and took the place of the Vermis as . . . intestinal parasites?"

This is why they wanted Evelyn. She's the key. Since she specializes in biomechanics, they think she can help them achieve perfect symbiosis with the dreadnaught. *Thank Mary she got away from them. Thank Mary we found her first.*

"I don't know." He touches the comm. "Hon, are you seeing this?"

The smuggler answers, "Seeing but not believing. We are *so* fragged."

"So that's it? They take Venice Minor? We're not even going to try." My voice sounds tight, even to my own ears.

Venice Minor is a pleasure planet, bereft of even rudimentary defenses. The Morgut must want some resource found there, or maybe they just want to colonize. This might be part of their mass exodus. Regardless, they're not the type to go for a relaxing beach vacation. Mining colonies invest in good SDIs because they have valuable ore to safeguard. Venice Minor has natural beauty, lush flora and fauna, and a proliferation of peaceful resorts. Mary, even raiders and pirates take holidays here. Nobody with any sense would attack such a place.

Sickness and dread roil in my stomach. If our weapons can't touch it, there's not a ship in the Armada that can stand against this thing. It won't matter if they all get here, courtesy of Dina's upgrades. We'll just all die together, then.

March slants me a look. "Give me a minute to think."

He knows as well as I do—all the thinking in the world won't change the reality. Argus touches me on the shoulder, and I turn to find him looking young and scared. Until now it's been one big adventure to him, I think.

"We're not going to win this one, are we?" he asks quietly.

I can only lift my shoulders in a helpless shrug. The dreadnaught hasn't noticed us yet, but when it does, the thing will annihilate us. That much I can guess from March's poorly concealed fear.

"Well?" Hon demands. "Do we stand or scatter? We have another ship coming in. Looks like . . . Yeah, it's the *Sweet Sensation*."

Oh, Mary. Hit and Kora are on that one.

"We have to try," he replies at last.

In this instance, try means die. I exhale heavily and resign myself to it. "Get Torrance on cannons."

March nods and calls med bay. "Doc, I need you prepared for heavy casualties."

"I'm ready," he replies.

Part of me wants to argue that it's ridiculous for us to wade into a fight we have no hope of winning. We should run, find a place to hide, and hope the trouble sweeps over us. That's what the old Jax would've done. She'd have had no problems letting everyone else fend for themselves. Right now I'm almost sorry I've changed.

We can't run. We're the only hope for Venice Minor and the larger galaxy as well. If the dreadnaught is a monstrosity like March believes, we must find a way to stop it.

March opens a channel to the *Dauntless* and the *Sweet Sensation*. "I'm going to bounce a warning to New Terra, then we're going in."

CHAPTER 52

It's rare that a person can say she gave everything.

I can now.

The ship smolders. We lost deck two an hour ago.

Fact: We cannot take many more hits. At March's command, the *Dauntless* and *Sweet Sensation* fled, leaving us to face the dreadnaught alone. They carry with them images and samples in the hope someone smart and innovative can come up with a way to hurt it. Maybe it will be Dina.

I'm happy Hit and Kora made it out safely, happy that Hon and Loras got out, too. If this space above Venice Minor is to be our tomb, then let the end come. Let this dark beast devour us, then, and someone else take up the fight.

The black ship carries the taste of grimspace, but twisted and tainted, as if they took someone like me and fed it to the dreadnaught over long years. Here, we are plankton before the leviathan. March was right. Our lasers do nothing. Our cannons glance off its skin as if it's made of dark matter. I keep firing, but I'm weary. Everyone is.

The *Triumph* rocks with yet another missile. They tear through our shields like they aren't there, and only the fact that our ship is more maneuverable—and March is an expert pilot—has kept us dodging for so long. But his reflexes are slowing. At this point, we're only delaying the inevitable. When it destroys us, it will turn its attention back to Venice Minor, and there's nothing we can do.

I resent the impotence more than the prospect of my own end.

I glance over at March, my heart aching. His hawk eyes meet mine, heavy with sorrow and regret; but it's not his fault I followed him here. In truth, I would follow him anywhere. He is not perfect, with all his dark shadings and the weight of duty on his soul, but I could never love anyone more.

There's no need to say it. He knows. At the end, he flows into me as he was always meant to be. I'm complete and at peace.

Ship alarms have been going off for a while. Torrance hasn't been able to turn them off, so we're spending our last moments with Klaxons in our ears, and red lights flashing overhead. It lends the cockpit a peculiar, infernal air.

"It was a hell of a ride," I say out loud.

Our coils are drained. I have maybe one more shot from the lasers, but no more. We don't even have juice enough left to run. Nothing left for a jump.

March smiles at me, love shining from him. There's no point in hiding anything now. "It sure was."

"Life support has been compromised," the computer tells us coolly. "There are two hours and fifty-two minutes of oxygen remaining. Sectors twelve, fifteen, and nineteen have breach. Lockdown in progress."

"Commander, LC, it was my pleasure to serve with you," Argus says.

He pushes out of the nav chair then and offers up a perfect salute. I've never seen anything so brave or so awful. Since the next hit will blow the ship wide, I get to my feet also. I don't take the last shot.

To my astonishment, it doesn't come because there's another ship on the horizon, coming from the planet and rising fast. The sleek, smooth lines identify as a pleasure yacht, and when it comes closer, I realize I've seen it before. I took a ride on that ship once.

I scramble for the comm. At this range, I don't need the codes. "Ramona?"

Her image flashes to life. As always, she's lovely. Her dark hair has been looped in elaborate coils, and she's dressed head to toe in white. "You're looking pale, darling. Happy to see me?"

I laugh unsteadily. "Right now? Not really."

"You will be. There's not much time now, Sirantha. Everything I have is yours. You'll find all the documents in order on Venice Minor. I think you know where, you've stayed at the villa."

"What are you talking about?" I ask, bewildered.

"In all these years," she says, as if I haven't spoken, "you've never asked me for anything. Not once. When I got your message . . . well." She lifts her slim shoulders in a shrug. "This is what I can do now. You'll be free to allot my assets as you choose. Believe what you may about me, but I have always loved you. Now, go." Her gaze focuses on March. "Take her away from here."

She smiles at me one last time, then the message shifts from private comm to open transmission, bounced to every satellite. Her very expression changes, becoming prouder, colder, and almost . . . majestic. "I am Ramona Jax," she tells the universe. "And I do this because this is *my* world."

At first I don't understand, but March falls back as instructed, as quick as our limping vessel will carry us. The dreadnaught focuses on Ramona as the greater threat. Her pilot, if there is one, doesn't try to dodge its hits. Instead, her ship sails directly toward the beast, gaining speed with every second. I watch in horrified silence.

"She's going to ram it," Argus breathes.

That won't be enough. It could never be enough. She'll break up on its hull, and leave it gleaming in its dark power. The dreadnaught doesn't try to take evasive action. Why would it? The thing's untouchable.

I close my eyes, unable to watch her die.

"No. Look." The demand in March's tone jolts me.

Impact. At first nothing seems to happen, then her ship splits wide, revealing the payload inside. She's turned her entire yacht into a bomb. Light radiates outward, almost like sunrise after the longest night. The dreadnaught crumples inward. I can't hear the force, but both ships go up, and the enormous shock waves ripple outward.

Dead. My mother's dead.

It's absurd, but I'm both proud and grieving at the same time. When I asked her for help, I never thought it would come this way.

"She saved us," I whisper.

March nods. "Probably half the damn universe, too. We have to find out if there are more of those. I took readings. We can scan for them."

"Not to be unheroic, but maybe we want to find somewhere with breathable atmosphere and fix the ship first," Argus suggests.

"Two hours and twenty-two minutes of oxygen remaining," the computer advises.

"Venice Minor is closest. I have a house there, apparently."

I can hardly assimilate her sacrifice. It goes against everything I thought I knew about her, but then, people are never precisely as we see them, for good or ill. Billions of people will see that transmission; Ramona broadcast every last second until her ship went up. Maybe now, going forward, I'll be known as her daughter. I find I don't mind at all.

"If you're not the luckiest son of bitch in the whole galaxy, then I don't know who is." Hon's voice crackles through our comm. "Remind me never to play cards with you."

March scowls. "I thought I told you to head for New Terra."

"I thought I'd hang around to watch you die first."

"We're here, too," puts in the captain of the *Sweet Sensation.* "What's our plan, sir?"

He answers, "We need to get on the ground. You two follow us in and pick up any pieces that fall off."

"Roger that," Hon says.

March flies with kid gloves. The nav com's shot, so he guides the *Triumph* on pure instinct and expertise. The landing is hell, but he manages to put it down outside my mother's private hangar with a minimum of extra damage. By the time he stands up, I've almost accepted that we're still alive.

Well, some of us. We lost deck two. That's everyone in maintenance and comms.

Foreboding ripples over me, then I realize who I know that works in comm.

Rose. We lost Rose.

CHAPTER 53

While everyone else is eager to see Venice Minor while the ship is being patched up, I head toward medical. By now, Doc has to know. Besides him and Rose, I'm the only one who knows what passed between them, so I'm the only one who can understand what he's going through.

Half the lights don't work, so I stride through a flickering wasteland of blown ceiling panels and loose wiring. Near med bay, the air turns acrid with the stink of charred polymers. The ship seems deserted; everyone else has disembarked, but I know he hasn't.

I find him amid the wreckage of his lab. Any progress he's made better be backed up in the ship's database because the physical samples have been smashed. Maybe the dreadnaught is to blame for that, but from his expression, I think not. His silver hair stands on end, suggesting rough, careless hands in it.

He's removed his white jacket and stands in his Armada uniform like a soldier, but his pose comes from anguish, not military bearing. That's when I realize he's not alone, at least not entirely. *He already went to get her.*

Rose's body has been laid out on one of the tables. Doc must have covered her face, unable to look at the bloodshot eyes brought on by asphyxiation. For a moment, I consider backing out of the room, then discard the notion. He senses me anyway.

"She died thinking I had been untrue—even, perhaps, that I didn't love her."

"I know. I told her you did, and that she needed to talk to you about it." This isn't the time to mention how spectacularly he mishandled the confrontation. I suspect he doesn't need me to figure that out; he's a smart man.

"So she discussed our relationship with you?" He sounds numb, quiet now that the initial storm has passed.

"Yes, she did." I summarize what she saw.

"The worst of it is . . ." He gazes up at the ceiling, hands clasped behind him. "She wasn't wrong."

I knew that by how you answered her, Saul. You're not too clever for me to read.

I lean my hip against a counter littered with broken instruments. "You don't have to tell me if you don't want to."

He shrugs. "Who else is there? If she confided in you, then it's fitting I do."

"Evelyn," I prompt.

"She is . . . intoxicating," he says quietly. "Her intellect shines like a diamond, but she's strong and resourceful, too. How many people could survive what she did? I enjoyed our work together . . . too much, perhaps. I would find myself watching her, the slope of her chin when she studied a specimen, the way she curled a strand of hair around her finger while she pondered a complex problem. I had never met anyone like her, and she struck me as brilliant, fascinating and new."

Whereas Rose was familiar, safe, unexciting. Yes, I understand how it happens. It's not really my business, but I can't help asking, "Did you—"

"No. But it wasn't for want of desire. It was for lack of opportunity and excess of work. Rose saw the height of it. Ev lost many friends to the Morgut. That day, grief overcame her, and I tried to comfort her. But in my heart, I wanted more."

So I was right about that part, but . . . so was Rose.

"Saul, I'm so sorry."

"Men can be very stupid," he says bitterly. "We cease to value what we have until it's gone, and only then do we realize the gold we glimpsed in distant hills paled as dross compared to treasure we had in hand."

"She loved you." It's a thin attempt at comfort because I'm angry. Things shouldn't have ended like this. He should have run after her and begged for her forgiveness.

"She wouldn't have been here but for me. I should have made her stay on Lachion."

There's nothing I can say to that, except: "I don't see how you could *make* her do anything. She was a grown woman."

"Perhaps you're right. Mary knows, she did as she wished without regard for my opinions. When I said I was leaving again, she wept. I could never stand her tears since she was always so fierce in other ways."

That offers a sweet glimpse of how they were together. I remember how Mair spoke in her journal of Rose fighting for him when the Lachion men challenged his beliefs. What does he believe now?

"How long were you together?"

I see him thinking back over the years. Memories sit heavily on him, pleasure and comfort now denied. "Twenty-five turns, but I knew her longer."

His broken aspect defeats the kernel of anger in me. I can't hold on to righteous indignation in the face of such obvious torment. Pushing away from the counter, I cross to him and put a hand on his shoulder. His muscles feel heavy and solid beneath my hand, evidence of a childhood on a high-G world.

Saul turns into my arms, much as Evelyn must have. The irony doesn't escape me. For endless moments, I hold him and feel fresh grief shaking through him in a silent storm. At length he steps back, and I find that his eyes are dry. Too many tears to shed.

"What will you do now?"

"I think you'd better leave me, Jax. I'd like to say good-bye to her." There's such awful composure in his face. I would feel easier if he screamed or raged.

As LC, I make a decision. "I'll go, but I'm setting the AI on watch."

"You think I'd do myself harm?" An ugly smile twists his mouth. "Then you don't know me. You see . . . I *deserve* to suffer."

In his eyes I see he believes he does. Nevertheless, I keep my promise with instructions to the AI once I leave med bay. From there, I pick my way to the exit ramp, negotiating bits of debris. It's going to take days to get us in the air again, assuming we have anyone left on board who knows anything about repair. The crew from the *Dauntless* and the *Sweet Sensation* may have to pitch in.

I come across Evelyn sitting just outside the ship in a pool of sunlight. Here on Venice Minor, the days are long and bright, the sky impossibly blue overhead. On another part of the world, a dreadnaught rain will be falling.

"He hates me now," she says without looking up. "I cost him everything he loved."

I wish I didn't feel so much sympathy for her. She didn't set out to come between Doc and Rose, but there's no doubt in my mind that she adores him. I suspect she even tried to keep her distance. She's no temptress. With her plain face, she would doubtless consider the idea laughable.

"You can't take the blame for this. Give him some time. I'm sure he'll realize it's not your fault. He's too logical for it to be otherwise."

She turns her face up toward me, younger in this golden light. Like me, she is a sole survivor, and that leaves a mark. Even now, she is searching for reasons why she's still alive, wondering at her own purpose.

"Do you think so?"

"But you can't push him," I warn. "It may be hard, but I think you have to wait for him to come to you, and there's no telling how long that will take."

She eases to her feet. "I'm patient. I have time, and there's a lot to do. How are you feeling, by the way?"

I shrug. "So far, so good."

Best not to think about all the things that could go wrong, the way all that technology could run amok inside my body. Fear could paralyze me if I let it.

"Advise me of any changes. And don't forget I need to check you out next week."

Her swift shift amuses me. She's too much the scientist to wallow long in her emotions, however powerful they may be. I do wonder if the same is true for Doc.

With a wave, I pass from the hangar along the path that leads to the gardens. Clansmen greet me with sharp salutes, most of them filthy, charred, and worse for the wear, but they're still here. They're still with us, *Lachion tried and Lachion true*. There's a certain poetry in their battle-stained faces, a refusal to bow before impossible odds. I can only take heart in their resolve.

The grounds are as lovely as when Ramona held us hostage here. A manicured lawn abuts an alabaster wall, wreathed in scarlet and fuchsia blossoms. A tree with purple flowers grows beside the villa, casting twilight shadows on the balcony where I once stood, the scent of peaches wafting on a warm wind. Vel's shadow stands with me there.

Nostalgia sweeps over me. I have my own losses to weather.

CHAPTER 54

March finds me wandering the halls inside.

I've already confirmed my mother's words. She transferred everything to me before her final act. Apparently I own nearly a quarter of Venice Minor, and Mary only knows what else. I didn't go through it all; I'm more than a little stunned.

"Jax," he murmurs, and opens his arms.

That's when I notice he isn't wearing his uniform. Instead of the midnight blue with commander's insignia, he's clad in black from head to toe, simple garments from the ward-rober. I run to him then.

He catches me close, but it doesn't stop there. After swinging me around, he cradles me against his chest and strides toward the room I used on my last visit. Of course, he knows, though he wasn't there. I can feel him coiling warm as sunlight through my head.

Once the door has closed behind us, he kisses me soundly. When we come up for air, I smile up at him. "Isn't this against the rules?"

"You're on leave," he answers. "So am I. So let's get you out of that uniform."

"Shower first?"

"I've already had one, but I'll help you, Lady Jax."

"Lady?" I arch a brow as he unbuttons my jacket.

"Your inherited a title from your mother, among other things. She accepted it in lieu of payment for a debt."

"I think I like LC better. Are you sure the title passes that way?"

"Uh-huh. I had a look at your assets." His hands curl around my bum.

"My assets, huh?"

"You also own the mine on Dobrinya and part of a moon. Most impressive." March works my trousers down my hips, only to find them caught on my boots.

"Are you seducing me for my credits?"

"Absolutely," he says, deadpan. "I had no interest in your body before now, did I?"

"You make a good point."

I hop on one foot, helping him. With equal measures of amusement and anticipation, we tug at each other's clothing until we're both bare. He follows me to the san-shower and helps me with lingering caresses that leave me wanting to get the hygienic portion of the entertainment over with quickly.

Afterward, he carries me to the bed. The window is open, a warm breeze blowing over my skin. He comes down to me with love shining in his eyes, sparking gold and amber. Though this is only the eye of the storm, he shows no sign of preoccupation. Every scintilla of his being focuses on me here, now. I run my hands over his shoulders, glad to have him hale and whole while others are alone and grieving.

"No," he whispers. "Don't think of that. Don't think of loss. We're together."

His head falls back at the pleasure in my hands. I touch him until he's shivering. The heat of him warms me, more glorious than the sun.

"I missed this. I missed you. Mary, the nights I couldn't sleep for it."

"Me, too, Jax."

March lets me feel it then. The walls come down entirely, and I see he suffered as much as I did. More, perhaps, because he had the quiet pain of wondering whether there was a limit to my patience. He knows now; there isn't. I'll wait for him and him alone until the universe goes back to dust.

"We'll have to go back to how things were on the ship when we leave here." It's not a question.

He touches his brow to mine. "Lady, you are the heart of me, but yes. It can be no other way during this war."

Which may never see an end while we are young enough to want.

March acknowledges that with a nod. Mary, how he burns, as if kindled from within by love of me. I remember its loss. I remember how I navigated him on Ithiss-Tor, filtering my essence through the dark spots in his mind, as though he were a series of broken beacons. I did it to repair him, fuse the damaged emotional connections, so he could remember what it was to feel and love. War killed that part of him. I brought it back. In doing so, I left some of myself behind, but I think I also took part of him with me. We are twined together inextricably now, and I wouldn't have it otherwise.

With tender fingertips, I find each scar, and he does the same to me, hands skating along my arms. I find the marks don't bother me anymore. Time has softened them to a purple patina, and I can view them as the Ithtorians do: mementoes of an interesting life.

His mouth finds each pleasure point, cherishing me. We kiss and touch until the slant of the sun changes. It has never been this slow between us, and the sweetness fills me like the juice of a ripe fruit. By the time he pushes my thighs wide, I'm aching for him.

In all ways, March fills me. He comes down to me, his lips warm against my throat. I hold him while he moves, wildness and adoration singing in my veins, but I can't stay passive long. Soon, my hands dig into his back, and I rock against him, my breathing coming in hard little moans.

But he knows I like femme dominant, and so he rolls to watch me at my peak. He holds me there for endless moments, arched above him. I can't speak or breathe. By the time he lets go, I'm starting to see starry sparks, and my limbs have gone lax.

Afterward, he cradles me against him, and I paint his skin with my fingertips. A near-forgotten thought—the way the beacons felt different the last time I jumped—tugs at my brain. It was like they answered my call—

I think my perfect relaxation helped. If I hadn't been floating, thinking of March, I would never have made the final connection. I've always thought I could float free of my body in grimspace and go sailing, and that's exactly what I did in the nav com. I navigated March, altered him from the inside out. Why can't I do the same to the beacons?

Kai and I used to repair them when the signal wavered. In fact, the last dream I had about him, back on Ithiss-Tor, had to do with our last run, before the disastrous mission that ended in the crash of the *Sargasso* and his death. If a beacon was permitted to wink out, it would screw up grimspace navigation permanently. Humans don't handle all the maintenance by themselves, of course. The other races help; we cooperate to keep the beacons operational. But if I can repair them, strengthen them, then I might be able to change them, almost like reprogramming.

If I can alter their pulse, even a little, it will be harder for the Morgut to navigate. Part of their fleet, if not all, might be lost the next time they jump. Who knows how many dread-naughts they have? And they may be heading for New Terra soon.

Of course, once I leave my body in grimspace, I don't know if I can come back. To my knowledge, it's never been done before. Maker records are spotty at best; we don't know much about the ancients who first traveled the star lanes, only what we can dig out of antediluvian ruins.

But the prospect of leaving him sends a spike of pain through my body.

He notices, of course. March levers himself up on an elbow. "You okay?"

Shit, I have to reassure him. I focus on blocking that part of my mind. Partitions, just like when we jump. *He can't see this. He can't know.*

"I'm fine." I manage a smile. "Just a cramp."

A grin spreads across his face. I once thought him ugly with his harsh features and broken nose. Now he's the most beautiful man I've ever seen.

"Are you saying I wore you out? Maybe you're getting old, Jax."

Jumpers don't die old and gray.

"Not even close. I'm just out of practice, and there's only one way to fix that."

I kiss him to distract him from poking around my head. Luckily, long abstinence makes him amenable to focusing on sex instead of what I'm hiding. We make love twice more, spending the whole day in bed. The last time, I weep silently when it's done and hold him to me, breathing in his scent. He is everything.

I assume he put Hon in charge of repairs, but right now, I don't much care if the *Triumph* never flies again. I would like to remember him here. I want to remember him silhouetted against the starry sky, smiling down at me. I want to remember his mouth on mine, his soul curling through every fiber of me. This is what I will carry away from this place. As he ever has, he will bolster and give me strength.

"I love you," I whisper into his shorn hair. I miss the silky length, though I'd never tell him so. It amazes me that a man so hard could have hair so soft. It's different from mine in all ways, but he always touched my head as though he loved the coarse feel of it.

He's sleeping now. I touch his features, featherlight, tracing the jagged lines, hard jaw, and unexpectedly sensual mouth. My fingertips brush his ridiculous lashes, fanned across his sharp cheeks.

I never had anybody love me like you do, he said back on Ithiss-Tor.

I hope he sees this for what it is: not abandonment, but a desperate act born in love. I can't consider what this may do to him. It's right. Even with the promised reinforcements, it may not be enough, and we certainly don't have time to develop weapons that can hurt the dreadnaughts. We can't count on anyone else reacting like Ramona. She was ever a force unto herself, inexplicable as the wind.

My mother gave all, whatever her reasons. Can I do less?

CHAPTER 55

I slip from the bed when I'm sure he won't miss me.

There's no way for me to gauge how long we have. Sooner is better. I scout the place quickly, looking for a ship. My mother had a number of them. There must be one left here suitable for our purposes. And then I find it.

Now I just need a pilot. It takes me only a couple minutes to locate Hit.

She's not sleeping. I find her standing on a balcony, face turned up. She's gazing toward New Terra, toward Dina. She turns to me in surprise.

"I'm glad to see you're all right. That dreadnaught . . ."

I hate what I'm about to ask of her, but I lay it out nonetheless. If I could see another way, I wouldn't be here. Hit knows as much. I can see it in her eyes. The fact that she hasn't sent me packing tells me she knows our situation is dire.

"You've thought about this a great deal."

I nod. "I won't lie to you. It may be our last jump."

Hit gazes at me squarely; she has a way of cutting to the chase. "Will it save her?"

She's thinking of Dina, the woman she loves. In my mind's eye, I see them as they are: dark and light, moon and night. Such things belong together. There is balance in it.

"Since it'll buy us time if it works, this may be the only thing that can. I don't know if I can do this, if it'll shake out like I think it will. It's a theory, no more." I smile at her. "But what the hell, you're a gambler, right?"

"Then Mary grant it's enough. I'm in."

"Excellent. There's a two-seater in the outdoor hangar. It doesn't have much juice left, and no comfort for a long haul, but the phase drive works."

"And that's all we need."

"Yeah. Meet me there as soon as you can."

I can't think about how March is going to react when he discovers I've gone. It's a good thing I learned to partition, or this plan would've been doomed before it got off the ground. That'd be too damn bad since it's our only hope.

"Understood." She pushes to her feet.

I hesitate. "It's okay if you take the time to send a message."

She inclines her head, so tall, proud, and brave that it breaks my heart. I don't want to take her out there with me, but I can't do this alone. March would never let me go without him, and the Conglomerate can't afford to lose him. They need his leadership now, and I—well, at long last, I'm expendable. That renders this suicide run an acceptable risk.

"I won't do anything to jeopardize the mission."

"I know you won't." With that, I turn and walk away, nothing more to be said.

I spend my last moments on Venice Minor, perhaps my last moments of life, contemplating the past. There are so many people whose lives have touched me, who moved me with their strength or kindness or wisdom. They've enriched me and made me better than I ever thought I could be.

The old Jax would never have considered this sacrifice. She considered everyone more disposable than herself; all that mattered was saving her own skin. I'm not that woman anymore, but there's enough of her left in me that I weep quietly at the prospect of my own end. But I keep my grief locked down, so I don't broadcast. He's more attuned to me than anyone else in the world, and if I scream in the silence of my own head even while he's sleeping, there's a chance he will hear me.

I can't let him stop me.

Feeling like this may be the last thing I'll ever do, I activate the terminal in maintenance. "Record on, highest encryption. This message should only be accessible to Commander March, first squadron, Conglomerate Armada, four hours after creation." That allows enough time to do what we must but not enough for him to prevent our departure.

"Acknowledged."

I should've checked my reflection before I started this message, but it's too late now. He'll see whatever's there: messy hair, tired face, shadows beneath my eyes. No point in trying to hide from him at this late date anyway. I never could. So I gaze into the vid and speak my piece:

"This is Lieutenant Commander Sirantha Jax, assigned to the *Triumph*, first squadron, Conglomerate Armada. You will take what I have done as high treason, but I hope you come to realize there was another purpose. I regret leaving you behind more than you know, but it is my hope that I can slow the gathering storm. I hold you in my heart in this final hour. Good-bye, my love."

That done, I use the indifferent AI to establish my testament, putting all my worldly goods in March's hands in the event of my death. Constance would've known there was something wrong, but she's on Emry Station, training new soldiers to replace those who fall in battle. Who could've ever dreamed that a little PA unit from a backward rock like Lachion would be so important?

Mair did, I expect. I find traces of her in everything we do, as if she looked forward and anticipated what we might need. It's a pity she didn't glimpse this and warn me. Then again, maybe she did. Maybe everything that's happened served to turn me into the kind of person who could step willingly into the abyss. And I only regret I must take Hit with me.

I spare a final thought for distant friends.

Vel is on Ithiss-Tor, putting the finishing touches on the first Ithtorian fleet. I find it ironic that they've made him their general after all those years in exile; but he knows what we're up against, and he can best coordinate their ships. There's a whole new generation of Ithorian hunters, eager to make their mark upon the galaxy. Their time has come.

Farewell, my dearest white wave.

As if Mary herself sanctifies our plan, I encounter no one on my way to the outdoor hangar. The rest of the crew sleep peacefully, recovering from constant days on call. Hit steps out of the shadows. Dressed in black, she's no more than a slim shadow herself. We've both discarded our uniforms. They have no place in what we're doing, and we want to leave no doubt that we acted of our own free will. No secret orders, no coercion.

"Do you have the codes?"

I nod. "We'll have no trouble getting out of here. The ship is authorized for travel, and I'm the commander's right hand if anyone inquires."

"You're his heart, too, and now you're going to break it."

"Hearts were made to be broken." I know that's not exactly how the quote goes, but it fits our circumstances well enough.

Hit gives me a wry smile, teeth gleaming white. "Then let's be about it."

I slide down the hatch behind her. This ship is tiny, hardly more than a skiff. It has no weapons or armor, which means it was the only one left unguarded. Kai and I took one like this when we went to chart a new beacon, and we didn't want to fool with a medic or a mechanic. It was risky, but that was part of the magic. I was never scared then; I don't think I had the capacity to see past the thrill: him and me against the whole universe.

It's not like that now.

She checks the instruments, verifying that the ship will fly. "Everything looks good."

At her nod I input the departure codes. I selected this

time of day for our getaway because there's only a skeleton crew on duty. By the time anyone realizes a ship has gone missing, it will be too late.

The horizon will be dark for hours yet. Stars hang heavy overhead, but I take no comfort in their beauty, knowing that the Morgut fleet will be mobilizing soon if we don't do something about it. Therefore, Hit takes us smoothly into the sky. We don't have the power to jet away from Venice Minor's gravity, but this little ship has heart.

She flies for a while in silence. Her profile is lovely. I watch her for a moment, trying not to let fear take root.

"How did you end up with Madame Kang?" It seems like I should know more about her if she's going to hell with me.

"She raised me. She took in street girls, trained them in her art."

"So you were taught to kill as a child?" I try not to sound judgmental.

"Among other things." She glances at me then. "You think it was a hideous life, but we were happy. She treated us well."

"You mourned when she died."

"Didn't you when you lost your mother?" Her mouth twists. "Eh, never mind."

I consider that. "I do, actually. But she died well."

It wasn't sacrifice. Ramona didn't have the heart for that. On consideration—and remembering her answer to my message—I know now why she did it. Defiance, pure and simple: *You shall not have what is mine.* That doesn't render it any less magnificent. For the first time in more years than I can recall, I am proud to be her daughter.

"That she did. Jax, watching that feed . . . I had chills."

"So did half the known universe," I admit. "So perhaps she got what she wanted in the end, pure renown."

She checks the instruments. "We're far enough away now, I think."

As the phase drive powers up, I see a shimmer through the view screen: scout ships, the vanguard of the Morgut

fleet arriving to renew their assault on Venice Minor. There
will be more dreadnaughts, more death. Once they win here,
they will push farther, all the way to our homeworld. We
have to stop them. Now. *Before* they leave grimspace. Or
New Terra is doomed, and humanity with it.

Such long odds. Such a dark prospect. Hit smiles at me
and touches my hand. In her eyes, I see all the reasons why
we're doing this: everyone we've left behind. They may
never know what we do out here. It will have to be enough.

I jack in. There's a known jump zone not too far from
Venice Minor, but we can't risk running into the scout ships,
so it has to be a direct jump. This little ship has no special coupling to open the way, so I do it with my body and
my will, grimspace blazing through me like a lover's touch;
Doc's implant regulates it for me, and the blockers take the
pain. We jump.

The colors fill my head in an incandescent rush: streak-
ing sanguine and silver, azure and viridian, until we pass
the corridor and enter grimspace proper, where the colors
become waves. It doesn't matter which beacon I target, so I
cue Hit at random. If this works, any of them will do, as the
new pulse resonates through the others, changing them with
its unique tone. They're a network, and they form a pattern;
most likely if I could view it in entirety, it would match the
one we've installed on the *Triumph* in miniature, what the
Morgut have on their ships. This will be a thousand times
more intense than the repairs Kai and I did, because simple
mental manipulation won't be enough.

I must commit to the task fully, and if I fail, then we die
in obscurity. We have precious little time now. Grimspace
will drain us fast.

But first I have to warn her. *I don't know what'll happen
when I leave my body. I may not be able to guide you back.*

She conveys a mental shrug. Her mind is disciplined and
steady; she has no fear. *I'm willing to make the ultimate sacrifice, if that's how it has to be.*

Fair enough.

Gathering everything I have, everything I am, I focus on the door in the far horizon, the door that isn't a door—that beckons yet I dare not answer—and the tethers holding me to my body give way. I sail out of the cockpit and into the crimson sea; it blazes through me, but there is no pain. Instead of letting the current carry me all the way out, I leap to the beacon and pass through it in my entirety.

Everything changes. I sense the new pattern echoing outward from ground zero, changing each in turn, and it fills me with elation. Because it's based on my energies, I'll be able to navigate these beacons, but nobody else will—until I train them. Which means I must get back, or not only will I have crippled the Morgut fleet, but countless human ships will be lost out here. I have to show all our allied jumpers how to read the new beacons. But the red current pulls at me, tugging me toward my final exit.

And I'm swimming against the tide.

**Explore the outer reaches
of imagination—don't miss these authors
of dark fantasy and urban noir that take you
to the edge and beyond.**

Patricia Briggs	Karen Chance	Anne Bishop
Simon R. Green	Caitlin R. Kiernan	Janine Cross
Jim Butcher	Rachel Caine	Sarah Monette
Kat Richardson	Glen Cook	Douglas Clegg

penguin.com

M15G0907